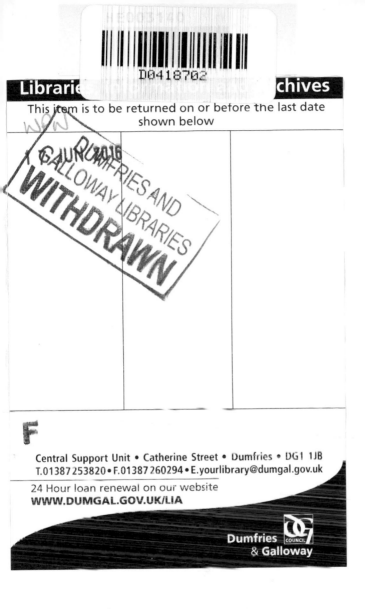

Librarie chives

This item is to be returned on or before the last date shown below

DUMFRIES AND GALLOWAY LIBRARIES

WITHDRAWN

F

Central Support Unit • Catherine Street • Dumfries • DG1 1JB
T.01387 253820 • F.01387 260294 • E.yourlibrary@dumgal.gov.uk

24 Hour loan renewal on our website
WWW.DUMGAL.GOV.UK/LIA

Dumfries
& Galloway
COUNCIL

D0418702

CRITICAL ACCLAIM:

'Simply brilliant . . . mesmerising, beautifully written and intelligent to boot. Sets the pulse racing and the mind working. A writer to watch'
Manchester Evening News

'This is a sensitive, richly atmospheric thriller . . . The story achieves a powerful momentum as the layers of deception are stripped away in this highly charged, beguiling debut'
Crime Time

'An accomplished writer . . . taut and suspenseful'
Publishers Weekly

'That it turned Kathy Reichs' blood cold is perhaps all that need be said about Lucretia Grindle's latest chiller'
Ottawa Citizen

THE
NIGHTSPINNERS

Lucretia Grindle was born in Boston Massachusetts and grew up spending half her time in the United States and half her time in the UK. Continuing as she started out, she still splits her time, but now calls the coast of Maine home.

Also by Lucretia Grindle

The Faces of Angels
The Villa Triste
The Lost Daughter

THE NIGHTSPINNERS

LUCRETIA GRINDLE

PAN BOOKS

First published 2003 by Macmillan

This paperback edition published 2004 by Pan Books
an imprint of Pan Macmillan, a division of Macmillan Publishers Limited
Pan Macmillan, 20 New Wharf Road, London N1 9RR
Basingstoke and Oxford
Associated companies throughout the world
www.panmacmillan.com

ISBN 978-0-330-49146-4

Copyright © Lucretia Grindle 2003

The right of Lucretia Grindle to be identified as the
author of this work has been asserted by her in accordance
with the Copyright, Designs and Patents Act 1988.

All rights reserved. No part of this publication may be
reproduced, stored in or introduced into a retrieval system, or
transmitted, in any form, or by any means (electronic, mechanical,
photocopying, recording or otherwise) without the prior written
permission of the publisher. Any person who does any unauthorized
act in relation to this publication may be liable to criminal
prosecution and civil claims for damages.

5 7 9 8 6 4

A CIP catalogue record for this book is available from
the British Library.

Typeset by SetSystems Ltd, Saffron Walden, Essex
Printed and bound by
CPI Group (UK) Ltd, Croydon, CR0 4YY

This book is sold subject to the condition that it shall not,
by way of trade or otherwise, be lent, re-sold, hired out,
or otherwise circulated without the publisher's prior consent
in any form of binding or cover other than that in which
it is published and without a similar condition including this
condition being imposed on the subsequent purchaser.

ACKNOWLEDGEMENTS

With special thanks to my father and husband for their patience and support, to my editors, Lee Boudreaux and Maria Rejt, for their unfailing good humour, and to my agent, Sloan Harris, who is simply the best.

THE
NIGHTSPINNERS

ONE

Shoo Fly. That was what my mother called me. Shoo Fly Pie. 'Shoo Fly – don't bother me, I belong to somebody.' I can hear her still in the southern nights of my childhood, nights that never seemed clear and clean like they do farther north, but were instead heavy and alive with fireflies, and nightjars, and all of the things that move and wind through the dark.

When I think of those nights now, I hear my mother's voice. She is standing in the kitchen, the soles of her Keds firmly planted on the linoleum floor. Her hands, narrow and long-fingered, move rhythmically and without thought, like something programmed. She is canning. She ladles whole peaches, squishy and bright yellow, into jars, pours syrup that will stick to you if it spills, and burn. She spoons piccalilli that is red and green and hot with pepper corns. While she does this, she sings.

Her thin, hopeful soprano threads its way through our house. Sharp and not quite right, her voice is out of harmony with Georgia. It does not match the long, green fields of the farm, the road, red with dust, the sun-blistered walls of the sheds, or the slow creak of our screen door. It is not some rolling bass, or sweet arc and swoop of a Baptist hymn, nor a sad, slow, sax note of the South. Her voice is not a knife wound. It is just something present and unseriously painful, like a papercut that stings and cannot be forgotten.

'Shoo Fly,' my mother sings, and sometimes in the night I feel that she's calling my special name. My mother didn't have a special name for Marina. I'm not sure why, perhaps because it was enough of a name in itself, enough of a distinction for Petamill, Georgia. We longed to be called Sue-Ellen, Carla-Louise, Mary, Daisy or, best of all, Elizabeth-Anne; but no, there we were in that town with those names, Marina and Susannah, the living evidence of our mother's optimism, of her double-dog-dare that in the face of circumstance we would 'become something'. It was as if, in naming us as she had, our mother had given us something grandiose, something to make up for the fact that we had no father. Or, to put it more accurately, that she had probably never been quite certain of who he was.

Not that our mother was wild anymore. Our birth must have cured her of that. With her bobbed dark hair and her pressed white blouses, the tiny gold earrings from the Five and Dime, and the mid-height heels that she wore to work, our mother's wildness was a thing of the past. It clung to her only in half-remembered stories, and hovered about her fine-boned beauty like a memory. I dream of my mother as a young girl, and when I do she is always wearing a candy-red dress with a wide skirt, and little flat shoes that are black and have bows on the toes. Her waist is tiny. Her hair is a glossy cap. I can hear her laughing. I dream of her in roadhouses, in those places by the side of secondary highways where the parking lot is crowded with pick-up trucks and lit by a neon sign, and where the noise from the bar and the jukebox lifts everything up and floats it out on to the heavy dark.

That is only my dream. I do not know what the reality was, and my mother never told. As I have grown older I have come to suspect that it had more to do with the back seats of Chevrolets, with beer cans and bottled cocktails, with truckers pulling through town. There was, of course, our hair, which was a color unlike any known in our family and was distinctive enough to have been something of a clue, if we had been looking for clues. But, now that I think of it, Marina and I were peculiarly uninterested in the possibilities of our parentage. We had very little, if any, interest in who our father was. Our world was closed and complete. Night after night we spun the threads of a cocoon around ourselves while, upstairs in our room, we listened to our mother's song.

In the dark we lay, stretched and still, in our twin beds, and if our mother had climbed the stairs and looked in on us, as she so often did, she could well have assumed, from the sweet tilt of our heads, from the motionlessness of our hands, that we were sleeping. Of course she would have been wrong. On those nights Marina and I are not drifting high above the farm on a cloud of dreams. We are not sinking and innocently lost in sleep. Oh, no. We are busy.

Without so much as a motion, and without a sound, Marina and I are weaving words between us. We are threading words through the soft shafts of shadow that lie across the window sill. We are sliding them along the bar of light from the hall that filters under the door. We are sending phrases, paragraphs, laughter,

faster and faster, like flights of moths across the dark
space of the room between us. Without so much as a
whisper, we are weaving the web that binds us, braid-
ing the strands of our secret cocoon. We are
nightspinning.

Not that our mother would know this. Not that
anyone would know it. It is our secret. No one guesses
that we are nightspinners. No one knows how much
we talk, or about the words we weave between us.
We work in silence, and when our mother eases the
door open she rewards us for what she assumes is
our sleep. She whispers, 'You are such a good girl.'
She says it just once, to both of us, as if we were one.
Which, in fact, we are. We are two peas in a pod,
Marina and me. We are bright as buttons. Cute as pie.
Mirror images. We are twins.

By the time we were nine or ten, Marina and I could
carry on complete conversations without speaking.
Our nightspinning that had begun in the dark had long
since grown strong enough to withstand the light of
day. I would feel a prickle on the back of my neck, a
subtle rising of the tiny, soft hairs that grew there, and
I didn't even have to look at her to know what she
was saying. Marina would send words and thoughts
and entire paragraphs into my head, whether I wanted
them or not. Permanently set to receive, I was a fax
machine that never ran out of paper. My mind was a
blank screen and, because we were the nightspinners,
Marina could write on it any time she chose. Mostly,
when she was doing this, she would not meet my eye.
She would look in another direction, her gaze fixed on

the wall, or the fields, her chin set stubborn, and the tiniest smile of triumph would flicker across her face because I could not stop her, could not turn her away if I tried.

To be honest, most of the time I did not try, and nor, in so far as I know, did she. For I used my privilege as a nightspinner too; I sent my share of messages across our private airway. I do not know if the back of Marina's neck prickled, or if she came to resent me for my uninvited presence in her head. I presume that that was what she felt, if only because it was what I felt, but I do not know, and since I never asked her, I will never know. My sister is dead. She was murdered eighteen months ago in Alexandria, Virginia. Now she is just a case number, an unsolved homicide. One of many.

It is going to rain, I can smell it. The high sashed window that opens on to the balcony of my apartment is raised and the sounds and the smells of the city drift into my rooms. There is not much traffic in this part of Philadelphia. Popular wisdom says the city is dying, and so perhaps that explains the quiet of it. It is only occasionally that I hear footsteps on the sidewalks below, or shouted laughter, or the rush of a car in the street like a great exhaled breath.

In the corner beyond the fireplace the dog moves restlessly. He is a German Shepherd, a leggy, two-toned wolf, black and tan with a bear-like snout and golden eyes. As I watch, he rises from his bed, stretches and regards me seriously. It is almost midnight and we are due to be abroad, to make our final patrol of the empty streets. He paces in front of me through the hallway and waits while I reach for my sweater and his leash.

We open the door and pause for a moment on the landing outside my apartment. Only five of us live in this building, and it is possible for a moment to imagine that the other three apartments do not exist, that the dog and I are completely alone, and that in stepping through the door and out on to the landing, we have crossed back over time, fallen through a hundred years.

The house is a brownstone, a dowager duchess of the Victorian past who has been only slightly modified in order to greet the modern age. The wall sconces, once lit by gas, are flame-shaped buds of glass. A brass chandelier, adapted uneasily to electricity, hangs in the stairwell. One storey above me a great skylight glows faintly, its smoky panes suggesting an eternal blanket of snow, or a Holmesian fog. The stairs, thick-carpeted in crimson, wind down four flights to the parquet floors below. The banisters are huge and ornately carved, and far too wide for me to wrap my hand around. This late at night, in the quiet, it is possible to feel that I am a small child and that the grown-ups are asleep.

The heavy doors swing shut behind us as the dog and I come down the front steps and on to the sidewalk. We pause to sniff the air, to listen, and then turn left, and a block later, left again. We have a routine, and it never varies. Along Delancey Place the dog inspects each set of iron railings, considers each gingko tree. He stops to peer intently at several sets of the wide front steps that lead to glossy black doors with knockers of polished brass in the shape of claws or lions' heads. One particularly ornate lintel is supported by a pair of caryatids. The dog gives them a conspiratorial glance in passing, and they look benignly down on us, as if their thoughts have room to wander while they hold the house on their heads. Even in the rain, or in the coldest wind, or in the powdery pinpricks of the snow, the dog never hurries this ritual. Sometimes his leisurely pace, his lack of urgency, makes me impatient, but not tonight. We are having an Indian summer, and even though it is mid-September the breeze is a warm breath that puffs in from the Delaware, bearing the promise of soft, overblown drops of rain.

On nights like this I sometimes think I can smell the sea. Though of course that is not true. The ports of Philadelphia are a long way from open water. Nevertheless, I like the idea enough that I often insist on it. 'You are lying!' George would say, when I claimed that I could taste the ocean, could roll its salt along the back of my tongue. He would smile, reach for my hand, raise his eyebrows at the horror of it, and exclaim, 'You are such a liar, Susannah!' Born and raised among the small towns of the mid-West, George found mendacity both beguiling and faintly erotic. Now I wonder about him, and if he misses the idea of the sea, and my lies. Then I remind myself sharply that George is no longer my business. He has decamped to Paris and I am not to wonder about him, not to indulge in fruitless speculation. I have given up keeping track of French weather and calculating time changes. That way lies the road to ruin. The dog turns left, and left again, and we are on the home stretch.

★

As I lock the door behind us the clock in the entryway strikes twelve. I slip the dog's leash off and let him run ahead of me up the stairs. He is on the landing when the phone begins to ring. He cocks his head and looks at me and I look back at him and shrug as I fit my key into the lock. He noses the door open and I wipe my feet and drop his leash on the table and follow him into the living room, past my desk where the phone rings and rings.

At first I used to answer it. 'Hello, hello,' I would say obligingly over and over again, but there was never anyone there. I even dialed star-sixty-nine a couple of times, but all I got was a beeping tone that the operator once informed me meant my caller had 'blocked' their line. Now I no longer bother about the calls. I have become used to them. Like our final walk, this mid-night call has become part of our routine. The phone will ring exactly five times, and then, just before my answering machine clicks in, it will stop. Even as I think this the noise ceases, and the first splats of rain hit the balcony window.

The dog makes a quick patrol of the apartment and returns to his bed in the living room, which is where he prefers to be. He does not sleep in my bedroom, he likes to keep his distance. He is aloof in his devotion, and not especially made to cuddle. His purpose is more serious and he has chosen it for himself. He is the watcher at my door.

His yellow eyes follow me. I can feel his cool regard as I stop in front of the hall mirror, caught by my own reflection. I am the only one left now, and I think that I look the same, and not the same. It is as if, now that

Marina is gone, I am more concentrated. I am both of us, doubled up, distilled.

I reach up to unclip my hair and stop in mid-action as my hand moves in the mirror. It is my mother's hand, exactly. Bony and long-fingered, it reaches into the air, a blank space on the finger where she wore her ring. It is spooky, and yet momentarily familiar, the claustrophobic way in which my mother and Marina have arrived to dwell in me. It is as if they have quit the game and left me here, the family representative on earth. I shake myself, push them away, and finish the gesture they have arrested me in. I remove the large clip and let the hair fall down around my shoulders. I am not a vain woman, but it is true that it is my pride and joy, this lion's mane of bronze and red.

I'm going to pour myself another glass of wine. The rain is picking up tempo now, bouncing on the lead wall of the balcony, spreading a thin sheen that glows a dull orange in the reflected city lights. I relish these last warm nights even while I look forward to the tanginess of fall. Sometimes I think I moved north for the seasons, but on the other hand, perhaps that is not true. Perhaps I just got this far, just hit this city and stayed. Perhaps I have no good reasons for being here at all and, like the taste of the sea, I just insist on the idea of them. Perhaps I make them all up. After all, it is indeed true that Marina and I were both terrible liars.

We would make up anything, any old story or excuse, just for the sake of it. I could always tell, of course, when Marina was doing it. I would catch the sly slide of her eye, taste the edge of her words, and without missing a beat I would join right in. My grandmother was particularly easy prey. We would go over to her house after school and just tell her any damn thing we pleased. Sitting at her kitchen table we would insist that we were getting a puppy, painting our bedroom turquoise blue, having nothing but angel food cake for dinner, and watching *Love American Style* on TV until midnight. Now that I think of it, she didn't really pay very much attention to us. Maybe we weren't actually very good at it, or maybe she honestly had better things to do than care about what we ate or watched on television. Or maybe she had heard it all before. There is evidence, after all, that my mother was no angel.

Momma herself always knew when we were lying. She would just look at us out of the corner of her eye, or raise her hand like a policeman stopping traffic, the wedding band that she insisted on wearing flashing in the light. Or she would simply say, 'Well, that's some tall tale,' which was immediately deflating. There is nothing on this earth to stop a good lie in its tracks like the conviction that you are not being believed, but, Momma aside, that was not usually a problem. Charlie and Dex Eames, and Sonny Delray, and Della Hervey and Anne Louise Blakemore, and anyone else who cared to listen, all believed that we would be getting a puppy any day, and that when we grew up we were both going to be ballet dancers.

We finally did start to take ballet lessons when we were ten. What my mother called her 'jam money' paid for them, along with her extra hours hostessing at the only fancy restaurant in town, which was called the

Coachstop. When the Coachstop got a liquor license in the summer of that year, it was a big deal because everybody made more money and all of the customers had a cocktail before dinner. I don't remember one reference, ever, to anyone in that town drinking wine. At home you drank beer, or peach cordial, or malt liquor out of long-necked bottles, and when you went out you drank bourbon, with or without ice, or martinis, or sometimes something like a Sidecar. If you were a lady, you might have a Tom Collins, or a SeaBreeze, or a Whiskey Sour.

I still love those names. I love the idea of Angostura Bitters, and maraschino cherries, and all the little colored paper umbrellas that anyone who eats in one of my restaurants would choke over. That's what I do, by the way, I design restaurants. I call them 'mine', but of course they're not. They are just my designs, my idea and artistic vision brought to life. You would recognize them. They are those places that offer small intricately designed towers of food on outsized plates, and wildly chic seating arrangements, where the size of the bill is diametrically opposed to the size of the portions served. That is what I do, how I make my way in the world. I create the ambiance, the look, the safe haven that you move into in order to be fed.

Anyways, that year, when we were ten and my mother had a good year selling her jams and relishes and chutneys, we finally got our ballet lessons. The Shall We Dance Studio, which was really just a big room with a mirror and a rail fastened along one wall, was on the second floor of the hardware building. You got to it by a rickety set of wooden stairs that ran up the outside wall of the building and that I am one hundred per cent sure were not safe and legal. We went there every Wednesday after school for our class. We pliéd, stuck our toes out like ducks, and whined for pink leotards and matching tights that our grandmother and Uncle Ritchie, who lived with her, finally bought for us. Our mother bought us little kid-soled ballet slippers that were shiny black and soft on the bottom and came pressed together like hands in prayer bound by elastic bands.

At the Christmas pageant we both wanted to be the Sugar Plum Fairy, but neither of us was. We were mice in the first part and candy canes later on, and I have hated *The Nutcracker* ever since. Marina said that it didn't matter. Lying in our beds one night after a particularly boring rehearsal in the church hall, Marina spun the words out to me. She sent them flying into the darkness, and said that it did not matter, that it was of no consequence at all, and that our day would come. She said that we would show them all, and that one day we would be perfect swans. We would dance *Swan Lake*, and one of us would be the black swan and one of us would be the white swan, each a perfect inversion of the other. 'Look,' Marina had commanded, 'look, you can see them.' And I could. Just as she had promised, the swans were dancing out there in the shadows. Leaping and fluttering across the web that stretched between us, they never put a foot wrong, until finally the poor prince was so besotted that he never even noticed that they were not one and the same.

*

I think of those swans still. I had forgotten them for years, for decades, but lately they have come back to me. I see them now in the shadows of a different room, one as far removed from our twin beds and sash windows and patchy screens as can be. The bedroom that I lie in now is a period gem. Its Victorian moldings and ceiling rosette have been lovingly restored by the architects who own this building and live on the ground floor. This is highly desirable, this live-in architectural arrangement. Or so I am told. It is a guarantee of good taste, so we can all rest easy now in the sure knowledge that the stairs will not be redone in a carpet of unfortunate pattern, or the etched glass panels of the vestibule doors be replaced by plywood.

The rooms of my apartment are painted in severely understated soft grays and mossy greens, colors I have always loved. Once, when I thought I might be getting married, I contemplated a gray wedding dress, something very pale and gauzy, like a spider's web. I did not get married, however, and so in my bedroom I am alone, except for the swans. They come into the darkness, or rather out of it, those two identical divas, one black, one white. They pivot and flutter and pirouette, but now, as they go to leap, there is no web to catch them, and they hesitate and falter, stalled, like figures on a music box whose time has run out.

You don't think about time running out, until it happens to you; and then you can barely get it out of your head. It is as if you are living with that hour glass and it is draining, draining, draining. All those grains of sand. You do not think when you are a child that your mother's hours may be limited, or that those long summers will not go on forever, or that there will not always be a second chance to make things right. You do not think of the not-so-slow corrosions of cancers, and it does not occur to you that on some March night, just as spring is seeping through, its colors spreading like a wash across winter, someone will ring your sister's doorbell, will step over the threshold.

You do not think of these things before they happen, and afterwards you cannot stop. Or at least, I can't. That is what I think of as I listen to the rain and watch the smeared glow of the city lights across my balcony. I think of nightspinning, and of broken webs, and of words that hang unheard in the dark, and are left, floating free, to be scattered across the night sky like stars.

TWO

On the night before our mother died, I was woken by Marina. The insistent tone of her voice, punctuated by a loud banging on the door of my dorm room, dragged me out of sleep. When we had gone to the University of North Carolina, Marina had suggested that we share a room, but I had promptly vetoed the idea. Chapel Hill was my first real time away from home, my first break for freedom, and I was determined to make the most of it.

I was eighteen, and it had occurred to me that my mind might not, after all, be a piece of communal property that I was forever sharing with my sister. By the time we packed our identical duffel bags in the fall of 1983 and loaded them into Momma's car for the trip to Chapel Hill, I had endured three months of Marina's hurt feelings and several lectures from my mother on the subject of cruelty. Neither had any effect. Within a week of my mother wishing me luck and kissing me good-bye, her eyes wide with hope and sorrow, I had cut off all of my hair. I looked like I had had a close encounter with a pair of hedge clippers, but I thought it was marvelous. Never again would anyone start a conversation with me, only to realize three sentences into it that I was not, after all, Marina.

Now, in the pre-dawn hours of this October morning three years after our arrival in North Carolina, Marina was hammering on my door, standing in my hallway, demanding my total attention. The moment I opened the door, she burst into the room like fury itself, the damp night smell of mown grass clinging to her. I watched as she began grabbing my things. Clothes, and hairbrush, and glasses, and shoes, all were stuffed into a blue canvas bag that she had come equipped with, and even as she was saying, 'It's Momma. Come on, we have to go!' I could feel my stomach constricting into a sour, bile-filled puddle of dread.

'How do you know?' I finally asked. She shoved a pair of jeans and a sweatshirt towards me and shook her head at my obvious stupidity, at the sticky slowness that I was mired in.

'Uncle Ritchie called me,' she replied. 'And if you had a phone like any normal person, he'd have called you too.'

I felt as if a bucket of glue had been poured over me and was hardening, but by now Marina was pushing me towards the door, urging me on as one does a large reluctant animal, a cow or a mule that, given half a chance, might suddenly sink down on its haunches and lose forward motion altogether.

'I knew anyways,' she added, as I had known that she would. My sister was still utterly determined in her conviction of her psychic powers, in her ability to communicate with me and Momma and God-only-knows-who-else at will. I felt like pointing out that that was precisely why there was no reason for me to bother to get a telephone, but I didn't argue. I was being hustled along the hall and down the stairs and pushed out into the street where Marina's old blue Honda sat like a matchbox toy, pulled up at a rakish angle on to the grass verge.

It seems to me now that drives like that are always kind of the same. They have certain characteristics in common, those moments in your life when everything is about to slip over the edge of change and there is not one single thing that you can do about it. There's an immediacy to every little detail. You notice with utter clarity the gas station that you pull into before hitting the interstate. You remember the neon sign with the letter missing, the attendant who slouches with the lethargic hostility of adolescence and smells vaguely of marijuana and spearmint chewing gum. You recall the disappointment of the night air that rushes in through the half-rolled-down window and fails to bring with it the shock of coldness that you had hoped would snap you into feeling something.

I slouched down in my seat and undid my seatbelt in a gesture of defiance, and I put both feet up on the dashboard. When I stared out of the half-rolled-down window, I could not see beyond the glass. All I could see was my own reflection staring back at me and, beyond that, trapped in the glass, Marina's profile as she drove.

I remember when I first knew that Momma was sick. It was during the spring break of our freshman year in college, long before anyone actually said anything, long before anyone actually 'knew' anything, in the diagnostic sense of the word. If I was Marina, I would probably insist that Momma had had 'a black aura', or some such thing, and that that was what I saw. But for a start I don't believe in that crap, and besides, I didn't need any supernatural indicators to tell me what was obvious.

I was standing in the dining room of our house where I had been working on a project. I had come back to Petamill for spring break because I had nowhere else to go. On arrival I had wasted no time in spreading my things over the entire dining room table, rendering it useless, and my mother and I had fought about it. It seemed like we fought about every little thing since I went off to Chapel Hill. Along with cutting my hair, I had developed a rigorous determination to rock the boat.

Turkey or ham for Easter, whether she did, or did not, have the right to send my high school clothes to the church charity sale, if I could, or could not, borrow her car, would, or would not, leave my shoes scattered around the living room. It wasn't, after all, the shoes or the car, and I didn't give a hoot about my old bell bottoms, or what we ate at Easter. It wasn't any of those things that I was fighting, it was Momma herself. It was her stoicism, her endless optimism, the way she just carried on, year after year, seating ladies at the Coachstop and recommending the club sandwich and the crab cakes, canning and jamming and saving pennies and hoping that somehow things would turn out and us girls would make something of ourselves beyond that tiny southern town.

Looking back on it now, I don't know what else I thought she could have done, but at the time her resignation terrified me. I wanted her to do something.

I wanted her to sweat, to fight, to struggle against circumstance. I was desperate for her to kick out against the dusty dirt-packed roads and the repetitive smack of screen doors, and the Sunday sound of Baptist hymns, and the billboard on the road out of town that said 'Jesus Saves'. But my mother did not believe in violent struggle. She believed that you played the cards you were dealt, that you took up your hand with good grace, and that that was just how life went.

The problem was that I didn't want my cards, I wanted a whole new deck, and I did not feel that my mother's message was one that I could afford to hear. Mired in the arrogance and the myopia of youth, I believed that my mother had no dreams, or that if she did, she did not dare to fight for them.

Anyways, on that particular spring afternoon, which must have been a Sunday because Momma wasn't at work, I was staring out of the dining room window when I saw her coming up the track that ran across the fields. She was walking very slowly and her head was bent, and once she paused and looked as if she was catching her breath. She was carrying a paper grocery bag that was probably filled with canning jars that had been stored in Uncle Ritchie's basement, and she kept switching the bag from arm to arm, leaning it against her hip as if it was heavy. Suddenly, I wanted to run out of the house and take the bag from her. I wanted to carry it back to the porch, walking beside her up the steps and chattering about my friends at Chapel Hill, and about my classes, and about all of the plans that I did not have for the future. But I couldn't. I stood frozen to the spot, as if I had been turned into a pillar of salt like one of those ladies from the Old

Testament, and as I watched her through the window I felt a burning in my stomach, and recognized the hideous knowledge that reaches beyond fear and into the certainty that nothing will ever be the same again.

The screen door banged in the kitchen when Momma came in, and I could hear her moving around. Then, after a moment, the noise stopped, and it seemed to take hours for me to walk out of the dining room and across the hallway to the kitchen door. The balls of my feet were tingling, and my ears were pricked like a cat's. I don't know what I expected to find. Maybe I just thought she'd be dead in there on the floor. So, when I pushed the door open and looked in and saw her sitting at the red-topped kitchen table, I was so flooded with relief that I picked a fight with her right off about whether or not I'd take a part-time job at the campus art store.

Marina came in right in the middle of it and, hard as I tried, I couldn't involve her. She got that stubborn look on her face and refused to say a thing, and finally Momma just stood up and turned away to the sink and started rinsing out jars. Then she looked up at me and shrugged and said, 'Oh Shoo Fly, you just do whatever you want', and that answer terrified me so deeply that I stayed awake all that night, listening to the peepers and staring into the hot dark.

By the time we got to the hospital in the late morning, there wasn't much of Momma left. She died quietly that afternoon with no fuss, playing out the cards she'd been dealt. Marina and I didn't know what to do, so we just sat there on either side of her bed, as identical and silent as bookends.

I gave Marina the house. Well, not the whole thing; I gave her my half. I didn't do it immediately, at least not before the funeral. The thought didn't even occur to me during those first, flat, white-light days when the world seemed as if it had no texture, no edges or rough surfaces, nothing you could get any purchase on. Everything had been robbed of shadow and was slippery to the touch, so thoughts just slid off, refused to stick or stay in any particular place.

Momma was buried in the Petamill Unitarian cemetery next to Grandma, something that, in itself, was not even a decision. Without ever saying anything at all about it, I knew that neither Marina nor I would ever have contemplated the idea of cremation. Actually, we probably did talk about it, since both of us were big on the idea of making informed decisions, even if we already knew what we were going to do. So we probably discussed the possibility of cremating Momma, regardless of the fact that we already knew we wouldn't do it. Perhaps Marina brought it up one afternoon when I was downstairs washing dishes and staring out of the kitchen window and she was up in Momma's room lying on the bed, or going through drawers deciding what Momma should wear for her journey into eternity. Most likely she telegraphed the words right into my head, saying something like, 'I don't even want to think about burning her up, do you?' And I probably replied, 'God, no. None of those urns and scatterings and ashes.' 'There aren't any ashes,' Marina would have said. 'At least that's what they say.

They say it's more like sand. Kind of grainy and heavy.'
That's probably how it went, and with us a floor apart
and not a word spoken that any other living person
could have heard.

Uncle Ritchie bought a new suit at the men's store.
It was light gray and vaguely shiny, and even though
I'm sure it fitted him, he looked uncomfortable in it.
He looked squeezed and buttoned and compressed, as
if he was being garroted. I didn't need to be told that
Uncle Ritchie wouldn't be around long. I don't mean
that it was the great hereafter that was beckoning him.
It was more like somewhere south of Miami, although
the possible similarity between the two does not escape
me. I pretty much knew that Uncle Ritchie had been
biding his time, just like the rest of us. Ever since his
wife, whose name I can't even remember, ran off with
somebody-or-other a long time ago, Uncle Ritchie
had been the ghostly pet of both my mother and my
grandmother. Now that Momma was dead, the whole
of Grandma's farm was his. The farm was nothing to
write home about, but it would probably set him up
for life in some halfway-decent Florida trailer park
where he could fish. Momma's house and its two acres,
for what it was worth, was ours.

I couldn't look at that house with its white clapboard and its porch and screen doors without feeling
something akin to a bout of panic. It was as if, one
day, I might walk in through the door and never be
able to get back out again. It was as if to be in that
house was to be fifteen, or sixteen, or seventeen
forever, locked into that Georgia town, the flat mud-
green lozenges of the fields and my mother's eternal

hopefulness. So, what I did next now seems inevitable, but it is not something that I am exactly proud of.

There's a weird kind of silence that comes down on the day after a funeral. I felt as if I'd been to a party and was slightly hung over from it, and so, sometime in the late morning, I went out on to the front porch and sat on the glider, which had been there since about 1965, and whose springs were squeaky, and potentially lethal. They gave you the distinct feeling that you might be gliding happily along when they would decide, entirely of their own volition, to give up the ghost and let go of their springy little lives and shoot you forward, right off the porch and into the driveway. I was contemplating this, and wondering how far I might fly, as my sneakered toe propelled me back and forth in a satisfyingly moronic stupor, when Marina came out and sat down on the porch step.

There were times when the sight of Marina still jolted me. Times when, no matter how much I ought to, I never could get used to the idea of a carbon copy of myself. No matter how short I cut my hair, or what I wore or how I spoke, I would always be her. If you ran an electrocardiogram on us, the peaks and troughs would match exactly, and so would our eyes, and the shape of our earlobes.

'What do you want to do with the house?' Marina asked after a while.

I stopped in mid-glide and looked at her narrowly. She wasn't looking at me. She was staring across the crab-grassy lawn and the track that led to Grandma's house, where this very moment Uncle Ritchie was probably packing his Bermuda shorts, and out into the field beyond. Her eyes were fixed on the crop of something that looked like kale that had been planted by the Herveys, who leased the land and all married each other and wore overalls and promised to buy Uncle Ritchie out just as soon as he named the day, which would probably be tomorrow.

'What do you mean?' I asked.

'Well,' Marina turned slowly and looked at me. She shrugged a little. 'I was thinking,' she said, 'that after we finished college, we could just come home.'

The words filled me with a distinct physical urge to leap up and start screaming and waving my arms in the air like a crazy person, but instead, I waited a moment and then I said, as calmly as I could, 'What?'

'Come back here,' Marina said, warming to her subject. 'You know, live here. Like we used to. Everything could be the same again. We could both get jobs around here. It wouldn't be hard. It would be just the same.' She repeated this insistently, as if it was a virtue, the main selling point of her master plan.

I stared at my twin sister, wondering if she was out of her mind. It was all I could do not to slap her, or shake her, not to lower my face to hers and scream that we were grown-up now, that we weren't the goddamn nightspinners anymore, and that besides, didn't she understand that I had spent practically my whole conscious life, at least since I could remember it, wanting, and then trying, and then succeeding, in getting out of here. I wanted to scream at her that 'just the same' was, to me, roughly the equivalent of dead.

Marina started talking then about how it would be, about which of us could have Momma's room, and how we'd repaint the downstairs and I could turn the

garage into my studio. Great. The thoughts filtered
through the buzzing that had begun in my head. I could
work out of here, and then I would never ever have to
leave at all, except to go to the Piggly Wiggly and to
collect my social security checks. I could see us sitting
right here on this front porch, on this same goddamn
glider, the two weird sisters creaking down into middle
age. Eventually we'd stop talking altogether and just
hold long conversations with each other through the
telegraph wires in our heads. Maybe of an evening,
Momma could join in too. Then we'd start dressing
alike, and local kids would stare at us when we went to
the bank and dare each other to ring our doorbell on
Halloween.

Without even looking at Marina I got up and went
into the house, slamming the door hard behind me.

It was late that night when I came downstairs. I knew
Marina had gone to bed because I'd heard her, and I'd
waited for a good long time afterwards before I came
out of Momma's room where I'd been pretending to
sleep and snuck along the hall without flipping the
lights. I even remembered to skip the tenth step on the
stairs where it squeaked. I had on my favorite red
shoes, just like Dorothy in *The Wizard of Oz*, but mine
were Keds, not ruby slippers.

In the kitchen I paused just long enough to drop an
envelope on the table. It wasn't addressed, but Marina
would know that it was for her. In it was as legal
sounding a letter as I knew how to write in which I
gave her my half of the house. I don't think even then
that I could have fooled myself that this was an act of

generosity, and instead of making me feel less guilty, as maybe I'd half-hoped that it would, it only made me feel worse. I was like a thief, except that what I was stealing was wrapped in an act of omission.

I was careful with the screen, easing it back so that it didn't bang, just like I'd learned to do when I was a kid, and in two steps I was on the back walk and tippy-toeing along the concrete path to the garage. Marina's Honda was parked on the driveway and, while it wasn't actually blocking the big barn-like doors of the garage, it wasn't exactly out of the way either. I figured that I'd only have to drive on the lawn a little bit to get around it.

I swung the doors back and saw Momma's icky green Impala parked right dead center, where it always was. One quick look reassured me that it had four inflated tires and a key in the ignition. I was counting on the fact that it would have gas in the tank too, since Momma always took care of things like that. I opened the driver's side door and threw my duffel bag on to the seat, and I was about to swing my big canvas purse in behind it, when something strange happened.

The next thing I knew, I was out of the garage and running back up the path and darting into the kitchen like something behind me was on fire. I didn't need to turn the lights on. I went straight to the cabinet, the one to the left of the sink where Momma stored her jams and jellies and relishes that we'd always made such a fuss over having to eat and been so embarrassed by. Before I even knew what I was doing, I had the door open and was reaching up for jars of red pepper jelly, and green piccalilli, and yellow corn relish, and sweet orangey balls of pickled peaches.

I stuffed as many jars as I could into my shoulder bag. They clinked and clanked, and the bag weighed about a ton, dragging on my shoulder. Then I grabbed a few more jars, as though they might be the last food in the world that I would ever have the chance to get my hands on. When I couldn't hold anymore I backed out of the kitchen door, leaving the cabinet wide open and letting the screen snap like a gunshot as I hobbled down the path and into the garage, bent double over my booty like Quasimodo.

I threw the jars and the bag on to the long slippery front seat of the Impala and climbed in. I said a prayer of grace and thanks to Momma as the engine turned over on the first try and the needle on the fuel gauge zoomed up to 'full', and then I put the car in reverse and went flying backwards out of the garage, just missing Marina's Honda, and driving a deep set of ruts into the soft earth.

I didn't turn on my lights as I shot out on to the road and made a three point turn. Nor did I look up. I didn't need to. I knew what I would see. I knew that I would see the white-clad figure of my sister standing like a specter in the upstairs window, staring down at me from the darkened house.

THREE

September fifteenth. I wake up early to pale, milky light that filters through the curtains. The material shifts and breathes in the gritty draft of air that sighs from the window. The pattern is crossed with green leaves and they appear to lift and float. The street below is utterly silent. I have dreamed of Marina.

When she was alive, I rarely dreamed of her. In death, however, she has chosen to make her move. She has infiltrated not only my waking hours, but also my sleeping ones. Now she moves through my dreams on a regular basis and in a variety of guises. There is almost never a night that goes by when she does not put in at least a cameo appearance. Last night I saw her standing in a circle of fire.

Uneasiness clings to me like a spider's web, but I do not know why. I can hear my heart, and on my tongue there is the metallic aftertaste of fear. For a moment I lie very still, watching the dust motes in the new day. I concentrate on the row of pictures that marches across my bedroom wall. They are antique prints, aquatints of historic houses in Britain. I find them soothing. Tiny people populate their scenes. Women walk across long lawns shaded by broad oaks. Children run, their minuscule hands raised, their voices locked in silent shouts and laughter. Men stand under willow trees beside ornamental ponds and step in and out of carriages. Merton House. Haddon Hall. Lanhydrock. I was only in England once and I never visited any of these places, but I like their names, and I repeat them to myself over and over again until I can no longer feel the beating of my heart.

I get up, and my feet feel for the grainy familiarity of my ancient and threadbare rugs. I invested early in 'shabby chic'. Initially it was a design choice that was a function of poverty rather than trend, but now that I could afford to get rid of them I have grown attached to my distressed tables, and my blotchy mirrors in their gilded frames. I pull on my jeans and shirt, dressing quickly. The living room seems reassuringly normal when I open the door, and the dog is waiting for me. He watches me from his bed by the fireplace. He might appear relaxed, lounging in his large fur coat, but I know that he is coiled like a spring. He calculates my every move, waiting for the faintest sign that I am ready to go out.

The dog was called 'Jaeger' when George brought him home for me, but I do not speak German, and I changed his name to Jake. 'Jake the Snake' I sometimes call him: 'My Yellow-eyed Friend', 'The Young Man in the Two-Toned Suit'. Still, at the time I wondered if it was bad luck to change a dog's name, the way that they say it is bad luck to change the name of a boat or a horse, and I worried that this might evidence itself in Jake's hating me, or being stolen, or hit by a car. I was sometimes afraid that I had bestowed misfortune upon him, and I was afraid that he would not understand words like 'sit', and 'dinner', and 'ball' in English. I feared that he would feel lost in a foreign world, that he would lie patiently on his bed, hoping that one day he would hear a word spoken in German.

If this was the case, if Jake was lost and teaching himself English, he was a quick learner. Certainly he never misunderstood 'walk' or 'park', words that throw him into a wild dance of anticipation. That is what he does as I gather his leash and his red rubber ball and a couple of the plastic bags that I steal from the vegetable section of the supermarket. Jake charges into the entrance hall ahead of me. He stations himself across the door, reaching up to nose the worn knob of the Yale lock, urging me on, butting against me as I bend to tie the laces of my sneakers.

As we come out on to the landing I can hear the stereo in Cathy's apartment. Our apartments share the top floor and are separated by the divide of the attic stairwell, so no noise carries from my kitchen to hers. This is merciful because she plays Celine Dion, Oasis, or Hooty And The Blowfish every morning while she gets ready to go to work. This morning Up Where We Belong filters out around the edges of her apartment door. I cast only a cursory glance at my mail from yesterday, which is still lying in a small heap on the landing table, before I follow Jake, who is already bounding down the first flight of the stairs.

Cathy is helpful by nature and she often collects my mail from the front hall when she comes in from work and leaves it on the table in the top landing. I know that she believes that she can lure me into active engagement with the 'real world' through these tidbits of telephone bills and Williams Sonoma catalogs, but I am uncooperative on this front and I often leave my mail on the landing for two or three days before I take it inside. Cathy does not quit though, and she would make a project of me if I let her. She knows that there is misfortune in my past, and while she considers me to be both odd and irresponsible, she thinks that I am worthy of salvation. She demonstrates this conviction by inviting me to the parties that she gives and introducing me to all of the single flight stewards and United Airlines ticket agents with whom she works. 'You have to kiss a whole lot of frogs,' Cathy told me once, lowering her voice to the whisper that many people feel the imparting of wisdom demands.

When Jake and I step out of the house the air is muggy. Far above there may be clear, crystalline blue, but you cannot see it; a thin veil of misty clouds whites out the sky. Jake and I start down the street. At the lights he stops beside me and my fingers rest on the sleek familiar fur of his head as if he were a seeing-eye dog. When the traffic stops people surge towards us. The women wear suits and running shoes and glance at their watches with peeved expressions. The men look drifty and sad and carry briefcases. Jake and I weave through them as if we are negotiating rapids, or drift wood on a river. We reach the other side in safety and continue down the five blocks that slope to the Schuykill.

Jake's park was once the province of junkies and hookers, a meeting place for the less savory side of the city's gay scene. Now it has been rehabilitated and peculiarly claimed for dogs. They come not just from this neighborhood, but from all over the city. Cars containing Labradors, Rottweilers, and Jack Russells park along the opposite street, their inhabitants wriggling with joy at the promised opportunity to run free. Young mothers push strollers and call to Golden Retrievers, and in the early morning and at sunset a fleet of vet students arrive and land like geese, all accompanied by the strays they have rescued.

Jake drops his red rubber ball at my feet, his eyes bright with expectation. Looking at him I feel a terrible pang of guilt. There is no reason for me to stay in the city. I should not have moved into the brownstone a year ago, when George and I went our separate ways. I should have moved to Bucks County, or to the Brandywine, or to somewhere out along the Delmarva Peninsula. I should have gone then, and I should go now. I should not linger, but instead should summon the energy required to step forward into my brave new future. This is what others tell me and, periodically, what I tell myself. I should not wait for George, and indeed, I am not. His intentions are declared and he has moved on, into the young and tender arms of one of his graduate students.

I know this fact, and I am surprised by how little it moves me. I blame this on Marina. I am quite certain that it is her revenge on me. She has reached down from whatever netherland it is that she now inhabits, and she has pulled some plug on my life. She has opened a valve, and then she has watched as feeling and color, and even pain, have swirled away. Jake gives a small moan of impatience and I reach down for his ball and throw it, watching as he races across the scrubby grass and leaps to meet it in mid-arc.

★

'You have an admirer,' Shawn says as I come through the vestibule doors. This morning he's wearing black jeans so tight they must have been spray painted on and a neon white T-shirt with 'Philly Rocks' lettered across his chest in purple. The color roughly matches his hair. Shawn's voice is high and sing-songy, and he waggles his index finger at me as if I'm a naughty child. I have no idea what he's talking about, but I don't say so, and he forgets to elaborate because Jake pounces on him and is busy sniffing the bottom of his pants and his running shoes.

'Jakey!' Shawn squeals, and Jake hops with pleasure.

Shawn's a relatively new addition to the household. I guess he's been a friend of Cathy's for a while; apparently they met at the gym where Cathy hangs out a lot, especially during the summer because it's air-conditioned and her apartment isn't. She told me she and Shawn became 'work-out buddies' because he has the best abs she's ever seen. 'Uuun-bel-ievable!' she'd said, rolling her eyes. I think she actually has a crush on him, but the evidence would suggest that not much is going to come of it. Still, I suspect that Cathy lives in hope, because last month she convinced Zoe, one of the architects who owns the building, to hire him as some kind of secretary. Now he seems to be ubiquitous. I almost fell over him last week when I came out of my apartment and found him on his hands and knees polishing the bottoms of the banisters, but he'd made up for it by kissing my hand and explaining that he was 'Zoe and Justin's new wife'. 'I can be your fiancé too, if you want,' he'd said.

In theory this marriage will enable Zoe and Justin to spend more time actually doing drafting work in the studio that they keep uptown while Shawn does things like call the plumber, and organizes what Zoe calls 'the quagmire' of her and Justin's paperwork. In practice, however, Shawn seems to spend most of his time dusting and polishing and rearranging the mail into little alphabetical piles that he stacks on the sideboard in the entryway. This last practice has already been the cause of some controversy. According to Cathy, last week, Gordon, who lives in the apartment below me, pitched a fit because he said that Shawn had opened one of his credit card bills. Shawn apparently told him to 'get a life', and later told Cathy that he was absolutely certain that Gordon was a 'closet case'. Now Gordon glares at him on the stairs, and Shawn is prone to sticking his tongue out at him when his back is turned.

Even so, Zoe says Shawn is 'A Godsend'. She told me this last week, and she'd widened her eyes and nodded her head just like a Virginia-Go-Faster as she'd said it, so I assume that his job isn't in jeopardy. Pre-Shawn, Zoe and Justin hadn't had an employee, and apparently that was a mistake. 'A big one,' Zoe had said, 'I have no idea,' she had added, 'how you do your thing all alone.' I assumed that by 'thing' she meant my so-called business, and I had refrained from sharing with her the fact that my idea of paperwork generally runs to a series of large brown envelopes. I label them and fill them up and stick them in a drawer. I'm sure the sight would make Shawn faint.

Now he's spraying Windex on the huge gilt mirror that hangs over the sideboard and rubbing at it with wadded up newspaper.

'I just cannot stand fly spots,' Shawn announces. He

glares at them in the mirror as Jake and I start up the stairs, and then he raises his eyebrows in mock horror so his tiny upright spikes of hair rise and fall like a crown of thorns.

'I like the new hair color,' I say. As far as I can remember, last week it was kind of blue.

'You should try it,' Shawn says, rubbing hard at a fly spot. 'It only lasts a couple of weeks and it doesn't even trash your hair.' He looks in the mirror and grins at me, 'I don't know what I'd do without that Miss Clairol,' he says.

A large florist's bouquet, shrouded in plastic and tied with a large orange bow has been carefully laid across the landing table outside my door. 'These Came For You!!!' Cathy has written in swirly letters on a yellow Post-it note. Obviously, this is what Shawn was talking about, and I can imagine the thrill it must have given both of them. Cathy has arranged the flowers so prominently that even I will not be able to ignore them, and when I take them inside and open them, two sachets of 'flower fresh' plop into my kitchen sink. I can't find a card. There's no hint of their provenance. They are lilies, a dozen stems in orange and yellow, and a deeper, almost brownish, red. They have been carefully arranged in a cascade, the darker colors at the bottom and the spikes of the paler blooms reaching up like tongues of flame.

The colors clash and are faintly disturbing. On the whole, I really don't like lilies. When we were small Momma planted a bank of them by the garage and they grew like weeds. I remember that their thin, dark green leaves were shiny, and that their orange, upturned faces were too sharp against the chipping white paint. Once Marina said she saw a copperhead in the lilies, but I knew that this was a lie. Black snakes lived there, and since they're the enemies of copperheads, I didn't think we could have both living in the lily bank. Even so, I preferred not to pick the flowers, and when I walked by the lilies on my way to the clothes-line, the plastic basket biting into my hip, and my feet bare in the sawgrass, I gave them a wide berth. I watched for a sudden motion, for a bobbing of their bright faces, or a ripple in the forest of their leaves that stood tall in the heat, and were so dark and shiny that they might have glowed with sweat.

I cannot imagine who might have sent the lilies to me. It seems unlikely that they are from any of Cathy's ticket agents. One of them had asked me out several months ago, but I had been evasive and rude and he had gone away with the faint and consoling impression that I might be gay. I look at the calendar over the stove, but Thursday, 15 September, means absolutely nothing to me. I start to go next door and ask Cathy if she is certain that she has not made a mistake, but then I realize that she will have gone to work by now. It would be pointless in any case. Before her present incarnation as a deputy supervisor for United ticketing out at the airport, Cathy flew the friendly skies. She eventually was promoted to Purser. Cathy was the smiling flight attendant who kept track of the vegetarian meals and made sure that the economy fliers weren't using the First Class bathrooms. She may be terminally perky, but she does not make administrative mistakes.

I stick the lilies in some water, and pour myself a cup of coffee. Then I call Beau.

'Did you send me flowers?' I ask.

'Why would I do that?' he replies, and I can hear someone in his office. I can see him raising his hand to them, index finger up to say 'just a minute'. I can see his unruly mess of blond hair, his tweed jacket hung over the back of his chair, his loosened tie, and I feel a small pang of disappointment. Even though I don't like the lilies, I realize that I was half-hoping that Beau had sent them.

'I have no idea,' I say, 'but somebody did.'

'Well Sugar, I would have if I'd thought of it,' Beau says. 'Have a beer with me and tell me all about it.'

I don't need to ask where, or even what time. It will be at seven and not six, because the first thing Beau likes to do when he gets home from work is watch *The Simpsons*, and we only ever go to one place. It's a mediocre bar called Sherlock's. It serves pallid, elongated burgers, yellow cheese nachos flecked with bright green pieces of jalapeno peppers, and cheap beer. There is guaranteed to be no live entertainment. '221b Baker Street', as Beau refers to it, has the sole advantage of being about four steps from his apartment and, since he is terminally lazy and not filled with the spirit of adventure, I always go there.

'Well,' I say, 'my dance card is free.'

I see him the minute I walk in. Beauregard. The first time I heard that name, I laughed out loud. George told me that one of the secretaries in his department was dating some guy called Beauregard from South

Dakota and wanted to bring him to our Christmas
party, and I laughed out loud. I didn't know that
anyone from South Dakota could be called Beauregard.
Oh, I knew Beauregards and Shelbys and Camerons all
right, up the yazoo, but they all came from my side of
the Mason Dixon. Until I met Beau, I'd never even
considered that you could grow up in Spearfish and be
called 'Beauregard'.

The secretary hadn't lasted more than a couple of
months, but Beau had. He'd struck up a vague, guy-
type friendship with George and used it as an excuse
to wander over to our apartment on the weekends and
play with Jake. Then, when George and I split up, I
got Beau, just like I got the sofa and the wok. Of
course, I had always known, in some secret part of
myself, that he liked me better than he liked George,
and besides I had Jake. I didn't fool myself about the
real nature of the attraction, but even so, I was pleased
when the first weekend I moved into the brownstone
I found Beau on my doorstep holding two tennis balls
and a six of beer.

I have pushed the door open and paused, not to
search among the crowd, or to scan the faces, but to
savor the comforting smell of beer and cigarette smoke,
and the babble of indistinct words and jagged lines of
laughter. Beau is leaning on the bar, his heavy-set
frame askew as he flirts with the bartender. She is petite
and butch, with a nose ring, and a slight air of menace.
When Beau turns and sees me his hair falls into his
eyes. He pushes it away, yanks at his already loosened
tie, and treats me to the cock-eyed smile that nurses in
the hospital where he works find so charming. This
otherwise potent weapon glances off me as though I

am Princess Leah and my shield is raised. One of
the more useful legacies of my southern past is that I
am immune to charm. God has not created the
crooked smile that can twist my hard heart, and Beau
knows this. Even so, he never stops trying. It's one of
the things I love him for, and he knows that too. I
slide on to a bar stool and Beau orders a pitcher of
beer.

'Suuusannah,' he says. 'Oh Susannah, don't you cry
for me.'

The first swallow is cold and familiar. I take my
time, drawing it out, knowing that I am not meant to
look forward to this as much as I do. Beau watches me
and lights a cigarette.

'So,' he says, 'someone sent you flowers?' I nod,
liking the cool way that the glass fits into my palm,
watching our reflection in the wood-framed mirror
behind the bar. The bartender catches my eye, glances
at Beau's cigarette and scowls in disapproval. I smile at
her, reach for Beau's pack, light one, and blow a quick
stream of smoke in her direction. Beau laughs and then
pretends he does not notice.

'So who?' he asks. 'Who is your suitor?'

'No one,' I say, 'probably. Probably something to
do with work. I dunno, they're testing a new arrangement for the opening and they forgot to include a
card.' Actually, this idea has not occurred to me until
this very moment, but it seems by far the most obvious
explanation.

'How is it?' Beau asks, 'Cambodia, or Laos, or
whatever the Hell it's called?'

'Indochine,' I say. 'It's good.'

Beau and I have laughed long and hard over the

restaurant project that I am currently working on. It's a big and expensive job, one of those east-west fusion cuisine places where everything is gussied up with lemon grass and ginger. The tension is rising because it is due to be opening on the Friday before Christmas and the contractors have been out on strike and have only recently returned to work. The owners often send me things in the mail, swatches of material, sample menus, lacquered red chopsticks, and forget to tell me their purpose or origin. I ignore these, leaving them in sad and unopened heaps on my study floor while I continue with the finishing touches of my designs.

When the owners initially explained to me that they wanted 'the concept to be steeped in the heritage of Southeast Asia', Beau suggested that they call the place 'My Lai'. I thought that the pictures from *Life* magazine would be a highly effective motif, and Beau pondered the possible ingredients of a house cocktail called the 'Lieutenant Calley'. The idea did not come to pass, and instead Indochine is black and white, startled only by the occasional livid burst of color. Huge lithographs of a woman who looks suspiciously like Catherine Deneuve cover the three-storey dining room wall. She will gaze down on miniature plates of tempura and survey spiky arrangements of elephant grass and orchids.

In all likelihood the lilies have been sent as a test run for my approval, a down-market alternative to birds of paradise. Beau begins to tell me a story about the hospital funding office that he runs, but I have become distracted and am not listening. I pour myself another beer and wonder if I can make all of Indo-

chine's wait-staff go barefoot and wear black pajamas
and coolie hats.

It is eleven o'clock by the time I leave Sherlock's.
Beau tries to persuade me to take a cab, but after a
second pitcher of beer and a plate of nachos that
neither of us was interested in eating, I wave him off,
telling him that I need the walk. At first there are
people on the streets. Voices bubble around me,
snatches of conversation wash up and recede. The gas
lamps in front of the opera house are flickering, giving
the illusion of wind on this still night, and above me
the lights of the tall buildings are silver streaks on the
sky.

As I head downtown the streets empty. The more
obvious theaters and bars cluster towards the historic
district. Down here they are more discreet. They are
tucked in behind the façades of the once great houses,
squirreled away in store fronts, recessed beyond court-
yards and awnings in the side streets. I skirt Rittenhouse Square, where at night the homeless congregate
and sleep on the ornate benches that old ladies occupy
by day. It is a lozenge of darkness canopied by trees
and I can feel eyes watching me as I cross the street.
For just a moment I imagine that I feel someone
moving behind me, a prickle dots the top of my
shoulder, and then I turn the corner and ahead of me I
hear a snatch of music.

There is a restaurant on the block ahead that was
one of my first projects. It seems dated now, but I still
stop to look at it. I know that beyond the doors there
are bare tables, wicker-seated chairs, stainless steel

buckets of flowers, round blue discs of plates. A group spills out on to the sidewalk, two couples, arms entwined, and with them comes a burst of light, a clatter of conversation, and the splurge of a saxophone. I walk on and my feet lift as if they are disembodied. My heels tap the pavement, moving of their own accord, bearing me along on the sweet jazzing riff of the city.

On my block it is darker. I have passed the little antique shop, the newspaper stand, and the video store, and now, quite suddenly, here are the heavy familiar blocks of the brownstones. My building is the last one, on the corner, and I must run the gauntlet. I have to weave under the trees and slip from streetlight to streetlight in order to reach it. Jake will be expecting me, and I am reaching for my keys, swearing yet again that I will clean out my bag, when the hairs on the back of my neck stand up.

It happens without warning and the sensation is so powerful that I stop in mid-stride, tip on the heels of my boots, and almost lose my balance. My body tingles and goes very still. I can hear nothing beyond the dim murmur of traffic streets away. A swathe of shadows stretches out in front of me. I take two steps forward, and I am sure that I hear two steps that are not my own. I stop and they stop. I know I hear breathing. I have just passed a street lamp and I do not want to turn around. Suddenly I'm too afraid of what I'll see. My throat begins to close and I cannot decide whether to spin and face the circle of light, or to run.

Then, a house ahead of me, a door opens and two men in jeans and polo shirts burst down the steps. A taxi whizzes down the street and stops as the lights turn to red. The men, whom I have seen before, raise their hands in greeting as they pass but do not break their stride. In my bag my hand closes over the cool lump of my key ring, and I step forward, shaking my shoulders, letting out something like a sigh, as if I have been holding my breath.

Jake is waiting for me as I come through the apartment door, and I pause only long enough to grab his leash. The sound of footsteps seems silly now that I see Jake again. He's my shield, my magic sword. No matter how late it is, or how dark, the streets never frighten me if I am with him. I am euphoric, unreasonably lit up, biting back a powerful desire to laugh. Jake tumbles down the stairs, and as I follow him I fancy that I can feel the house quivering with life. Soft music comes from behind Cathy's door. On the next floor down I can hear the TV playing in Gordon's apartment. Gordon works in a bank and is deeply attached to Jay Leno. Someone has put flowers on the sideboard in the front hall, and the etched glass in the vestibule doors looks as if it is made from spun sugar.

I let Jake take his time. There is a parrot who lives in a basement apartment on Delancey and sometimes it sits in the window and talks to people's feet as they walk by. Tonight, from behind its sheer white curtain, it talks to Jake, yammering at him like a fortune teller at the fair. He stands on the pavement, looking from me to the shadowy figure of the bird, cocking his head and raising his eyebrows in amazement. It is just before midnight when we get back and I am standing on the balcony when the phone begins to ring.

In the pause between the shrill tones of the fourth
and fifth rings, I hear the front door of the house slam
closed, and a moment later Zoe and Justin appear on
the sidewalk below. They are carrying neatly arranged
bundles of rubbish. Tomorrow is Friday, garbage day.
Any time after midnight black plastic bags and neatly
folded newspapers and cardboard boxes may be piled
on the far side of the street. There is an unwritten rule
that if you have anything particularly good to get rid
of, shoes, or an old overcoat, or left over party food,
or an uneaten pizza, you do not wait for the morning,
but take it out the night before. You arrange these
things carefully, allow them to protrude from the
corners of bags, place them discreetly on altars of
bottles and tin cans, so that in the deepest hours of the
night they can be picked over, adopted, accepted or
rejected.

Zoe and Justin have left what looks to be a hat, a
torn blanket and a box, possibly containing food.
Halfway up the street another door opens, another
couple appear bearing bags. I realize that this week I
have nothing to leave, no broken-handled saucepan,
worn out jeans, or single gloves. I step back into the
apartment, leaving the balcony window open, and
decide I will take down the ordinary rubbish anyways,
then I do not have to worry about missing the collection men in the morning.

I have tied the two bags and collapsed several wine
cases and tied them with brown string, when I notice
the lilies. Their spikes reach upward, and the blooms
are garish against the soft gray of my walls. Even
though it is not hot in my apartment their inky, dark
leaves glisten, and for half a moment I think I see them

quiver. I still have the big ribbon they came in and I snatch them out of the vase, letting them drip on the hardwood floor while I bind their stems and crimp the edges of the bow.

Outside, Jake and I dart across the street. Other people are coming out of houses now, carrying boxes of bottles and bags of trash, and the atmosphere is almost festive. Jake and I place our bags and our cardboard carefully beside Zoe and Justin's, and then I lay the lilies on top. I set them gently, as if they are the centerpiece at a funeral.

Back upstairs, before I close the window, I step on to the balcony again. More black mounds of rubbish are appearing, more squares of cardboard and gift-like bundles of tied paper. In the shadows and under the trees they are all dark lumps, but I can pick ours out. It is topped by a paint splash, by the flame-colored streak of the flowers and the burst of the orange bow. I turn away from them and close the window, quite certain that they will find their home, that my offering will be accepted, and that long before dawn the lilies will vanish into the night.

FOUR

'And, so?' Elena's voice comes to me from a long way off, as though she is calling out from behind a wall or speaking from the end of a long hallway, instead of from the smooth leather armchair where she sits not six feet from me. The sleek Swedish lines of the chair do not suit Elena's bulk. The paisleys of her skirts and the layered brocades of her jackets threaten to spill over its slim arms, to break free of the dour lines of tubular steel and flood across this room where we sit, watched over by the mandatory dusty ficus tree and bounded by book shelves and the smudged dirty window that looks down on to the quiet street below.

'You should get bars,' I say, dragging my eyes away from the window and looking at Elena. 'It really isn't safe.' She smiles, her heavy, aging face creasing and bending at all of its accustomed points.

'Are you still so worried, Susannah,' she asks, 'about safety?' There is a light in her eye, a glint of mischief as sharp as the high-pitched ring of a bell. The question is a joke, a self-parody. I am the doctor, you the patient. The cigar is not a cigar, and your slip is showing.

'Of course,' I say, and I am tempted to add, 'Aren't we all? Shouldn't you be?'

I have been coming to Elena for just over a year now. A psychotherapist of the old school, she is a genuine Viennese, the widow of a professor at Penn. She is a big woman, and in her luxurious patterned clothes she looks slightly not-human, like something designed and painted, an aging Klimt or the sculpture of a woman made by Gaudi. This image is enhanced by the fact that Elena often sounds like an imitation of Anna Freud. Even after years in the United States her accent is pronounced enough to be hokey. In fact, everything about Elena could appear to be fake, a self-dramatized concoction, except that she is real. There have been times when Elena has seemed more real to me than I am to myself. Every Friday for the last thirteen months I have sat in this room and asked her to make sense of the tangles in my mind. Sometimes she has been more successful than others. Today we have been talking about one of our favorite subjects, an old sore we return to again and again. We have been discussing Marina's death.

It happened in the spring, on 17 March, a Friday. In the evening, to be exact. Or at least that's what they think. That's their guess, the best they can do on the evidence which, surprisingly, given the gruesome nature of the crime, is slim.

It was, by all accounts, a beautiful night. The moon was half full and the air was soft and warm, brushed with those southern puffs of promise that reach even as far north as Alexandria, Virginia. Cherries would have been in blossom, their petals drifting down and landing on the cobblestones, dotting the water of newly filled fountains, and the windshields of the cars parked along the streets. On a night like that, a Friday night at the end of a long winter, people would have been going out, walking to the restaurants that sit on the piers along the Potomac, buying a bottle of wine, collecting a pizza, lingering on their doorsteps to sniff the air. Or so you would have thought. You would have thought that in a courtyard of fancy townhouses like the one where my sister lived, people would have been around. You would have thought that they would have stopped to talk, to greet one another, to comment on the flowers that had recently been set out in window boxes and stone urns. You would have thought that they would have noticed a stranger. But, on that count at least, you would have been wrong. Apparently they did not.

By the time she was found it was hard to fix the time of death. On that Friday, she was seen at six-fifteen, shortly after she garaged her car. She was carrying a briefcase, wearing a suit. Her winter coat was still flung over her shoulders. She said 'good evening' to several people, and smiled, and walked into the courtyard and, presumably, through her front door. It was not until she did not turn up at a dinner on the Saturday, not until the hostess in question had called five times and gotten no answer, not until she failed to appear at her job at the World Bank on Monday morning, that anyone became truly alarmed. By the time the homicide detectives of the Alexandria Police Force called me on Monday night, they figured that Marina had been dead for as much as three days. She fought hard, they could tell that much, and it might have been a close run thing. But he slit her throat, and in the end he stabbed her more than twenty-five times.

I say 'he', but it's a generic form. I have been assured that there is no reason to assume that the killer might not have been a woman. This idea, naturally, does not go down well. Most people don't like to think of women killing other women, and especially by a method that is quite so gruesome, but nothing can be counted out.

'Everyone is concerned about safety, my dear,' Elena says gently. She is not joking now. 'At least everyone who thinks,' she adds, 'but we have to live in the world, after all, don't we? We ride the bus. We cross the road. We even walk our dogs at night. What happens if we allow our fears to govern us?'

'We become cripples,' I say, rewarding her with a smile. 'We become prisoners.' I know these responses well. Elena nods, pleased with my progress.

'And, so?' she says, 'What else? What is it, Susannah, that is bothering you?'

'Nothing,' I reply. 'I'm sorry.'

'George is back?' Elena asks, 'No?'

'Yes, I guess so. I mean, I don't know.' In fact I do know. I know perfectly well that he's back because Beau has told me, and because the term has started, and that means that George will be teaching again. Fresh from his year in Paris, he will stand behind the lectern and perhaps will occasionally affect an accent not unlike Elena's. He has brought with him the wife that he acquired on what Beau terms his 'Junior Year abroad'. She is very young, and very gamine, and speaks with an accent of indeterminate European origin. Beau suspects her of coming from Oklahoma. I know this because he ran into them on his lunch break. In the bookstore. In the Philosophy section. Holding hands.

Beau was briefly introduced, and insists that the wife's name is Vignette. His rendition of this story, delivered earlier this afternoon by telephone, was complete with descriptive flourish, and it made me laugh, which was the point. It was also a warning. The Devil is abroad and Beau doesn't want me to be taken by surprise.

'And what do you think about that?' Elena asks. She cocks her head on one side, encouraging response. She's finding me heavy going today.

'I don't care,' I say. 'Really, Elena. I do not give a damn, and that's the God's honest truth.'

'Good,' Elena says.

'It's brought things back, that's all,' I say, 'but it was bound to wasn't it? I mean, everything happened when George was here, and then he was gone, and now he's back again.'

'So it takes you back to what happened before he left?'

'Of course,' I say. 'I mean, Marina, and everything falling apart, and then the fight.'

At the mention of 'the fight' Elena and I both smile. It was 'the fight' that brought us together, 'the fight' that propelled me to her door. As usual with things like that, it was the catalyst, and turned out to be the least of my problems. Now I can smile about 'the fight'. At the time I believed that it was conclusive evidence that I was going out of my mind.

This thesis was suggested by George. It was George who, one August night a month before he was due to leave for his year in Paris, told me that I had become 'as-crazy-as-my-crazy-fucking-sister'. Shortly afterwards, I slapped him. And then he slapped me back. And then I broke rather a lot of things that we had either purchased together or that I had given him as gifts. And then he packed a bag and went to a hotel. And then he called the next morning to tell me that I was going insane, that my rage at being left behind while he went to France for a year was conclusive evidence, both of the fact that he had made the right choice in deciding to go alone, and was now making the right choice again in leaving me. And incidentally, he had added, since Marina had been killed, and actually, probably, for some time before that, I had been as crazy as a bug. In fact, given the way I had behaved towards Marina even before she was dead, given the fact that I had refused even to speak to her on the telephone, given all of that, not to mention the way that I behaved in general, I had probably always been as crazy as a bug. Marina and I were probably both crazy as bugs, George said, and always had been. He just should have seen it earlier.

His argument had seemed so persuasive at the time that it had caused me to seek out Elena. Elena, who, having listened patiently to the details of 'the fight', shrugged her shoulders at the broken china and asked me about Marina.

'What could you have done?' she had asked, after I had told her about the knife wounds, about the lack of evidence, the front door that was not forced, the blood smears that said nothing, the fingerprints that could not be matched, the startled look on the detective's face when I arrived to identify the body, and the joke that I had made, asking if he needed verification that I was 'next of kin'.

'How could you have saved her?' Elena had asked, after I had told her how I had stood and stared at Marina's ruined face. 'What do you think you could have done?'

'Talked to her,' I had finally replied. 'I could have talked to her.'

But I didn't. On that count, George was right. I had refused even to pick up the phone.

Although we had been almost completely estranged in the ten years since Momma's death, in the weeks before Marina died, she had suddenly tried repeatedly to reach me. The first time she called I really was on my way to a meeting, and I spoke to her only briefly, but from the very first instant that I heard her voice on the phone, heard her demanding my attention, and my time, and possibly my entire life, I felt something close to panic. I recognized the insistence in her tone, and I felt her sense of ownership, this thing she believed she held over me because my heartbeat was the same as hers. I felt it as surely as if it had been a hand laid across the back of my neck. In that instant I knew that if I let Marina back into my life she would nightspin her web around me until I was paralyzed.

So when she called again, I said I was too busy, or promised that I would call back, but I never did, and she kept calling. Finally, I told George to say that I wasn't home, and when he wasn't there to lie for me, I stopped answering the telephone altogether.

She caught me only once, on a Saturday, a week before she died. It was in the evening. I was making dinner. George had taken Jake to the park and we were expecting guests, and when the phone rang I reached for it without thinking. My sister's voice was edgy, high pitched and angry.

'For Christ's sake!' she had exploded across the telephone line. 'What the Hell is the matter with you? You just don't return phone calls?' A glass of wine was sitting on the counter, light glimmering off its liquid surface, and as I reached for it I could feel my pulse begin to hammer. 'Damn it!' Marina was saying. 'Damn it, Susannah! You can't do this! You can't block me out, and you know it. You have to talk to me!'

'No,' I said, hearing my own voice as if it was disembodied. Hard and flat. 'No, I don't. I don't have to talk to you.' There was a silence then, just the slightest breath of one, before I heard Marina's voice again. This time it was quiet, not much more than a whisper.

'It won't do any good, Shoo,' she said, and I could see the beginnings of her smile. Over hundreds of miles I could sense the slight, twisting rise of her lips. 'You know it won't do any good,' she said. 'You know that if I want you to, you'll hear me anyway.'

And then I leaned over and pulled the phone plug out of the wall.

It is four o'clock when I leave Elena's office. I follow her down the narrow back stairs of her house and along the hall to the front door where she lets me out on to the street.

'Remember,' she says, standing on the step, her

heavy hand resting on the cut-glass of the door knob, 'I will be here next week, and then I am gone. To Austria, for a month.'

'I won't feel abandoned,' I say.

Elena goes home for a month twice a year, to stay with her sister, and this is another of our jokes, that I will become an orphan, that I will seethe with quiet rage because she has abandoned me. I have read enough contemporary fiction to know that this is what patients often feel. I have even heard that all Manhattan therapists decamp to Long Island and upstate Connecticut for the month of August, and that the steaming city is then regularly abandoned to the grieving, the orphaned, and the angry. However, I have previously assured Elena that in my case this is not a concern. By now I know that she agrees with me, and that what truly worries her is not that I will be enraged at her desertion, but that I will simply forget to come again on her return, that in her absence I will drift away, I will slip my moorings and float, unguided, out towards the flat plate of the horizon that is the edge of the world.

The first hints of twilight thicken the late afternoon as I weave my way in and out of the narrow streets of the historic district where Elena lives and head downtown. It's just after five p.m. and things are closing. Normally, I might walk from Elena's, but today I have brought the car. I have a meeting at Indochine that even now I am late for.

The car's big engine hums, and for half a moment I close my eyes and breathe in the comforting smell of its leather seats. I do not need an old Mercedes Benz. I could easily do with a Honda, or one of any number of small, fuel-efficient vehicles that would require less care, take up a smaller and cheaper space in the garage, be easier to park. But I love my car. I bought it from a secondhand dealer, a shyster mechanic in a dubious part of town, who assured me that it had once belonged to his mother. It is a big old sedan of the deepest midnight blue, a color that they do not make anymore for the American market.

I pay my garage to wash my car regularly, to polish its beveled chrome lines, wax its doors, and roof, and hood. I know that this is vanity, and that it may seem incongruous, given how I look myself, but I am fussy on this score. To me my car is akin to an ocean liner, large and ungainly, verging on ugly, but grand, and I treat it with all the care accorded to a species on the endangered list. The garage attendants agree with me. They are sick of rounded Saabs and tank-like SUVs. 'That car has style,' one of them tells me, and when they see Jake jump into the back seat, they shake their heads in disapproval, even though he sits on a folded blanket.

There is a parking space of sorts in the alley behind Indochine, and I pull in there beside two dumpsters full of pieces of plywood that sit under a sign reading NO TRESPASSING — DANGER ZONE — PRIVATE PARKING. Lolly's white Lexus has already taken the prime spot and I am forced to the outside, blocking her in. This doesn't actually matter, since we'll be leaving at the same time. There is no sign of Lolly herself, and I assume that she's already inside talking to the construction manager, and feeling superior because I am late.

Lolly is one half of the partnership that owns Indochine, and is therefore my employer. This is not

the first time that I have worked with Lolly and
Richard Thomson, who may or may not be her
husband. I am not entirely clear on the status of their
personal relationship, and she has never cared to
explain it to me. They were married, or are married,
or might be about to be married. The difference to me
is minimal. Thomson Inc. pays its bills, avoids bank-
ruptcy, and occasionally makes money, all of which
could be considered a rarity in this business. They own
another restaurant in the city that I designed for them.
On the top floor of an old warehouse looking out on
the Schuykill, it is a pretend-punk martini bar with
red leather couches and serves Cal-Mex nibbles, baby
lobster tacos, crab and black bean enchiladas, and
hollowed out limes filled with margarita sorbet. Basically it's a safe place for single bankers and the younger
Penn professors to hang out and feel that they are hip
and marginally dangerous. Indochine will be the
Thomsons' upscale showcase. No whiff of punk here,
and you have to eat at a table.

'Put a hard-hat on,' Lolly says as I approach. 'We're
under-insured.'

She is wearing a pink suit, a buff, baby color that
hints of a pearly dawn. The skirt is mid-calf length, a
wrap around that she has made no attempt to secure.
Her long stockinged leg emerges from the resulting
gap and ends in a high-heeled shoe of the same pink
color. I have seen this before, this predilection of
Lolly's for perfectly matching footwear, and I have
always assumed that she has her shoes specially dyed.
Two by two, I envision them lining her closet shelves.
Baby blue, pearly pink, buttermilk yellow, they're
every color of the pastel rainbow. She glances up at me

and taps her head reprovingly. Lolly likes swift adherence to the rules. The hard-hat which tops her silver pageboy is a spotless white and has the word 'Boss' lettered across the front in red.

'Go look in the front room,' Lolly says when I join them. The construction manager smiles at me and shakes my hand.

'Lookin' sharp,' he says, and I assume that he means the front room of the restaurant, not the too large hard-hat that I have put on and must hold with one hand to prevent it slipping down over my eyes.

I leave Lolly and the construction manager, whose name I vaguely remember as Earl, or maybe Al, in what will one day be the restaurant's reception area where they are absorbed in some sort of wiring diagram, and pick my way down the short hall into the main dining room. The hall makes a little angled turn at the end, a ninety degree dog-leg. I had specified this particularly, insisted on it. I pulled a minor artistic tantrum when it looked briefly as if it might be too difficult to do. The point is that this way the entire back wall of the two-storey room will be intact, unbroken by doors.

The impact on turning the corner and entering the room is what I had hoped for. There she is, my black and white lithographed lady. Head and naked shoulders only, she stares out from the wall. She's replicated eight times in her series of panels, four on top of four, spreading from the ceiling down to six feet off the floor. The wall has been lacquered black, and the tables and chairs, when they are set in place, will match.

'What do you think?' Lolly asks. She has snuck up behind me. 'Please, dear God,' she adds, 'tell me they got the lighting right. It cost a fortune. If they didn't, I'll have to slit my wrists.'

'They got it right,' I say. 'It looks good.'

'She's not too creepy is she?' Lolly has raised this question before, as if she's mildly afraid that the woman's blank eyes will put people off their food. I shake my head.

'No,' I say. 'And even if she is, by the time we get this room finished, get the tables and chairs, and the bamboo tree, and everybody in here, believe me, she'll only be background.'

This seems to reassure Lolly, and we spend the next hour and a half sitting on metal folding chairs in the reception area going over orders for plates and cutlery. Not for the first time I talk Lolly out of knives, forks and spoons with bamboo handles. I put my foot down too on the issue of square plates. I do however allow her to have round ones in the deep, lacquered red that she favors.

By the time we have reviewed the linens it's near seven o'clock.

'I don't suppose we could only hire Asians?' Lolly asks as she squares the edges of her papers and fits them neatly into her document case. 'No,' she says, glancing at my face, 'I didn't think so.'

We switch out the lights, leaving on only the night lamps, and Lolly removes her hard-hat and slips it into a plastic bag. I leave mine where I'd found it, lying on a trestle table by the entrance to the kitchen, which is virtually finished and already slated for inspection. The heavy steel door that leads to the alley shuts behind us, and Lolly sets the site alarms.

'I would never have believed it,' she says as she

punches the last numbers in on the electronic pad, her manicured hand swift and sure, 'but I actually think that this thing is going to be done on time, easy.'

'Don't jinx it.'

She rolls her eyes at me.

'I guess you knock on wood all the time too,' she says.

'You bet,' I say. 'Doesn't everyone? Don't you?'

'Susannah! I was born in Jersey. How can you be born in Jersey and be superstitious?'

By this time we are walking towards our cars and Lolly laughs, her voice high and unexpectedly girlish.

She is still saying something to me, something about sending me swatches for napkins, and I am nodding in reply as I cross the front of my car and reach the driver's door. There is a security light mounted on the building across the alley, one of those yellowish sodium lights that give the aura of eternal fog, or malaria, and throw strange shadows, so at first I do not see it. Lolly is already getting into her car when I begin to swing the driver's door open, and then freeze in mid-motion. She looks up and sees me.

'Susannah?' she calls. 'What is it?'

I cannot answer her. I cannot move. I am embarrassed as tears begin to prick behind my eyes.

'Oh shit!' Lolly says. She is standing beside me now, and together we stare down at the beautiful, lustrous blue of my driver's door where someone has carved deep, long scratches, and engraved the single word, 'BITCH'.

FIVE

'I'm not sure what it is that you expect us to do, Ma'am.' The cop's voice is low, unexpectedly melodic, and accentless, as though he has been trained at a drama school or to speak on the radio. He is young, black and handsome, and for an absurd moment I picture him playing Othello, his long-fingered hands holding Desdemona's handkerchief instead of his police notebook and a blue Bic pen.

'She doesn't expect you to do anything, she just needs the police report for the insurance,' Lolly says. Her voice is shrill and she stresses the words 'do' and 'insurance', as though she's said this four times before, which she has, and as though she's talking to an idiot, which she isn't. Her tone isn't lost on the cop, who glares at her and focuses his attention on me.

'You arrived at five-fifteen, and you didn't come out of the building again? Didn't come to get anything from your car? Until you came out at approximately seven p.m.? And that was when you noticed the door? Is that correct Ms—?' He has given up on 'Ma'am', and his voice fades off as he hunts among the scratchings in his notebook for my name. I am beginning to feel faintly ridiculous.

'deBreem,' I say. 'Susannah deBreem, and yes, that's

right.' I don't even know if Lolly is right about the insurance, although it has the ring of truth to it. Presumably, if I don't get this in writing from the police, my insurance company will posit the theory that I did it myself in order to get them to pay for a new driver's door.

'A boyfriend?' the young cop is asking. 'Someone who you recently broke up with? Could this be personal? Someone who would have a reason to do this to you?'

'Like what?' Lolly asks. I shake my head. I can hardly believe that this could be one of Cathy's friends feeling snubbed, and the idea of George creeping around back alleys in order to carve the word 'bitch' in my car door is almost enough to make me laugh out loud.

'No,' I say. 'Look, it was probably just some kid.'

Lolly is fidgeting behind me, and I want badly to get out of here. Over the cop's shoulder I can see his partner sitting in the cruiser that they've parked on the far side of the alley. He's big and heavy set, the caricature of an Irishman, and he looks as though he would be pissed off with all this if he could spare the energy.

'OK,' the policeman is saying to me. 'I don't see that there's anything more we can do. I'm sorry about your car, Ms deBeer. We'll file the report.'

'Great,' I say, 'thanks very much.' I start to say that it's 'deBreem', that deBeer is a diamond, but it's a losing proposition, and instead I stick my hand out. When the cop shakes it, his grasp is weak, and his fingers feel floppy. He takes an awkward step backwards and then turns away.

'There goes Philadelphia's thin blue line,' Lolly says, as the cruiser slides out of sight along the canyon of the alley, leaving nothing in its place but the sickly yellow light of the street lamp falling on brick and pot-holed tarmac. 'I'd take you out for a drink,' Lolly goes on, 'but I have to be in a meeting fifteen minutes ago. It's the symphony ladies, and if I don't get there they'll screw up the catering for Yo-Yo Ma and there'll be hell to pay.'

For some reason it always surprises me when I remember that Lolly is the head of a high-powered volunteer group that seems to be responsible for vir-tually everything that happens at the Philadelphia Symphony. Already she has opened her car door and is stretching one long, high-heeled leg towards the well of the driver's seat.

The lights of her Lexus flare up in two white beams as I unlock my door, sliding my eyes over the deformed panel, trying to avoid looking too closely at it, as I imagine a lover avoids a new scar. I back out into the alley, and Lolly whizzes past me.

After she is gone I sit in my car without moving. There is an unnatural calm in the alley after the strobe of blue lights, the cop's questions, and the streak of the Lexus. The engine hums, and I cannot hear any other sound. I try to imagine the scrape, or was it more of a rip? I envision a sharp edge, or a pointed tool, running down through the layers of buffed wax and the deep midnight blue of the paint. It bites metal, and spells out a B, an I, a T, the hissing sound of CH. I imagine that if I held my hand against the letters on the car door I could read them as if they were braille, could read the hatred that must rise up from them, and that would brand my palm like a burn.

Jake threads himself back and forth around me, urgent and sinuous as a snake, nearly knocking me off my feet as I reach into the closet for his leash. While we waited for the cops I used Lolly's car phone to call Beau and ask him to come over and walk Jake, but there had been no answer, and clearly he didn't get my message. Now it's past eight-thirty and Jake has been sitting alone in the darkness, waiting for me. When I open the apartment door he rushes out on to the landing and flings himself down the stairs. I trail after him, glad that no one seems to be around. I run my fingers along the banister, trill them across the fruit and leaves carved into the newel posts. I let the leash drag behind me on the new crimson carpeting and its heavy brass clip falls from step to step in a drumbeat.

Jake and I make our escape on to the street without being seen, but when we come back from our walk we are not so lucky. We step into the front vestibule, and through the frosted panels of the inner doors I can see figures standing in the entry hall. I can hear the sharp, high ring of Cathy's laugh. I don't know who she's talking to, whether it's Gordon, or Shawn, or Justin, or Zoe, but I do not want to meet any of them. I am in a terrible mood and all I want is to be alone. I consider retreating back out of the front door, dragging Jake down the steps and on to the sidewalk, but they will have seen me by now, and besides, it is way past Jake's dinner time and I am dying for a drink.

'Hey!' Cathy says, as we come through the doors, stepping from the faintly grimy marble of the vestibule on to the polished parquet of the entry hall, 'How was your day?' Jake wriggles away from me and goes to greet Gordon who is sorting through a stack of mail that is piled on the high, polished sideboard. He's thumbing through Shawn's neat piles as though he's certain that something of his is missing.

'Lousy,' I say. 'My day was lousy.' My voice is louder than it should be. Gordon turns to look at me, and Cathy's face collapses. The words came out more harshly than I had intended. Cathy looks as if I have slapped her, as if she has made my day lousy. A swell of guilt and irritation rises in my chest. It's a familiar shadow of suffocation, a resentment at the weight of other people's feelings. With it comes the guilt that Elena insists is sometimes good for us. It keeps us kind, she says, when by instinct we might be otherwise.

'I'm sorry,' I say. 'My car door was gouged.'

'Oh!' Cathy exclaims. 'Oh, no. Not your gorgeous car! I love that car! Was it deliberate?'

'Yes,' I say. 'Very.'

'You're sure?' Cathy asks. Crystals hang in the windows of her apartment and tiny cherubs armed with bows and arrows dot her notepaper. Pointless vandalism is not part of the world that Cathy wants to believe in. 'It couldn't have been an accident?' she asks.

'Not unless someone accidentally wrote "Bitch", no.' My voice has become waspish.

'Oh my God!' Cathy says, her eyes widening. 'You're kidding. In your garage?'

'No, uptown. It was my fault for leaving the car on the street.'

'Wow,' Gordon says.

'I can't believe that,' Cathy says. 'Poor you.' She is anxious to offer me her sympathy, to salve my wound.

'I'm fine,' I say. 'It was just stupid, that's all.'

The doorbell rings and I realize that Cathy must either have given up on Shawn or be hedging her bets, because she's obviously waiting for a date. The blue coat she has on is new, she came in and showed it to me when she bought it on sale a week ago, and she is wearing shiny black trousers. Her dark hair is puffy with mousse and she smells vaguely of fruit chewing gum.

'I have to go,' she says, 'or else we could have a drink. I'll call you!' and I nod as she slips through the glass doors. Gordon and Jake and I stand listening to the rise of her voice and to the lower rumble of the man's as they greet each other and then disappear out on to the street, the heavy front doors clunking closed behind them.

'Well,' Gordon says. I am not sure if he is referring to Cathy, or to my car door, or to the pile of mail he has assembled.

'Are you missing something?' I ask, nodding at the mail.

'No,' Gordon says. 'Just checking. After last time.'

'Did he really open your credit card bill?' I'm not even sure why I'm asking this, except for the fact that I don't want to talk about the car door anymore.

'Damn right,' Gordon says. 'Nosy little fairy,' he adds as he taps his mail into a neat pile, squaring the edges. 'He's like goddamn Tinkerbell. All at once he's everywhere with his feather duster.'

'I guess he does a good job for Zoe,' I say. I'm not sure why it is that I feel like I have to defend Shawn, but I do. Maybe it's because I don't like fly spots either. Gordon makes a humphing sound, and I decide to drop it. Jake's hungry and he's already halfway up the stairs.

'Is there anything there for me?' I ask.

'Nope,' Gordon says, 'not one itty-bitty little thing. Maybe the good fairy already took it up for you.' I ignore this and begin to climb the stairs behind Jake. Gordon follows me.

'You know,' he says, 'that kind of thing, I mean that someone wrote that on your car door, that's really kind of scary.' I cannot see Gordon as he speaks, and his voice rises from behind me, as if someone is broadcasting it over a loudspeaker. 'You're a woman in the city' the message says, 'be afraid.' I understand that it's well meant, but I'm already pissed off by the way he's talked about Shawn, and I feel my hackles rise.

'No, it isn't scary,' I hear myself saying. 'It's just really stupid, and a big pain in the ass.'

We have reached the first landing and I turn around as Gordon stops in front of his door. The doors on this floor are huge. Once they must have led into the upstairs parlors and the master bedrooms of the house. Their lintels are heavy with mahogany vines, fruit and leaves.

'Are you sure you don't want a drink?' Gordon asks. Standing in front of his door he looks momentarily dwarfed, although he is not a small man. From where I am, two steps above him, I can see the smooth wave of dark hair across the top of his head and the slightly heavy set of his neck, which is still tanned from the summer and exposed where it meets the collar of his plaid shirt. He pulls his key out of his pocket and it slides into the lock without a sound.

'I have a bottle of wine open,' he says, and suddenly I feel bad that I've been so short with him. If I thought that somebody had opened my mail, I'd probably be nasty about it too.

For half a second I hesitate. I have glimpsed the front room of Gordon's apartment on the odd occasion when I have been passing and he has left the door ajar. I have seen the large bowed window with the mahogany window seat, and caught sight of the side of the fireplace which is of the same carved wood, dark and masculine, and utterly different from my apartment's delicate moldings and soft moss-greens and grays. I imagine the feel of the wineglass in my hand, the half-hushed music from the stereo. Then I remember that Gordon would be there too, and that I would have to make conversation and behave myself. I decide I prefer my bad mood and go up another step.

'Jake,' I say. 'Thanks a lot, but I have to feed Jake.' Gordon looks at me for a minute, and I can feel my face getting hot. Then he nods and steps inside, and without a sound the heavy door swings shut.

'Dr Doom has a crush on you.'

The words float down from above my head, and at first I can't tell where they're coming from. Then I look up and see Shawn's face above me. For a second he appears to be disembodied, as though he's become one of those cherubs that the Renaissance painters were so fond of, nothing but wings and a head hovering above the Virgin Mary.

'What are you doing up here?' I ask, and I wonder how much of the conversation downstairs he heard.

'Creepy-Weepy,' he says, ignoring my question, and grins at me. 'Want some popcorn?'

As I climb up the stairs I see that the door to Cathy's apartment is open, and I smell the fake buttery scent of those bags that you buy in packs of six in the supermarket and put in the microwave.

'My TV's dead, and Cathy, bless her little heart, said I was such a nice person that I could use hers,' Shawn explains when he sees me looking at the door. 'Don't worry,' he adds, 'I'll lock up on my way out. Zoe gave me keys. I got your mail,' he says, and he bounces back into Cathy's apartment and re-appears a second later with a copy of *Architectural Digest* and a couple of bills. 'Great article on the Georgians in Dublin,' he says, as he hands me the magazine and the envelopes. 'I knew you wouldn't mind if I peeked.'

I start to say that I do mind, actually, but it seems too petty, even for me, and so instead I say, 'Of course not,' and reach for my keys. Jake is sitting at our door, looking at me beseechingly.

'There's a *Star Trek* marathon on Fifty-Six, but,' Shawn adds, glancing over his shoulder into Cathy's apartment, 'my guess is you're probably not a Trekky.'

In my earliest memory I am lost. Before this I remember fragments, a door, a window, a patch of color, but this is my first real memory, the first whole story that I can recall where I played a part. We must have been on a picnic, or on one of Momma's excursions. Typically, these were trips to a battlefield, or a state park. Momma and my grandmother would sit on a blanket on the grass and eat sandwiches, and Uncle Ritchie would bring a portable deck chair of yellow webbing, and his fishing line, and the tin cash box where he kept lures, and pieces of wire, and cutters, and the tiny flies he made from tufts of feather.

I do not remember exactly where we had gone that day, but I do remember the heat, because at lunch Marina and I had had a fight over which of us should get the last cup of the lemonade that Momma had made fresh that morning and put in the cooler with plenty of ice cubes and slices of real sugared lemon. We had both refused to share, insisting on all or nothing, and the fight had nearly reached the hair-pulling stage when Uncle Ritchie settled it by flipping a coin. Marina chose heads, and I chose tails, and I won. I drank the lemonade in one long gulp, and then I licked the sugar off the lemon and slurped out all the pieces of pulp right in front of her.

Later, when everyone had finished eating and the grown ups had fallen asleep, I wandered off by myself. I remember that one of my feet hurt, as if I had a stone in my shoe, or had been bitten by a spider, and I sat down. I bent my head back and the light seemed to spin above me, as if I was still and the world was moving. I could smell pine, and the soft scent of scrub grass. There was no suggestion of fear in this perfect moment, just a sense of weightlessness, and I know now that what I felt, but could not then name, was freedom. Reveling, I watched the patterns of light above me, the fractured lines of blackness, and the greens that twinkled and revolved like stars.

Then, suddenly, the world went still. The light stopped dancing. The boughs of the trees grew thick and heavy, and the sun turned white. It was very hot, and all at once I knew that if I got to my feet and started to run, I would not know which direction to go in order to find my mother.

I sensed Marina's presence like a smell, and when I looked around I saw her standing in the forest, not four feet from me. She was wearing a yellow T-shirt, and the same pink shorts that I had on, and the same pink dime-store sneakers with beads tied into the laces. Utterly immobile, she was framed by the undergrowth that brushed at her bare arms and legs. At most, we were five or six, and my sister's face was narrow and freckled, her hair tied back in a neat pony tail. She was staring at me the way a cat stares at a bird that is wounded: with great interest, and a significant measure of detached malice. I wanted to say her name, but the words dried out and died in my throat.

'They all love you better,' Marina said, quite clearly. 'But I hate you.' Then she turned back into the bushes and was gone.

I was screaming when my mother and grandmother found me. I had worked myself into a frenzy, and although I was probably not more than a hundred yards from them, I had been unable to find my way back. Frantic, I had thrashed at the bushes, scratching my arms and face. I had lost one of my pink sneakers, so that I was half-barefoot and streaked with dirt. 'Shoo Fly, Shoo Fly,' I can hear my mother say, and I can still smell the sweet scent of her bath soap as she wiped my face with the edge of a napkin dipped in iced water, and smoothed the tangled hair from my eyes.

The yellow swatch of watered silk that I am working with is exactly the same color as the T-shirt that Marina was wearing that day. I did not realize it until now, until I held it up here against the paper of this color-board that I am composing, and saw that it was not warm, and golden, and deep, as I had hoped, but sharp, a thin, sunshine yellow. Looking at it, I hear Marina's voice. It is clear, as a child's voice is, but each of her words is as complete as a pebble dropped into a glass of water. I. Hate. You. It was quite dispassionate. It was obviously something that she had considered. On that particular afternoon it was something that Marina knew without a doubt. She never said it to me again, but I never got the feeling that she was sorry either. I never had the impression that my tears, or my subsequent hysteria, or the loss of my pink sneaker, had moved her.

The color-board is my first gesture towards the project that will follow Indochine. It is a 'tea garden', a glass-topped pavilion in the courtyard of a small museum where ladies who appreciate art and students in black leather jackets can purchase herbal infusions by day and white wine by night. I have put off working on it for so long that I am behind with the designs, and I cannot procrastinate any longer. Such is the faith of the board of directors that they have given me a free hand. Carte Blanche. So I have no one to blame but myself. The yellow was entirely my idea. I

wanted to pair it off with mint greens, with something
cool and faintly Edwardian. The result is a failure. The
colors, the swatches of material, the blobs of paint,
remind me of nothing so much as water-logged petals
or colonies of algae, things that grow and float on dead
water.

I reach for my glass, realize that it is empty, and get
up to pour myself another drink. My back and my
knees are stiff, as if I have been exerting myself, or
have just sat through a long flight. I drop three ice
cubes into my glass and swirl them in the amber liquid
of the whisky, listening to the satisfying cluck-cluck
they make as they knock against the side of the glass
and against one another. Returning to the living room,
I pace the rug. I place my bare feet carefully in the
squares of the faded Turkish pattern. I rattle the ice
cubes and let the scotch burn the back of my throat,
and silently I curse Marina.

There was nothing wrong with my design. I had
been happy with the greens and known that I'd had
the right shade of yellow, until she had emerged in her
child's T-shirt and gazed upon me from the shadows,
dropping her words like stones. Now it will all have to
be redone. The colors will have to be scrapped, the
idea erased. I will have to start over. I will have to find
a combination, a pattern and colors, that Marina has
no claim on.

'Crazy,' I say out loud to myself.

Anger boils up in me. It rises through my body like
mercury, burning, until I have to blink in order to
focus, have to take a breath and step back. I close my
eyes, take a deep swallow of the scotch, and the phone
rings.

My reaction is so fast that I am not even aware of
it. It's as if something inside me is exploding. I don't
even know if it's midnight, or ten-thirty, or one a.m.,
but I grab the receiver from my desk and I scream into
it, 'Leave me alone!' Then I send the phone sailing
across the room. It hits the arm of the couch and
bounces back on to the thick pillows.

I am shaking all over, trembling with rage and
surprise. The scotch has spilled out of the glass in my
hand and is running down my wrist, and I am staring
at the phone, facing it as if it is a living adversary,
which is patently insane.

The realization takes a second to sink in. I lick the
liquor off my arm, and when I go to pick up the
phone, I hear a voice coming out of it.

'Susannah? Susannah?' the voice is saying. 'For
Christ's sake, are you there?' It's Beau.

'Yes,' I say, raising the phone to my face, 'I'm
here.'

'What in God's name is going on?' asks Beau. 'Are
you OK?'

It is a moment before I say 'yes', and then I add, 'I
thought you were someone else.'

'Who?' Beau asks.

'I don't know,' I say. Beau clears his throat.

'Well, then,' he says, 'do you want some Chinese
food?'

Ever since I moved into the brownstone, Beau and I
have kept keys to one another's apartments. We assure
ourselves that this equal access is necessary in order to
subvert disaster. What we have in mind is heart attack,

epileptic fits, fire, sudden death. I read an article once
about a woman who choked on a plum stone and lay
dead for a week. It was winter, and with the full blast
of central heating she had begun to smell before anyone
found her. In the wake of George's departure for Paris,
I occasionally viewed my new apartment as a potential
mausoleum, a sort of personal necropolis. It was this as
much as anything that drove me to surrender a set of
my keys to Beau, who suggested that I steer clear of
unpitted fruit.

In reality, our comings and goings, our crossing of
one another's turf, have been more geared to the
collecting and depositing of mail, and to the occasional
delivering of dry cleaning, than to emergency interven-
tion. The greatest beneficiary has been Jake, whom
Beau often walks or feeds if I am held up with Lolly,
or kept late working at a site.

Now, as a result of this ability to come and go
at will, Beau has surprised me. The first notice that
I have of his arrival in the apartment is not the ring
of the front door buzzer, but Jake's squeal of welcome. The second is the distinctive smell of Chinese
food. This is followed shortly by the sight of Beau
himself leaning around my kitchen door. He thrusts
a large brown paper bag towards me and says,
'Beware of hospital administrators bearing Kung Pau
Chicken.'

We spread the white cartons out between us across
the kitchen counter and perch on my two high stools.
We swing our feet in the air, like children at a soda
fountain. Yellow and orange blotches blossom on the
sides of boxes that hold pineapple shrimp and chicken.
Beau picks one of them up and roots in the bottom of

it with his chop sticks. He reminds me for all the world of a cartoon bear peering into a discarded can.

'So you don't know who the creep is who calls?' Beau asks. After shrieking at him on the phone, I have been forced to tell him about the phone calls, and about what has happened to my car door. It seemed thinner in the re-telling, and filled with the potential for self-dramatization.

'Nope,' I reply. 'I don't even know if it's the same person. They don't always call either. This week they've slacked off.'

'He, she, it, hasn't called tonight?'

I shake my head and, as if on cue, we both turn to look at the wall clock, which reads twelve-twenty. If the telephone was in the room we would probably stare at that too, but it isn't, so we can't. Instead, Beau puts down the sticky container he has been examining and reaches for my beer.

'That's mine!' I say.

'I know,' he replies and winks at me. 'What about Star. Six. Nine?' he asks, making it sound like a game show introduction. I shake my head.

'I tried that once, but I got a weird tone that the operator says means the line is blocked.' Beau shrugs.

'Well, I guess if I was into making pervert calls I'd block my line too,' he says. 'Actually, you can buy those things at Radio Shack for twenty bucks. They're called the Phone Zzzapper, or something. They work on caller ID too.'

'How do you know?' I ask. Beau shrugs.

'It's the kind of cool stuff that cool guys like me know,' he says. 'What you should do is change your number.'

'I know,' I say, 'I know, but everybody I know has this number, and so do all the contractors and everybody from work.' I get up and get myself another beer from the icebox, since Beau is drinking mine. 'I'd unlist the number, but obviously whoever it is who gets off on doing this has already got it.'

'Excellent point, Watson,' Beau says. I flip the cap off the bottle and throw it at him.

'I figure they'll just get bored,' I say. 'Eventually.'

'It's a tele-marketer gone berserk,' Beau announces. He considers this for a moment, rolling the neck of the beer bottle between his palms. 'I love the word "berserk",' he says. Then he treats me to his best cock-eyed grin. 'Suuuusannah,' Beau asks, 'if I walk the dog, can I get really drunk and sleep on your couch?'

By the next morning he is gone, vanished as if he had never been. The dishes are scrubbed clean of duck sauce, and of the gummy shreds of dumpling, and the bits of hardened rice. 'Dog fed' says a note taped to an empty can of Alpo that sits on the counter. 'If he says otherwise, he lies.' A similar note is taped to Jake's leash, which has been looped through the handle of the refrigerator door. It says, 'Dog walked'. Both of the notes are illustrated, and I study them as I pour my coffee. On the first, a stick figure dog eats a hamburger that he holds between his front paws. On the second, a stick figure man and dog walk arm-in-arm together while a round, child's sun shines overhead.

I don't find the third note until I go to rub Jake's stomach as he lies on the living room rug. I come face to face with the square of paper as I bend over. This one is taped on to the pillow that Beau used, which is, in turn, piled on top of a neatly folded Hudson's Bay blanket that I bought long ago on a college trip to Montreal. A stick figure man is jumping in the air. 'Thanks!' the note reads, and then it says, 'Don't forget – Church concert tomorrow night – 7.30'.

I had forgotten. Beau has never invited me to go to a church service with him, and even if he did, I would not want to. Try as I might, I do not agree with Beauregard. Every day as a child, I sat on the school bus and read the billboard on the road into Petamill, Georgia, and I still do not think that Jesus Saves. The church concerts, however, are an exception to my rule of abstinence. Beau's choir gives three a year, and every time he sings a solo, and every time I go to hear him. I have a routine now. I linger outside the door until the music starts, and then, on the first strains of the organ, I slip inside. Sitting on the back pew in half darkness, I raise my eyes to the lurid stained glass above the altar where a yellow-haired Christ tends his lambs on a pasture of neon green. The choir begins, and I tap my foot to the familiar words. Rock of Ages. Bide With Me. The Lord is My Shepherd. Then I wait for the moment when Beau steps forward, his ungainly bulk shrouded in the sky-blue nylon of his choir robe, and as he reaches the lectern and draws himself up, I close my eyes. Sometimes I think I hold my breath until I hear Beau's voice, and then I feel it lift me up, and I surrender. As Beau sings I rise beyond the dull gray walls of the church. I let him carry me away, and we spiral above the city, borne upwards on his soaring, hopeful notes of praise.

SIX

'So how the Hell did this happen?'

It is as much a statement of outrage as a question, and Benjy scowls at me over his shoulder as he asks it, as if I might have taken a screwdriver and done it myself. His dark, beetle-browed face compresses into a frown, making him look fierce like billy-goat-gruff in the fairy tale. I shrug, but Benjy has already turned back to the car. He bends down, examining the door and muttering to himself. The garage smells of oil and the black sludge at the bottom of the Mr Coffee machine on Benjy's old wooden desk. A stack of semi-clean looking styrofoam cups sits beside the machine, and I half-consider helping myself, but then think better of it. I am mildly hung over after last night's Chinese food–fest and I am not sure if the thick, toxic liquid would kill me or cure me.

'I don't know how it happened, exactly,' I say. Although, of course, I have a pretty good idea. The mechanics of the act, the 'how' and the 'what', so to speak, are not terrifically difficult to figure out. 'I've parked it there before,' I add, as if this is some measure of self-defense. Benjy sold me this car, and he takes its well-being personally. 'Can you fix it?'

'No, I can't fix it.' Benjy straightens up and wipes

his hands down the front of his boiler suit, which is so filthy that it's hard to imagine what it might once have looked like. It is the only thing that I have ever seen him wear, and while I suppose that Benjy must have other clothes on underneath the boiler suit, I can't swear to it. 'What I can do,' he says, 'is try to find you a new door, but it'll take a while.'

'How long?' I ask. The idea of being without my car makes me feel stranded and vaguely panicky.

'I dunno. It's vintage, and it's not the easiest color in the world to match. And it'll cost, Miss Cheap.' This is Benjy's pet name for me, 'Miss Cheap'. He smiles as he says it. I'm not sure exactly what I've done to deserve this nom de guerre, probably just coming to him in the first place instead of going to what Lolly would call 'a real garage'. Benjy has few illusions about the nature of his establishment. He goes to the desk and pours himself a cup of coffee, then he pours a second one and hands it to me. It's lukewarm and feels furry against the roof of my mouth.

'Where's my man Jake?' Benjy asks, sitting down in a chair with wheeled feet and scooting himself backwards towards a dented filing cabinet that is stacked with phonebooks. I point out that I have to take a cab back, since presumably he will be keeping the car.

'So cabbies won't take mutts?'

'Not big ones, no.'

Benjy considers the injustice of this for a minute before he digs a pair of thick-rimmed glasses out of his pocket and perches them on the end of his nose. The heavy black lines of the frames make him look like a cartoon character. Regarding him over the edge of my coffee cup, I imagine that I have drawn the glasses on to Benjy's face with a magic marker and that I could lean forward and add a mustache, or pointy ears, or small curly horns coming from the top of his head.

'All right,' he says, 'so, in the meantime, until I can match up the door for you, I'm gonna put a new one on. I know you get hairy without your wheels, and you can't drive around town with that written on the side of your car, people'll think you're a pervert. It won't look great, but I'll try to find a dark color until we come up with the real McCoy.'

'Thanks,' I say.

'For you, Doll, anything.' Benjy winks at me and shrugs. 'What can I say?' he asks, 'my mother was a red-head.'

I finish the coffee and drop the cup into a trash can that is already filled with balled-up candy wrappers and Dr Pepper cans. Benjy has already embarked on his search for a 1972 Mercedes door. He's ferreting through a pile of papers and reaching for the wall phone that lurks behind an outsized Nascar calendar. He waves to me, and just before I leave I ask, 'Do you see a lot of this kind of thing?'

'All the time, Doll,' Benjy says. 'All the time.' I'm not sure if this reassures me or not, and I think it over as I step outside into the afternoon sunshine.

I have to walk almost as far as the museum before I see a free cab, and by the time I've gone that far it seems pointless not to walk the rest. It's Saturday, and the city is busy in a different way from usual. People are out on the streets, but they're wandering, slowed down, feeling the last of this warm autumn sun on their shoulders. The parking-lot of the big new Fresh-fields supermarket is jammed. A couple of cars cruise around like predatory fish, waiting for spaces to open up, and a child squeals as his mother loads him into a cart and pushes it, running, towards the revolving door.

I pass by the small, solid block of the Rodin museum and come up short, stopped by a river of traffic. A fleet of runners pound along the opposite sidewalk. They're all guys, six or eight of them. From the easy way that they bunch together you can tell that they're office-mates, friends, a set of buddies who egg each other on, and fight the dreaded paunch and the first gray hairs together for an hour every weekend. George used to run with a group like that, a covey of the suddenly-not-so-young professors from the University. Every Saturday morning he would leave just before ten, yelling to me from the front hallway as he laced up his shoes, the last words muffled as the sweatshirt went over his head, and cut off altogether as the door slammed.

These guys will be lawyers or bankers, though. They're better dressed than the Penn professors. I can see their mouths move as they talk to one another, passing words back and forth, laughing, until the light changes and the cars come to a halt. Then the men move forward in one compact body. At the same moment, I step off the curb into the street. We meet, and they divide and flow around me. As they pass I hear laughter, and smell the slight, mingled scents of aftershave and sweat.

The shadows lengthen through the afternoon until the tree that spreads above my balcony casts a long, dark pattern that falls like a spider's web through the window and on to the living room floor. Jake is snoring. It's a comforting sound, a soft, slow, drawing in and out of breaths which shudder at the end, as if he cannot quite bear to let them go. Occasionally, he yips in his sleep and scrabbles his paws against his bed in a little running motion that sounds like mice. I watch him for a moment as I stand with the laundry basket balanced on my hip. Earlier in the day, I gave him a long run in the park, and now he is so peaceful, so absorbed in his dreams, that I tiptoe away and slip through the door without him, turning the handle slowly, so the latch falls silently back into place.

The lamps on the landings have not been turned on yet, and above me the frosted panes of the stairwell skylight seem to glow. In Cathy's apartment I can hear music playing, a soft thud, thud, overlaid with the tinkle of piano keys. Far below me, Zoe crosses the entryway and her heels clack on the parquet. She calls out the beginning of a question to Justin, and the words are lost as the door of their apartment swings shut. Gordon is listening to the TV, or to the radio, I am not sure which, as I pass his door and make my way downstairs, my slippered feet whispering on the carpet.

The laundry room is in the basement, down a warren of corridors that run under the house and converge on a heavy metal door that leads into the back garden. The half window of the door is criss-crossed in metal mesh, and though we all have a key to it, so in theory we may bring our bicycles, and our skis, and our boxes in and out, I cannot remember ever seeing it used. Now, as I stand at the top of the steep stairs that lead from the entryway down into this minotaur's maze, I see that the lights are already on and I can hear the swoosh and growl of the washer and dryer. I hold the laundry basket out in front of me, which means that I cannot reach for the banister, and must feel my way, lowering each foot in turn, swinging it back and forth, dusting for the hard surface of every narrow step.

At the bottom of the stairs a hatch-like doorway is set halfway up the wall. On my inaugural tour of the house, Zoe had informed me that it is a laundry chute. A whole system of chutes runs through the walls of the house, and they are wide enough to hold a small child. Zoe had showed them to me with great pride, pointing them out as part of the house's collection of period features. She assured me that they had not been blocked up, that domestic authenticity was still intact in the wake of restoration, and that each of the original bedrooms still had a hatch similar to this one, a mouth that once swallowed soiled sheets and damp bath towels, and spat them out down here. The one in my bedroom is behind the bathroom door, but I have never opened it. It is tastefully painted to match the molding, and I imagine that if I shouted down it, or even whispered, anyone standing in the dark, subterranean hallways could hear my voice.

I am half tempted to put down my basket of dirty socks and jeans, and to lift the iron door of the laundry hatch. Perhaps I could hear Gordon's TV. I could shout back up the chute in French or Pig-Latin, and make him blink, spin around, wonder at these disembodied voices. The idea is enough to make me laugh out loud, but then the noise of the washer rumbles and dies, and I turn away from temptation, realizing that I must seize my moment or lose the opportunity to Cathy's towels, or Zoe's Merrimekko sheets.

A bare bulb hangs in the long corridor. Presumably, its lack of any shading is another of Zoe's gestures towards authenticity. The end of the hallway disappears in shadows, and I can just make out the square of dim light that is the window in the garden door. I take only a few steps towards it before I turn right down another passage, and then left into the windowless square of the laundry room. A year ago, when I first moved in, I wondered if I should leave a trail of breadcrumbs when I came down here, or tie a scarlet thread to the bottom of the banister in order to find my way back, but over time I have grown fond of the basement. Now I think of it as the honeycomb, the secret terrain of the worker bees who labored here, who once scrubbed and mended amid shadows and ugliness, in order that above them delicacy and fine manners might flourish.

The bulbs in the laundry room do not have shades either. There are three of them and they are each at least 100 watts. I stand in the doorway and blink, wondering if Whirlpool white enamel can induce snowblindness. The strength of the bulbs suggests Cathy's handiwork, and so does the new folding laundry table, the iron and ironing board, and the bottles of spray starch that are ranged along it. 'Anyone can use these!' a Post-it note stuck to the wall says. A smiley face beams out from below the exclamation mark.

In the light of this generosity and goodwill, I have no choice but to be helpful. I take a load of pink and baby blue towels out of the dryer and dump them on the table. Then I transfer the white wash that has just

finished into the warm drum of the dryer, and I even
remember to change the heat setting to 'delicate'. I stuff
my own washing, higgle-piggle, into the machine, and
as I pour the soap powder I deliberately ignore the
manufacturer's advice and handy measuring scoop. I do
plan to fold the towels, but first I peruse the various
dials on the machines, wondering if the air supplied to
'delicate' is really warm enough, and if 'cold' will
actually clean my clothes. I make my decision, and I
am leaning over and am about to push the appropriate
buttons when the lights go out.

At first the darkness freezes me. Like a sci-fi character
who has been hit with a stun-gun, I'm stuck on tippy-
toes, bent across the washing machine with my arm
pointing aimlessly into pitch black. It is so dark in the
room that I cannot even see my own hand. I withdraw
it slowly, and rock back on to my heels, placing my
slippered feet fully on the stone floor. I straighten up,
and then, although I cannot actually see it, I turn
instinctively towards the door. And that is when it
happens. My shoulders tense. My fingers go stiff. The
back of my head is suddenly cold, and feels electrified.
I am not alone. Someone is standing in the doorway.
   My first instinct is to close my eyes, to play possum,
to block out this world, but I can't. Instead, I am
riveted, staring and unable even to blink, as if I do not
dare to take my eyes off what I cannot see. The person
is facing me. I know it as surely as if there is a taut
string, running through the space between us, carrying
the vibration of their heart. A surging sensation pulses
through me, and at the same time my muscles lock and

turn solid. This is what it must be like to die of electric shock, to feel voltage coursing through you and yet to be unable to move.

I don't know if I am breathing. I'm not sure, because I can't hear anything. I'm suddenly conscious of the fact that there's not a rumble of traffic, not a drip of water, not even the whisper of breathing. The air between us is thick, and I cannot draw it into my chest. There is not so much as a glimmer, or a reflection of light, but I know with absolute certainty that if I could force my feet to move, if I could step forward and stretch out my hand, my fingers would travel through nothingness and then meet the density of human flesh.

We stand there for seconds, or for minutes, I don't know, and when the noise does come, it is just a rustle. It is so small, and so slender, that it might not exist, except that I know that now the doorway is empty. Then, from the hall, I hear something else. Slow, and very deliberate, it is the sound of humming. The voice caresses the tune. It is high pitched and faintly mocking, and it takes each note and lingers over it, making it full and fat, before releasing it and moving on. Leisurely, and insistent, the voice takes its time. It rolls out the little song, allows it to swell, pushes it to become louder and louder, stronger and stronger, until I scream.

My eyes are closed tight and the screams go on until they are broken by the sound of running feet, by clattering, and bright lights. I hear Cathy's voice, and someone is trying to put their arms around me, to catch me, but I push them away. I can't be touched. I am doubled over.

People shout my name, and finally, when the screaming slows and draws itself out to nothing but an embarrassing gasp, there is a babble of voices: Cathy's, Zoe's, Gordon's, and Justin's. They have all come running. They are all here, gathered around me in the too small laundry room, jostling the ironing board, tipping the folding table, knocking the towels and the bottles of spray starch on to the floor.

When I tell them what has happened, they look back and forth to one another, and then Justin and Gordon search the basement. They carry a tire iron and a hammer. They turn on every light. They tell us that they opened old cupboard doors, looked behind bicycles and skis, forced themselves to walk into the ancient meat locker, and to stand underneath the iron hooks where hams and dead birds were hung a hundred years ago. What they found is that the door to the garden was open.

It was not wide open, Gordon says. Not, so to speak, blowing in the wind. It was just cracked, only a thin line of light down its edge gave it away. It was as if someone had taken their time, as if they had been leisurely in their departure, and careful to pull the door closed behind them.

The police come, but not for an hour and a half. On a Saturday night in the city, an open basement door is not a priority. No one can remember quite when they had used it last, and no one can swear that they had been certain to turn the locks. At some point, Justin had swept leaves off the patio, and Zoe had planted bulbs, but both of them thought they had used the

doors that open from their own living room on to
their thin sliver of a deck with its four little steps.
Cathy remembers seeing them out of her window, but
she cannot say on which day, or which door they
might have used, or even if it was the week before last,
or the week before that.

'Garden wall,' the policeman says. This time he is
white, tired, and middle-aged. 'Any kid could climb
that garden wall.' He suggests that we consider a roll
of silver razor wire, and Zoe scrunches up her face in
disgust. Or possibly broken glass. We could break wine
bottles, and slather cement along the top of the old
brick wall, and stick the pieces in. Then the shards,
brown and bottle green, would stick up like rotting
fangs, their tips showing above the climbing rose and
the grape vine that Zoe plans to plant. Twice the
policeman asks if I could identify 'the suspect', and
twice I have to say 'no'. Twice I have to tell him that
I saw nothing.

'Then how do you know someone was there?' the
policeman asks.

'I heard them,' I reply. 'After they stood in the
doorway, I heard them humming.' The policeman
writes this down and shakes his head.

'In the future,' he says, 'be more careful with that
door.'

The blanket that I have wrapped around me now is
old. It is crocheted, a pattern of gaudy flowers in the
bright oranges and cheap greens of acrylic wool. I push
my fingers through the holes in the weave, and when
I bring the material up close to my face I smell moth
balls, and the vague, musky scent of things locked away
in suitcases. My grandmother made this blanket. It is

one of a dozen that she hooked and gave to us. They had lain over the back of every chair, along the arm of every sofa, across the beds in the house that Marina and I grew up in. It is phenomenally ugly, and I do not know why I kept it. Since Chapel Hill it has stayed in the bottom of my suitcase. Tonight, if I stretch out my arms, it hangs from my shoulders like a cape.

I have called Beau. I left him a message saying that something had come up, lying, and making it sound as if I had urgent work to attend to. He will not call back tonight. I have told him not to, led him to believe that I will not be here. He will go to his party after the concert, and drink beer and eat chips with a clean conscience, sure that he is not abandoning me.

Gordon offered to walk the dog with me. He longed to extend the wing of his protection over me, but I would not let him. I dug my hand into Jake's ruff, ran my fingers along the saddle on his back where the hackles rise, and told Gordon that I have my guardian. Earlier I had accepted Zoe's tea, and later, Cathy's wine. Now I am sated with concern, and all I want is to be alone.

It is past midnight now, and the phone will not ring. I walked Jake early, at eleven-thirty. I made sure I was back in time, just in case. Tonight, of all nights, I wanted to answer. I wanted to shout into the telephone, to scream that I refuse to be cornered like this, but no call came, and as the hours have passed my anger has faded into fear. Sitting on the sofa, my hideous flowered wings wrapped around me, I replay the darkness. I wonder if I heard the flick of a light switch, if there was the faint sound of a footstep that I have forgotten. If I had turned, spun away from the dials, in the second before the lights went out, would we have come face to face?

My own bottle of wine is almost empty, and I cannot sit still any longer. I gather the blanket and stand up. I walk carefully, counting eight steps to the carpet's edge, and then four steps beyond to the cool of the window pane and the gray of my balcony. Its colors shift in the mottled shadow of the tree and the city lights. I turn and count six steps back to the phone that will not ring, and to the question that no one asked.

'Where were you?' the policeman asked, and 'What time was it?' and 'Were you alone?' and 'Do you know who it was?'

He asked me all those things, but there is one question that he forgot.

'Humming, Miss deBreem?' the policeman had said, and I had nodded, holding my breath, but he never thought to ask the next question. He never thought to ask me if I recognized the tune.

And I did. Until this afternoon I had not heard it for over twenty years, but even so, I could sing it now. I could sing it just the way I remember it, in that same high, southern voice of my childhood. 'Shoo Fly,' the words go, 'don't bother me. Shoo Fly, I belong to somebody.'

SEVEN

The touch of his skin had been cool and unexpectedly smooth when he shook my hand. A moment later, when he passed me his card, I had noticed that his nails were pale and clipped. I had noticed his cuffs too. They were bright white and stiff with either starch or the sizing that comes in new men's shirts. I remember thinking that altogether, he looked too clean for his job.

'Homicide Division, Special Detective Mark Cope,' the words on the card say. Embossed above them is the seal of the City of Alexandria, and at the bottom of the card, in the small, scratchy letters of Special Detective Mark Cope's handwriting are the numbers of both his office extension and his home telephone. 'You call me,' he had said, when he handed it to me on the day of Marina's funeral, 'You call me, Miss deBreem, if there is anything at all that I can do for you.' He had been the officer in charge of the investigation into Marina's death, and I could tell, even then, that he felt bad. That he had no words of reassurance to give me.

I have considered Special Detective Cope's offer over and over again since I took the card out of the envelope where I have kept it for the last eighteen months. Now I pick it up and bend it back and forth, as if the feel of it in my hand will suggest to me what I should do. At times his invitation seems more tempting than others. At times I imagine that he could rescue me, and then I stop and ask myself, 'from what?' Will Special Detective Cope rescue me from a telephone that rings and a caller who does not speak? Will he save me from the word 'bitch'? Will he defend me against a nursery rhyme? And how, exactly, am I supposed to tell Special Detective Mark Cope of the Alexandria Homicide Division about what I heard last night in the basement? How am I supposed to tell anyone?

I loosen my fingers and let the card fall to the floor. It flutters, drifts like a snowflake on the way down. I have had far too much to drink. My mind feels soft and blurry at the edges, and the sharpness of everything, even the terror that I felt in the laundry room, is dulled. Only a few things still stand out. 'We're the Nightspinners,' I hear Marina's childhood voice say; and then I hear her again, but this time she is older. 'You know it won't do any good, Shoo,' she whispers. 'You know that if I want you to, you'll hear me.'

'Marina is dead.' I say it out loud, and I like the sound of the words. They have a shape and form of their own. They are tangible and I can reach out and hold them in my hand. Marina is dead, and there are no such things as ghosts. 'No such things,' I say aloud.

I am repeating assurances that were offered on a regular basis by both my mother and my grandmother, neither of whom believed in 'the shining', or in spectral figures of confederate soldiers, or in any of the other stories we traded at school when we were ten, and eleven, and twelve. In the summer twilight, groups of kids would gather in the haylofts and the shadows of the barns, and trade ghost stories before running home across the fields, giddy with the frisson of fear.

'Nonsense,' my mother would say, when I woke with nightmares, when I ran along the hall in my bare feet and begged her to let me climb up into her high bed and seek sanctuary there for the night. 'Nonsense,' she would repeat, even as she pulled back the soft linen sheet and let me climb in beside her. 'I don't understand, Shoo,' she would say, stroking my hair, 'where these nightmares come from. You know those stories are silly?' And I would nod, letting her believe that it was some stupid story of Della Hervey's, or of Sonny Delray's, about a headless cavalry rider, or a spectral dog, that had wakened me, heart hammering, and left me staring into the dark while Marina lay, still as death, in her bed across the room.

I pull Grandma's blanket around me, covering myself with her flowers, and I listen for the echo of my mother's voice. 'There are no such things as ghosts,' she says. I lie down on the couch, and my head hits the soft pile of cushions with a 'poof' as their down collapses. In the corner, Jake shifts and stretches and falls asleep again. 'There are no such things as ghosts,' Momma says. 'There are only memories, and they cannot hurt us.'

We must have been fifteen in the summer of the fires. They began, I think, in May or June, and at first they were so inconsequential, so possibly the result of dry lightning strikes, or of courting couples smoking and throwing the still-lit butts out of car windows, that no one paid them much attention. They were just circles of hot orange light and blossoms of white smoke that punctuated the early summer nights. They seemed to disappear before the fire engine was ever called, and to leave nothing but a round devil's footprint blackening the corner of a local farmer's field.

By July they had become frequent enough to elicit comment from the fire chief, who was also our school principal, and he wrote a column in the *Petamill Times* warning his students to be careful, and urging farmers to keep a sharp eye out for wandering strangers or hippies who might be camping in the woods. The fires became a topic of conversation, and as the weather grew hotter and the nights thickened into summer, people grew jumpy. After dark they took to peering out of their windows, to scanning their fields, or the back lines of their woods for anything brighter or larger than a firefly. By August, as the fields dried and the rains stopped, farmers began to sleep with one ear listening for the low, cackling laughter of spreading flames.

Yet the fires were infrequent enough, and apparently inconsequential enough, that it was still possible to dismiss them as a series of accidents, to think of them as nothing but a strange chain of coincidence: one of those inconvenient flukes of nature, like a year of heavy ticks, or a fall when too many deer get hit on the road. This theory was backed up by the fact that no real damage was ever done, until the morning when the Eames' barn burned to the ground.

In other circumstances the barn fire at the Eames' might have been a routine kind of tragedy, the sort of thing that every farm both necessarily courts and dreads, but in the edgy atmosphere of that summer, and in light of what happened afterwards, the fire seemed to take on special significance, as if it was a climax that we had all somehow been expecting.

I was never sure, even at the time, which came first, the acrid whiff of smoke on the heavy August air, or the screech of the farm whistle that meant somebody on our road was in trouble. What I do remember is that it was hot, and that a faint uncharacteristic breeze ruffled the heartshaped leaves of the lilac bushes and ran its hand across the tops of the alfalfa that was just coming into second crop in Uncle Ritchie's front field.

Momma and I were in the vegetable garden that ran out from the side of the house. The plot spread itself in a patchwork of purple-veined beet greens, thick splotches of red radish, and thin wavy fronds of carrot tops. Momma and I were standing in a cloister of vines that morning, picking out the crop of runner beans and dropping them into brown paper bags from Food Fayre. Dilly beans. Beans packed into jars with slivered almonds. We would eat them all through the winter. I was contemplating this fact, silently ridiculing Momma's emphasis on what she called 'home grown goodness', when the single shrill note split the morning.

I remember that instinctively I turned towards my mother, seeking confirmation of what we had just heard. The whistle was the sound of calamity itself. It could mean that a tractor had turned over, trapping Lou Delray, or Tom Hervey, or even Uncle Ritchie, compressing his chest against the rock hard summer soil, squeezing the air out of him while someone ran for help. It could mean that a man had caught his hand in a baler or a wood chipper. It announced that a child had stumbled on a dead log and surprised a copperhead or, worse, had wandered into the muddy shallows of the creek and come across a cottonmouth.

When the whistle sounded, Momma stopped picking, her hand raised in mid-motion. Then, as I watched, she tilted her face to the wind, scenting, like a dog. She was still for a moment, and by the time she swung towards me, I could smell it too. The whistle shrilled again. 'Fire!' Momma yelled, her voice melding with the high, urgent note, and then she was running down the bean row, tipping the bag as she went, spilling shards of green on to the newly watered soil.

When I caught up with her, Momma was standing on the front lawn and Marina was beside her. They were staring towards the dark band of pine that ran along the far end of Uncle Ritchie's front field and marked the boundary of our grandmother's land. Rising from beyond the trees I could see a gray haze of smoke that seemed to shimmer and thicken even as we watched. There was something mesmerizing about its density, about the way the smoke formed itself into a cloud and puffed itself out at the edges, the way it wavered in a mass, rippling when the breeze hit it.

'It's the Eames' barn,' Marina said. Her voice was barely a whisper, and if my mother heard her, she did not acknowledge it. I looked at my sister, inclined to argue, to point out that it was more likely to be the hay store that Uncle Ritchie shared with the Delrays, but the look in her face made me stop. While Momma and I were beaded with sweat, our foreheads creased and our bodies fidgeting in the anxiety and excitement of disaster, Marina was absolutely still. A smile twitched the corner of her mouth, and she did not so much as slide her eyes towards me. Instead, she watched the cloud of spreading smoke. She concentrated on it as if it were alive, as if she could mold it, and cause it to grow and blossom against the limp blue of the summer sky.

A pick-up raced by on the road and another followed it. I saw Uncle Ritchie in the first, clutching the wheel with both hands. His soft bulk bounced and met the wide front seat again as he hit the pot hole opposite our driveway and sped on. The second truck was the Herveys', and I had just time to glimpse Della, and to be jealous of the fact that she was standing up in the truck bed, clutching the back of the cab, her hair blown straight up from her head, before the plumes of dust rose in the road and swallowed them.

'Come on you girls, come on now. Hurry!' Momma called. I had not seen her move, but when I looked around she was trotting towards the garage, grabbing the big door with both hands and swinging it open, and a moment later our old Country Squire was flying backwards out of the dark. Momma slammed on the brakes and leaned across to open the passenger door, yelling at us now to get in. I went first, and despite the cool of the shadows it had been parked in, the station wagon's front seat was warm and stuck against the back of my thighs as I scooted along it to make room for Marina.

We followed the pick-ups, veering past the hay store, which was not burning, and down the old county road that was in even worse shape than ours and dead-ended at the Eames' farm. As soon as we came around the corner we could see the feathers of fire that were waving from the barn's roof, and the heat hit me even before I slammed the wagon's door and followed Momma and Marina as they wove through the collection of cars and trucks that had pulled up in the Eames' yard.

A bucket chain had been started from the house, and I saw that Grandma was already there. She was up towards the back with the other old ladies, while younger people had joined in in the middle of the line. They were passing heavy black rubber buckets hand over hand, trying not to slosh the water out, while the Eames boys, Charlie and Dex, grabbed the empties and ran back up the line to the house with them. The men were down at the front of the line, closest to the wall of heat that seemed to move steadily outwards from the barn. Each man would throw a bucket and then they would jump back, cursing and hopping as if the ground itself was scalding their feet. Marina ran down to help Dex and Charlie, and when Momma and I joined the line we felt the heat press itself towards us, felt it reaching out and stroking our faces, and the flat planes, and secret deep slopes of our bodies.

It wasn't until I heard a shout and looked up that I realized that people were on the roof of the Eames' house. Mr Eames and his brother, Royce Jr, and Joe Cappel, who did laboring work for Uncle Ritchie and whose wife took in laundry and sometimes gave Marina and me hard candies when we walked past her yard on the way home from the school bus, were up there. They had rigged up a hose and they were spraying the top of the roof, soaking it as best they could so that when the barn finally went maybe its sparks wouldn't set the house on fire too. Down below, Mrs Eames was watching them. Her hand shielded her eyes as she looked up, and the thin material of her dress fluttered against her shoulders as people ran back and forth around her.

At some point the fire engines arrived, and the bucket chain stopped, and we were all commanded to move back. They were still running out the big black hoses and yelling about getting water from the cow pond when the silo caught and went up. The torch of flame was so bright that the day dimmed around it, and even the firemen stopped to watch.

I could feel everyone round me holding their breath as the huge burning pillar seemed to lift off and hover above the earth. It paused as we watched, looking for a moment as if it might take flight, as if it might simply continue to rise into the sky and then spin like a giant roman candle. Momma reached out and clutched my arm. Her fingers dug into the flesh above my elbow, and I was about to complain when she let go anyways and covered her mouth with her hands as the silo tipped sideways and crashed on to the barn roof.

For a second there was something like silence. Then the barn let out a great sigh, as if it was finally giving up, and a terrible cracking, like the sound of hundreds of bottles breaking, made me reach to cover my ears before it was drowned in the sudden thundering of the barn walls as they fell in on themselves and lit the sky with a storm of sparks.

After the barn collapsed, Momma walked over to Mrs Eames and put her arm around her shoulders. They had grown up together and been best friends in school, and Momma rubbed little circles below the back of Mrs Eames' neck the same way she used to when Marina and I were little and had heatstroke or a headache and would still let her touch us. The men were coming down from the roof of the house, and the sun caught the drips from the gutters and spangled them with colored prisms of light. Behind the crowd, the firemen moved in on the collapsed timbers and criss-crossed them with high, arching jets of water. The crackling of flames died to a hissing sound, and the plumes of smoke turned darker and rose in columns from the embers and the ashes and the soggy blackened piles that had been the Eames' new harvest.

Mr Eames was the last of the men to come off the ladder, and when his work boots hit the ground, he stood still for a minute, still holding the wooden rungs as if he could not bear to turn around and face the barn or the neighbors and friends who stood watching and pitying him. He was a tall man, and gangly, with a neck that seemed too long, and arms that seemed too narrow to support his paw-like hands. No one came near him while he rested his forehead on the ladder's rung, but out of the corner of my eye I noticed Charlie, who was a year or so older than us. He sidled up to the edge of the crowd and stood beside Marina. She did not look at him, but she moved her hand in a slight beckoning motion, as one might to a well-trained dog. It was almost unnoticeable, but I saw it, and Charlie sensed it. Without taking his eyes from his father's back, he ran his fingers quickly down her wrist and across her palm.

The sight fascinated me. It was no more than a brush, a quick, furtive stroke, and it might have been a mistake, except that it wasn't. The gesture was as

intimate, and as full of history and promise, as a kiss.
I felt myself flush under the layer of dust and sweat
that rimed my body. I was suddenly and inexplicably
embarrassed, and yet I could not look away from them.
Until that moment I had thought that I knew everything about Marina. I had taken it for granted. It had
never once occurred to me that she might have secrets,
that someone could be close enough to her to touch
her that way without my knowing about it, or that
some part of her life could be going on without me,
but clearly it was. I felt the flush on my skin deepen
with confusion, for in the next second, as Charlie bent
forward, leaning down to tie his shoe lace, the bright
coin of a medallion swung away from his neck.

He grabbed it almost instantly, shoving it back
down inside his collar, but he had not been quite fast
enough. I had seen the bright gold chain, seen the
scalloped edge of the disc clearly, and even from that
distance I had recognized it. I would have known it
anywhere. It was a St Christopher medal, and I had
saved for four months to buy it for Marina on our
fourteenth birthday.

'It's for safe journeys,' the sales lady in Jordan's
Quality Jewelers had told me, when I had first noticed
it in the glass case by the window. Her name was Mrs
Pease, and her daughter, Danna, was two years behind
us in school and picked her nose. I had gone into
Jordan's with my mother, who was getting the clasp
on her pearls fixed for the umpteenth time, and while
she discussed this with Mr Jordan, Mrs Pease had lifted
the St Christopher medal off its velvet pillow and
dangled it in front of my face. It was the size of a
quarter, with ripply edges, and on it a big man wearing

what looked like a mini-skirt stood knee deep in the middle of a bunch of wavy lines holding a baby on his shoulders.

'That's St Christopher carrying the baby Jesus across the River Jordan,' Mrs Pease had informed me. 'It's a real nice thing to give someone you love. It means they'll always travel safe.' When I had asked her how much it was, she had replied, 'Twenty-five dollars with the chain, which is solid gold.' Then she had put the medal back on its velvet cushion and snapped the glass lid down, turning the lock with a little silver key that was chained to her wrist.

By that time my mother was done, and as we had stepped out of the store, I had said to her, 'Do you think Marina needs to be kept safe?'

At this, Momma had given me one of her looks and said, 'Shoo Shoo, you are wise beyond your years,' which annoyed me, and was really no answer at all, but, all the same, I decided then and there to save up and buy Marina the St Christopher medal.

I did it partly because I could tell by the way Mrs Pease had locked it up that she figured I'd never be able to afford it, and partly because I was in one of my semi-Baptist fits, and I feared that Marina was Godless. The 'M' that I had engraved on the back had cost me an extra seven dollars, which meant that I'd taken Grandma's garbage out a lot more than I'd needed to.

Now, the sight of that medal swinging back and forth around Charlie Eames' neck was almost more than I could bear, and I willed Marina to look at me. I stared at her with every ounce of concentration I could summon, until, finally, she turned slowly towards me. She did not want to meet my eyes, I could tell. Her jaw was stubborn and set, and she was as intent on blocking me out as I was on prising her apart, cracking her open like a clamshell. Furious, I spun words out across the hot, muggy air, but the contest between us never got going, because in that instant, just as Marina turned to me, presenting me with the defiant, blank mask of her face, Mr Eames let out an unholy yell.

It was like the sound a bull makes when it is pawing and lowing in rage, a deep rumbling that rises to an incoherent bellow. Mr Eames raised his head from the rung and made the sound a second time, and then he swung back from the ladder, pushing it away so that it fell and clattered against the porch rail, and turned towards us. The third time he bellowed the sounds formed themselves into words.

'Boy!' Mr Eames screamed, 'Boy, I'll kill you!' and before any of us understood what was happening, Charlie Eames was running, skirting around the burning debris of the barn, and making for the open field beyond. He tried to vault the high board fence of the paddock and failed. Stumbling, and too frantic to think of turning to the gate, Charlie threw himself at the gray splintered timber, scrambling, his feet and arms moving like an over-wound toy, but he could not move fast enough, and he was only able to climb a few feet when his father caught up with him. The two huge hands fastened on the boy's scrawny shoulders, and grabbed him by his overall straps. For a moment Mr Eames held him up, dangling him, almost as if he was showing him off, like a possum or a rabbit he had just pulled from a snare. Then he flung his son down on to the ground, roaring again with rage. Drawing his foot back, Mr Eames aimed for the boy's head, but

Charlie twisted in the puddles of water and ash and raised his arms in time. Even so, Joe Cappel and Mr Delray, who had almost reached them by then, said they heard the bone in Charlie's arm snap like a gunshot.

It wasn't until an hour or so later, when we got in the car to go home, that I realized that my mother was crying. Joe and Mr Delray and some of the other men had pulled Mr Eames off Charlie, and shortly after that his Uncle Royce and his mother and our grandma, who had once been a nurse, had taken him off to the hospital. Mr Delray and a few other men had walked off into the fields with Charlie's father, and everyone else had milled around for a while, too startled and embarrassed to know exactly what they should do.

'You know the Chief came and talked to Charlie and to some of the other boys. He warned them about those fires,' I heard Mrs Hervey say to my mother.

Then I saw her shake her head and mutter while my mother shook her head and said, 'That's no excuse, Ruth Ann.'

It was well past noon when we finally got back into the station wagon, and the long bench of the front seat was so hot that it was hard to sit on. At first I tried to hold myself up with my hands, pushing my palms against the squishy plastic so I could raise the back of my thighs where the skin felt as if it might be peeling off, but Momma turned the key hard in the ignition so it made a grinding sound, and then she backed up too fast, and jerked the car around into the road, and I tipped over sideways. I looked at her to complain, but the words stopped in my mouth.

Tears were pooling above the high ridges of her cheek bones and leaving pale stripes as they ran down her face. 'Damn it,' she was muttering, 'damn that son of a bitch.' She stepped on the accelerator so that the car bounced forward, and I fell up against Marina, who was staring straight ahead and still refusing to look at me.

If the heat was burning the back of her legs off, she did not seem to care or notice. Without watching what she was doing, Marina fiddled with the button on the door lock. She was pushing it down and plucking it up again with increasing savagery, until I was afraid that she was going to open the door accidentally and fall out of the car and into the ditch. I looked at my mother, who did not usually approve of this kind of behavior, but she was intent on the road and was still shaking her head, twitching it from side to side as if she had a bug caught in her ear. Then Marina stopped anyways. Suddenly she sat quite still with her hands limp on her knees, and I could hear her humming to herself, singing the notes of a tune that I couldn't quite make out. They rose and fell and were lost in the wind that blew through the open window and whipped Marina's hair across the sharp angles of her face.

Elena leans back in her chair and gazes at me with all the detached interest and impersonal attention to detail that I imagine painters and pathologists reserve for their subjects. At first I had found this scrutiny of hers unsettling. Now I have grown used to it and usually I just stare back at her, waiting for her to deliver the pearls of insight and wisdom that her not insignificant fees suggest she keeps handy at her fingertips – but not today. Today, I lean forward, anxious.

Elena looks at me for a long time, and then she finally says, 'So, you are frightened in the dark by someone you cannot see, someone who is humming a song that was familiar to you as a child. Then, you tell me a story. It is a terrible story that is very frightening, about a fire, and about violence, and about betrayal. The violence is to a child, your age, by a man, in this case his father. The betrayal is that of your sister beginning to live a life that is separate from yours. As you realize that this is the case, that she is moving away from you, that she is, in some sense, abandoning you, she sings.' Elena raises her hand and the dusty glow of the amber ring that she wears catches the sunlight that filters through the window of her study, 'I am sorry – she hums.'

Elena drops her hand to her lap and studies it for a moment. Then she says, 'Fear is a strange thing. Of all of the human emotions, it is perhaps the most power-ful, and often the most apparently irrational. It is also the most insidious. It can stay with us for years, and arise with all its power when we least expect it. The irony is, of course,' she says, smiling, 'that so often our fear says more about what is inside us than the thing outside that we perceive to threaten us.'

Our hour is over, and Elena leads me down the narrow back stairs. I will not see her again until early November, and although I have reassured her that I will be fine in her absence, I am not so sure. All at

once, I feel reluctant to leave her, to walk out of the
door and turn my back on the comforting bulk of her
tapestried jackets. Standing with my hand on the cut-
glass of the door knob, I already miss the familiar jangle
that her jewelry makes when she moves, and long for
the reassuring opiate of her perfume.

Elena knows this, but there is nothing that she can
do about it. So she smiles, and says, 'Nothing will
happen to me,' as if she can read my mind, which is,
after all, what I pay her for. 'I will see you at four
o'clock on Friday, November the second.'

'Go safely,' I say, and I open the door.

'Susannah,' Elena says, 'nothing will happen to you,
either. You are fine. You know that.'

'I know,' I say, and I wish that I believed her. She
reaches out and touches my face. Her fingers, soft and
worn as leather, brush across my cheek.

'Tell me,' she asks, 'what happened? To the boy?'
She is trying to focus me, to bring me back to the
reassurance of the real world, and even though I
recognize this, it takes me a moment to realize that she
is asking about Charlie Eames.

'Oh, nothing,' I say, trying to play along with her.
'I mean, he ran away. And everybody knew, after that,
that he'd been setting the fires. No one ever saw him
again.'

'November the second,' Elena says. Then she closes
the door behind me.

EIGHT

Of course, it is not entirely true, what I have just told Elena. It was not intended to mislead, but it is an abbreviation. It's the sort of jumping from 'A' to 'C' that we all indulge in from time to time in order to get to the point. To say that no one ever saw Charlie Eames again does have a kind of accuracy, in the long run. In the short run however, in the final hours before he boarded a Greyhound bus and set out for the oilfields, or for the flat, pale waters of the Gulf, or for wherever it was that he went to find his future, it couldn't have been farther from the truth.

After all, Charlie did not run away from the hospital, where I gather they set his broken arm. He came home. We heard later that he braved his father, who had cooled off enough by then to walk out into the field and stand there, smoking cigarette after cigarette and staring at the ruin of his barn, until Mrs Eames went out and took him by the arm and led him back inside for supper, where he sat as docile as a child with Dex, and Charlie, and his brother Royce. After supper, Mrs Eames later told Momma, her head shaking and her voice faltering on the memory, Charlie's dad sat on the steps and offered him some bourbon 'to kill the pain', which was the closest he came to apologizing to his son for accusing him of burning the barn down and breaking his arm. So, all of those people saw Charlie Eames before he went, and I know for certain that two others did. One was Sonny Delray, who lent Charlie the fifty dollars he had saved up, and 'borrowed' his father's pick-up truck to drive him to the bus station, and the other, of course, was Marina.

As soon as we got home from the Eames' on the day of the fire, Marina jumped out of the car and went up the porch steps and into the house, moving as fast as a scalded cat. Momma herself went straight into the kitchen and picked out one of the ice cold Miller beers that she kept lined up in the refrigerator door for Uncle Ritchie when he came by. I heard the bottle cap click on to the counter, and as I came through the hall, I saw her take a long drink without even bothering to pour it into a glass. This in itself was so unusual that I was tempted to stop and see what she would do next, but that would have meant abandoning Marina, who was already halfway up the stairs, and who I was determined not to let out of my sight.

All the way home in the car I had been sending her words, demanding to know what was going on between her and Charlie Eames, and how she could possibly have given away my St Christopher medal, but she had blocked me out with her humming. She had used it like static or a radar scrambler, and I hadn't even been able to get her to glance at me. It was the first time that she had tried this trick, and I was almost as intrigued as I was enraged by it.

The rebuff had only increased my determination to get her to talk to me, so I took the stairs two at a time until I was right behind her and could see the dark half moons of sweat that had formed under the arms of her T-shirt and the bumpy outline that her bra straps made across her shoulders. She must have all but felt my breath on her back, and her long braid hung inches from my nose, swinging like a pendulum. I was sorely tempted to grab it and pull hard, but I knew that if I did she'd hit me, and I didn't want to get in a fight while we were on the stairs and she had the advantage of height.

She grabbed the newel post at the top of the banister and swung around it into the hall. She was almost running now, and I think she would have sprinted for our room, but part of ignoring me required not running, not acknowledging that I was there at all. I knew that once we got into our room I would have her cornered and that she would have to face both my presence and my demands, so I may have slacked up a little in following her the last few steps.

What I didn't count on was her shutting me out. We had chased each other before, and when cornered, we always turned and fought. The pursuit was just a preliminary drama, a sort of ritual whereby we got as far away from Momma as we could, and then jockeyed for an advantageous position before striking or receiving the first blow, which might be either verbal or physical. So it never occurred to me that Marina would simply refuse to engage, but that is exactly what she did. When she reached the door of our bedroom, she stepped inside and then, very slowly and very deliberately, she turned around and stared at me. I had to stop abruptly to avoid running into her, and I might have pushed past her if it hadn't been for the look on her face.

Long ago, Marina had mastered the trick of turning her face into a mask. She could render it utterly immobile, as if it was suddenly no longer flesh, but a solid, cold substance, something like Plasticene or agar gel that had been poured into a mold and left as a decoy while the soul inside retreated. She did this now, but the look in her eyes carried, not contempt, which I had seen many times before, but something completely new. This time it was a warning. With all of the power of her being, my sister was telling me not to come one step closer.

Despite the heat, I felt cool and slightly sick, and I stepped unsteadily backwards. We stood there staring at one another for a few more seconds, and then, very slowly, Marina closed the door. I heard the latch click as she turned the handle, and I waited to hear her slide the bolt of the lock home, but we both knew that that was unnecessary, and she did not do it. I stood where I was for a little longer, waiting to hear her footsteps as she moved away from the door and into the room, but they did not come. Finally I turned away from her and went back down the stairs and straight across the entryway and out of the front door into the sunshine.

I finished the beans that afternoon. I picked up the ones Momma had spilled when the fire whistle went, and I stripped the rest of the vines clean of everything except the few late, weanling babies that wouldn't be ready for another week or so. All of the time that I was doing this, I kept an eye on the upstairs windows of the house, half-expecting to see Marina looking down at me, or at least to catch the bulk of her figure moving behind the screens. I saw nothing, and at dinner time I was half-surprised when she came downstairs as usual and laid the kitchen table and helped Momma make chicken on the barbecue as if everything was perfectly normal.

It was late that night when I heard her moving around. I knew better than to roll over, or even to try to get a peek at what she was doing. Besides, I didn't need to. We had snuck out of the house hundreds of times together after Momma was asleep, and I knew perfectly well that she was pulling her jeans on underneath her night gown, which she would wear all the way downstairs, and possibly out to the garage, so that if she was caught she could say she was getting a drink of water, or in the worst case scenario, that she had heard a strange noise, or been sleep-walking. I heard her reach for her sneakers, which she'd tucked under the edge of her bed, and then there was the almost imperceptible 'swoosh' of the door opening and closing again, followed by the soft pad of feet on the hall's bare boards, and the conspicuous absence of the squeak from the tenth step of the stairs.

I waited until she was downstairs before I got up and tiptoed to the window, and I made sure I stayed to the side, in the shadow, so she would not see me if she looked up. I didn't hear the kitchen door open, but in a few seconds I saw the white flash of her night gown as she darted into the darkness of the garage. I guessed that she must have left a T-shirt stuffed into one of the tool boxes on the shelves, or in one of the buckets that Momma used to store her gardening trowels. A few seconds later she emerged. There was a little moonlight, but I couldn't make out what color she was wearing, of if she had put on anything extra-fancy. Even so, I was certain by now that she was going to see Charlie because she had unbraided her hair. That was what Marina always did when she wanted it to look special. In the pale, white light of the moon, it hung, thick and heavy, in a sheet that fell down over her shoulders and reached almost to the middle of her back.

When she reached the middle of the driveway, Marina stopped and looked back, as if she had sensed someone watching her. I ducked, but I could still see the white triangle of her face as it turned upwards, searching the windows of the house. She waited for a moment, pausing, cat-like, and then, apparently satisfied, she walked to the end of the drive, passed our mailbox, and broke into an impatient trot. By the time she crossed the road and hopped the ditch into Uncle Ritchie's field, she was running. I knew that there was no danger now of her looking back, and I knelt on the window seat, pressing my hands and face against the screen, watching my sister as she moved away from me, following her receding figure as she ran through the new alfalfa, and slipped into the far shadow of the trees and was lost in their long band of darkness.

She did not come back until just before dawn. The fields were lit in a wavering gray half-light when I saw her. She must have left the tree line sometime before, and she was in the middle of Uncle Ritchie's field when I picked her out. I pulled back from the window then, and withdrew myself into the shadows. I stood in the darkened bedroom and watched her approach the house, hovering just far enough back from the screen so I could see her, but she could not see me.

She made her way across the field, her hands in her pockets and her head down. She had tied her hair back with something, but some of it had escaped and hung down across her shoulders. She stopped once, suddenly, as if she had heard something, and looked back towards the woods and then out at the road. My eyes followed hers, and I thought I saw it too, a darker bulk where the bushes rose in a tangle. For barely a second a light burned. It was an orange pinprick, so small that it could have been the flaring of a cigarette. Most likely it was nothing but a late firefly sparkling in the darkness before dawn, and when I looked away from it I saw Marina shrug and pick up her pace a little as she walked on. Then she hopped the ditch and came on down the road towards the house.

I got back into bed then, and kicked the sheets around, and made sure to throw the neatly folded coverlet half on to the floor so it would look as if I had been dreaming. Then I closed my eyes and waited.

I had begun to wonder what she was doing, and I was nearly caught watching the door, when I heard the tiny clicking sound of the latch. She had been so quiet that I had not heard her in the kitchen, or on the stairs, and as the door made its gentle swooshing sound and swung open, I lay as still and as hushed as a rabbit with its ears folded back when it senses the approach of a cat.

She stopped just inside the room, and then I heard her footsteps again, but they did not pad towards her bed as I expected. Instead, I felt her as she came towards me. Her breath made a soft puffing sound, as if she had been running, or as if the effort of so much silence had exhausted her, and at first I thought that she might snatch the sheets away, or say something to me, but she didn't. She just stood there looking down on me, commanding me to look at her. I turned stubborn to the core, and refused to open my eyes and give her the satisfaction of sharing her adventure.

It was Monday before we heard that Charlie was gone. On Sunday morning Momma had finally rousted us out of bed and marched us off to help Grandma chip paint off the outside of her house. Our family had given up going to church long ago, which at times I almost regretted because now, instead of observing Sunday as a time to do our duty towards Jesus, we observed it as a time to do our duty towards whatever Momma and Grandma decided to get done. As a result, not only did we have to get up early but, more often than not, we had to spend the day raking, or weeding, or painting, or doing some other such job that was almost odious enough to make getting dressed up and singing I am the Lamb of the Lord look good. Even so, I now half-dreaded getting my driver's license in a year's time. I could only imagine how much that would widen the scope of Momma's ambition, and how she'd have me and Marina spending all our free time driving back and forth to the dump, and doing good-deed things like delivering meals-on-wheels to old Mr Marmion who clacked his teeth and spat at you when he talked.

As the result of our paint-chipping, Marina and I didn't get a chance to see anyone, or hear anything at all that Sunday. Sonny Delray did not even stop by to make fun of us, which in itself was somewhat unusual.

I kept an eye on Marina, but she didn't do or say a single thing out of the ordinary, and she was even friendly. So much so, in fact, that I might have forgotten that Charlie Eames even existed if I had not seen a path of broken stalks in the alfalfa when we drove back past Uncle Ritchie's field at dinner time.

Nothing unusual happened that night either. I set the table while Momma and Marina made dinner, and later all three of us washed the dishes. It was hot, and while Marina watched television, and Momma did things at her desk, I went out and sat on the porch steps and watched the stars and tried to shake off the uneasy feeling that was clinging to me like the muggy, still air. Finally, I got up and walked away from the sound of the TV laughter and the lights in the house. I turned out of the driveway and on to the road until I reached the thick tangle of wild berry bushes and old rose that still stood by the ditch. Grandma said that roses meant a farm house had been here once, and that if you dug down far enough under the alfalfa field you might find goodness knows what, a silver spoon, a broken dish, some fragment from the lives that had been passed here.

Turning around, I saw our house, with the lights shining yellow, and Uncle Ritchie's alfalfa field spreading away to the right of the road. I dropped on to my hands and knees then and, spreading my palms across the flat edge of the road and the dusty band of scrub grass, I searched. It was a moment before I found it, but when my fingers hit the soft, spongy cylinder, I knew exactly what it was. I picked the cigarette butt up and dropped it into the pocket of my shorts.

Marina read *Jamaica Inn* in bed that night and she

fell asleep with the light on so that the moths batted themselves against the screen and I had to get up and take the book out of her hand. I knew from looking at her that she was fast asleep, and that she was not going to move again. So, I turned off the lamp, and got into bed and half-listened through the night, skimming the top of dreams, and wondering who it was who had stood by the old rose bush, smoking, and watching my sister come home in the dark.

I was still thinking about this, in a half-hearted kind of way, on Monday afternoon when we found out about Charlie Eames. It was Sonny Delray, of all people, who was the unlikely bearer of the momentous news. I saw him coming down the road while I was sitting on the glider, pushing myself idly back and forth, wondering how long I could put off mowing the lawn. He swung around our mailbox, rapping the top of it with his knuckles, and I could tell, just by the way that he was walking, that he had something important to say.

For as long as I could remember, I had never heard anyone call him anything but 'Sonny', and although I must have been vaguely aware that he had another name, I had no idea what it might have been. He was a big boy, heavy with puppy fat that had lingered through adolescence and padded his body, making him look soft and squishy. Sonny was one of the people who never could tell us apart, and over the years Marina and I had occasionally amused ourselves by confusing him deliberately. He had a terrible crush on her, when he could figure out which one of us she was, and at the Memorial Day Picnic that spring, we'd actually gotten him to kiss me when he thought I was Marina. In the midst of this clutch, which I had submitted to only after significant bribery, Marina and Della Hervey, and Charlie and Dex Eames, and a bunch of other people, had jumped out from behind some trees and all but landed on top of us.

Sonny had been so mad that he'd run off and had barely talked to any of us until after the Fourth of July fireworks, but by that Monday afternoon in late August all had been forgiven, and as I watched him come across our lawn, I thought that he looked as if he'd been plumped up like a down pillow. He was positively inflated with importance, and completely forgot to try to figure out which one of us I was.

'I came over to say how real sorry I am,' Sonny announced.

He had come to a halt right in front of the glider, and I had to put my bare foot down hard in order to stop it from ramming into his knees. The sun was behind him, but in the shadow of his baseball cap I could see that his face was creased with the kind of exaggerated concern that means people are secretly happy about bad news. A flicker of interest tickled my chest, but I had no intention of giving him the satisfaction of asking what he was talking about.

'I mean, I did ask him if he wanted to leave anybody a letter or anything,' Sonny went on, 'but he was in one real hurry, and I knew he'd told you himself anyways.'

At that moment I felt Marina come around the side of the house. I couldn't see her, but the dense summer air had been disturbed, and I knew that she was there.

'I tried to talk him out of it,' Sonny was saying, 'I surely did. I said, "Charlie, you're crazy, man", but he said there wasn't a single thing, in this damned town that he cared about, and that all he wanted was never to see this place or anyone in it again.'

'What are you talking about?' Marina asked, and Sonny's head swung around, making him look like a surprised tortoise.

His face registered the momentary confusion that came with understanding that he had not known who he was talking to, and he blushed deeply at being caught out again. Then he said, 'Well, Charlie Eames, of course.' His embarrassment made him aggressive, and the words came out like a challenge. 'I drove him to the bus station yesterday morning.'

Something like a smirk began to creep across his face, and I saw Marina stiffen.

'I was at home taking care of that heifer when he came over,' Sonny said. 'Everybody else was at church. Except you of course, since you guys don't go to church. I told Charlie that we could go by your grandma's where you were probably working, if he wanted, but he said he was in too big a hurry, so we took Daddy's old truck. Charlie drove over, 'cause he has his permit, but I drove all the way home by myself.'

He flopped down on the grass at my feet. Smiling up at us, he took his cap off and ran his hands through his hair, reliving his moment of glory in driving the six miles back from the bus station without a learner's permit. I was secretly impressed with this, since the only place I'd ever driven was up and down the road in front of our house, or around Uncle Ritchie's farmyard, and that was always with Momma and

Marina in the car yelling instructions at me and grabbing the side of the seat or the doorhandles.

'I knew nobody would catch me,' Sonny said,
'because everybody was in church, including Dick-
Head.' 'Dick-Head' was Dick Burns, who was Petamill's local cop. He was actually an all right guy who cut
most of the kids in town a lot of leeway in buying
cigarettes and drinking beer, but we felt like we had to
call him some kind of bad name anyways.

I had to admit that Sonny had been exceptionally
daring, and he was so pleased with his retelling of the
adventure that both of us had nearly forgotten Charlie
Eames altogether. We were discussing the route he had
taken, and what it had been like, and what he would
have done if somebody recognized him, when Marina
said, 'But when is he coming back?' Her voice was
higher than it should have been, and Sonny and I both
stopped talking and looked at her. 'When did he say
he was coming back?' Marina asked.

Sonny stared at her for a minute, and then he said,
'He isn't coming back.' And for a change he looked at
Marina as though he thought she was stupid. 'Don't
you get it?' he added. 'He's gone. He left, man. He's
history.'

The words hung in the air, and suddenly I wanted
to tell Sonny to shut up, but the sounds died in my
throat, and I couldn't. I just sat there, with little waves
of excitement slapping at my stomach, while I watched
Marina.

'He said he just wanted to get the Hell out of this
town,' Sonny was saying. 'He borrowed my fifty
dollars. That was all my summer money.'

There was a pause, and then Sonny started pulling

up the dandelions that grew around the legs of the glider and popping their heads off with his thumbnail.

'He promised when he got a job he'd mail it back,' he said, and then he added, 'It wasn't the first time his dad hit him, you know. That's why he burned the barn down.'

Silence hung in the air.

'Firebug, firebug,' Sonny said, and a funny little smile played around his mouth. I might as well not have existed. He was staring right at Marina. 'Crackle, crackle,' he said.

For a second I thought that she was going to say something. She opened her mouth and closed it again. Then Sonny shrugged, and pulled up another dandelion.

'Said he was going on down to Baton Rouge, or maybe to Texas.' The head of the dandelion went flying into the air. 'I've thought about maybe I'd do that myself,' he added, 'after high school. They say that—'

'Shut up!' Marina shouted. She glared at both of us as if it was our fault that Charlie Eames had burned his father's barn down and then just decided to leave without telling anybody.

'Just shut up!' she yelled again, and then she turned on her heel and started down the driveway.

Sonny looked as if he'd been slapped.

'Marina,' he called after her. He began to get to his feet, pushing himself up in an ungainly motion, like an old dog that is too big. 'I'm sorry,' he called. 'Hey, I—'

'Shut up!' she yelled again, without looking back, and then she started to jog.

I stood up too, and Sonny and I watched as she went up the road, and jumped the ditch, and started to run across the field, heading for the band of trees, just like she had two nights before. Sonny's round, pudding face was as hurt as if she had thrown something at him, and when he finally turned to look at me I said, 'What did you mean about the fires?' But Sonny just shook his head, as if he didn't understand me, and threw the last dandelion he was holding down on to the grass.

'Nothin'. Nothin', Shoo,' he said. Then he started to walk off down the driveway, his head all hunched down and his hands dug in his pockets, and left me standing there by the dumb old glider feeling like I didn't understand anything at all.

As that Monday afternoon went on, I found that I was secretly pleased by Sonny's news. I liked the drama of it, but even more than that I liked the fact that Charlie Eames was gone. As I considered it, as I looked back over the summer while I pushed the mower across our browning front lawn that Momma made such a fuss over, I still could not tell when Marina had abandoned me. I could not pinpoint the day, or even the week, when she had entered a world that I was not allowed into. Although I was still not sure of the exact nature of the exclusion, I could smell the betrayal of it like a hound smells a skunk. The bright coin of the St Christopher medal, which was even now probably hanging around Charlie Eames' neck, speeding him in safety to wherever he was going, was proof enough of that. To make things worse, even fat old Sonny Delray seemed to be a part of it.

In fact, I thought, not only had I been denied the vicarious thrill of Marina's stupid old love affair, and whatever else she and Charlie'd been up to, which probably included fire-bugging, if Sonny was to be believed, but I hadn't even been able to figure out that I was being excluded. This in itself presented problems of a logistical nature. I felt like a general who had been betrayed by his allies, and ambushed at the same time. How could this have happened? I asked myself as I stopped the mower and pulled a plug of grass clippings out from between the rotors. Not only had I been outmaneuvered, but I had suffered an absolute failure of intelligence. I had been totally unaware that anything was even going on. The net result was that Marina had both betrayed me and made a fool out of me in the process. That, I thought, as I started the mower up again and lunged it dangerously close to Momma's flower bed, added insult to injury.

So I decided that I was glad that Charlie Eames was gone, and I hoped that his vanishing act would inflict upon Marina the rash of betrayal, and the sting of humiliation that she had inflicted on me. I was glad that her heart was broken, too. I was glad because right then the only thing I was interested in was revenge. And because I smelled the possibility of power.

If I was the only person who knew about Marina's secret, I thought to myself, as I wheeled the lawn mower into the garage, then I was the only person who could comfort her for the loss of it. Aside from Sonny that was, who I knew damn well Marina wouldn't turn to if he was the last person left on earth. So I decided, then and there, that I would exact my revenge by being extremely kind and generous to

Marina. I would bestow my pity on her, and then, sooner or later, I told myself, whether she liked it or not, she would be grateful.

I didn't lose any time putting my plan into action. The idea of Marina being beholden to me was too sweet to squander for a moment. She was back in time for dinner, and when Momma asked her twice what she had done that afternoon and twice she did not answer, I leapt in before the question could come up again. I said that we had trimmed the edge of the flower border, and weeded around by the vegetable garden, but that then Marina had gotten a headache and gone to lie down. I went on with great confidence, rambling about the corn, and about how I'd had to pick nine ears just to get these six we were now eating because there had been weevils and corn worms in almost every other one. I did not glance at Marina even once as I said all this, but I could see her looking at me out of the corner of her eye. In ordinary cir-cumstances she would have been highly suspicious of this impromptu defense, but I could tell by the look of her that she was all wobbly inside, and that she had been crying and could not be bothered to suspect my motives.

She went upstairs before I did, and it was not until after *Charlie's Angels* that I followed her. She was sitting up in bed reading again, or pretending to, her book propped on her knees. I watched her for a minute, until she looked up, and then I said, 'I'm sorry. You know, about Charlie. I'm sorry he left.'

She started to shrug and go back to her book, to let me know that neither Charlie Eames nor my sympathy mattered to her, but then she stopped. She watched me for a second, tugging on her braid, wrapping its long coil around her hand and pulling to see if it would hurt.

'I don't know why he didn't tell me,' she said, and the misery and need in her face were both so strong and so unfamiliar that I felt uncomfortable. 'Why didn't he tell me?' she asked, and this time I shrugged.

'I don't know,' I said. 'Maybe he didn't have time.'

She was still looking at me, and I began to fidget. Suddenly I felt that in saying I was sorry I had somehow volunteered to provide her with answers to her questions, and the fact that I couldn't made me feel unaccountably guilty. It made me feel as if I had somehow caused Charlie to leave, or told him not to warn her that he would be going. A jolt of anger ran through me as I looked at her. All summer long Marina had kept Charlie a secret from me, and now that I had found out by chance, and everything had turned out wrong, she wanted me not only to explain what had happened, but to salve her wounds for her.

Despite the fact that this was exactly what I had wished for, the situation was nowhere near as rewarding as I had thought it would be, and I began to wish instead that I'd never even noticed her and Charlie Eames, or that I could go to Momma and get her to take care of Marina. I stripped my T-shirt off over my head and wriggled quickly into my night gown. Then, before she could ask me anything else, I turned my light off and rolled over. I could tell that she was watching me, that she was contemplating saying something else, and I was relieved when I heard her close her book and turn out her light, and no words came fluttering at me through the darkness.

It was hot, and I had rolled my coverlet all the way down to the bottom of my bed. When I heard Marina get up, I thought that perhaps she was taking hers off altogether, or that maybe she was going down the hall for a glass of water, or to talk to Momma, but instead she stood in the middle of the room and whispered my name.

'Susannah, are you awake?' Her voice was quavery and I knew that she was almost crying again. 'Shoo?' she asked.

'Uh huh,' I said without turning over.

'I'm sorry I gave Charlie the necklace,' Marina said. 'I know I shouldn't have done that.'

'That's OK,' I grunted.

By this time I was wishing that she'd just shut up about it all, but she didn't. Instead, she sniffed and said, 'Can I get in with you, Shoo? Please, just for tonight?'

When we were very little, we had often slept in the same bed. No matter how many times Momma separated us, she would find us in the morning curled into each other, our hair spread across the pillow, our hands sticky with sweat where our fingers had locked together. Now, the sound of the night peepers filled our room, and somewhere across Uncle Ritchie's field I thought I heard an owl.

'Please,' she said again. Without speaking, I threw my sheet back, and Marina slipped into my bed.

NINE

I do not think about Charlie Eames now. Until the barn burned, and his father broke his arm, and he ran away, until I viewed him as a cause of Marina's behavior, I really never thought of him much at all, even back then. After all that, after he disappeared, I viewed him mainly as an object. He was a thrill I had been denied, a secret that Marina had kept from me. Charlie was on a par with a five-dollar bill that she had once hoarded, and with eyeshadow that she had stolen from Woolworth's and didn't share. He was like the dirty jokes that she sometimes whispered to Della Hervey on the bus and refused to let me overhear. So, I remember the fact of Charlie Eames, but do not recall him as a person. I do not recall the way his hair might have fallen, or the sound of his laugh, or the shape of his hands and face. Those are not things that I remember.

What I do remember is the feel of Marina's body on the night when she came into my bed. It was too hot and too heavy. She was a weight that was tied to me, bound to me by arms as slender and as supple as vines, and by tendrils of need that wound themselves around me, and by all the webs that we spun in the darkness.

I feel her sometimes still, and on these mornings I wake panting and lie slick with sweat, even though it may be cold in the room and frost spangles the windows. The air that I am conscious of breathing on these occasions is particularly sharp and clean. It tastes to me as it must to a swimmer who has been trapped, who has been fettered and tangled by weeds, and who has struggled to rise and crack the shimmering surface of the water. On mornings like that, when my body finally cools and I have caught my breath, I feel a buoyant sense of freedom, a release as sweet as a puff of summer air. This morning it lasts until I look in the mirror.

'Go away,' I say to the face that looks back at me, and I feel instantly embarrassed, although there is no one to hear me but Jake. 'I don't have time for you,' I tell Marina, and then I open the medicine cabinet with more force than is necessary. I brush my teeth and braid my hair and get ready for the morning meeting that I have with Lolly.

Mint green is the color for today, a shirt and headband and flat shoes that match. The headband and the collar and shoulder pads of Lolly's shirt have tiny fake pearls sewn on to them, and although I understand that the intent is something along the line of strewn stars, the overall effect is of bits of rice, or confetti, as if she has just come from a wedding, or a parade.

'The napkins have arrived,' she announces as soon as I open the door and before I even have a chance to get out of the car. 'I'm sure they're going to be totally fabulous. I can't wait for you to see them!'

I don't point out to Lolly that I have seen them, that, in fact, I designed them and that this is what she pays me for. Instead, I get out and stand on the sidewalk, scrabbling in my bag for my glasses' case. We are on our way to the Design Center, which is housed in a strange windowless block of a building that hangs over the edge of the Schuykill. There is a lurid mural of whales and dolphins painted on the side of it, which is justified by the fact that it was originally intended as an aquarium. The only available parking for the Design Center is along the University Bridge, where we are standing now. Lolly must have arrived just seconds ahead of me, because the Lexus is tucked in two cars back and she was waiting when I pulled up, gesturing to where I should park, as if I might not be able to figure it out for myself.

'Oh,' she says now. She has just noticed my new car door, which is blue, sort of, but nothing like the blue of my car. It's obviously spray painted, and the best Benjy said he could do in the circumstances. 'Well,' Lolly says, 'that's not too bad.' Which means, of course, that it's awful. 'When is the new one coming?' She glances over her shoulder as she asks this, as if she's afraid that someone she knows might see her standing beside my disfigured car. 'Soon, I hope,' I say, gathering up my briefcase and locking the car. 'Don't worry,' I add. 'In the meantime I won't go around telling anybody I work for you.' This causes her to grimace, and take me by the elbow. Lolly marches me along the sidewalk as if I am a naughty child.

'Come on,' she says, 'we can't keep the Dragon Lady waiting.'

The 'Dragon Lady' is actually Mrs Koom Wai, a

diminutive and terrifying Korean woman who owns one of the best textile places in the Center. This morning she has just received a new shipment of tapestried silks and, if Lolly wasn't with me, I would easily spend several hours pawing through them, feeling their smooth, cool, weight, watching the flash of their gaudy turquoises and magentas, and tracing the paths of the tiny embroidered figures who scurry across bridges, racing from pagoda to pagoda. As it is, I wink at Mrs Koom Wai, meaning that I will be back, and she fetches the tablecloths and napkins that I have chosen for Indochine. On her return she lifts each one neatly folded, and then, like a magician, she releases the fabric with a snap of her wrist, and sends it rippling in a wave of black and scarlet across the broad, polished surface of the display table. A '10 out of 10' is Lolly's verdict, and she takes me upstairs to lunch on the strength of it.

'This is to make up for the car, because I didn't have time the other night,' she insists as I protest, and when the menus arrive she orders us both a dry martini. 'Just show it the vermouth bottle,' she says to the waiter, 'and for God's sake, no olive.'

The drink leaves me feeling lightheaded and irresponsible. I should be hurrying home to work, but after Lolly leaves, kissing me incongruously on the forehead since she cannot be bothered to lean down far enough to reach my cheek, I linger for a cup of espresso and then wander downstairs. The Center is laid out like the interior of a big hotel, and I stare idly through the thick-paned display windows of the shops that line either side of the carpeted hallways.

I drift aimlessly, and finally come to rest in front of

a window lettered with the words 'Ultimate Kitchen'.
Beyond the glass there is a riot of Provençal fabric.
Dishcloths, oven gloves, tea cosies and bread baskets
are all made up in vivid yellows and electric blues
dotted with small red flowers. Dried boughs of olive
branch and grape vines climb a central pillar, and
copper bowls, and pans, and molds in the shape of
hearts and fishes hang from racks along the ceiling.
Below them are stacks of wicker baskets, but what
draws me, what catches my eye, is the bright glint of
stainless steel, the polished gleam of the knives.

Like jewels, they are locked behind glass and backed
by black velvet. My request to touch requires a key,
the opening of a padlock, and hovering supervision.
The blades range from long, rounded at the end and
paper-thin, for slicing smoked salmon, to a fine, eight-
inch boning instrument with a point sharp enough to
etch glass. There's a short, stubby, serrated blade whose
twist will zest a lemon or curl frozen butter into a ball.
The handles are ebony, molded in the grip, and
somehow already warm and welcoming to the touch.
When I pick each knife up the handle folds into my
palm, locks into my grip with all the familiar solidarity
of a handshake.

The girl offers me a cutting board and a sacrificial
tomato, but I don't take her up on her invitation to
slice its skin. I'm feeling fickle, and I've been lured
away by the poultry shears. My old ones disappeared
some time ago, and the scissors that I have been using
since then are fine for snipping chives, and worse than
useless for anything else. Deboning a chicken is out of
the question.

This would not be true of the shears now before

me. Two pairs are laid out in the display case, and I lift them both. I snap at the air, hearing the quick swish, the delicate 'click' of the blades as they meet. One set is serrated, the other smooth, and it is these I am drawn to. When I run my finger along the edge of them I can feel just how precisely, and just how quickly, they will cut.

'I'll take them,' I say, and the salesgirl slips the shears into a plastic sleeve and wraps them carefully in tissue paper that she ties with a raffia bow. She tucks a little piece of lavender into the knot. I can smell it as I take the package, and when I leave the shop the shears sit in my shoulder bag, giving it a new and satisfying weight.

Outside the wind has picked up. The overripe mugginess of the Indian summer has been chased away, and for the first time it feels like fall. The slight, metallic tang of autumn clears my head, and I pause in the middle of the bridge to watch a train creep along the tracks on the far side of the river and disappear into the tunnel that runs under the Penn Hockey rink and skirts the tall white buildings of the University.

I used to know them all, those buildings. I used to know their names, used to weave in and out of them expertly, dropping George off, or picking him up, or going to meet him for lunch, or a drink. Now their familiarity has begun to fade, and I am no longer certain that I would know which alleys are one way, which parking lots are safe, or which gates close at dusk. It is as if a part of me has slipped away while I was not looking, and, like amputees who sometimes feel pain in a limb long after it is gone, I feel a sudden lurch of sadness.

All at once I'm caught in a short, sharp riptide of regret for all the things that I would wish undone, and for all the moments that I would wish rewritten and relived. For just a second the feeling is so all encompassing, so complete, that it takes my breath away. But then I force myself to walk on, to put one foot in front of the other, and to feel for my keys, and think of Jake, who will be waiting for me. I reach the car, and have just decided that this afternoon we will go for a long walk in the Wissahickon Park to celebrate the coming of fall, when I look up and see George. He's not ten yards away and coming straight towards me. For half a second I wonder if my thoughts have actually brought him into being, if I have somehow inadvertently conjured him up from some deep, hidden pool of longing and nostalgia.

The sight of him is at once so completely familiar, and so utterly strange, that I freeze. I knew, of course, that he was back from Paris, and that, one day, inevitably, I would run into him. I have envisioned our meeting. I've played it out carefully, and run through the possibilities, the coming around an aisle and seeing him in the grocery store, the bumping into him at a bar, or at a party, the unexpected sound of his voice during an intermission at the theater. Even so, I feel unfairly trapped, bullied, as if the past has broken through its barriers and elbowed its way into the present. I'm not ready for this sudden, spinning sense that life has gone nowhere, that the last year has crumbled and I might just as well be standing on another sidewalk, under streetlights this time, two days before he's due to leave for Paris, wishing him 'Good Luck', and then watching him walk away.

His hair has grown a little. The wind lifts it up and blows it sideways. He's still wearing his old tweed jacket, one of several that he adopted as a uniform after he started teaching at Penn, but he's switched from khakis to black pants, tightish jeans which, I guess, must be the influence of his new wife. He is, thank God, alone, and since I have seen him before he sees me, I have a chance to take in the look of his face, and to compose my own. I have the chance to arrange my mouth and eyes, to rest my hand on the car door so he will not see it shaking, before I say, 'George?' and his step checks at the sound of my voice, and he looks up to see me standing in front of him.

'Susannah!' His voice hasn't changed. He doesn't sound like Inspector Clouseau or Vincent Price, but I can't tell whether there's any pleasure in it, or just surprise.

'How are you?' We both ask it at once, and stop at once, sounding like a badly scripted sit-com.

'Fine,' I hear myself saying, and I know I'm nodding like one of those dog things that sit in the back window of trashy cars and wag their heads up and down. 'And you?' I'm asking. 'And Paris? How was—'

'Great,' George says. 'It was really great.' He's nodding too. 'I mean, it's just a whole different scene, you know, Suze.'

Suze was George's pet-name for me, his diminutive, like the ones they are so fond of in Russian novels. George is the only person who ever had a name for me, other than my mother and Marina. Once I thought 'Suze' was sweet, a sign of intimacy. Now it

crosses my mind that it was probably just a convenience, something that was faster and easier to say.
I've been asking George more questions, almost without realizing it, appropriate things about his book and
his teaching, but I'm not really listening to what he's
answering. Instead I'm slipping away. I'm wallowing
in the familiar sound of his voice, drifting on the
memory of his touch, and catching the half-forgotten
echo of his breath against my skin.

I want him to keep talking so I can watch the
familiar planes of his face a little longer, but he's
stopped. I'm vaguely aware that he might have asked
me if I'd read something in the *New York Times* about
the Pompidou Center, and so I shake my head, which
seems to satisfy him. Then he looks around, reaching
for another subject.

'Is this yours?' he asks, pointing at the Mercedes,
and I realize that he's never seen it, that I bought it as
a treat for myself after he left.

'Yeah, I'd always wanted one. Well, an old one.'

'So work must be going well?' George runs his
hand along the car's roof, then he looks up at me and
grins. 'Shame you couldn't afford all four doors,
though.'

'Well,' I say, 'just a casualty of city life.' George
furrows his brow in concern.

'Accident?' he asks. 'I hope you're OK? Or should
I see the other guy?'

'No, no.' I say it too fast, but for some reason it
annoys me, as if he assumes I deliberately invited
someone to run into me, and as much as I'd like to, I
don't trust the concern in his voice. I'm beginning to

feel uncomfortable, and I start to fumble for my keys.
'It was just some little jerk being artistic,' I say. 'Letting
me know what they thought of me.'

'They wrote on your door?' Perhaps things like this
don't happen in the City Of Light. George's voice
sounds incredulous.

'Carved.' I get the door open and throw my briefcase across the console and into the passenger seat.
'"Bitch", to be exact,' I add, straightening up and
smiling. I expect George to laugh, but he doesn't. He's
staring at the door as if he could see the word, and he's
furrowing his brow again. His face is creased in concern, and I know him well enough to know that this
time it's for real.

'"Bitch"?' he asks. 'That's really weird,' and I feel a
hollowness blossoming in my stomach, because now
there's something else moving across George's face. It's
like a shadow on water, almost not there, but unmistakable at the same time. It's a slight shimmering suggestion of fear.

I don't want to ask, but I know that I have to.

'What? What's really weird?'

The bridge seems to have gone quiet, as if the
people walking past us are bouncing on air, and finally
George says, 'Marina.' He looks right at me and the
space in my stomach collapses in on itself, it implodes
like a star.

'What about her?' Somehow I know the answer to
this even before he says it.

'Somebody did exactly the same thing to her,'
George says. He looks at me. 'Don't you remember?'

'When?'

My voice sounds croaky, like something's stuck in

my throat. George shakes his head and looks at his feet. Like a kid, he's drawing a little circle on the pavement with the toe of his shoe, tracing it over and over again. 'George,' I say, 'when?' My hands are dug into my pockets and it's everything I can do not to reach out and shake him.

'Maybe I didn't tell you,' he says. 'I can't remember. You guys weren't really talking at the time.' He stops the circles and looks at me, shrugging. 'She told me about it one of those times when she called. When you wouldn't talk to her. She was pretty pissed off.' He shakes his head, as if he could clear it of the memory. 'She said it was going to cost her a fortune,' George says. 'Some asshole had carved the word "Bitch" in her car door. It can't have been more than a couple of weeks before she died.'

TEN

I pressed George after that. Standing on the bridge yesterday I grilled him, my voice unnecessarily shrill, demanding to know whether he could remember anything else, anything at all, that Marina had said, but he couldn't. Or so he claimed. It was probably the truth. His eyes had begun to flicker by then, and he just wanted to get away from me, to dart like a fish through reeds back into the unsullied waters of his new life.

The mention of Marina's name had curdled the momentary warmth between us. It had always been like that, even when she was alive, and George and I had already discovered once that being murdered in no way diminished her powers. On the contrary. No longer constrained by the mortal world, Marina was now free to be everywhere, always. Yesterday, as we stood on the bridge, our eyes watering in the bright wind, her ghost had erased time and returned us to ground zero. Rising like a phoenix, she had left us once more knee-high in the ash-heap of anger and guilt that was finally all that had been left of our five years together. By the time he kissed me goodbye, leaning forward and pecking each of my cheeks quickly, à la française, the brush of George's lips had not felt welcome and familiar, as I had expected they would. Instead they had been reduced to something dry and foreign, and they brushed like paper against my skin.

Now, I try to blot out the corrosive effect that Marina's death had on us, and I play George's words back in my head while I watch the flat glare of the light on the Delmarva Peninsula. Jake lies on the back seat and from time to time I can hear him snuffling. Occasionally he sits up and looks out of the window, and I catch a flash of black and a rapid swipe of sable, and see his earnest golden eyes in the rearview mirror. The road ahead is a soft gray strip and the fields that border it have not yet turned fallow and dead. Soon the metallic blue-green of the wetlands will appear on our right, and shortly after that Jake and I will get our first glimpse of the Chesapeake.

Kathleen Harper's directions were extremely accurate. She detailed churches that I will pass on the left or right, and roads that have county numbers and animal names like 'Fox Way' and 'Mallard's Lane'. If the woman who had been Marina's best friend in Washington had been surprised to hear from me when I called her last night, she had given no hint of it. There was nothing in her voice to suggest that she had forgotten me or that she found the fact of my calling in any way strange. Instead she had been ready with her directions, and she had treated my request to come and talk to her about Marina as if it was the most natural thing in the world. She had sounded, in fact, as if she had been waiting for me all this time.

I have met Kathleen Harper only once before, at Marina's funeral, a dingy affair at a crematorium somewhere near Reston. Less than a dozen of us stood in a modern white stucco chapel and sang All Things Bright and Beautiful, which was the only hymn I could think of at the time, while my sister's coffin was propelled, as if by magic, down a sort of conveyor belt and disappeared behind a navy blue curtain. Kathleen had come up to me afterwards, and I remember her as brunette, well-groomed, and tall. She had introduced herself as a colleague and friend of Marina's from the World Bank, and like Special Detective Mark Cope, she had given me her card. She too had scribbled her home number on it, and murmured, 'If there's ever anything . . .' Now, since my meeting with George on the bridge yesterday, it suddenly feels as if there is something.

As I walked Jake through the Wissahickon Gorge an hour after leaving George, I played his words back in my head over and over again: 'Someone wrote "Bitch" on her car door a few weeks before she died.' But of course she didn't just die. The woman who was my mirror image was cut to pieces. She was stabbed more than twenty-five times.

The house is big, and modern, and on the water. Jake watches me from the back seat as I stand on the terracotta steps and ring the doorbell, which chimes three times like something out of Edgar Allen Poe. I can't hear footsteps inside, and if it wasn't for the tail-end of the car that I can see sticking out of the open garage, I'd think that the place was empty, like a house that is waiting to be sold.

I try to remember what I know about Kathleen

Harper, and come up with not much. She had worked with Marina at the World Bank, and I'm pretty sure that I remember the mention of kids and a marriage, or maybe of a divorce, but beyond that I don't know anything about her. So, when the door swings open, catching me by surprise, the woman who stands in front of me is a complete stranger.

I am right in remembering that she is tall and dark. She's also big-boned, and too thin, so the immediate impression is somehow two-dimensional. She looks flat, as if she's a cardboard cutout. This illusion may also have something to do with the blank sheet of light that floods in from the glass wall behind her, back-lighting her like a prop on a stage. She had mentioned last night that she had stopped working, and, freed from the obligation of going to an office, she is no longer well groomed. Her skin is pale, as if she's a recluse or an invalid, and her hair is cut short, almost like a boy's. She brushes it back from her forehead in a choppy, nervous gesture, and I notice that she chews her nails. Two livid spots of color appear on her cheeks as she stares at me. She opens her mouth and closes it, and then gives herself a visible shake.

'I'm sorry,' Kathleen Harper says, 'I don't mean to be rude. It's just that sometimes I forget that there were two of you.'

The house seems to be a series of glass rooms, some of which look into each other, and some of which look out over the water. There are minimal rugs on the floor, and all the couches are low and rectangular and very Bauhaus. In the center of the living room there's an upturned tea crate with a bowl of jelly beans and some magazines on it, which suggests that her

husband got the coffee table. I follow Kathleen into
the kitchen, turn down her offer of a sandwich, or
coffee, and then accept a beer when she says she's
going to have one.

'It's after two,' she says. 'I don't usually drink in the
afternoon, but it is one of the pleasures of being at
home.'

The kitchen, which is predictably sleek, is made
almost entirely of blond wood and stainless steel. A
row of narcissus bulbs sit on the window sill above the
double sinks, and a child's pink knapsack with pictures
of Barbie on it lies on the edge of the island beside a
knife block and a halogen stove. Pots hang from a rack
on the ceiling. They're highly polished, and graduated
in size, and show no sign of having been used in the
recent past. It's not hard to see this room as a bastion
of take-out sushi, and white wine in mini-bottles, and
children who nibble chicken fingers and other tubular
things that go into and come out of the microwave on
plastic trays. Kathleen opens the refrigerator, and when
the door swings out I see the picture of Marina.

It's one of several of what appear to be family
photos that have been slipped into plastic sleeves and
stuck in place with magnets in the shape of sunflowers.
In it Marina is sitting on the steps of a deck, which I
guess must be at the back of this house. Her arms are
looped around two small girls, and she is smiling. One
of the children holds a brown labrador by the collar,
twisting its head around in an attempt to make it look
at the camera. Despite myself, I'm fascinated. The
picture looks like my sister and not like her at once, as
if someone else has invaded Marina's body.

'They adored her,' Kathleen says. She's watching

my face intently, and I feel myself color, as if I've been caught peeking through a keyhole or listening at a door. She flips the tops off two bottles of Rolling Rock.

'She used to spend a lot of time here. This was our weekend house, pre-divorce.' Kathleen hands me one of the beers. 'We taught her to sail,' she says. 'You know, we'd have cook-outs, go over to the marina, all that sort of stuff. The girls got a big kick out of that: her name Marina, and marina. I told them it was a car accident.'

Kathleen adds this quickly, and a little half-smile plays around the edges of her mouth when she does, as if she's both confessing and apologizing to me for this whitewash of Marina's death.

'I know you shouldn't lie to kids,' she adds, 'but I could hardly tell them the truth. That's one of the reasons I started working at home after it happened, so I could be here for them. Poor little guys. They were having a hard enough time as it was, with the divorce.' Kathleen takes a quick swallow of the beer and swings the refrigerator door shut. 'Would you like to go outside?' she asks. 'We could walk.'

Jake runs ahead of us down the lawn. Kathleen watches him with the combination of nostalgia and envy that is usually reserved for old boyfriends who have moved on to other women.

'I miss my dog,' she says, as Jake finds a stick and then drops it and heads into the tawny colored band of tall grass that fronts the water. 'My husband took him and the boat. I kept the kids.'

'That must be hard,' I say. I don't know her well enough to add 'I'm sorry', or to know if she'd rather have had it the other way around and kept the boat and the dog. Jake erupts from the long grass and hops over a stone wall at the bottom of the lawn, racing back towards me to make sure that I'm still in sight. A dock runs out over the water, and by the time we reach it he has trotted out ahead of us and I can hear his claws making little ticking sounds on the weathered silver planking.

Kathleen leans against the railing and watches the water, which is still and smoky in the late afternoon.

'Treasure the Chesapeake,' she says, quoting the license plate slogan, the one that has a picture of reeds and a loon, and that you see mostly on the back of 4x4s. 'It's polluted, you know.' She stretches her hand down towards the water, as if she could stroke it with the tips of her fingers. 'They say they're trying to clean it up, but every time they do, you read about another company pouring crap into it. Marina loved this place. She said it was "peaceful". That was the word she used. She said it like it was something incredibly valuable. I worry about that.' Kathleen pauses. 'I worry about whether she's at peace now.' She finishes her beer and sits down on a board locker box where boat fenders and single sneakers and tangled fishing line probably end up. 'So,' she says, 'you drove two hours down here. What is it you want to ask me?'

The question comes out almost as a demand, and when Kathleen looks up at me, her expression has changed. All at once it's a mixture of inquiry and defensiveness, like a child's, as if she expects me to accuse her of something or to hurt her feelings. Marina had perfected this same look when she was in her teens, this same guilt-inducing combination of naked-ness and hostility, and with a flash of clairvoyance I can see why she and Kathleen were such good friends. I can read it on Kathleen's face. The two of them must have recognized one another instantly. They each must have realized that they'd found a buttress, a sister-in-arms in their battle against the world.

I'm unprepared for this sense of familiarity, for this weird sensation that I'm talking to Marina by proxy, and that I'm right back in a place that I've run so far to escape. I'm equally unprepared for my response to it, for this old resentment that I thought I'd left behind forever, the one that's ballooning in my chest. I open my mouth and then close it again. I have to stop myself from stepping backwards.

'I'm sorry,' I say, and then I'm annoyed with myself for saying it. It's not, after all, as if the woman can read my mind, but she's thrown me totally off balance. Suddenly I think that this might not have been such a good idea, and I'm half-tempted just to put my beer bottle down and leave. Then I remember how deep the scratches of the letters on my car door were, and the look on George's face, and the darkness of the laundry room that was as thick and perilous as the river that runs underneath us now. So I pull myself together. I tell myself not to be ridiculous, and finally I just spit the words out.

'I need—' I say, 'I mean, I want to know what happened before Marina was murdered.'

Kathleen looks at me for a moment.

'Before she was murdered?' she asks. She seems genuinely surprised by this, and slightly disappointed, as if it was something else entirely that she'd expected me to ask.

'In the days before, the weeks before.' I'm talking faster now than I want to, shoving urgency into the words until they sound as if they're piling up on each other. 'Someone wrote on her car. I need to know if there was anything else like that. Letters, or phone calls. A break-in, maybe. Anything. Anything at all that she mentioned.'

Kathleen is watching me. She looks incredulous, and vaguely sly at the same time. The uncomfortable thought that I'm being an unbelievable idiot, and that she may somehow be able to turn that fact to her advantage, occurs to me. When she finally speaks there's something close to disdain in her voice.

'You don't know?' she says. She draws it out, and looking at her I realize suddenly that for some reason I don't understand, Kathleen Harper dislikes me intensely. 'I can't believe that you don't know,' she says again. She's going to make the most of this. 'Marina went to the police and the whole nine yards. I mean, you're her sister, I assumed that she told you all about it, that you knew. She called you, didn't she?'

'Yes,' I say, and the word is tight in my throat. It's barely a sound. It's choked off by the memory of Marina's voice, and by the popping sound that the phone plug made when I pulled it out of the wall.

I'm sure Kathleen knows all of this. I'm quite certain that she knows the whole story, but that she wants to hear me tell it. It's important to her to humiliate me, and she's been planning this for a long time. What she wants is to hear me confess to total ignorance of the facts of my sister's life, to indifference

in the face of her anguish, or worse, to willful aban-
donment. I can smell Kathleen's jealousy as surely as if
it's perfume. For some reason she's desperate to hear
me admit that, in the end, Marina was closer to her
than she was to me.

'She called but we didn't get much of a chance to
speak,' I say. Kathleen glances at me sideways and gives
a sour little smile and a knowing nod.

'There were phone calls,' she says. 'Chocolates.
Flowers. Sometimes she thought somebody was following her. At the end there was the car, and somebody broke into her yard, threw garbage all over the
place. I can't believe you didn't know. It had been
going on for months. Marina was being stalked.'

I sit down on the locker and close my eyes. I can
feel splinters through my jeans, and I imagine that you
wouldn't want to sit here wearing shorts in the summer
time. The edge of the railing bites into the back of my
head, and I push against it, welcoming the distracting
line of pain, the same way you do when you dig your
nails into your palm to stop yourself from sneezing or
laughing in church. The heat has gone out of the sun,
and for a few seconds the world seems utterly silent.

'She must have tried to tell you,' Kathleen says.

'She did,' I say. 'I didn't feel like listening.'

'Marina wasn't always the easiest person in the
world,' Kathleen's voice has modulated. She's scored a
couple of points and now she's willing to demonstrate
her intimacy with the workings of my sister's soul.
'You just had to understand where she was coming
from,' she adds.

In this moment the urge to slap Kathleen Harper is
almost overwhelming, but I refrain. Instead, I sit up

and finish my beer. I don't have the energy to be interested in the vendetta that Kathleen seems to be conducting on Marina's behalf. I just want to get what I need and get out of here.

'Look,' I say, trying to keep my voice even and neutral, 'could you tell me what happened, Kathleen? Please. I'd really like to know.' I attempt to sound like a supplicant, as though I'm eager to atone, and on a pilgrimage here that has nothing to do with self-interest.

'I can't see why it matters to you,' she says. 'It's a little late now.'

She pauses, but I don't say anything. I have the distinct feeling that Kathleen knows, or at least suspects, exactly why it matters to me, but I'm not going to give her the satisfaction of saying so. I'd leave right now, but I really need to hear what she has to say. She's the only person I have access to who knew my sister in the last months that she was alive, and she'll talk to me because her desire to show off is even greater than her desire to punish me. As far as Marina goes, I'm the best audience Kathleen Harper's ever going to get, and she knows it.

'It started,' she says, 'I don't know, maybe six months before Marina was killed. At least that's when she started to notice it. At first it was nothing, really. Phone calls, nobody saying anything when she answered, that kind of thing. To be honest, at first I thought that maybe she was being paranoid, except that Marina wasn't particularly paranoid. She got Caller ID and stuff, but it wouldn't work. The line was blocked, or something. Anyways, I finally told her to change her number, and she did, but the calls kept coming. Then he, or she, I guess, whoever it was, started sending her things.'

'Things?' I ask, 'what kind of things?'

'Well, I know there was a bottle of champagne, and then some flowers. That kind of thing. It was like she had a secret admirer. In fact, I teased her about it. There was a valentine.' Kathleen stands up and puts her hands in her pockets. 'One of those frilly satin hearts with chocolates inside.' It's a second before I realize that she's crying. She wipes the tears away quickly with the back of her hand.

'I didn't take it very seriously,' she says. 'And neither did she. She didn't even call the police until the car.'

'And that happened when?'

'After Valentine's Day. The end of February, maybe.'

'Was she scared?' I'm not sure why I ask this, but it seems important. Kathleen wipes her eyes again and shakes her head.

'No,' she says. 'That's what was weird, looking back on it. Even after the car, even after it got ugly, it was more like she was really annoyed, not scared.' She sits down on the bench next to me and I find the closeness of her vaguely repellent. When she leans forward to rub Jake's ears it's all I can do not to knock her hand away. 'It was more like that after she came back from Georgia,' Kathleen says

'Marina went down to Georgia?'

The shock in my voice must be unmistakable, although the fact shouldn't surprise me. I knew that Marina hung on to the house, but somehow it never occurred to me that she actually went down there.

After she died, the property reverted back to me, and I sold it to the Herveys lock, stock and barrel, through lawyers, and without ever setting a foot out of Philadelphia. Now the idea of Marina going back there, of her sitting on the porch by herself, or sleeping in Momma's bed, seems at first macabre, and then almost unbearably sad.

'Not too often, but sometimes,' Kathleen is saying. Her voice makes me jump, as if I had forgotten that she was sitting beside me. 'She went there when she wanted to get away,' Kathleen's voice slows down, caresses these last memories. I'm irrelevant now. She's just drifting, playing out this particular loop of the past.

'The last time, she took a week off from work. It was in early March,' Kathleen says. 'Just after the car thing happened. I didn't know until she got back that she'd even been in Georgia. I guess she went down on the spur of the moment, she'd do that sometimes. She just left me a phone message saying she was going away, and I thought maybe she was going to the Bahamas, or something.'

She pauses, and I nod, even though I cannot begin to imagine Marina in the Bahamas. Pictures are swirling around my head like the white bits in a snow-globe, and the only thing that I can hold on to is that she must have been there the last time she called me. When I unplugged the phone, Marina must have been standing by Momma's desk in the living room, or staring out of the window above the kitchen sink. I can see her twisting the old yellow cord in her free hand, concentrating on the dark rings that Momma's jam jars left on the countertop linoleum, or watching the tall, smooth fronds of the lilies as they throw spiky swords of shadow in the back door light.

'I only saw her once more after that,' Kathleen adds. 'It was a few days before she died. The kids were on spring break. She came with us, and we went shopping at Crystal City and then we took them to a movie.' She's staring out across the water now, and I can see the track her tears have made on her cheek, and the slight smudge where she wiped them off.

'What was she like?' I ask, 'when she came back, when you saw her that last time?'

Kathleen thinks for a minute. 'Smug,' she says finally, 'you know, the way someone is when they have a secret. When they know something you don't know. And there was something else.' Before I can ask her what, Kathleen goes on. 'She had this little place,' she says, 'at the townhouse. It was a corner of her garden that was fenced in. She kept her garbage cans in there, and when she came back she found it wrecked. It meant that somebody had climbed over the wall from the alley. There was a padlock and it had been forced. There was garbage all over her garden, and she was really angry about that, but she was calm too. It was like she was determined.'

'Determined?'

'Yeah,' Kathleen says, 'like she was very focused on something, very preoccupied. She could do that. She could just close you out.' She looks at me for confirmation, for reassurance that Marina could hurt, that she could turn herself to stone.

'But she wasn't scared?' I've ignored the question in Kathleen's eyes. I don't want her wheedling through the doors of my memory. She shakes her head. 'Did she tell the police?' I ask.

'Oh sure,' Kathleen says. She looks at me. 'They didn't do anything.'

Kathleen's eyes are wide and green, and she's so close to me that I can see where her bottom lip is chapped. The skin is dented and cracked, as if she's been chewing it. 'You know,' she says, 'I read this piece a while ago, in *Harpers*, or the *New Yorker*, about this woman who was stalked.' She doesn't take her eyes off my face. 'This guy followed her. He called her, and sent her stuff, and broke into her house. She went to the police, and they said there was really nothing they could do. Finally she gave up her job and moved to another city and changed her name. The article said that the case was considered a success because he didn't kill her.'

Fear is a ripple on water. Any pebble dropping, any tiny thing, the ring of a telephone, the slam of a car door, or the shift of a shadow can start it off. And when it's not like that, when it's not endless spreading rings, it's an undertow, a swift current that runs, lethal and unseen, below the surface of the day. Just now I can feel its pull, I can feel it teasing at me, trying to swallow me whole.

I stop for a moment and take deep breaths. It's late afternoon, and Jake and I are about five miles from Kathleen Harper's house. I've stopped at one of the churches that she listed as a way-marker in her directions. It's small and brick and, most importantly, it appears to be deserted. Which, right now, is crucial, because I don't want anyone to witness this panic that's moving in on me, that's gathering inside me like a storm.

I sit down and put my head between my knees, the way teachers at school used to tell us to do if we threatened to faint. When I look up Jake is weaving in and out of tombstones, pausing occasionally to sniff the ground in front of them, or to study them as if he can read the inscriptions. The overgrown lawn that stretches out under the old trees of the churchyard has the reassuringly familiar smell of damp earth and old leaves, and the blankness of the tall white framed windows promises anonymity. I can guess what's behind those windows, the plain rectangular room, the lines of dark wood pews, the pulpit and the hymnals, and the stone baptismal font, and I wonder if I can be cleansed. If so, I want the memory of this afternoon rinsed off me. I want to be washed clean of it the way you want to be washed clean of a hang over or an unwelcome kiss.

I close my eyes and I can see Kathleen Harper's face. She's up too close. She's bending down to look into the car window, and her cheek is almost touching mine. She's completely determined that I understand how important she was to Marina. When she speaks I can smell her breath.

I dig my hands into my jacket pockets, feel the warmth of the worn material, and let my fists unclench. Overhead a jet cleaves the late afternoon sky, but it's high up and silent. I squint to watch it, and in my mind I fasten Kathleen's voice to it, and will it to diminish. I will her words to get smaller and smaller, and to spread themselves thin and fade away like a vapor trail, but they're stubborn and they won't go. They hang before me in the autumn air.

'Aren't you going to ask me?' Kathleen Harper demands. 'Isn't that what you really want to know, whether or not Marina and I were lovers?'

It's dark by the time we get home, and I'm tired. I feel drained, worn out by Kathleen's anger, and by her insistence, and by my own fear. Part of me thinks that if I came face to face with Marina herself at this moment, I'd hardly care. I fumble with my keys, and forget which one fits in the front door lock, and then I drop them and have to start again while Jake sighs and sits down on the steps to watch me.

I barely register the sound of Gordon's TV, or notice what is playing on Cathy's stereo as Jake and I finally come through the entryway and climb the stairs and reach our landing. Now that I am home, I want to block the afternoon out. I want to have a long shower and wash Kathleen Harper off my skin. Maybe, I tell myself, I've settled something. Elena would probably say that I'm exhausted because in facing Kathleen, I've finally somehow faced Marina. Maybe she would be right. Maybe just by hearing the story, even if it is eighteen months too late, I've atoned, laid to rest the ghost that has been trailing after me, or at least appeased it.

It certainly feels that way, because, strangely enough, just at this moment Marina seems quite close. She's been with me all the way home, and for once, I'm glad. This is not Kathleen's Marina, this is another one, a private childhood Marina who had special names

for the stars, and who I see too rarely. This is the
nightspinner who could make swans dance, the little
girl Grandma called 'Brave-as-Lion'. She does not visit
me often, but this evening something has brought her.

I undo the yale lock on the apartment door and
Jake trots in ahead of me. I don't bother to switch on
the lights. I like the glow of the street lamps and the
dusky light that filters into the apartment. I'd like to
capture this light, with its woolly yellow softness, and
I wonder if it would be too dim to eat by, and, if not,
how, exactly, one would reproduce it.

In the bedroom I take my jacket off and drop it
across the bed. Then something happens. It's almost
nothing. It's just the tiniest motion, just a quaver, as if
the air has been disturbed. That's when I realize that
someone else is in the apartment.

ELEVEN

This time no electric current pulses through me, maybe because I can see, or because this time I'm not cornered in the basement, not boxed into the darkness like an animal brought to bay. Up here in the half-light I'm on my own home ground. I strain to listen, trying to pick up the signal that alerted me, but there's no specific sound, there's nothing in particular beyond the slow purr of six o'clock traffic in the street below. Unlike last time, I can't tell how close this person is. I only know that they're here.

My shoulder bag is on the dressing table and I inch towards it, sliding my feet over the rug, trying not to lift them up and give myself away with a step. I keep my eyes on the bedroom door, on the patch of gray wall, and the corner of a picture frame beyond. It's important not to be taken by surprise. The mouth of the bag is open and my hand snakes into it. I'm watching the hallway and holding my breath while my fingers move slowly, carefully, past my wallet, and my hairbrush. It's an act of will not to scrabble. Not to grab, or to scream. Then my fingers find the tissue paper package, and something inside me relaxes as my hand closes around the blades.

There's a faint smell of lavender as I raise the shears

level with my shoulder, adjust my grip, and step into the hallway. It's empty. The archway to the living room and to the kitchen beyond is four paces ahead of me on the left, and that's the space that I have to get past. I can see the glint of my keys on the half-moon of the hall table, but I know I won't need them. I never throw the bolts on the door, or place the chain. It will only take me one second, one turn of the wrist to open it, and then to erupt on to the landing, to scream for help. But one second can be all it takes. I remember the white sheet in the morgue, and what was left of Marina's face.

I know I have to move. I have to take a first step, and I tell myself to resist the seduction of panic. It won't help me now. I'm quite certain that my life rests on the next ten steps I take. I raise the shears up and back, straining my arm like you strain a spring, priming it for maximum thrust. Out. Down. Hard. Then a shadow moves at the edge of the arch and a man steps into the hall.

A noise rises in me, something unplanned and loud, but my mouth goes dry at the same time. I can't move forwards or backwards. My lungs feel as if they're going to burst. And then Jake scoots into the hall, he races towards me wriggling with pleasure and Beau says, 'Susannah?'

'Don't!' I'm yelling. 'Don't, don't, don't! Don't you ever do that again!' And then I'm banging on him, hammering at his shoulders with my fists, and he's trying to apologize, trying to explain that he let himself in and fell asleep on the couch waiting for me. Jake's circling us, whining in distress and confusion because Beau is the person he loves best in the world after me.

'Susannah! For Christ's sake,' Beau says. 'Calm down!'

It's the wrong thing to say. I'm seeing Kathleen Harper's face, feeling her nasty little smile, and remembering the morgue room in Alexandria, and the phone ringing, and the crackle of cellophane around lilies. Marina runs through high grass. Yellow light falls on the word 'Bitch'. George shakes his head. The lights go out. It's as if someone has busted open a box inside my head and a slew of pictures has come spilling out, all mixed up, and all linked together.

'Get out!' I yell at Beau. 'Just get out and leave me alone!'

I see the words hit him and he recoils from me. He drops my wrist, steps backwards and opens the front door. Even as it swings closed, I know I've made a terrible mistake.

'Beau,' I call, 'wait.' But my voice has gone limp and useless, and suddenly I feel limp and useless with it, as if I've been dragged under by a wave and spat back up, waterlogged and bedraggled. Jake is turning in circles in front of the door, whining, and the sight of him makes me start to cry. The shears are underfoot where I've dropped them, and I trip on them and kick them aside as I open the door. I call Beau again, and when I lean over the railing I can see the top of his head. He's a ball of blond hair and black shoulders growing smaller, hurrying downwards, and he's not about to listen to me. Jake sets off after him, tumbling down the stairs, and I follow, going two steps at a time, which is almost too much for me, and I nearly fall over when I crash into Gordon.

He emerges from his apartment just as I reach his landing, and we collide, me flinging myself down from above. For a second I'm in his arms, and then he backs up a little, concern written all over his face.

'Susannah,' he says, 'are you all right? I heard—' I'm embarrassed at being so close to him, and at the fact that he's heard me yelling, and that now he sees me crying. In other circumstances, it might be funny, but it isn't. He starts to say something, to reach out towards me, but I don't want Gordon's sympathy, and in that moment I hear the sound of the front door closing, and I jerk away.

'I'm fine,' I say as I push past him, more roughly than I mean to, and I don't look back, or say 'sorry', as I run down the stairs.

When Jake and I get on to the sidewalk, Beau is already across the street. He's only a few yards away from us and he's walking with his head down. This time when I call him, his step falters, and then he stops and turns around. Jake and I wait for a cab to come by and slow down for the light, which is turning, and then we dart across the traffic.

'I'm sorry,' I say, as we come up to him. 'I'm sorry, I'm sorry.' I'm saying it like a kid, fast, throwing it out in front of me as I approach him.

'It's OK,' he says, but his voice is dull and flat. 'I have no business letting myself into your apartment without asking you.' He recites this as if it's something that he's memorized, and then he bends over and strokes the top of Jake's head. The sight of his big hand between the dog's ears is such an ordinary gesture that it fills me with relief.

'It's not you,' I say. 'I was just so scared.'

'I'm not surprised.' Beau looks up at me, and I realize that he's angry. 'Why the Hell didn't you tell me?' he asks. It takes me a second to realize that he's talking about the laundry room, but I don't have time to wonder how he found out because he's saying, 'I mean, for Christ's sake, Susannah, some lunatic breaks in and terrifies you in the basement, I can't believe how scared you must have been, and you won't even tell me? Me. Beau, Susannah. I love you, and you call up and you lie to me. How am I supposed to feel about that?'

He straightens up and crosses his arms, and I have no idea what to say. We stare at each other until, finally, I stutter, 'I meant to—' But Beau cuts me off.

'No you didn't,' he says. 'Don't lie to me, Susannah. You did not mean to tell me. You weren't going to say anything, the same as you didn't say anything about the phone calls, the same as you wouldn't have told me about the car if I hadn't called that night. You were just going to deal with all this by yourself, just like you always do. You like to think that means you're strong, but it doesn't. It just means that you're too goddamn insecure to trust anyone. You certainly don't trust me.'

The words have come out in a rush and I'm stunned, partly because they're true, and partly because of Beau's hurt and anger. I've never seen him mad before. I expect him to turn on his heel and walk off now, but he doesn't, and for some reason the fact makes me feel like crying again. He just stands there on the sidewalk with his arms crossed, staring at me, waiting for me to say something, while Jake gets tired and sits down, and people walk past us and give us knowing little sideways looks because we're fighting in public.

'How did you know?' I finally ask.

'Captain Bubbles told me,' Beau says.

'Captain Bubbles' is what Beau's taken to calling Cathy since he found out that she used to be a stewardess, and as he elaborates he's torn between telling his story and holding the high ground of being mad at me. A smile sneaks up on the corner of his mouth.

'It was a classic guerrilla action,' he says. 'I made the tactical error of taking too long getting the key into the door and she and the Toy Boy ambushed me. They told me all about it. Full flight update. They were both dressed in spandex. It was ugly. Early Sarah Brightman was playing in the background, I Lost My Heart To A Starship Trooper.'

'It was not,' I say.

'OK,' Beau admits, 'I made up that part. Actually, I think it was Yanni At The Acropolis, but they were both wearing muscle man outfits, including headbands.'

'He's her work out buddy,' I say.

I can see Cathy popping out of her doorway in the gym gear that she sometimes wears after work. The sweatshirt is red with an airplane on it and the leggings are silver and have UNITED written in big scarlet letters down the sides of the thighs. She has red slippers that match, and I imagine her telling Beau all the lurid details of my adventure in the laundry room while Shawn looks on, nodding, behind her.

She would have impressed upon Beau the drama and the gravity of the situation, and summed him up as potential boyfriend material for me at the same time. Probably she saw it as doing me a favor, bringing out Beau's protective instinct, casting him as the white knight and me as the damsel in distress. Cathy reads articles in *Cosmo* that advise this kind of thing. 'Five Steps To Being More Vulnerable', they are called, and 'How To Put The Pride Back In Your Lion!'

'She says I should take better care of you,' Beau adds, and I snort. 'Come on,' he says, 'I'm getting cold. Let's go have a beer,' and he puts his arm around my shoulder as I reach for Jake's collar.

'Beau,' I say before we cross the street, 'what you said before? About you love me? Is that true, or did you just say it to make me feel bad?'

'It's true, and I said it to make you feel bad.' Beau's looking up the street for a break in the cars that are slowing for the light, and I can't see his face.

'Well I love you, you know,' I say.

'Damn right,' Beau says, and then we step off the sidewalk and weave through the stopped traffic.

The air between us is fizzing. Beau keeps his arm around my shoulders and by the time we get to the front door both of us are giggling. It's not until we try to get inside that we realize that neither of us has keys. I left mine upstairs, and Beau's are in the pocket of his jacket, which is still draped over the back of my couch, so we buzz Cathy to let us in. She apparently doesn't hear us, and a second later we try Gordon.

After my earlier performance I feel like a complete horse's ass when I have to tell him that I don't have any keys, and could he please let me in. He does, of course, and when we get to his landing he pokes his head out of the door while I apologize for being rude earlier. He looks as embarrassed as I feel, and the soft red tinge of a blush begins to creep above his collar. To make it worse he tries to reach out and pat Jake, who skitters away and hides behind Beau, giving him a doe-eyed look of adoration and leaving Gordon's hand hanging in mid-air.

'So much for enhanced security,' Beau says, as we come up the stairs and see my apartment door wide open. We're both feeling giddy by now, and we laugh at this as if we've made an elaborate joke.

'Hi, Love Birds!' Shawn says.

He leaps out of Cathy's door and on to the landing just as we get to the top of the stairs, and for a moment I think he's going to end up in Beau's arms, which might be more than Beau could handle. The first time I introduced them, Shawn took Beau's hand and said, 'That's S-H-A-W-N. Shawn, like the Dawn.'

'I was just going to come downstairs and let you in,' he announces, 'but Doctor Dirty got there first.'

Shawn's in his gym gear too, just like Beau said, and he's dancing from foot to foot, like a kid who has to go to the bathroom. He's wearing a rhinestone stud earring that exactly matches the purple color of his hair, and I'm about to compliment him on it when Cathy appears and demands that we come out and have pizza with them.

'We've been lifting weights,' she announces, 'so we deserve a treat!'

She flexes her arms above her head like Wonder Woman, and I notice, not for the first time, that she's in impressively good shape. So, for that matter, is Shawn. I'm not exactly sure what being a work-out buddy involves, but I can imagine them being incredibly competitive at the gym, running beside each other on those machines, going faster and faster, or lying on their backs side by side pushing huge dumbbells into the air.

'What do you guys like best?' Cathy is asking, 'Quadro Staggione, or those Mexicali things with roasted corn? We're going to Mario's, they have awesome margaritas.'

'They don't want to eat with us!' Shawn says, turning to her. 'They want to be alone. Look at them!' He gives us an exaggerated wink and takes Cathy by the shoulders, pushing her back through her door, 'Say Bon Voyage and Have a Nice Flight,' he commands.

The door closes behind them and Beau and I stand for a second in silence. I wonder if I'm embarrassed by what Shawn said, but then I look at Beau and decide I'm not.

'Do you think they're, you know?' I whisper, nodding towards Cathy's door.

'No!' Beau whispers back, 'don't be stupid. He's her lap dog, that's all.'

'I don't know,' I whisper back, 'I'm not sure—'

'Oh, Susannah!' Beau hisses, and then he pushes me through my open door.

'So why did you come over anyways?' I ask.

The question is less than gracious, but it doesn't

matter. We're sitting on the living room floor in front of the gas fire. Beau winds his arms around me as I lean back against him. I can feel him plucking at my hair, he's pulling it out of its braid strand by strand. Neither of us has mentioned what we said on the street. We don't have to, it hangs between us like a sweet smoky cloud. We've finished off a Thai take-out, and are working on a six of beer. Red and blue flames flicker behind the glass coals in the grate. I keep moving my foot up in front of them and then yanking it back just before it gets burned. On another night I might light candles, but not tonight. Tonight we've left all the lights on. Jake's lying on the rug with us, and we're playing old Beatles songs on the CD. Yesterday. All My Loving. I Wanna Hold Your Hand.

'So,' I ask again, 'why did you?' I twist my head around to look at Beau. He's suddenly sheepish, which of course makes me more interested.

'What?' I ask, 'what?'

'You didn't come to my concert,' he says. 'You were busy with the ax murderer in the basement.'

'Norman Bates,' I say, 'please. Show some respect.'

'Yeah, right,' Beau says, 'doesn't his mother run a hotel?'

'No, a laundromat.'

'Ah,' Beau says. 'But you still missed my piece. My solo. So I was going to give you a private per-formance.'

'You were going to sing? Just for me?'

Beau has never offered to do this before. In fact, I've never heard a note come out of his mouth except in church. He plays the piano, but it's as if he needs that lurid blue choir robe and the doleful eyes of Jesus's

sheep on the neon green meadow in order to find his
voice. Now he's looking at me out of the corner of his
eye, gauging my reaction to this gift he's offered.

'Will you?' I ask. 'Please. For me and Jake?'

I lean over and switch the CD player off. John
Lennon's voice stops in mid-word. I curl my legs
underneath myself, and Jake puts his head in my lap,
and both of us watch Beau. He's thinking this over,
and when he finally makes up his mind and gets to his
feet, he's as awkward as a bear. He stands above me,
and straightens his shoulders. He gives his arms and
hands a little shake. And then he sings.

'I looked over Jordan,' Beau sings, 'And what did I
see, Coming for to carry me home?' His beautiful
voice swells and fills the room. It balloons around me
and Jake and Beau himself, and rises up until we all
seem to be rising with it. 'A band of angels,' Beau
sings, 'were coming after me, They were coming for
to carry me home.'

I've written 'Kathleen Harper' in big block letters on
my graph pad, and I'm filling them in, shading the
sides and making them cast a shadow across the little
blue boxes on the paper, while I listen to the phone
ring. It rained last night and a bright watery light plays
over the living room floor. The lead on the balcony
has turned dark, and the puddles on it shine white and
ice blue, as if a mirror has been flung down and its
broken pieces lie face upwards to the sky. The phone
has rung fifteen times, and I'm about to hang up when
somebody answers.

I can tell right away that it isn't him. I remember

his voice quite clearly, and it was measured, low and precise. The words were as clean as the bright white cuffs of his shirt, as precise and neat as the card that I now have in front of me, the one with the words Special Detective, Homicide embossed on it in navy ink. 'I want you to call me,' he'd said. 'Any time, if you have any questions. If there's anything you think of, or anything I can do for you.'

I'd put the card in my desk and almost forgotten it, but I remember the words clearly, and I can't imagine the voice that spoke them ever sounding as staccato as the one I'm hearing now. This one barks. It sounds both harsh and matter of fact, and it spits out, 'Alexandria. Homicide,' as if I've called a taxi stand or a sports bar.

When I ask for Detective Mark Cope, I can feel a pause come down the line, and for half a second I imagine him dead, shot in an alleyway while in pursuit, or retired, moved to the mid-West to become a Police Chief in some suburb outside Fort Wayne or Des-Moines where his kids can ride a bicycle in the driveway and walk to the White Hen Pantry. In fact, neither of these things are true. Detective Cope is in court for the day is all, and I can call back tomorrow, or leave a message.

I choose the latter, partly because I promised Beau this morning before he left that I will do this, and partly because I'm afraid that if I don't leave a message I'll lose my nerve. I'll decide that just because somebody vandalized my car and Kathleen Harper's a headcase there's no need to waste Detective Cope's time and patience. I'll decide that this is stupid after all, that maybe what I really need to do is to get on with my life, and go out to dinner, and buy a new dress. And if I do any of those things, I'll never call again. So I leave my number, area code first, and spell 'deBreem' twice, just to be certain that there's no mistake.

I devote the rest of the day to the Museum Tea Room. This time I'm trying a light blue, two shades short of turquoise, and a lot of silver gilt. It's like Elgar played on electric instruments. I want the result to be both refined and tangy, to go with the lemon tea and cold white wine that these places demand, and I wonder if all the chairs and tables could be made of bright stainless steel, with curlicues.

I don't think of Marina, which is a relief, and it's mid-afternoon before I take a break. Jake is asleep on his bed, stretched out like a rag creature, his legs extended and still, his head flopping slightly on to the floor. Beau took him to the park very early this morning while I was still in bed. They came back with croissants, and I find buttery little flakes of pastry in the sheets when I make the bed.

Beau circles around the edges of my mind, but I don't let him come all the way in. I know that everything between us has shifted, that we're lovers now, and not just friends, and I'm not sure I want to think about what this might mean. At least not just yet. I put some clothes away, fold up the Thai food cartons that still sit by the sink, and startle myself with the sudden noise that the top of the garbage can makes when it snaps closed on top of them. Then, for some reason, I picture Kathleen Harper.

It's her height that comes back to me, the way I looked up at her when she opened her front door. It's a certain loose-jointed power that swung through her stride, and echoed in her arms when she walked that I find suddenly disconcerting. Like the Cheshire Cat's, her smile materializes in front of me, that curving of her mouth that couldn't wipe out the way she looked at me, couldn't counterbalance the shadow behind her eyes, or the chapped, chewed, mottled skin of her lips, or the pungent smell of jealousy that rose off her like steam.

I know, I'm absolutely certain, that I turned the deadbolt and latched the chain on the front door after I brought Jake in mid-morning, but all of a sudden I'm out of the kitchen, and crossing the living room. I'm almost tiptoeing, as if I'm afraid that the air might jangle if I bother it. And I'm hurrying. I'm tugging the chain, pressing the screws that hold the lock plate with my thumb, testing how much weight they'll take, and then I'm turning the key. I release the deadbolt, and put my ear down and listen as it turns over. Then I unlock it and lock it again. Just to be sure.

TWELVE

By late afternoon there's a taut silence in the apartment. Every particle of air seems charged with possibility, and none of it pleasant. Detective Cope still hasn't called back, and as much as I'd like to call Beau, I don't want to tie up the phone even for a minute. Finally, I can't concentrate on the Tea Room at all anymore, and I decide to give up and take Jake to the park. Reaching the street is like stepping back into real time. I feel as if I'm re-entering life after being trapped in some kind of suspended animation. Jake and I pause at the top of the steps above the sidewalk while I clip his leash on and arrange his selection of tennis balls in my pockets.

It's four-thirty and children are coming home from school. Mothers walk by in pairs. They grasp children by the hands and talk together as they go, their glossy heads nodding, and their long woolen dress coats flapping open to reveal blue jeans and running shoes underneath. At the lights a long line of little kids, all holding hands, comes to a halt. The two women shepherding them clap like cheerleaders and nudge the children into order, bending to adjust flopping back-packs, and pick up drawings of pumpkins, and black cats, that have slipped out of mittened hands and wafted on to the sidewalk like leaves. The traffic streams by and then slows, collecting itself into a solid block of taxis and delivery vans and cars as the lights turn yellow and then red again against the graying sky.

I don't think it's going to rain, but a mist seems to be descending on the city, as if a cloud is slowly lowering itself until its underside rests on the peaks and spires of the buildings. The sound of footsteps always seems to be slightly muffled in this kind of weather, and as Jake and I head down towards the Dog Park, turning away from the busy cross streets, we seem to be moving in silence. The people that we meet, men in business suits coming home early, women with grocery bags balanced on their hips, pass by us in a whisper, accompanied only by a 'swoosh' of clothing or the rustle of a newspaper. Invariably, their heads are bent, and sometimes I think I recognize someone, only to find as they come closer to me that they are total strangers. Occasionally a child shouts or calls out, and the small, high voices sound as if they come from far away.

The Dog Park is alive with activity, and even before we cross the street Jake is straining at his leash. This is one of the busiest times of the day here. Mothers and kids bring their dogs after school, and the vet students and their foundlings are here too. The instant that we get across the road, Jake begins to hop in excitement. When I do not let him off his leash immediately, he turns and sits, staring at me imploringly, his gaze shifting from my face to my pockets where the tennis balls rest. When I release him and throw one, aiming it in a long lob towards the top of the closest little artificial hill, Jake gives a squeak of delight and bounds after it, his ears flattening in anticipation.

I see several people I know, a sculptor who is

accompanied by his St Bernard, an accountant who practices t'ai chi on the tennis courts watched by his Old English Sheepdog, and a woman whose name I can never remember who has an Airedale called Elsa. We greet one another and form a little circle of talk. We walk a circuit or two around the park together, discussing the weather, or the likelihood that the leash law might actually be enforced, or the absurdity of the advance marketing for Thanksgiving, and even, someone says, Christmas, which has already started.

A pack of dogs whirls around the central patch of grass, chasing the tennis balls that someone inevitably throws for them. They race backwards and forwards and around in circles, shifting their pattern and direction like a flight of ungainly birds. We watch them while we talk among ourselves, and are only dimly aware of where our own dog actually is in the group. So, when I am finally ready to go home and call Jake, it is not surprising that I can't find him immediately.

Occasionally, if Jake's having a good time, he pretends to ignore me, but I still expect him to peel off from the main body and come to me eventually, and I'm a little irritated when he doesn't. I whistle again, scanning the dogs, and it's a second before I realize that I don't see him. I can't pick out his tall pointy ears, or the black tip of his tail from the midst of the barking, woofing herd that surges past me, and then spins around and surges again.

'Jake!' I call, 'Jakey!' and then I whistle for good measure. The sculptor and the Airedale woman have located their dogs and are brandishing leashes, and I've walked down the path a way, wondering if Jake's gone off under the stand of squat little blue spruce trees that sit beside the boundary fence. I keep calling him and clinking the end of his leash, as if somehow he might hear and recognize it.

Small petals of anxiety are beginning to unfurl inside me when I finally see him. He must have got sidetracked and gone after a squirrel. He's coming around the edge of the tennis court, where he knows he's not allowed to go because the tarmacked yard beyond is derelict and edged on one side by heavy scrub and on the other by a warehouse. He looks suitably abashed. In fact, he looks so sheepish that he could have committed a serious sin, like going after a cat, but I know that this is unlikely, if only because no kitty in its right mind would come within a mile of this place.

'Jaake,' I say as he comes close to me, drawing the 'a' out into a question, and he flattens his ears down on to the sides of his head, the way he did when he was reprimanded as a puppy, the way he still does when he hears thunder.

We make it home in record time because I want to watch the six o'clock news, and I just manage to mix Jake's food, and slap his bowl on to the floor, and pour myself a drink before I hear the sober tones of Jim Lehrer issuing from the living room.

'Today,' Jim says, 'the Attorney General appointed an Independent Counsel—' and I leave the cupboards swinging open and abandon the kitchen, making for the couch, where I slump and stretch my legs out in front of me, and take a first cool sip of wine.

It's an hour later, after a round table discussion on the Balkans and a piece about geese migrating, when I notice that Jake hasn't eaten his dinner. In fact, he hasn't moved. After we came in, he'd followed me into the kitchen and then left and flopped down on his bed, and he's still lying there, curled up like a giant fox, his nose tucked in between his hind paws and his tail. Something makes me say his name, and even as I say it I'm getting up, I'm crossing the room towards him, moving too fast because something is wrong.

Jake just barely lifts his head, and his eyes are dull and glassy. Beads of white foam are coming out of the corners of his mouth. I grab him and force his jaws apart to see if there's anything in there, although I'm not sure what I should be looking for. I try to lift his head up, but it's heavy in my hands, as if it's stuffed and weighted, and when I pull on Jake's collar and call him, my voice high and frantic, he gets up, takes a couple of steps, and lies down again, flopping back on to the floor with a thud so hard it must be painful.

My fingers turn fat and rubbery when I punch Beau's number, like in one of those bad dreams when you're trying to call the police, but you can't hit the right buttons no matter how hard you try. Then I hear ringing, and any second I expect to hear Beau's voice, but when I do, it's on the answering machine.

'Beau!' I shout into the phone, 'Beau it's me!' I realize that he must be watching *The Simpsons*, and that that's why he hasn't picked up, and I know that if I shout loud enough, if I tell him what's going on, he'll hear me and answer. His phone is on the table right next to the couch, so even if he's asleep, the ringing must have woken him.

'Beau!' I shout, 'Beau, there's something wrong with Jake!' Beau still doesn't answer, and in a couple of seconds I hear a long beep that cuts me off. I don't know where he can be. At Sherlock's? Still at work? I have never known Beau to work a minute after five-thirty, but I start to punch his work number anyways, and then remember that he has a new extension and I don't know it. As I reach for my address book, scrabbling in the drawer of my desk, I glance at Jake and realize that I don't have time for this. Instead, I call the garage and ask them to get my car out. Then I grab my keys and I'm racing down the stairs.

Tony, my night garage man, raises his eyebrows when he sees me coming running up the sidewalk. It's only four blocks and around the corner from my front door to the converted carriage houses that once held pony carts and four-in-hand coaches and now hold a cross-section of Saabs and SUVs with the occasional Volvo and Audi thrown in.

'There's something wrong with Jake,' I say, by way of an explanation for the fact that I'm not even wearing a jacket, although it's begun to rain, and not handing him the usual two-dollar tip that I give him when he has my car ready and running.

'Don't you worry,' Tony says. Jake is a big favorite at the garage, and Tony's concern is all over his face. He closes the door for me as I pull out into the street and I say a prayer to the God of Parking that there'll be a space in front of the house. There is. I see it as soon as I turn the corner, and I slide the car into it, hugging the curve with no space to spare on the first try.

Jake doesn't want to get up at all now, and I have to drag him to his feet. There's more of the white foamy stuff along the edges of his mouth, and he hangs his head down as if he's about to be sick. I half pull and half shove him out on to the landing, and I only just remember to grab my shoulder bag before I slam the door. The stairs are easier, but he's still like a big, floppy toy. He goes a few steps and then he wants to sit down. When I push him from behind he wobbles and looks as if he's going to stumble and fall all the way down, so I have to grab him from in front and try to hold him up and pull him at the same time. I'd pick him up in my arms if I could, but at one hundred pounds Jake is too big for me. At some point I think that I ought to get help, but there's no noise from behind any of the doors, and I'm afraid that explaining would take too long.

Zoe and Shawn come in through the front door just as we reach the entryway.

'Susannah!' Zoe says, 'My God, what's the matter?'

'I don't know,' I say. 'I'm not sure. I have to get him to Penn. The car's right outside.' Zoe drops her briefcase on the floor and moves instinctively to grab Jake, who is three steps up, and has started to wobble again, but before she can reach him, Shawn jumps up the stairs and catches the big dog up in his arms. Jake doesn't like to be cuddled by strangers, and he tries to struggle, and even gives a little growl, as Shawn lifts him up. Zoe grabs his head which is hanging down at a horrible angle, and I can't help but notice that pale, sable colored hair is getting all over the front of her pretty black overcoat.

'Where's your car? Right out here?' Shawn asks, and I nod and open the vestibule door, and together the three of us cross the cold damp marble, and go down the steps to the sidewalk. I get the car door open, and when Shawn tries to slide Jake on to the back seat, his legs drop and drag, and his nails make little screeching sounds against the wet stone. Zoe and I run around to the other side of the car, and as traffic whips past we lift and pull Jake on to his old folded blanket. By now his eyes are closed and his lips are twitching up into a funny little snarl. I turn down Zoe's offer to come with me, and ask her instead to call the vet school and tell them I'm on my way. She obviously thinks that Jake is dying, and I do too.

She leans in the car's open window, and grabs my hand on the steering wheel. Tears are pooling on the rims of her wide, blue eyes. 'I'll tell them you're coming, I'll call right now,' Zoe says. Then she lets go of my hand and runs back up the steps. Shawn stands in the road and raises his arms like a traffic cop. A car skids to a halt and the driver swears, and I just see Shawn swearing back at him as I pull out and slot myself in behind a cab and run the tail end of the light.

I make it to the vet school in eight minutes flat, and by the time I get there I don't think that Jake's breathing anymore. Zoe's been as good as her word, and a bunch of people are waiting for me. When I stop they come running with a doggy stretcher. A vet is asking me questions while they lift Jake out of the car and take him away. The last thing I see is his tail. Just before they go through the big swinging doors, it flops off the stretcher and hangs down like something dead.

*

I sit in the waiting room. I've filled out forms giving permission for Jake to be anaesthetized, and operated on, but I have no idea if he's even still alive. The wall opposite me is papered with posters giving information on worming, and pet care, and adoption, and I stare at them as though I'm memorizing every word, but the letters slide into meaningless jumbles. In my mind I go over and over the contents of the cupboards under my kitchen sink. There are bottles of Ajax and Lysol, and possibly tiny cartons of rat poison. I keep my paints and solvents in a box in the hall cupboard, and I'm not careful with it. I often leave the door open when I get a jacket, or boots, or even Jake's tennis balls. For that matter the balls could have rolled in something in the park. God knows what. Drugs. Poisons. Anything.

When Shawn comes in and sits down beside me, it takes me a second to realize that it's him. It's not until he offers me one of the Starbucks cups he's holding and says, 'Here, this is for you,' that I even look at him. He's wearing a black leather jacket and a baseball cap, and without his purple hair he looks pretty much like everyone else. He's changed his earring too. Now it's a discreet gold stud. I want to ask him what he's doing here, and possibly to tell him to go away, but he doesn't give me the chance.

'You shouldn't be here by yourself,' he says, and he peels the plastic top off the cup and hands it to me. 'Mocha Latte,' Shawn whispers, 'with a shot.' He winks at me and opens the pocket of his jacket so I can see a little silver hip flask nesting there. 'Never want to be without it,' Shawn says, 'it's good for the soul.'

The faint whiff of brandy curls towards me as I raise the cup, and he's right, it tastes good.

'Thanks,' I say. Shawn nods without looking at me and takes a sip from his own cup.

'Do you know anything yet?' he asks, and when I shake my head, he doesn't say anything else. He just sits there beside me in the waiting room, staring at the worming posters and sipping his coffee.

'You don't have to stay,' I say, finally. 'This could take a long time.' Shawn shakes his head.

'If you don't mind,' he says, 'I'd like to. I had a dog once, a retriever. Her name was Jess,' he adds, as if this explains his desire to sit here with me in the vet school waiting room, which, in a way, I suppose it does.

From time to time, I glance at him out of the corner of my eye. He's a bigger man than he seems to be on first glance, and the bulk of him seems more solid, somehow more real, now that he's not camouflaged in one of his outfits. I wonder where he came from, and why he's here in Philadelphia, and some other time I might ask him about this, and about Jess, but at the moment it doesn't seem to matter very much.

When my name is finally called, I hand my empty cardboard cup to Shawn and follow a young vet who is tall and pale and sounds Russian, through a set of swinging doors with 'Personnel Only' written on them in chipped red letters. I think at first that I'm going to get to see Jake, and that he's going to be dead, but instead the vet leads me down a corridor and into what is clearly his office.

The room is tiny, with just enough space for a desk

with two chairs in front of it. It doesn't have a
window. Instead of daylight an X-ray box glows
behind the vet's head. A nameplate on his desk reads
'Dr Vincent Gurewich, DVM'. He gestures for me to
sit down. There's no sign of Jake.

'Jake is in shock,' Dr Vincent Gurewich says. He is
holding a clip board with papers attached to it and he
looks at them, not me. 'We don't know, exactly, what
is wrong with him. We've pumped his stomach, but
he seems to have had some kind of seizure. We're
trying to stabilize him now.'

Dr Gurewich speaks in very precise sentences.
When he finally glances up at me, he looks exhausted,
and I wonder how long he's been here, stitching up
cats and dogs and telling people that their pets are
dead. 'It's possible,' he says, 'that he could have had a
stroke, although at five, he's very young for that.'

'You mean a heart attack?' I ask. It sounds
unbelievable.

Dr Gurewich shrugs. 'It's possible,' he says. 'It could
have been brought on by some form of poisoning, or
he could have a congenital heart defect, and there would
be no reason for you to know. Nothing you could do.
On the other hand, it could be colic. It happens more
frequently with horses, but also with large, deep chested,
dogs. Their intestine becomes blocked and can twist
and turn septic. Does Jake bolt his food?'

'No,' I say. 'At least, I don't think so.'

'Do you remember when he last drank?' I think
back. Usually Jake has a long drink and splashes water
all over the kitchen floor when he comes back from
the park, but this evening I can't remember whether
he did or not.

'Maybe two or three this afternoon,' I say, 'I'm not sure.' Dr Gurewich nods as if this has been helpful, then he stands up, and so do I.

'They should be X-raying him now,' he says. 'If there's a blockage, it will show up and we'll operate on him to remove it. He couldn't have gotten into rat poison? Anything like that?' I remember the little cardboard tray of DeCon that I'd placed under the sink pipes at the back of the cupboard right after I moved in, but in order to get to it Jake would have had to plough his way through a whole collection of cleaning fluids and old sponges and unused shoe polish kits, and I'm sure I would have noticed.

'I really don't think so,' I say. Dr Gurewich nods and almost smiles as he opens the door for me.

'There's nothing more you can do for Jake, Miss deBreem,' he says. 'Go home. We're sending the contents of his stomach to the lab for testing, and we will call you. As soon as we know anything.'

I feel as if I'm being dismissed, which I am, and I can't think of anything else that I can ask or say. I'm just about to step past Dr Gurewich and into the hall when he darts back into his office.

'Oh, I nearly forgot,' he says. He reaches into one of the drawers, and hands me a large manila envelope. When I look inside I see that it contains the dark leather coil of Jake's collar.

THIRTEEN

Shawn is waiting for me. He stands up expectantly as I come through the swinging doors, and at the sight of him I feel a quick, mean stab of irritation. The concern written all over his face embarrasses me, and even as I think this, I tell myself to grow up. He's only trying to be kind. He didn't have to bring me coffee or sit here wasting an hour. I tell myself I should appreciate the gesture, and then I try to convince myself that I do.

'They think he might have had a seizure, and they're keeping him for a while,' I say, as blithely as I can. 'They think he's going to be fine, though. I'm sure he will be.' Shawn doesn't smile. He can tell that I'm lying about Jake being fine, and the fact half-irritates me and half makes me like him.

'Come on,' I say, 'let's get out of here.' I figure the least I can do is buy the guy a beer.

Bruges is a dark, wood paneled place with stained glass windows and pew-like booths. They specialize in Belgian beer, and the pitcher on the table between us is filled with something that I can't pronounce. Shawn ordered it. In fact, he picked this place out. It's only around the corner from my garage and the house, and although I've walked past it probably a million times, I've never been in it before. I wonder if Shawn and Cathy come here, if they sit in these booths and eat Moules Frites and argue over who gets to read the *Inquirer*'s Sunday Style section. Or maybe they get sloppy drunk and kiss in the shadows. Booths can be good for that sort of thing. No matter what Beau says, I'm still not entirely convinced they're just gym buddies. Now Shawn takes off his baseball cap and runs his fingers through his short, spiky hair so it stands straight up on end.

'Here's to Jake,' he says, and raises his glass. We clink edges, and I take a mouthful of the tepid deep amber liquid. I don't like the taste much, but the color's beautiful.

'Do you live around here?' I ask.

'Kind of,' he says, 'about ten blocks away.' He smiles as he says it, and lowers his glass. 'So, I guess the answer is really, "Not Really",' he adds.

'I guess so,' I say.

'It grows on you,' Shawn says, nodding towards my glass. 'I thought it was gross too, at first. Now I'm a convert. They say it has more vitamins than Budweiser. Actually, I think I'm just proud of the fact that I can pronounce the name. I always wanted to be a European.'

'Have you been there a lot?' I ask. The question sounds ridiculous, but for some reason I have begun to feel incredibly awkward, as though I'm on a high school date. This makes me wonder again if I've got Shawn wrong. Despite the skin tight jeans and the hair, despite the rhinestone earring, which he isn't even wearing right now, I've never been entirely

convinced that he's gay. Maybe Cathy's on to something and he's straight after all, I think. Or, Hell,
maybe he swings both ways. Who knows? It does
occur to me to wonder if he's making a pass at me,
and I just hadn't noticed.

Then he says, 'Not a lot. I mean I went on the
post-college-grand-tour-railpass-trip. You know, back-
pack, Paris, Berlin, London. Then, a couple of years
ago, we spent some time in Italy. Me and Bill. He was
my partner. He died last year.'

'Oh,' I say, 'I'm very sorry.' Now I feel horrible.
Shawn shakes his head and actually smiles.

'It's OK,' he says, 'well, I mean it isn't. Especially
not for Bill. What I mean is, it wasn't Aids. He had a
heart attack. It had been coming for a while. He was a
lot older than me.' I'm not sure what I'm supposed to
say to this, but Shawn rescues me before I have to
worry about it.

'Yeah,' he says, 'Florence was incredible. Have you
ever been there?' I shake my head. 'Amazing,' he says.
'Bill and I only spent a week or so, but, man, would I
love to go back there. You know, get an apartment for
a while, just live? It's like, if you could do that, you'd
become a whole 'nother person. You know?' He
reaches for a beer mat and pulls a pen out of his
pocket.

'Well,' I say, 'lots of people think that about moving
somewhere.' The specter of George in a beret is
hovering above my head. 'Sometimes maybe it's even
true,' I add. Shawn looks up at me and grins. He
finishes the little drawing he's been making on the beer
mat and pushes it towards me.

'Here,' he says, 'for you. In case you don't ever get
to Florence. That's the Palazzo Vecchio, the Medici
digs where they hung their enemies out of the windows. They were all wearing red stockings. The
enemies,' he adds, 'not the Medici.'

'Cool,' I say. The picture is of a square castle with
a tower. Shawn pours more beer into my glass.

'I mean,' he says, 'I happen to think that people can
reinvent themselves. If they want to. I'm trying it next
in Mexico, but I'll have to be quick, I only have a
week.'

'Oh yeah?'

He nods and puts his glass down.

'I'm going down for the Day of The Dead, it's on
November second, and it's kind of like Halloween, but
not really. It's basically a big party. They take all this
food to the cemeteries, and lay tables and have feasts
out there with all their ancestors and their dead friends.
I mean, it's cool. It's as if, once a year, the dead aren't
really dead anymore. Like, you can sit down and have
dinner with them, and work out all the stuff you didn't
work out before they died. Sort of like an annual
second chance.'

I have a sudden vision of myself sitting down to a
big meal with Marina. I wonder if we'd be our adult
selves or our childhood selves, if we'd be eating roast
lamb and a spinach soufflé, or hotdogs and dilly beans.
If we're grown-up, I can't decide if she'd look like she
did before she was murdered or after, and this bothers
me. Either way, I think, it's not my kind of thing.

'Sugar skulls,' Shawn says.

'What?' I ask.

'Sugar skulls,' he repeats. 'That's what they make for the dead. With black licorice holes for eyes. I'll bring you back some.'

I realize that he's been talking on about his trip to Mexico, and that I haven't heard a word. Now his face collapses, as though I've been a terrible disappointment.

'Look,' I say, 'I'm sorry, I—' But Shawn cuts me off. He leaves my apology, if that's what it was, hanging in mid-air.

'That's OK,' he says quickly, 'really Susannah, that's OK. You know, you've had a lot of shit around lately. First your car, then the laundry room thing, and now the dog. It must be really scary.' I realize that this is virtually the same thing that Gordon said to me, and I wonder why it is that men, of whatever sexual persuasion, need to convince themselves that women are frightened all the time.

'I don't really think they're related,' I say, but even as the words come out of my mouth, louder than I mean them to be, my stomach shifts. Shawn shakes his head.

'Of course not, I didn't mean that,' he says, even though we both know that he did. 'It's just that, well, you should be careful.' He laughs and grabs my glass again. 'Hell,' he says, refilling it, 'we all should. Did you know that Cathy went on, like, some airline assault course? So she could jump hijackers and that sort of stuff. You would not believe what that woman can bench press.' Shawn raises his eyebrows and flexes his muscles. 'Probably, she's the only one of us who could actually defend herself if she had to.'

I look at him for a second over the top of my beer.

I'm wondering if he's going to tell me how much he can bench press, but he doesn't. He doesn't have to. I remember the tight jeans and the lycra. Beau and Gordon may call him Tinkerbell, but the guy looks to me like he's one solid muscle. He smiles at me, and I avoid his eyes and concentrate on my beer, but it's too late, he already knows what I'm thinking. To my horror I feel the heat of a blush creeping up my neck, and I hope it's dark enough in here so he can't see.

'I mean, I don't see Zoe or Justin standing up too well,' Shawn says, laughing. 'Their idea of being attacked is somebody taking the sugar off their table at Starbucks without asking, and as for Gordon, well, maybe he's got some secret kryptonite in there, but I still don't want to see him in his long underwear.'

'Did you really open his credit card bill?'

The words are out of my mouth before I even realize I've said them, and I stare at Shawn, mortified, my hand frozen in mid-air with my glass half raised. He looks at me and laughs.

'The expression on your face is worth one million bucks,' he says. 'Sure I did,' he adds. 'Opening people's mail is fun.'

'Fun?'

'Sure,' he says. 'You know, with a kettle and steam, just like in the movies.' He grins. 'I bet you never did anything like that, did you Susannah? I bet you were always a good girl. Besides,' he adds, 'I wanted to know what Gordon was up to.'

'Shawn!' I put my glass down. I can see him, bending over the electric kettle in Cathy's apartment. 'Do you open my mail too?' I ask. 'And everybody else's?'

'Naw,' he says. 'I read Cathy and Zoe's anyways, and you and Justin don't get anything interesting.' He winks at me, but I'm not entirely sure he's joking.

'I only did Gordon's 'cause he's such a putz,' Shawn says. 'Besides, I wanted to know what he does in there in his apartment by himself all the time. I thought maybe he was putting call girls on his Mastercard, or spending all night jerking off to those nine hundred numbers.'

'Is he?' I can't believe I'm asking this. Shawn shakes his head.

'Neh,' he says, 'nothin' that good. Nothin' good at all, actually. I'll tell you one thing, though. Our Gordy is a weirdo.'

'What do you mean?' I ask. Shawn shrugs.

'He just is,' he says. He's serious now. 'I've told Cath, and she doesn't believe me, but I can sense it. You know, I get vibes from people.' I'm staring at him and he looks at me and laughs. 'What do you want me to say?' Shawn says. 'Maybe it takes one to know one?' He shrugs. 'I'm just waiting for the day the teenaged hooker turns up at the house. That, or the vice squad. Can you imagine Zoe's face? In her perfect brown-stone restoration? It'll happen, I bet you. And I cannot wait.'

Shawn is still talking. Now he's asking the waiter for a menu and announcing that he bets it's years since I had a good meal. I stand up fast, and my full glass of beer spills and pools across the table.

'Oh,' Shawn says. He stops in mid-sentence and stares at the glassy amber liquid as though it might be blood instead of Pilsner. The waiter comes over with a big cloth and starts making clicking noises with his

tongue, and I grab the beer mat with the picture on it
and try to blot it against the leg of my jeans before the
ink on Shawn's castle runs.

'I'm sorry,' I say. 'I'm really sorry, but I have to
go.' I'm starting to babble. 'They're going to call from
Penn,' I say. 'Maybe some other time—' I gesture at
the beer that is being sopped up by the waiter, and at
the half-empty pitcher.

'Don't worry, Susannah,' Shawn says. He is smiling
at me, and under the yellowish light his hair looks
more purple than ever. 'I understand, really. I hope
Jake is OK.' I nod mutely and back up a step. 'It's
OK,' Shawn says again. He waves at the table. 'It's just
water and grain.'

I smile and nod, my head wagging, and then I turn
and start for the door, and it seems as if my boots make
way too much noise on the dark, polished floor.

Back at the house, I sneak through the entryway,
hoping there's nobody home, and run up the stairs like
a coward. When I pass Gordon's door, I try not to
quicken my pace, but I can't help it. There's no sound
coming from inside, and I'm glad. I don't want Gordon
to be home. A 'Get Well' card addressed to Jake and
signed by everybody has been left on the landing table,
and I take it inside and prop it against my cookbooks.
Part of me feels like such a heel for bolting out of
Bruges that I actually consider going all the way back
there to apologize to Shawn again, but I don't know
what I'd say.

I tell myself that I should go and thank Cathy for
the card, but I don't. I don't think that I could stand

her sympathy just at the moment, and I even feel half-guilty for having a beer with Shawn behind her back. What I do do, finally, is pick up the phone and call downstairs, because I promised Zoe that I would, but she and Justin aren't in, so I leave a message. Some very mundane part of my brain still seems to be functioning, and as I hang up I remember the matte of pale hairs on Zoe's coat and wonder if I should have offered to have it dry cleaned.

The light on my answering machine is blinking, and the little red number two is lit up. The messages must be from Beau, and I start to call him, but when I'm halfway through punching in his number, I put the phone down. I know it's not fair, or even particularly rational, but some part of me is really mad that he didn't somehow figure out where I was and come down to Penn, and that instead I had to listen to Shawn talk about sugar skulls and dinners with dead people. I'll call him tomorrow, I think, when I can trust myself to be nice.

I pour myself a drink and sit on one of the high kitchen stools. The scotch burns slightly on the back of my throat and when it hits my stomach I can feel it glowing, flickering against the darkness inside me like a little bonfire. There's a picture of Jake, in a silver frame that says 'woof' on the bottom, on the counter beside me, and I take another sip and promise that if he lives I'll leave this city.

I should have left here a long time ago. When George went to Paris I should have made a clean break. This is my punishment for not doing it. This is my punishment for penning Jake up in an apartment, for making the highpoint of his day the worn grass and paved paths of the Dog Park. This is my punishment for hanging on. I have money in the bank. I'll move to the Blue Ridge Mountains. Or to the Great Smokies. Or maybe to a farm on the banks of the Shenandoah or the Potomac. I'll turn my back on this place. I'll walk away from the heavy façades of the brownstones, and from the lacy spread of the trees in Rittenhouse Square, and from the memory of George's touch, and from the lights that reflect at night like fireworks on the black, oily water of the Schuykill. I'll leave it all behind if Jake lives. I swear. And we'll go somewhere, just the two of us.

The pills are right where I left them, stuffed into an old cosmetics bag at the back of my top drawer. Elena prescribed them for me right after I moved in here, over a year ago, when I was having trouble sleeping. The truth was, I didn't really mind being awake, so I never used them much, but I didn't throw them out either. Sleeping pills are the sort of things that might come in handy. These are small and pale blue, presumably to conjure up the picture of sleeping on puffy white clouds in innocent skies, and I'm shaking two of them out into the palm of my hand when the phone rings.

At first I think it might be the vet at Penn, and then, as I'm about to answer it, I look at my bedside clock. It's midnight. One, two, zero, zero, the red letters read. I watch the phone. It rings five times, and then, just as my machine is about to come on, it stops.

I stand there for a second, then I give it the finger and pop the pills into my mouth.

The phone is ringing again, and that's what wakes me. Shrill and long, it feels like a thin, bright chain yanking me up from thick darkness. My hand finds the receiver before I open my eyes, and it takes me a minute to understand that I'm hearing Dr Gurewich.

'Not colic,' he is saying, 'and so there was no need to operate on him. It was very lucky really—' I've opened my eyes now and I'm focusing on the tiny figures running across the pale green lawn in the picture of Merton House that hangs opposite my bed, and that is when I say, 'Lucky?'

'Yes,' Dr Gurewich says. He pauses, as though he's slightly annoyed with me for being so slow. 'In cases like this we don't always get to pump the stomach fast enough, but as I was saying, Jake didn't ingest much of whatever it was. We don't think there should be any long-term damage internally, but I'd like to keep him here for a few more days, until we get the full toxicology reports.' My brain feels as if it's been doused in syrup. It's sticky, and nothing seems to connect very well.

'Did Jake eat something?' I ask.

'Probably,' Dr Gurewich replies. 'We won't know what, exactly, until after we get all the tests. I wish I could tell you that that would be today, but the lab is very backed up. Of course, I'll call when I have the complete results, but for now I would like to keep my eye on Jake. It's not cheap, I'm afraid. The cost per day—'

'It doesn't matter.' I cut him off. I'm remembering Jake's picture in the frame that says 'woof', and the manila envelope with his collar in it. 'I don't care what it costs,' I say. 'I want what's best for Jake.'

'I'm glad,' Dr Gurewich says. 'We'll call you, tomorrow, Mrs deBreem. I'm sure Jake will be fine,' he adds, almost by way of an afterthought, and then he hangs up.

I lie in bed for a minute, holding the phone. The sleeping pills have made me feel as if my entire body has thickened, as if I've grown enormously fat over-night, and I keep blinking my eyes. It would be easy to slide back down into sleep, but I decide instead to get up. I should call Beau because he'll be worried by now, and besides, I want to tell someone the good news about Jake. The bedside clock says seven-forty, and I switch the radio on to hear the news. Someone on NPR is talking about farming as I get out of bed and turn on the lights and walk into the bathroom.

My eyes feel distinctly gummy and I'm still blinking like an owl when I lean over to turn on the cold water. It's odd that my new kitchen shears are lying on the edge of the sink. I don't remember leaving them there. The pills have made me groggier than I thought, and I splash cold water on my face. Then I reach for a hand towel, and look up.

The hair is long and copper colored. It's a thick strand, half a handful, what the Victorians would have called a 'lock', and it's mine. It loops over the tape that holds it to the mirror and hangs down like a tail, and now I understand why the shears are here.

My own face comes into focus slowly from behind the hair, as if I'm far away and getting closer. I watch my hand in the mirror as I raise it to my forehead. I watch as my fingers find the fringe that is little more than a bristle. They brush the spot, feeling for a nick, or a scrape on the skin, but there isn't one.

It was done carefully and, thanks to the sleeping pills, I probably didn't even move. I didn't even sense the person standing beside my bed in the dark. Or the hand that reached down and lifted my hair. Or the shears that came so close that they must have whispered against my face as the blades made their sharp, clean cut.

FOURTEEN

'So you're not actually certain that you locked the door?'

This time the policeman is a woman. She's about my age and she's not wearing a uniform, which I assume means that I've gone up in the world. Her partner doesn't wear a uniform either, and he's prowling around the apartment jiggling window frames while she talks to me and writes things in her notebook. Her name is Detective Aaronson. Now she raises her eyebrows and inclines her head towards the front door. She's asked me this question before.

'I think I did,' I say, 'but I'm not sure. My dog was—'

'Right, right,' she waves her hand in the air, 'your dog was sick.'

Her partner has raised the living room window and stepped out on to the balcony where he's examining the tree and peering over the balustrade. Detective Aaronson walks past me and I follow her as she goes down the hall and into the bathroom. The lock of hair is still taped to the mirror. She looks at it for a moment and then flips through her notebook.

'So,' she says, 'let me just get this straight. You arrived back at your apartment at approximately ten p.m. last night and saw no one. The phone rang at midnight, but you didn't answer it. Shortly afterwards you went to bed and fell asleep. When you woke up this morning you found the kitchen shears here, by the sink, and this piece of hair taped to the mirror. Then you called us.'

'That's right,' I say.

'And you heard nothing in the course of the night? You didn't wake up at any time?'

'I'd taken a sleeping pill, well, two actually.'

'And is that normal? That you take sleeping pills?'

'No. I was upset because of my dog.'

Detective Aaronson and her partner have already examined the bathroom, and I have already told her all of this once, but she seems to want to hear it again. She flips through a few more pages in her notebook and nods to herself, as though she's come to some kind of decision. Then she glances up at me, and her eyes are hard. They're a flinty blue and ringed by lush, dark lashes that seem somehow unnatural. The eyes are an extravagant ornament in her otherwise unremarkable face.

'Miss deBreem,' she says, 'ten days ago the police were called to an alley off Chestnut Street where you claimed that someone had scratched the word "bitch" on your car door. Two days after that, you claimed that someone had broken in and sang to you in the basement. There were no witnesses to either of these events. Now you claim that you've been receiving phone calls, which you've never reported, and that last night someone entered your apartment, cut some of your hair off, and taped it to your bathroom mirror, although there is no evidence of a forced entry, nothing was taken, no harm was done to you, and you are not even certain whether or not you left the door open.'

A wave of anger rolls through me and I feel myself begin to tremble, which I do not want to do in front of this woman.

'What, exactly, are you suggesting?' I try to keep my voice even, to stop it from creeping up above the red line that registers distress. 'That I'm making this up?'

She doesn't reply, which is obviously a technique that she learnt in cop school, or from watching *Law and Order*.

'Are you seriously suggesting that I cut my own hair off?' I realize that I'm sounding hysterical now. 'That I carved "Bitch" on my own car door? That I made up someone coming into the basement? Why the Hell would I do that?' I stop and take a deep breath. I'm trying to regain my cool, and failing. Detective Aaronson looks at me for a moment and then she says, 'You have a drunk driving conviction, Ms deBreem, October of last year. Is that correct?'

'Of course it's correct,' I snap. It happened about a month after George left, during a period when, to put it mildly, 'I wasn't doing too well'. I'd been out to dinner with Lolly and drunk too much, which was par for the course at the time, and on the way home I ran a red light. Luckily, I was only marginally over the limit, and it was two a.m. and the cruiser was the only other car around. In less auspicious circumstances I might well have killed someone, or at least lost my license. As it was, and given the fact that it was a first offense, the Judge accepted my plea, and doled out a hefty fine.

'I don't see what that has to do with anything,' I add. Detective Aaronson consults her notes again.

'At the time you told the court that you were under extraordinary stress, your husband had left you and—'

'Fiancé,' I say. 'He wasn't my husband, he was my fiancé.'

'—and that you were seeing a therapist, a Dr Schulberg. Are you still seeing him?'

'Her,' I say, 'and I don't see what that has to do with this.'

'Have you ever heard of Munchausen's Syndrome, Ms deBreem?' She asks the question so fast, that at first I'm not sure that I've heard her correctly.

'What did you say?' I ask, and I can hear my voice beginning to quiver.

'Munchausen's Syndrome,' she repeats. 'That's what it's called when people hurt themselves in order to attract attention.' It's her trump card, and she almost smiles when she says it, as if she took Psyche 101 and she's proud of herself. Suddenly I hate this woman with an intensity that startles me. I'd like to fling myself at her, to scream into her patronizing, supercilious face. I'm literally speechless, and before I can recover, she tacks off on to another course.

'Do you have a boyfriend?' she asks. I shake my head.

'Any exes? Anyone who might have reason to—'

By this time I must look like a dog with a flea in its ear. No, no, no, I'm shaking my head. I can't believe that she's treading up this path, especially after I've already told her about Marina, which I did practically the moment she walked through the door.

'You don't understand,' I insist now, and this makes

her look pissed off, which actually pleases me, although I barely have time to think about it. I feel as if I'm awash with words, as if they're rising through me, propelled upwards by a tide of anger, and frustration, and fear, and spilling out of my mouth in no particular order. 'I told you already,' I say, sounding like a kid who is about to cry. 'I had a sister, a twin. Identical. She was murdered. Stabbed. Someone came into her house and killed her. Eighteen months ago. In Virginia.'

Detective Aaronson is staring at me impassively, which, so far, has been her reaction to just about everything, from the hair, to the shears, to Marina's murder. Maybe she only has two emotional levels, this patronizing stare and sleep. Maybe she isn't real. Maybe if you cut her she'd ooze hydraulic fluid instead of blood.

'My sister was being stalked before she was killed.' I say this slowly. I'm trying to catch my breath and I want the words to sink in. I want them to penetrate, to make ripples, waves, any kind of froth on the calm surface of Detective Aaronson. 'She looked just like me,' I say, 'and someone was calling her, following her. Don't you think —'

I don't have a chance to finish because Detective Aaronson's partner, who is tall and very pale, and sort of like an albino vampire in his long dark coat, appears in the bedroom behind us and says, 'Could have been the balcony, easy. Window wasn't locked when I tried it.'

This is presumably further evidence of the unlikeliness of my story, one more fact to convince Detective Aaronson that I'm doing all of this, cutting my hair off and vandalizing my own car, making up men in the basement and murdered twin sisters in order to attract attention to myself. She steps past me and follows the vampire up the hall and into the living room.

'How many people have keys to this apartment?' Aaronson asks while she rattles the window frame. She's already gone out on to the balcony and looked over the edge as if she expected to see a rope ladder, or knotted bedsheets hanging from the railing. She's asked me this before too. In fact it was her first question. I didn't give her Beau's name then, and I'm certainly not going to now.

'No one,' I say, just like I did the first time, and she can tell that I'm lying. She smiles slightly and shakes her head.

'You might consider getting the locks changed,' the vampire says, and they begin to move towards the front door. I can't believe that they're simply going to leave after being here less than fifteen minutes.

'Don't you want the hair?' I ask, 'or the shears? Aren't you going to try to take prints?' They exchange glances.

'Strictly speaking Ma'am,' the partner says, 'there's no evidence that a crime has taken place here. There's no sign of a forced entry, nothing stolen, and no threats have been made.'

'No threats?' I'm practically yelling, and I'm glad that everyone else in the house is at work and no one can hear me. The partner nods sympathetically, clearly he's the good cop. Aaronson is buttoning up her coat.

'Look,' he says, 'most likely it's a practical joke that got out of hand.' He reaches out to touch my arm but I jerk away from him. He nods his head and looks both sympathetic and slightly hurt at the same time. 'If you can think of who might have done this,' he says, 'we'll be happy to talk to them.'

Tears of rage and humiliation flood up and blur my vision as the door clicks shut behind them. I can hear their murmuring voices from the landing as they start down the stairs and I don't even want to think about what they're saying. I close my eyes, resisting the temptation to sink on to the hallway floor, or beat the walls with my fists. I can hear Kathleen Harper's words, hear her saying, 'She went to the police, but they said there wasn't anything they could do.'

'No,' I say out loud, and I open my eyes. I'm stuck with Marina's face, and with her body. The same dips and valleys charted the beating of our hearts, but I'm damned if I'm going to share her death.

The card crumples in my hand when I grab it, and I hope that I haven't creased up the number, or rubbed out the name. On the stairs I take two steps at a time, and once I land sideways on my slippers and almost twist my ankle.

Aaronson and the vampire are just opening the vestibule doors when I come flying down the last flight, and he starts to say something, but I don't give him a chance. They've turned around to face me, and I shove Special Detective Mark Cope's card into Aaronson's hand.

'Here,' I say. 'Since you don't believe me, call him.'

As hateful as she is, I know that she's the one I have to convince. She stares at the card and starts to ask me something, but I've already turned my back on her.

'Just call him,' I say.

A

'Done in a jiffy,' the locksmith says.

He keeps glancing at me nervously as he works on the living room window, as if he's afraid that when he turns his back I'm going to start foaming at the mouth, or leap at him, springing across the room like Cat-woman. I can hardly blame him, my appearance prob-ably isn't reassuring. I've wrapped a scarf around my head like a turban, and I can't sit still, so I walk up and down the hall, and back and forth across the living room, and in and out of the kitchen, patrolling the rooms of the apartment. The only place I don't go is into the bathroom, where the hair still hangs from the mirror and the shears lie by the sink.

The phone's rung three times since the locksmith's been here. Once it was Lolly, and twice it's been Beau. I don't answer it. I just stand beside the message machine and listen while, in Lolly's case, she asks where I am, and in Beau's case, he asks about Jake. His voice is increasingly worried, and it swings between anxiety and anger when I won't pick up.

The first time this happened the locksmith was in the bedroom or the hallway, but the last time he was in the living room and he watched me out of the corner of his eye while Beau pleaded with me to either pick up the phone or to call him back. By now I'm sure the locksmith thinks that Jake is our child and that Beau is my husband who's done something terrible to him, which is why I'm locking him out of the house, and wearing a scarf on my head and refusing to answer the phone. I don't make any effort to enlighten him.

Now he finishes the window and picks up his tool box.

'Okey-Dokey,' he says. 'What do you want on the

front door? New locks?' he suggests, 'Everything changed?'

'New locks. Everything changed,' I agree. 'And then some.'

I manage to perch on the arm of the couch for a minute, but I can't stay there, so I get up and walk back and forth across the rug while the locksmith opens my front door and examines it. He whistles as it arcs outwards on to the landing. He appreciates the possibilities of this. The locksmith swings the door back and forth, testing the hinges and the weight, and then he nods and says, 'Some of these old interior doors in conversions do that, open outwards. You've got some depth in the frame here. I can mount an inner grille if you want.' He turns and looks at me. 'I've got one in the truck that should fit. It'll cost you, but nobody gets in or out of here.'

Zoe will have a fit. Vault-type grilles hardly go with her idea of sympathetic conversion. If I live through this, I'll have to take it down. Then I think of Marina. Against the courtyard light the figure would have been just a dark bulk, nothing more than a shadow on the threshold. She probably couldn't even see the face. I imagine her opening the door slightly, and then I imagine it pushed. I imagine the quick thrust of a hand, the sudden step, a shoulder maybe.

'I don't care what it costs,' I say. 'Go ahead and do it.'

I wait until after the locksmith has left to examine the windows and the door. I didn't want him watching as I run my fingers over the solid brass locks that he has fitted on to the window frames. I didn't like the thought of his eyes on me as I caress the door's edge, as I weigh the new key in my hand, and listen for the smooth whir, the deep click of the bolts sliding home when I turn it in the lock, which I do again and again, my ear pressed against the varnished wood as if I'm listening for movement in a pregnant animal's belly.

It's only three o'clock and the house is still empty. I can sense it when I step out on to the landing. As far as I can remember, Shawn doesn't come today, but you can never tell, so I lean over the rail to check for shadows moving below. I listen, but there's nothing. There's no muffled radio or television. No slam of a door. No footstep cracking against the high gloss of Zoe's parquet. There's not so much as the distant hum of traffic. Satisfied, I turn and admire my door.

It looks exactly the same, from the outside. No one could possibly guess at what lies behind it. I'm the only one who knows. When I swing it open, the grille is dark and heavy looking. It's as if someone's drawn a grid, hung black lines in the air to separate my world from the world out here. The squares are big enough to fit a hand through, and an arm, maybe. Up to the shoulder, say, but nothing more. A face could press against the squares. It could stare in at me. It could get as far as the eyes and the hands, but no other pieces could follow.

I select the right key and unlock the grille carefully. It's a little stiff, but I like the feel of it. When I push it, it swings inward on silent hinges. The grille meets the wall, and makes a dark graph against the pale gray paint. Then I pull it towards me. I give it just the merest tug, and it swings back. It's perfectly balanced.

The tongue meets the groove. The lock sets and drops home. Nobody gets in, or out.

First I call Lolly's office number, not her pager, since I don't actually want to speak to her, and leave a message saying that I have to take Jake to the vet and that I'll be gone all day. Then I call Beau. I try to make my voice sound as normal as possible when he answers the phone, and I know that if I do this well he won't suspect that I'm lying. Beau doesn't lie himself, so he's not very good at figuring out when other people are doing it. Besides, he's too busy asking about Jake to be suspicious of me. It was nothing, I tell him. Just me being ridiculous. Just a worried mother over-reacting.

'The way women do,' Beau says, and I can see him smiling.

'The way women do,' I agree, and I smile too. If my face falls into the appropriate mask, my voice won't give me away.

When Beau asks me if I want to meet him at Sherlock's after work, I demur. I say I'm going out to dinner with Cathy, and that as much as I'd like to get out of it, really, I can't. Beau says that those are the breaks, and that he'll live with being stood up. Will I call him tomorrow, he asks, and I promise that I will. I even say something about the weekend, about how maybe we could take Jake to the Wissahickon, let him run and have a beer at the Valley Green Inn. I'm drawing it out. I'm giving Beau plenty of time. Ample opportunity. But still he says nothing, and after he hangs up I admit that I've won my bet with myself, but it doesn't make me happy. Instead my stomach dips and the light in the room seems duller. Beau never told me where he was last night. 'You don't trust anyone,' Beau had said to me two days ago, 'You certainly don't trust me.' And he's right. On both counts. I don't, not anymore. I can't afford to.

The call from Detective Aaronson comes just before five o'clock, which is, frankly, sooner than I'd expected. She doesn't apologize to me. In fact, she doesn't say much. Her voice is clipped and businesslike, and I can tell that she's pissed off at having to make this call. Then again, I knew that she would be. I knew that Humble Pie was not her favorite dish, but I also knew that she'd eat it.

She's utterly graceless, and there's a distinct whiff of sarcasm when she asks if it would be convenient for me to come down to the station. Say, tomorrow? Say, nine a.m.? Then, after she tells me where to park, and which desk to sign in at, I ask her if there's anything I should bring. Say, a lock of hair? Say, a pair of shears? She pauses for a second, and then she says, 'No.' Someone will be over to collect those. In the next hour.

It's the vampire, but this time he comes with another man. Detective Aaronson is not present. They flash their badges, and when the vampire sees the grille he gives a small whistle. He nods in approval.

'Good girl,' he says, as though I did it for him. 'That was fast.'

They go down the hall and into the bathroom, and

this time I don't follow them. I don't even linger in the bedroom watching them. I just sit on the couch waiting for them to be finished. It doesn't take long. When they come back the new man is carrying a brown paper bag. He holds it carefully, and a little away from himself, as if he has a dead rat in there. There's a white tag attached to the side of the bag which says 'Evidence' on it in square black letters and below it I can see initials written in red ink, and the time and date.

The vampire comes into the living room, and without even glancing at me he goes to the window and checks the new locks. He jiggles the window frames, which barely move now. He peers out on to the balcony. He's feeling proprietary.

'Good,' he says. 'Very good.' Then he gives me a big smile. 'You take care of yourself, Ms deBreem,' the vampire says. 'Don't you hesitate to call us if you need anything.'

I stand in the doorway and listen as they go down the stairs. The policemen aren't talking, but I hear someone come in, and from the voice I realize it's Gordon. He says 'hello' to the two cops, and there's a little expectant pause after it, as if he expects them to explain themselves, but as far as I can tell they don't. Still, I can tell that Gordon's wondering who the hell they are, and I duck back inside and close the door and the grille before he can catch sight of me and decide to come up and ask about them, or about Jake.

As it turns out, Gordon doesn't come, but Cathy does. She knocks on my door and calls my name about a half-hour later, as soon as she gets home from work. Shawn is with her, I can hear him.

'Susannah?' Cathy calls. 'Do you want to come and have dinner with us?'

I stay very still. I freeze in the hallway, which is where I'm standing at the time, as if I'm playing statues. I don't even rattle the cleaning bucket that I have in my hand. It's full of Windex bottles and Ajax cans and old wodged-up pieces of paper towel. I've been cleaning. I've been disinfecting and scrubbing and polishing. I've been rubbing and rubbing, and then using a razor blade. I've been scraping away the gluey band that the tape left in the middle of the glass, the line that sat on my cheek like a brand, imposing itself like the mark of Cain every time I looked at my face in the mirror.

When I don't reply, Cathy waits for a second and then she calls my name again. This time I hear Shawn say, 'She's really upset about the dog.' I can almost see Cathy nodding in agreement. I can sense the glossy crown of her hair dancing back and forth. A second later their footsteps cross the landing and I hear the jingle of Cathy's keys, and then the heavy click as her door swings shut.

The phone rings just before ten, and as soon as I hear his voice on the machine I answer it.

'It could be almost any kind of commercial stuff,' Dr Gurewich says. 'It's widely available, in any hardware store. The only contents of his stomach were a couple of uncooked sausages. Luckily he wolfed them down and didn't chew too much. The casings probably saved him.' He is calling to tell me that the toxicology reports have come back on Jake. He was poisoned. But I already know that.

A police car goes by, and for a couple of seconds waves of blue light pulse across the ceiling and wash up against the living room walls. When it's gone, the sound of the siren lingers. I can hear it wailing down the streets of the city. It's after two a.m. and I keep my eyes fastened on the dark lines of the grille. I watch the polished brass orb of the door knob. It picks up light from the window and glows a little, like a magic egg in a children's story, one of those things that comes alive at night and grants wishes.

I've pulled an armchair into the corner of the living room beside Jake's bed, and from where I sit I can see through the archway to the front door and watch the window and the edge of the balcony, too. I've been waiting for some time now for the door knob to move. I expect it to twist silently. I expect to hear the faint scrape of a key in the lock, and then I expect to feel a vicarious frisson of disbelief, a jolt of frustration, when the bolts don't turn. Failing that, I expect a shadow on the balcony. I've memorized the pattern that the tree branches throw, and I'm alert for any change. There's no wind, so the first thing I may see is motion, or possibly just a thickening of the darkness.

Whichever it is, I'm ready. I opted, in the end, for the stiletto of the boning knife, rather than the hatchet-like carver, and now its long blade lies in my lap. Occasionally it glints, it almost sparkles in the dark. The blade is paper thin and very sharp. Already I've run my finger along it once and drawn blood.

Earlier, I'd heard the faint thud of Cathy's stereo as I stood in the kitchen, and I'd found myself drawing the blade back and forth in time to it against the whetstone. For a moment that was comforting, and so was the murmur of Gordon's TV. I could hear it occasionally too, filtering up through the heat vents from the floor below in a sort of warm mumbling. They'll hear me scream, I'd thought then. Of course they will. If I get the chance.

FIFTEEN

His hand is as smooth and as cool as a stone.

'Miss deBreem,' Special Detective Mark Cope says, 'I want to thank you for coming in to talk to us.'

He's flown up from Washington this morning, and another man, who is introduced to me only as 'Phil Dorris, who has been helping us with our investigation', is with him. Dorris is thin and olive skinned, and his long horse-like face has trouble breaking into the obligatory smile when he meets me. The vampire is here too, and Detective Aaronson since, presumably, this is her party. She merely nods in my direction when I come into the room. She's wearing a blue pantsuit, and she's folded her hands in front of her so she looks peculiarly demure, like one of those ladies who work as guides in the Art Museum.

The room we're in isn't small and dark and cramped like those featured on *Homicide* or old re-runs of *Hill Street Blues*. There's not a leaky radiator or a piece of watermarked plaster in sight. Instead, it's more like a conference room at a bank or an advertising agency, and the walnut veneer table and matching chairs make me feel slightly under-dressed. In fact, I have the surreal sense that I've come here to pitch a project to a bunch of backers, to discuss seating numbers and color schemes, instead of the similarities between the events that led to, on the one hand, my sister being hacked to death with a butcher's knife and, on the other, to someone creeping into my apartment to cut my hair off and tape it to the bathroom mirror.

Even as I think this, my fingers move towards the brim of my hat. So far I've been unable to stop this involuntary reaction, this need to feel the short bristly fringe that rises above my forehead in a ragged arch. I've given up the scarf for this meeting and opted for a hat instead. It's black felt with a narrow brim, and once it had a pink daisy pinned to it. I removed that this morning and threw it out. Flowers hardly seemed suitable for the occasion.

As I sit down I realize that Mark Cope and Phil Dorris are watching me intently, as if the expression on my face or what I've chosen to wear this morning might give some hint, some vital clue, as to why all of this is happening. Detective Aaronson moves down the table and sits on her own, while the vampire takes the chair next to mine. He gives me an encouraging little smile as he sits down, as if he's a coach and I'm a not particularly promising athlete about to enter the ring.

'It's the same person, isn't it?' I say. 'That's why you're here?'

At this, Mark Cope and Phil Dorris exchange glances with Detective Aaronson. The vampire studies the edge of the table. The point seems elementary, but all the same, their discomfort would suggest that I'm not supposed to have mentioned it.

'We can't be certain of that,' Phil Dorris says. He makes a tent out of his fingers and wiggles them back and forth. Then he says, 'But, given the nature of the circumstances, it's a possibility that we have to consider, yes.'

'Because Marina and I were identical?'

Dorris nods.

'That, and the pattern that's developing,' he says.

Clearly, he's the front man on their team, and now I understand who, and what, he is. He's a shrink. A profiler. He's one of those guys they make TV series about who specialize in psyching out serial killers and rapists and every other sort of criminally inclined weirdo. I wonder if he's Alexandria Police or FBI. Maybe he's been drafted in specially from Quantico now that we've crossed state borders. If this is the case, I guess it means that I'm privileged. All the same, his presence doesn't make me feel better.

'There are similarities,' Phil Dorris says, 'which I'm sure you've already recognized.' It's my turn to nod. 'It's exacerbated, of course, by the fact that you look alike. Most people like this go after a type, but in this case it may be something a little different. If it is the same guy, he may be trying to recreate some scenario in his head that centered on your sister.'

'Like what?' I say.

'I don't know,' Dorris shakes his head. 'The telephoning, the flowers, even coming into the basement. He's letting you know he's there. They may be a kind of courting ritual. It looks like he did the same thing with Marina. Then things started to go wrong. Probably she didn't respond the way she was supposed to. In a lot of cases these people are convinced that their target is, in fact, in love with them, and they're very deliberate. What they do may seem random to you or me, but it isn't to them. They have scenarios, ways they need things to work out. When the picture doesn't play right, they feel like they're losing control. And then they get mad.'

'So, he's doing this because I'm Marina all over again? Because he sees me as a second chance?'

'It's possible,' Dorris says. 'Given the parameters of this case, it's certainly something we have to consider.'

I'm trying to digest this. The suspicion that had fluttered in my stomach when I ran into George on the bridge, and that had unfurled and grown in me like an incubus as I spoke to Kathleen Harper, now seems intent on spreading its wings, on stretching and flexing until I split open and fly to pieces.

For the first time, I understand clearly that I'm going to die, and that there's nothing I can do about it. It's inevitable, like being diagnosed with MS or Parkinson's, or any other fatal genetic disease. It's no fault of my own, it's what I carry inside me. I'm going to be carved up by some maniac because I was born with Marina's face.

'Ms deBreem, Susannah,' Mark Cope is leaning across the table towards me. 'We need your help. That's why we've come up here.'

I look at his earnest face and I feel laughter rising, exploding like fireworks, inside me. I want to point out to him that that's my line, but he starts talking again before I have the chance. I'm only half listening. Right at this moment, I'm spending most of my energy trying not to squeal. I'm trying to preserve some shred of dignity by not doubling up over the table and laughing until the tears run down my cheeks.

I can imagine Marina watching me, daring me to meet her eye, and I hope she's here somewhere, flying around this blue carpeted room with its fake walnut table and chairs, and reveling in what a joke all of this is. But, of course, she's known the punchline all along. This is what she spent her life trying to make me understand: that no matter where I have my dorm room, or live my life, or how far I run, we're always together. We're two peas in a pod. We're bonded. In life, and in death, we're one.

'As I told you at the time,' Mark Cope is saying, 'we're convinced that Marina was killed by someone she knew, at least well enough to let into her house. She may have been expecting them, or they may have just dropped by. It's even possible that she invited them, although we can't find any trace of that in her phone records. So, we need to look for anyone, anyone at all, who has a connection to you now, however slight, and who your sister could have known then.'

I shake my head. The laughter seems to have dried up as quickly as it sprang to life, and I'm amazed that my voice sounds perfectly normal.

'We weren't friendly like that, Detective,' I say. 'I told you. I didn't know her friends. I really didn't know much at all about her life in Washington.'

'So you haven't thought of anyone,' he asks, 'anyone at all?'

'I told you at the time, there's George, but—'

'Who's George?' This is Detective Aaronson. She's pounced on his name like a cat and her pen is poised in mid-air.

'George Collier,' I say. 'He's a professor at Penn, and he was my fiancé when Marina was killed. She met him a couple of times, years ago, when we first started going out. But it's ridiculous. For a start, we were living together and we were up here the whole weekend Marina was killed.'

She glances at Cope and he nods, but she asks for George's address anyways. I give it to her, even though I'm not sure if it's right anymore, because I know she's going to find him if she wants to. Penn is hardly shrouded in mystery.

'And there's Gordon, downstairs,' I say.

'Wallingford,' Detective Aaronson says. 'We're looking at him.'

'Ms deBreem,' Phil Dorris says, 'there's a good chance, in fact a real likelihood, that whoever this person is, they knew your sister, but that doesn't necessarily mean that you'll recognize them.'

'You mean it could be anyone?'

'Well,' he says, 'not anyone. We can narrow the field a little. Whoever it was who killed your sister was probably living in or around Washington eighteen months ago. Or, if they weren't living there, they may have traveled there regularly for work.'

Lolly travels all the time, I think. And Beau goes to conferences. And so does Elena, and virtually everyone else I know.

'What else?' I ask.

'The method of attack,' Dorris pauses, 'the, well, frenzied quality of the stabbing. That's rage. Pure and simple. And rage usually stems from the personal. A spurned lover, someone your sister, perhaps unwittingly, insulted or damaged in some way. For instance, take the fact that her face was disfigured, that's a classic indicator of a connection that at least the attacker perceived as intimate. On the whole, I'd guess, white. Male. Between twenty-five and forty-five. Possibly professional. Possibly affluent. But not necessarily any of those things.'

'Oh great!' I say. 'Great. That really narrows the field! That leaves approximately, what? Two-thirds of the population of Philadelphia who may be trying to kill me? Or is it only twenty-five per cent? And by the way, are you so certain it's a man?'

'All we're certain of,' Phil Dorris says, 'is that whoever killed Marina was taller than she was, and right handed.'

'So it could have been a woman?'

He considers me for a minute before he replies, and then he says, 'Yes, it could have been a woman, if she was tall enough and strong enough.'

I lean back in my chair and close my eyes. For some reason, I feel as if I've won an important point here, as if we're scoring against each other, rather than pulling on the same side.

'It's not that bad,' Mark Cope is saying. 'The police here are going to do everything they can. They need you to give them your address book, your business contacts, a list of everyone that they should cross-check to see if there could have been any link with Marina.' He pauses, and I open my eyes and stare at him, like an obnoxious pupil staring at a teacher. He stares back at me, and then he says, 'In the meantime, we need you to be very, very careful, Susannah. This guy is close to you, and he wants you to know it. He's playing a game here. He's got a plan, but we don't know what it is. Yet. So you need to keep your eyes open. You need to look for a face on the street, a delivery boy, a postman, a guy in the video store – anyone who you see more often than you should.'

I glance at Detective Aaronson, but she's not looking at me, and I know right then that they're not going to do a damn thing. Despite Mark Cope, and Phil Dorris, and the fact that they flew up here, I'm sure that Aaronson is less than convinced that I'm in mortal danger. She's probably still betting on Munchausen's Syndrome, or PMS and the power of coincidence. Even on the off chance that I'm wrong, I'll bet that the Philadelphia police are just as under-staffed and as over-stretched as everybody else. Even if they are convinced that I'm about to be killed, there's probably precious little that they can do about it. All that giving them my address book is likely to mean is that I'll never see it again, and that they'll have it handy after I'm left chopped up in little pieces in a garbage can somewhere.

Suddenly, all of this is too real, and for some reason I think of Jake, and of the soft, dark triangle between his ears where he still smells like a puppy when I bury my face in his fur.

'Ms deBreem?' Phil Dorris is saying, 'Susannah? What is it? What's the matter?'

'My dog,' I say, and I can't finish the sentence because my voice is jumpy and unreliable. Like an electric current with a bad connection, it seems to be flickering in and out.

Phil Dorris is sliding a box of Kleenex across the table towards me, and when I reach out to take one, my hand shakes and the white tissue waves like a surrender flag before I can get it to my face.

'We'll get him,' Mark Cope says. He's probably one of those men who can't stand to see women cry. 'I promise you, Susannah,' he says, 'we'll get him.'

The vampire makes some reassuring noises too, and Cope is leaning towards me, trying to get me to look into his eyes, but I can't. I can't stop watching Phil Dorris's long, horsey face, and realizing that he and Detective Aaronson aren't saying a thing.

All I want to do is get out of this god-awful building. I've surrendered my Filofax to Aaronson, and I pulled myself together enough to shake everyone's hand and thank them, although I'm still not certain for what, and I'm walking across the lobby, making for the three sets of revolving glass doors that give on to the street, when Mark Cope catches up with me. I hear him call my name, and when I stop and wait for him, I see that he's slightly out of breath. He must have missed the elevator and run down three flights of stairs.

'Susannah,' he says, 'wait!' I can't decide, watching him in his starched white shirt and his red power tie, whether it's his pride or genuine concern that's made him come after me. Maybe my obvious fear is a blow to his ego, since it implies that I have less than one hundred per cent faith in him.

'Why didn't you call me?' he says, when he finally stands in front of me. 'Why didn't you call me as soon as this started happening?'

'I called you after I went to see Kathleen Harper,' I say. 'I left a message.' He shakes his head and looks away from me.

'I wish you hadn't waited,' he mutters. 'This

guy—' He doesn't finish the sentence, and I want to ask him, 'What? This guy what?' but the words die in my throat. 'Look,' Mark Cope says, 'back there, when you asked Phil if it could be a woman, did you have anyone in mind?'

'How closely did you check Kathleen Harper's alibi?'

I can see her standing on the step above me, see the shoulders that would have been powerful, a year and a half ago, from a summer's worth of sailing on the Chesapeake. I can see her flipping the bottle opener up in the air after she gave me the beer, and catching it again with her right hand. Mark Cope is watching me.

'I think you should check her out,' I say. 'Carefully. I think she and Marina were close. Really close.'

'We did,' Cope says. 'Her and her husband. They'd been friends of your sister's and so we looked at them both, but there was nothing concrete. Her fingerprints were all over Marina's townhouse, but she says she used to visit all the time, and her kids' prints were there too. We can't pin her down for all of the Friday, but we haven't turned up a sighting in the area either. No sign of her car or anything like that. Of course, the window is big, which is a real problem. It's really any time between six p.m. on the Friday, and eight p.m. on the Saturday when Marina didn't show up for her dinner date. We figure she was dead by then, but it would help if we had been able to make a more accurate time of death.'

I look out through the glass doors. A thin drizzle has started to fall and the sky looks white and fuzzy. The doors whoosh when they spin around, and people drop out of them and land in the marbled lobby. Some of them are clutching their coats and carrying briefcases as if this is an ordinary business office, and some are in jeans and sneakers with their hands dug deep into pockets and their faces turned down. It seems to make no difference that it's the weekend, the doors never stop. They could almost be automatic, the way they keep picking people up and spinning them out on to the sidewalk, and scooping others up and dropping them back into the lobby as if they're candy pieces in a machine, or cogs in a wheel.

'Just after eleven-thirty,' I say.

'What?' Mark Cope's voice seems indistinct and far away. People walk past us. A group divides and flows around us as though they're borne by a current and Mark Cope and I are two stones in a river.

'That's when she was killed,' I say.

I'm not watching Mark Cope as I say this, but I can hear him take a deep breath, I can almost feel him resisting the urge to reach out and grab me, to stop me, as if I might flee, as if I might slip into one of the door's glass cubicles and vanish with a 'whoosh' out on to the street.

'How do you know?'

He asks it very carefully, and when I finally turn and meet his deep brown eyes, I almost feel sorry for him.

'Because I heard it,' I say.

SIXTEEN

The scream was high pitched, and very loud. It exploded without warning inside my head, detonated in a blinding fireball of sound that, quite literally, knocked me sideways. For a split second it seemed to gather pace, to rush towards me, bearing down like the whistling roar of a night train. And then it stopped. The shriek hung in the air, ringing, before it died away, and echoed into a ragged, gasping squeak.

Of course, I later understood that the squeaking sound was because her throat had been cut, because the blade had bitten into her larynx and severed her vocal chords even as they still attempted to protest. At the time, as I grasped the edge of the kitchen counter, hung on to it as if it was the rail of a pitching ship, and watched the glass that I had dropped shatter, and the wine pool on to the floor, in that moment, I only knew that I had been winded. I felt as if someone had socked me in the stomach, or grabbed me by the throat, and I was choking.

In the seconds that followed, as the sound faded and the room came back into focus, I looked for her. I absolutely expected to see her feet planted on the brick patterned linoleum. I knew that as my eyes traveled up I would see Marina's legs, her body, her face, as she rose above me like a pillar. When I found that she was not there, I spun around, certain that she must be behind me, that somehow she had arrived at the apartment, and come into the kitchen. But the room was empty. There was no trace of her. There was nothing but the high ring of her scream, and the dying echo of a gurgling sound, something like water running and bubbling down a closed drain.

I felt as if I had been momentarily deafened. It was the same sort of sensation that Uncle Ritchie warned about when he was shooting doves, the tinny ringing and the breathlessness that comes from being too close to the crack of a shotgun. A few seconds passed before I could hear again the ticking of the big yellow clock on the wall above the stove, or the rhythmic drip of the sink faucet. A moment later I was aware that the slightly fuzzy sound of voices was coming from the living room, and I remembered that George had just put a tape into the VCR.

'Aren't you coming?' he had called, and right then I realized that he hadn't heard a thing.

'Suze?' George yelled a minute later, as I was stooping to mop up the spilled wine, 'are you OK?'

When he finally appeared in the doorway and saw the glass and the wine on the linoleum, he laughed and said, 'Oh, thank God. I always hated those glasses. One down, five to go.' He threw the broken crystal stem and the petal shaped pieces of bluish glass into the trash, and then grabbed the opened bottle and a new glass and said, 'Maybe we can smash this one too. Come on, the beginning's the best part.'

In the next second he was gone, and when I came out of the kitchen, he was back on the living room

couch watching Tom Hanks struggle towards the Nor-
mandy coast on D Day. I almost opened my mouth to
say something just then, but George glanced up and
patted the cushion beside him and said, 'Come on, or
I'll eat all the popcorn,' and then the moment passed
when I might have been able to explain to him that I
had dropped the glass and spilt the wine because I'd
heard Marina screaming.

My telepathic conversations with Marina were not
something that I had ever tried to explain to George. I
had told myself at the time that those were not the sort
of ideas that interested him, but of course the real
motive for my silence on the subject was more complex. He didn't like Marina, for a start, and beyond
that, I didn't want him to think that I was out of my
mind. The truth was that I was just as happy to forget
about them myself. I was delighted when, in secret,
I looked up studies on identical twins that said this
phenomenon was not entirely uncommon, and almost
always ceased after the onset of puberty.

    In our case, this had actually been more or less true,
and, of course, by the time we were in our thirties,
and admittedly well past puberty, we rarely had conversations at all, never mind ones that ignored the
banalities of speech. The era of our private communi-
cation had really only lasted until our teens. In fact,
when I thought of it at all, I realized that our secret
wavelength must have begun to take on heavy static
sometime during the summer when the Eames' barn
burned. At least that was when I first became aware
that Marina had figured out how to deploy some kind

of scrambler, some kind of blocking device to keep me out. By the time we graduated from high school it was over. Along with our old ballet tutus and our dreams of being swans, the nightspinning was a thing of the past.

Or so I thought. Until the night she died. Then, in her last moments on this earth, Marina screamed for me, and, just as she had promised, I heard her. Loud and clear.

Much later on that Friday night, after I had sat for two hours on the couch beside George, and after we had drunk the wine, and gone to bed, and made love, and fallen asleep, I woke up again and asked myself if I had really heard anything at all. Lying in the shadowed room with George beside me, I tried to convince myself that it had been nothing. I told myself that it had been the television, or a siren. Or a smoke alarm downstairs, or tom cats fighting on the fire escape. I told myself what I wanted to believe, that the sound was nothing more than the sound of the city at night.

Unable to sleep, I got up and walked into the living room. Gray light wormed its way through a crack in the heavy curtains, and I slipped between them, and opened the window, and leaned out and breathed in the first soft greenness of spring that you can only smell in the city in the early hours of the morning when everything is still. I closed my eyes then, and thought I caught the faint, sweet, scent of my grandmother's lilacs drifting up from the street, and the fecund, damp odor of the dark earth that had been broken and turned under Uncle Ritchie's plow. In that second, I almost turned back into the room and reached for the phone to call Marina. I felt a sudden urge to wake her up, to ask her if she remembered the smell of the farm at night, and the way the moonlight turned the stunted pines behind the barn taller and spikier than they could ever claim to be in the daylight. For the first time in years, I yearned to hear her voice, to hear the round, familiar, sound of her words. I longed for her to spin out some old story about the Delrays, or about Della Hervey, or about the ghost of a white horse that she once swore she saw, galloping in the moonlight and flying over the rotting, snaggle-toothed rails of Uncle Ritchie's paddock.

Then I closed the window and I told myself not to be ridiculous. I was far away and grown-up now. So I went back to bed. I lay there and listened for a while to the soft blow and whistle of George's breathing. Then I fell asleep, completely unaware that my connection to Marina had been so completely severed that in the moment when I had missed her the most, I had not even realized that she was dead.

Special Detective Mark Cope is watching me. We're sitting in a tiny hole of a cafeteria across the street from the police station, and he's holding a styrofoam cup of coffee with both hands. Steam rises out of it in a little tail of smoke. I have a cup of coffee too, and when I lift it to my lips the liquid is so hot that it burns the top of my mouth and I don't taste a thing.

I have told Mark Cope the whole story now. Sitting here in this booth, watching cops and old men come in and out of the steamed-up door, I have explained that Marina and I were nightspinners. I have described how we could send each other words, and even dreams and nightmares, and the way each of us could tell what the other one was thinking. I've told him all of this. And I've told him about that final, ripping scream.

Now he sits staring at me. His dark, handsome face is as still as a statue's. He's trying to decide whether or not he thinks I'm completely crazy. He's weighing up the possibility that Detective Aaronson might be right after all. He probably wishes Phil Dorris was here, and that they could exchange a look, or a secret hand signal. Or, better yet, that Dorris could take over completely and he would not have to say anything to me at all.

'Susannah,' Mark Cope says finally, and I have to give him credit for the fact that his gaze does not shift from mine, 'why didn't you tell me all this before?' I begin to laugh.

'Would you have believed me?' I ask.

The apartment is empty. It has never felt like this before. Even when I first walked into it and saw its unfurnished rooms, it didn't feel so totally uninhabited, so completely devoid of any kind of life. It's as if, in the few hours that I've been gone, someone's switched off a current and deprived this place of some unseen element that allows for the clack of footsteps, the shuffling of paper, water being turned on and off, the phone ringing. Perhaps, ironically, it's the grille that's done it, or the new sets of locks, but I can't imagine music, or laughing, or even the sound of the radio here now.

I move carefully. I don't want to disturb anything.

I feel as if I have to slip through the air in these rooms without displacing it. There's a thin rime of dust on the surface of my dressing table, and although it's probably been there for weeks, I notice it now, and the way the drip of the kitchen tap makes it sound as if nobody lives here.

Anger hits me, and it's as hot and as vibrant as lightning across a darkened sky. Right now I know that if I could get my hands on this son of a bitch, whoever he is, I'd kill him. I'd get him before he could get me. 'Come on, you fucking coward,' I want to scream, but then the words choke on the still air of fear, and I have to hurry. Because, despite the change of the locks, despite the grille, despite Shawn, and Cathy, and Justin, and Zoe, and yes, even Gordon, who is probably harmless, despite all of them so close around me, and despite Mark Cope's best assurances and the three copies of his card that I now have in my shoulder bag, I can't stay here a second longer.

I get my duffel bag down from the hall closet and open it out on the bed. Then I stand staring at my clothes. I'll have to be careful here. I have no real idea what I might need, or how long I'm going to be away.

'What should I do?' I'd finally asked Mark Cope after he'd heard the whole story and we had finished our coffee. 'It's great if you believe me,' I'd said, 'and if knowing a closer time of death will help, but while you're trying to find out who this guy is, what do I do? Send him a message? Ask him to wait?' Mark Cope had shaken his head.

'No,' he'd said. 'What you do is disappear.'

★

Now, sitting in the back of a taxi going uptown, I'm surprised at how much better I feel. At least I'm doing something. I have a plan that I've worked out with Mark. That's how I think of him now. No more of this 'Detective' stuff, we're on a first name basis. He and Phil Dorris are flying back to Washington. They're in the air this very moment, recharged, re-enthused, determined to go through every single alibi, every move of Marina's again. 'With a fine tooth comb', Mark Cope had said, and 'We'll find something.' 'We'll nail him.' 'I promise.'

My part of this plan is not to get killed, and in order to facilitate that, I'm checking into the Marriott. Only Mark and Phil Dorris and Detective Aaronson and the vampire know this. I'm not allowed to tell anyone else. I'm not even allowed to talk to anyone else until, one by one, Detective Aaronson tells me that the alibis of all the people I know, Zoe, and Lolly, and Beau, and even Mrs Koom Wai and Tony at the garage, and Shawn with his purple crew cut, have been cleared. Only after we know that none of them could have been in Alexandria on that fine spring night, am I allowed to return phone calls, or to put in the occasional appearance. In short, only then am I allowed to emerge from this dark wood into which I've wandered.

It won't take long, Detective Aaronson has promised me. In our second meeting of the morning, after Mark Cope and I had sat in the café, and then made our way back to police headquarters, she had regarded me with something close to grudging sympathy. I assume that this change of heart is due to the fact that Mark, and Phil, who is from the FBI after all, seem to be taking this so seriously. They've formally asked for Philadelphia's cooperation on their investigation, and it will take just a few days, Detective Aaronson assures me, to run through what she calls 'The A List', those closest to me. After that, I can speak to them again. I can have a white wine with Lolly, or a beer with Beau at Bella Italiana, safe in the knowledge that they are not about to leap up and cut my throat with the pizza knife, or garrote me in the ladies' room, or run over me in the parking lot, or even try to poison my dog. In the meantime, however, I have to disappear.

The cab flies through a yellow light just as it turns to red, and I hear a screech of brakes behind us and a horn honking.

'Goddamn women drivers!' the cabby says. He looks at me in the rearview mirror and laughs, and for some reason I do too. My duffel bag's in the trunk, and my portfolio is resting against my knee. I've called the vet school and arranged for Jake to stay there until I come for him. I've told them I have to go out of town. I've wiped all the messages off my answering machine, and I've thrown the perishables out of the fridge. Eggs have gone into the garbage, and milk down the drain. It's almost like I'm going on vacation.

'All of it?' the girl says. She's chubby and dressed entirely in black, like everyone else who works here. Her own hair has blue highlights, and the stud in her nose sports a stone of a similar color. I wanted to ask her if it was a real aquamarine, but I was afraid it might be rude. Her name is Joyce, I think, and she is holding a large hank of my hair up in her hand. Her nails are blue too, and when her eyes meet mine in the salon mirror, they're full of questions.

'Are you sure?' Joyce asks, and I realize that she's not half as tough as she looks. She's probably a Penn student, just a nice girl studying art history and shaving people's heads to work her way through college. 'This is a big step,' she says. Maybe she does some counseling on the side: gives advice on tattoos, and whether or not to drop French. 'We could go by degrees,' she points out, 'give you bangs first, and then try the color. Or go to shoulder length and see if you like it.'

I shake my head.

'All of it,' I say. 'Right now.'

'OK,' Joyce says.

She drops my hair and stands back.

'I usually cut dry,' she says, 'and then we do the color and then I clean it up again after. Is that OK?' I meet her eyes in the mirror and nod, and a second later I hear the swish and click of scissors.

My hair makes a whispering sound as it slides over my shoulders and slithers on to the floor where it lands in a thatch of copper, like the cut silk of dead corn. As I watch in the mirror, my neck, freed of its protective ruff, seems to grow longer, and my head and face appear stuck to the top of it. I emerge, shorn. Like a stick figure in a child's drawing, I'm as scrawny and ragged looking as a baby chicken.

Detective Aaronson doesn't know I'm here. I didn't ask her permission because I was afraid that she'd say 'no', so I came straight here in the cab. At least I've chosen a salon that I've never been to before. Not that I was fussy. I took the first one in the *Yellow Pages* that had an appointment open. It's called 'Avanti', which I think means 'fast-forward', or something to that effect, and by the time Joyce has finished, I'm certainly streamlined.

She's done exactly what I asked her to, which is cut the hair all over my head to the same length as the fringe I'd been left with. Then she sent me to someone called Heather, who painted my head in a helmet of goo that she promised would turn it black. She suggested giving me some green shading, which she said would match my eyes but I turned it down on the grounds that it would have been too flashy.

As it is, I look weird enough. Even I have trouble recognizing myself in the mirror behind the receptionist as I hand over my credit card, which is exactly what I'd hoped for.

'That looks really cool,' the girl who hands me back my slip says, 'really short hair is so sexy, and it's great with your eyes. You should come back for highlights.'

'Maybe I will,' I say, and I write in a big tip for both Joyce and Heather while the receptionist calls me a cab.

Sleep is the most wonderful thing in the world. By eight p.m. I can barely stay awake to eat the chicken salad and drink the wine that I've ordered from room service, and by nine I've stuck the tray back out in the hall and climbed between the slightly stiff hotel sheets. I've brought Elena's sleeping pills with me, but there's not a chance on earth that I'm going to need them after the combined effects of today and spending all of last night awake. When I had packed the bottle and thought of her, my hand had shaken. I would have given anything to be able to run to the safety of her office with its dusty ficus tree and messy, stuffed shelves of books. I'd cursed her then for being in Vienna.

My head feels strangely light on the pillow when I turn over, and I'm half-aware that I miss the heavy drag of my hair. I am wondering if I even have to brush the few spikes that I have left, or if I can just run my hand over it and be done, when I begin to drift off. Here in this anonymous room with its sealed windows and fifteen floors of people around me, I feel entirely safe. I feel as if I could sleep forever.

From what I can see of the morning outside, it looks bright. I've just lifted my brush to my head when there's a knock on my door, and a voice calls, 'Room Service,' and I realize that I've forgotten that I ordered breakfast and the newspaper before I went to bed last night.

I can hear people walking up and down the hallway, and the 'ping' of the bank of elevators around the corner as I go to the door, and so I think it's probably safe to open it. Even so, I look through the fisheye. All I can see is a piece of a small blonde-haired girl in a red uniform. When I undo the chain and swing the door back she's facing me, and holding a huge tray. On it there's a coffee pot and a dish with a metal cover, and a neatly rolled copy of the *Philadelphia Inquirer*. There is also a basket of flowers.

'What's that?' I ask, pointing. I know it sounds unnecessarily brusque, but I can't help myself. I'm hoping this is a gift from the management, but even before the girl opens her mouth I know it isn't.

'They just arrived for you, Mrs Thomson,' the girl says, using the not very inventive alias I checked in with. 'The front desk sent them up with your breakfast order.'

She smiles and starts to come into the room, but instead of backing up to let her past me, I reach for the basket. I don't actually want to touch it, so I grab the wicker with the very tips of my fingers, as if it might be toxic or hot enough to burn.

'Is there a card?' I hear myself ask.

By now the girl knows there's something wrong, and she just nods mutely. I turn the basket around, gingerly, holding it by the handle. They're African violets, and nestled between their little purple faces and the broad spongy green of their leaves, I spot the white corner of an envelope. There's nothing written on the outside, and the message inside is computer generated and printed on cheap paper.

'Bad Girl. I don't like the hairdo at all. You should have asked me first.'

SEVENTEEN

I did manage to bolt the door and to swing the U-shaped security lock closed. It's not a big achievement, but it gives me a disproportionate sense of pride, as if I have the right to congratulate myself for moving at all. That was in the first moments of frenzy, when I couldn't do anything but move. Then, it seemed entirely possible that I might begin to scream, that I might burst out of the door and race down the hallway and out into the street. In those minutes, after I had scribbled something on the bill and shoo-ed the poor room-service girl back out of the door, I dragged the desk chair into the tiny hallway and shoved its back up underneath the door knob. I drew all of the curtains. I yanked them together and crimped their gaps closed, as if I could stop someone from looking in, stop them from observing me through this panel of sealed, tinted glass twelve storeys high in the air.

After that I had picked up the telephone receiver and punched Detective Aaronson's number. Or I'd tried to. The first two times I got it wrong. I forgot that I had to dial nine, and when the polite, cheery tones of the hotel operator asked if she could help me, I almost dissolved on the quivering, helpless edge of tears. It was the cool sound of Detective Aaronson's voice on the answering system, the easy, clipped assurance in her syllables as she told me to leave a message or dial her pager number, that brought me around like a slap in the face, and made the words I had been so ready to babble die in my mouth.

As I had looked at the telephone receiver in my hand, I was certain that I could actually feel my blood slowing, could feel it thickening, turning viscous and heavy in my veins. 'Take a deep breath,' I had told myself then. It's the sort of thing my mother would have said. 'Take a moment,' I advised myself, 'to consider the facts.' Only four people knew where I was staying last night. They were Mark Cope, Phil Dorris, Rebecca Aaronson, and the vampire. This morning a basket of African violets and a note arrived on my tray. Someone who knew where I was and what name I was using had sent them.

The phone made a small, indignant chirping sound when I hung up.

The little patches of sweat that had bloomed across the back of my neck and between my breasts have cooled now and turned clammy. My shirt is sticking to them and the room feels cold. I pick up the thermos pot of coffee and pour myself a cup. It's thick and inky brown, and it smells bitter, but I force myself to drink it anyways. It's not until the second cup that I remember to add sugar, which is supposed to be good for shock.

The flower basket is sitting in the center of the desk, and I stare at it. I can't take my eyes off it as I force myself to lift the cup to my mouth and swallow.

The newspaper is on one side of the basket of flowers and the thick block of the Philadelphia *Yellow Pages* is on the other, and it looks perfectly innocuous, even pretty. It might be a welcome gift, in fact, to the naked eye, to the uninformed. It hardly seems to be an obvious object of threat. And maybe, I think, that's the point. On the surface, things look minor, innocent, but it's what's underneath that counts.

I can feel a presence in the room. It's here as surely as a whiff of perfume or of body odor. Whoever it was who killed Marina is close. I don't need Mark Cope or the FBI to tell me this. I know. I can sense them just as surely as if they're looking through the key hole. I put the coffee cup down slowly, reluctant to make any noise. I almost believe that if I closed my eyes, I could hear breathing.

'House Keeping,' the maid calls as the noise of her cart, which has at least one squeaky wheel, echoes down the long tunnel of the blue-carpeted hallway. I have been listening to it for the last half-hour, standing behind the door and measuring the intervals between the clanks of cleaning buckets and the muttered words of Spanish as the staff pass one another in the hallway and rap on doors.

There has been no rap on my door, and no call, because I left the 'Do Not Disturb' sign turned outward. Even so, the maid paused outside, and I could hear the small snifflings, the rustle of her, as she contemplated knocking despite the sign. Then she thought better of it and moved on. Now I can tell that she's gone around the corner, that she's parked up by the ice machine beyond the bend of the corridor, and I lift the 'U' lock and slide the security chain gently out of its berth.

I've abandoned my portfolio, and my duffel bag isn't very heavy. I can easily carry it on my shoulder. I check quickly to make sure that no one is around, and then I close the room door behind me softly, and hurry down the hallway. Almost as soon as I touch the button, the elevator door pings and opens and I step into it. It's as empty as I had hoped that it would be at ten in the morning, and it whisks me straight into the basement parking lot, zooming downwards on a whoosh of air, plummeting past eleven floors and the lobby.

When I get there, the hotel garage appears to be empty too, except for two guys at the far end doing detailing, and the girl in the ticket booth who looks like she's doing her nails. Even so, I lurk around for a good long time, and only when I'm certain that I haven't been followed, that no one is shadowing me from behind concrete pillars or parked Windstar vans, do I slip out, walk up the ramp-way, and duck around the corner, heading for Independence Plaza and the Liberty Bell. A taxi is waiting right where they usually are, and I slide into the back seat, and ask for the Rodin Museum.

Mid-morning is a busy time for Rodin, which is what I'd been counting on. When the cabby lets me out I cross the sidewalk and fall in with a bus tour from upstate that's pushing its way, like some kind of huge pulsing amoeba towards the entrance. Just before we get there I peel off and scoot around the corner of the building. A bunch of teenaged girls who look as though they might be on a school trip from out of town are leaning against the wall, passing a cell phone back and forth between them and talking to somebody called Rick. While one talks, the other three giggle and roll their eyes. I look back past them towards the entrance, but I can't spot anyone I remotely recognize. Even so, I think, as I hitch my bag up on to my shoulder, I'll thread in and out of Freshfields before walking the six blocks north to Benjy's garage.

'Doll,' Benjy says when he sees me standing in the machine bay, 'what's shakin'?' He's bent over the engine of a BMW, and he looks at me sideways so when he raises his eyebrows it looks as if they might shoot right off his face. 'What're you doin' here on a beautiful day like this? You wreck your wheels altogether this time?' I shake my head. I've made a decision to trust him, and I hope that I'm right.

'Benjy,' I say, 'I need a favor.'

He straightens up and looks at me, his eyes riveted by my hair.

'For you, Miss Cheap,' he says, 'anything. Whadda you need? A new Bose stereo, no questions asked?' He smiles when he says it, but I know that he's heard something in my voice, that he scents trouble and his antennae are up.

'Not quite,' I say. 'I need to rent a car from you. Something with out of state plates.'

Benjy looks at me for a minute, and I look straight back at him. I can see him start to ask me what's going on, and then he changes his mind. He wipes his hands down the front of his incredibly filthy boiler suit and says, 'How long are we talkin' here?'

I shrug.

'I'm not sure,' I say. 'Maybe a week, maybe two. I'd have to let you know.'

'But not months?' Benjy says.

'No, nothing like that.' Unless I'm dead, I think. In which case you'll probably get the car back anyways. Benjy considers me again for a second and then he says, 'You need it for now?' His eyes go to the bag at my feet, and I nod. 'OK,' he says. 'Lemme see.'

The bulletin board behind Benjy's desk is covered in old bills and receipts and flyers from pizza places and Chinese take-outs. He stares at it for a second, looking for something in the hanging mess of paper, and then he spots it and grabs a set of car keys. He turns to me and holds them up and grins.

'Who loves ya, baby?' Benjy says.

The car is an old model pale blue Ford Taurus wagon that's parked behind his building. It's completely nondescript and, even better, it has Illinois plates.

'She's got some dings,' Benjy says, 'but she runs good.' He bangs the hood of the car with the flat of his hand as if to prove this. 'I got her for my sister's kid when she went off to Northwestern. I mean, a kid can't go to college these days without a car, right? Anyways,' he says, 'the kid's on junior year abroad or some kinda thing. You know, livin' with a French family, learnin' to eat snails. My sister's that pissed she wouldn't go to Italy.' He hands me the keys. 'You get stopped, you just say she's your god-daughter, or your niece, or something. Registration's in the glove compartment.'

'Thank you,' I say. 'I'll be careful with it, I promise.'

'Hey, I can use the cash.'

I reach for my check book that I have ready in the pocket of my jacket, but when he sees it, Benjy waves it away.

'I don't know what my rental rate is yet,' he says. 'I'll think about it while you're gone.' Then he looks at me, and this time his face is serious. 'Just tell me one thing. You in trouble bad, Miss Cheap?'

I nod and swallow. Suddenly I'm afraid that if I actually try to say anything I'll start to cry.

'This got anything to do with the perv who wrote on your door?'

'I think so,' I manage to say. Benjy nods and takes my duffel bag from me without asking and throws it into the back seat of the station wagon. Then he opens the driver's door and holds it for me.

'You need anything else?' he asks. 'You got money?'

'I got money,' I say, and for the first time we both smile.

'Good,' Benjy says. 'Money's good.'

I get in the car and he closes the door. The ignition turns over on the first try, and I roll down the window.

'Benjy,' I say, 'I can't tell you how much I appreciate this, but if anybody comes here, if anybody, even the police ask—' Benjy lays his index finger by the side of his nose.

'I never saw you,' he says.

The water in the shower at the Paoli Holiday Inn is hot and I turn the pressure all the way up. I pour too much shampoo into the palm of my hand, I'm still not used to my brush cut, and I rub it hard into my hair, causing a great froth of bubbles to wash down over my body, and cascade off my shoulders as if I'm in a car wash. I scratch the top of my head on purpose. I dig my nails into my scalp and rake my fingers down my neck so when I dry off there'll be red marks on my mottled skin.

I'm trying to make my body kick back against this weight that's descended on it like a virus. I have to jolt myself out of numbness. I'm fighting the rabbit reaction, the desire to freeze in the face of a predator, just to hunker down and hope that you don't get killed.

Before I got into the shower I made myself do thirty push-ups. Then I did the same number of sit-ups. I want my arms to hurt and my stomach muscles to ache. If I could have turned the television up and screamed as loud as I could without attracting undue attention, I would have, just to feel the air going in and out of my lungs, just to know that I can still make that much noise. Instead I walked up and down the length of the room. I flexed my fingers as if they were claws.

When I get out of the shower the room smells like Italian food. I stopped somewhere at a strip mall, one of those nondescript, interchangeable places that are made up of acres of movie theaters and Pier Ones and Bloomingdales' stores, and drove around until I found a branch of the Olive Garden Restaurant. There's almost always one in places like those, and I was so hungry that I thought about actually sitting down and eating right there. But Paoli is the sort of commuter suburb where I just might run into someone I know, and I didn't dare take the risk, so I ordered take-out.

Besides, I'd already spotted the Holiday Inn out on the highway, and I wanted to get locked into a room where I could take the time to figure out what the Hell I was going to do next.

I know that the first thing I have to do is take care of Jake. He's OK where he is right now, but I can't leave him at the Penn Veterinary School forever, and it isn't safe for him to stay with me. I sit down on the bed with a towel wrapped around me and pick through the remains of a 'Viva Italiana Antipasto Selection', and think that that is one of the things I hate the most, the fact that I have to be without Jake. Then I pull the phone book towards me, and start making the only arrangements I can think of that will keep him safe. Protecting myself, I think, is going to be a lot more tricky. All I can say so far, is that I'm pretty sure no one followed me to Benjy's, or here. That means that at least I've bought myself some time, so I may have a slight advantage over my opponent in this game. Now all I have to do is figure out how to use it.

Sometime around our junior year in high school Uncle Ritchie taught Marina and me how to play chess. I remember that, even at the time, the gift was unexpected. I found it strange and a little alarming that my perpetually overalled and overweight uncle, who seemed more interested in the workings of his John Deere than he did in the people who surrounded him, should be the keeper of such arcane knowledge. In teaching us the opening gambits, the moves of knights, and pawns, and Queens, Uncle Ritchie revealed an aptitude for strategy, and for devious and forward thinking, that neither of us had ever suspected he possessed.

Needless to say, Marina was better at the game than I was, at least initially. When it came to both the required concentration and the necessary ruthlessness, she was a natural. To be fair, every time she beat me, she went back and explained how she'd done it. Just as if she was winding back a film, my sister could reconstruct the board and point out to me exactly where I'd made the one irretrievable move that had led to my downfall.

At first, I was amazed at how early in the game these gaffes could take place, and how inconsequential they could seem at the time. It seemed almost unbelievable to me, on re-examination, that in the wake of one of these cataclysmic moves I could have continued to play, and even, sometimes, to suffer the delusion that I was winning when, in fact, the whole situation was irretrievable and the game was already over.

Over time, however, and with Marina's tutelage, I got better. I learnt the lessons she taught me, and I came to understand the two things that she had always known instinctively: that no move was inconsequential, and that in order to win you had to take control of the board.

Kathleen Harper's words have gone around and around in my head. 'Determined', that was the exact term that she had used, she said that after Marina came back from Georgia that last time she was both smug and determined. I thought of this while I was doing push-ups; I repeated the word in time to my own motion, broke the syllables down, and recited them in my head, as if they were the beats of a metronome.

At first, the significance of Kathleen's phrasing, of her exact terminology had escaped me. I had assumed that what she was describing was merely my sister's ordinary knowing confidence and stubbornness, the all too familiar sight of Marina digging her heels in. It was exactly the sort of response that she would have had in the face of garbage being strewn all over her garden, so I had assumed that what Kathleen had told me was nothing out of the ordinary, but now I suspect that I was wrong.

Now, I suspect that something happened on Marina's last trip back to Georgia. Something that she either knew I would understand, or wanted to ask me about. Something that caused her both to feel smug, and to try to call me one last time. Something that made her believe that she could take control of the board.

This feels like the hardest thing that I have ever had to do, even though I know it isn't. It isn't as hard as burying Momma, or seeing Marina on that mortuary slab, or watching George walk away through the yellowing glow of a street lamp, his step already jaunty in the anticipation of the Sainte Chapelle, and copies of *Le Monde*.

But somehow I was prepared for those. This feels as if it's snuck up on me out of nowhere. Last night even the Holiday Inn room had seemed empty without the slight rattle of Jake's snoring, or the sound of him padding across carpets, and when, in the early hours of this morning, I was jolted out of sleep into the too still darkness of a strange room, it had taken moments before I realized that it was not an unknown presence, but an absence that had set off the alarm bells in my head. It was the fact that I could not hear the soft, shifting sound of Jake's body or catch the gleam of his yellow eye in the shadows that had pulled me out of my dreams with an undertow of loneliness so profound and so frightening that I had felt tears welling, and had had to turn on the light and sit up in bed clutching a balled Kleenex, reassuring myself that I still existed.

Now I bury my face in Jake's ruff, and he's embarrassed. He doesn't like to be held this close and he turns his face away, as if I'm doing something vaguely shameful. He wriggles away from me, and when I look up I see the sun filtering through maple trees, pouring a thick, golden syrup of lights across the afternoon. Leaves drop. Red and languid, they ride on the warm air and scatter themselves across the tasteful gravel parking lot. The Val Marie Kennels are way up in the Brandywine Valley, over an hour from Philly. It's a place that specializes in highly strung gun dogs, setters and pointers that need to be spoken to and stroked and walked on a regular basis when their parents are away, and it's where I'm going to leave Jake, maybe for the last time.

This is where Dr Gurewich recommended when I called him from the Holiday Inn yesterday afternoon and explained that I needed somewhere to leave Jake, maybe for as long as a few weeks. I think in some crazy part of my mind, I had hoped that Dr Gurewich would offer to take Jake himself, that he would say in his stilted European accent, 'But Miss deBreem, I will take care of your beautiful dog', and that he would actually mean 'But Miss deBreem, I will take care of you.'

That's how desperate I'm getting. I'm clinging to a fantasy about a vet at the Penn Animal Hospital because he's a doctor, if only a dog one, and his pseudo-Freud accent reminds me of Elena, and right now he's about the only person I can think of who might not be trying to kill me.

'Get a grip on yourself, Susannah,' I mutter aloud, and I snap Jake's leash on and start towards the newly painted red door that has a sign on the outside in the shape of a dog's head that reads 'Office'. Despite my best efforts, when we go up the steps and into the nice wood paneled room, I feel queasy. When this woman who is getting up from behind a desk and smiling at me reaches out and takes Jake's leash, I will feel as if I'm letting go of everything.

I sign the papers, and hand her his medical records, and I even smile. Then we go outside, and I hand Jake over, and stand beside the rented car and watch her walk him away down a path that leads towards a fenced-in set of runs. Jake looks back at me just once before he disappears. Then I feel as if I'm falling, as if I'm spinning in the darkness, as if, like Alice, I'm going down, down, down the rabbit hole.

EIGHTEEN

The house is shadowed and smaller than I remember it. Momma's lawn is spangled with dew, and puddles have formed in the driveway, so I guess it must have rained earlier. I stop the car on the far side of the dirt road and kill the engine and the silence around me seems total. I stick my hand through the open window. The air lies in my palm as soft and as thick as cashmere. No wind moves through the ropey, overgrown stalks that litter Uncle Ritchie's old field. In this suspended hour that comes between late afternoon and early dusk I feel as if I've entered a dreamworld, a place where the past winds on and on, and never reaches the present.

I'm tempted to turn the key again. I'm tempted to put my foot down and rev the engine, to back into the driveway, spinning my wheels and throwing up a plume of mud, before I turn and race down the road, back out towards the interstate, making for Louisiana and the gulf beyond Baton Rouge, or for the riotous noise and the fine decay of New Orleans. I could lose myself in either of those places. I could change my name, and erase my life. I could bury my trail – until whoever it is that cut Marina into pieces and tried to poison Jake picks it up again.

I open the car door and step out gingerly, as if I'm afraid that the ground might give way under my feet. Then I stand looking at the house that I was born in. My eyes slide along the porch rails, and across the clouded glass panes of the front door, and travel upwards as if by their own volition, searching for the tiniest movement, for the twitch of a curtain, or the half-motion of a drawn shade, anything that will betray the shadow of my sister, that will reveal her, looking down on me from the bedroom window where I left her standing fifteen years ago.

I got drunk last night, well and truly, in a ground floor room of a Red Roof Inn, one of those places by an exit on the interstate. I drank a cheap bottle of red wine, the kind that makes your head throb and dries the back of your tongue out so it feels like fur when you wake in the early hours of the morning. Anger drove me to it, I suppose. Just like I was a teenager again, or a truculent college student, I threw one last petulant tantrum on the highway going south.

Before I finally fell asleep, tangled in cheap sheets and drifting on the endless hum of the room fan, I got up and went into the bathroom. The walls were white-tiled, and as antiseptic as an operating theater, and the glass of water that I poured myself was almost fizzy and tasted faintly of sulfur. I caught my own eye in the mirror as I raised it to my mouth, and the face that looked back at me was narrow and mean.

'Don't gloat,' I said, and my voice was thick, 'you've got what you want.' A second later, while Marina was still looking back at me, I put the glass down and pointed at her, and said, 'Congratulations, you win. Game. Set. Match. I'm coming home.' And the flicker of a triumphant little smile played across her face.

The mailbox is tilted, as if someone has whacked at it half-heartedly with a baseball bat. As I step past it I reach instinctively to push it upright and my fingers meet the outlines of raised letters that still read 'de-Breem'. This seems strange to me, since we haven't lived here for a long time.

As I walk down the drive I can see that the garage door has new hinges. They're still shiny and silver against the graying wood. Although it's overgrown, it hasn't been too long since Momma's main flower bed that runs up the side of the front lawn has been edged in big, painted white, rocks. As I get closer to the house, I can see that a new bluestone square has been laid under the outside faucet by the kitchen door, and the step has been replaced too. The wood is still raw and pale, and now it's staining: the sides are riven with dark threads of damp because it never got painted.

For one terrible moment it occurs to me that maybe the Herveys have sold the place or rented it out, and that someone is living here, that even now they are watching me from inside, or may be about to drive in. Any second they might come back from the Piggly Wiggly or Food Fayre. They might get home from work in good time to make dinner and find me standing here. Then I look at the lawn, which is long and crab grassy, and at the puddles in the drive, and at the mailbox. I notice the padlock looped through a chain on the garage door, and I know it isn't true. The place hasn't been sold and the Herveys haven't rented it. No one is living here. No one has lived here since Marina was killed. The improvements that I'm seeing were hers.

All at once I can see her here, shed of her expensive city clothes and crouched in the driveway, spray painting rocks to line Momma's flower bed. She must have planted it too. She must have bought trays of pansies and marigolds from the hardware store, because, sure enough, when I go over to the bed and part the thicket of weeds that have grown up there I can make out the heart shaped leaves of black-eyed Susans, and the thick woody stems of peonies. A bramble rose snags my finger, and creeping out across the white stones I see the snaky stems of a clematis whose trellis has collapsed or been taken away. The blue star of its flower rests beside my shoe in the damp grass.

The porch must have been painted too, sometime in the autumn, or in the first days of that early spring before she died. When I run my hand along the railing it feels almost soft, and the ridges of brush marks trapped in the thick paint ripple and read like braille underneath my fingers. The glider is gone, but there's a jute doormat in the shape of a fancy flat knot outside the front door, and as I round the corner of the porch, I can see, even after eighteen months of semi-neglect, that Marina had been at work here too.

The chicken wire fence around Momma's vegetable garden is relatively new, and, although clover weed has covered the vegetable rows, as I walk down the fence I can make out a tangle of squash and cucumber vines that lurk at the bottom of the garden. They've twisted themselves against the wire, and their now dead tendrils still grab at it, as if they've been frozen, caught in the act of climbing desperately.

She must have worked here when she came down from Alexandria. She must have hoed, and tilled, and dug. The thought seems utterly bizarre, since I cannot once remember Marina evincing any interest in the garden when we were children, and yet at the same time, I know that it's true. I can sense her here as strongly as if she is standing behind me. In this silent, dying light, I can see her.

My sneakers and the bottoms of my jeans are sodden from the long grass, but even so, I pick my way towards the back of the house. I know now that nothing I see here will be new. I understand that everything that Marina did was an effort to keep things just as they had been. The peonies will still be next to the roses, and behind the locked doors of the garage, the rake, and the pointed spade, and the short handled pitch fork will still be hanging from the nails that Uncle Ritchie drove into the back wall one Sunday afternoon thirty years ago. This was my sister's secret life. She was recreating the past. Month after month and year after year she labored to turn back time.

The pines that edge the back lawn and spread out behind the garage have grown dense and they block out what light there is left and throw a long cold wall of shadow. The back windows of the house reflect the trees, and have turned black and staring. They're shiny, like ice, and anything could be behind them. It occurs to me suddenly that I have no idea how long I've been here. The warm, thick air seems to have thinned and turned chilly, and it's almost dark. A tingling feeling runs through my shoulders, as if someone's breathed on the back of my neck, and all at once I want to be back in the car, with the doors locked and the radio on.

I'm tempted to run, to fling myself forwards and sprint up past the kitchen door and down the driveway, groping for my keys and not looking back, but instead I make myself walk slowly, as if I don't care, as if with sheer bravado I can stare down the ghosts that lurk here.

The bank of lilies that has always been against the garage wall is thick and dense in front of me. It's grown wild and unruly without supervision. A couple of pointy orange blooms are still hanging on, this late in October, and they almost glow against the inky dark green of the foliage. The lily bank is now so thick and wide that the path has been swallowed and bodies could be hidden in there just as easily as snakes. I stop and realize that it will be impossible to pass through without losing sight of my feet, without the spiky tips of the flowers fingering my jeans. For just a second I look back, and over my shoulder I can see that the darkness has gathered and thickened in the pines. I tell myself not to be ridiculous, but, even so I don't want to walk back through the shadows behind the house. Out on the road I can see the pale gleam of the Taurus. It's maybe a minute away from me.

I don't take my eyes off the white shapes of my sneakers as they rise and then disappear, sinking down into the wet tangle of the leaves. I place each foot carefully, and then lift the other quickly. Intent on not tripping, I continue in this kind of high-step until I'm past the edge of the garage, so it's not until then that I look up and see the figure standing in the driveway.

It's a silhouette really. Just a solid shape between me and the car. I can't tell if it's a man or a woman, and I can't hear anything, no sound of footsteps, no engine in the road. Then a voice that I don't recognize says, 'Hey, girlfriend. Long time, no see.'

'I don't understand how you knew it was me.'

I sound more petulant than I mean to, and I smile to cover it up. I'm not sure if the whiny edge in my voice is because I'm tired, or because I just had the shit scared out of me, or because I never particularly liked Della Hervey in the first place and now I resent the fact that I'm sitting in her kitchen. My first instinct, when I figured out who it was who had snuck up on me, was to slap her. That, of course, was just adrenaline, and would have been pretty stupid, since, technically, it was her property I was sneaking around in the dark. Even so, I don't like the idea that Della's caught me red-handed, that she's seen me so obviously terrified. And I hate being called 'girlfriend'. By anyone.

In Della's case it's particularly inappropriate, since when we were teenagers Della was Marina's special friend, not mine. Of course, that didn't really mean that Marina liked her either. It just meant that Della could be easily deployed as a weapon for Marina to use against me when she felt like it. Now, watching Della as she fiddles with a coffee filter, I can remember the two of them sitting on the bus a few seats ahead of me.

In this very second, I can hear Marina and Della whispering together. Their shoulders shake as they giggle. Then they twist around to look at me. They crane their necks, making sure that I understand that I am being left out.

I hated Della on those afternoons, and later I would get my revenge on her by generously providing the wrong answers when she asked me for help on her math homework. She was thin back then, a pale girl with round brown eyes and the kind of fawn colored hair that bleaches almost to white in the summer time. She was always getting sunburned or having nose bleeds, and I also recall that she was remarkably stupid. So it really does annoy me that she managed to recognize me, given that it was dark, and that I've dyed my hair and all but shaved my head, and that we haven't laid eyes on each other in fifteen years.

Irritation is fizzing inside me. It's all I can do to sit still. I can't figure out if I'm exhausted, or if being here, sitting in the Herveys' old kitchen, which doesn't seem to have changed one iota since we were little, is just freaking me out in general. Upstairs I can hear a television playing, and it reassures me. In my frazzled mind it seems somehow less likely that Della's going to turn around and beat me over the head with a rolling pin while her kids are sitting upstairs watching some Baptist cartoon station or the Pokémon movie.

'Are you OK?' Della asks. I realize that she's been looking at me, watching me as if I'm an interesting and potentially dangerous animal that's wandered into her kitchen. I smile, way too brightly.

'Oh sure,' I say. 'It was a long drive. You know.' I

start to finger the heavy glass salt and pepper shakers that flank the paper napkin dispenser on the table. Della nods.

'Well,' she says, 'you know, I think I'd just know you anywhere, Shoo.' I guess she means this as a compliment, the same way that she probably means to be friendly by using my baby name. 'You know how it is,' Della says gravely, 'with people you grew up with and all.' Then, before I can say that I don't, she turns back to the coffee machine and flips a switch, and in just a second there's the dribbling sound of water and the whole room starts to smell like Maxwell House.

I could hardly get out of the invitation to 'visit' after she found me standing in the driveway. She told me walking back up the road about how she'd married some guy from Louisiana one summer twelve years ago, and how after that her parents had let them buy the farm cheap so they could go on down to Florida where her aunt and uncle already had a place on the Gulf. 'My husband, he's gone now,' Della had said as we walked through the dusk and turned the corner so we could see the lights of the Herveys' old house. 'My brother, Tommy, you remember him? He was older than us. He does the farm, but we kept the house, the kids and I,' she had added, as though this was the best that could be said for her marriage.

The kitchen's quiet. Della moves without making a sound. She doesn't crinkle paper, or knock into things, or bang the mugs that she's reaching for down on the counter. Even the drawers she opens and closes don't make any noise. She's over-careful, almost stealthy in her movements, and it's making me nervous.

'So what are your kids' names?' I ask. The question's inane, and I think she's told me anyways, but I forgot.

'Shelby, he's ten,' she says as she's reaching for a bag of Oreo cookies and arranging them in a circle on a plate. 'And Karen. She's eight, and looks just like her Daddy.'

'That's nice,' I say, even though I suspect that it isn't.

'Uh huh.' Della nods and puts the plate on the table. 'They go to our old school and everything.' She smiles at me. 'They even ride the bus, remember?'

'Oh, sure.' I smile back.

'I used to be so jealous of you,' Della says suddenly. She's still smiling, as though this is joyous news. 'You two, with your long red hair. The way you could wear it in a big long braid and tie a ribbon on the end. I was so jealous of that.' Before I can stop it, my hand rises to my head, and Della starts to laugh. 'I'm sorry,' she says, 'but it is just not how I think of you. You look sort of like a porcupine, Shoo. Like you did that time when you came home from college. Except now it's black.' I can't really think of anything to say, so I reach for an Oreo while Della giggles.

'Guess you knew me anyways, though,' I say after I've eaten my cookie.

'I guess so,' Della says. 'It's the way you stand, and walk, or something. I don't know. I just – well, when I saw you coming through those lilies, I knew it had to be you. Nobody else was ever so terrified of those darned things.'

Della's body has thickened. She's not fat, exactly, just wider. She looks as if she's been somehow compressed, as if someone put a weight on the top of her head, and as a result things were forced to grow sideways instead of up. I can remember this look. It's as familiar as a smell, or an old piece of clothes. Momma always said that one of two things happen to farmers' wives. They either get whip thin and hard, so the sinews on their arms and necks stand out like wires under the skin, or else they muscle up. They turn solid and broad, like stones.

'I knew you'd be comin' anyways,' Della is saying. She's still smiling at me. 'You know, after Marina died, and all that stuff. I knew you'd show up here someday. So, when the kids said they saw a strange car over there, I thought I'd better go take a look. It's almost like I've been expecting you. People always seem to come home.'

She slides a mug that has 'Got Milk?' written on it across the table towards me, and then she sits down and reaches for the sugar bowl.

'So,' she asks, 'how long are you here for?'

I realize that I'm staring at her again, and I have to force myself to answer.

'Oh, a day or two,' I say, trying to keep my tone matter of fact. 'I've got work down in Florida, and I decided to drive. I thought it would be nice to see the place again.'

Della nods, as if this confirms something. She's stirring her coffee, and I can't figure out if she knows that I'm lying. I'm afraid that any minute now she's going to ask me what I'm doing here, exactly, but the idea doesn't seem to occur to her, and instead she jumps up and opens one of the kitchen drawers. When she sits down again she pushes a set of keys on a pink plastic key ring towards me.

'For the house,' she says. 'You can stay in it if you want.'

The idea is so awful that I laugh. It's a kind of barking noise and it's embarrassing, so I reach for another cookie and make sure my fingers avoid the key ring.

'So you haven't rented it or anything?' I ask. Della shakes her head and takes the Oreo I'm handing her. She peels it open and bites one half.

'No,' she says. 'It was the land, really. The well. The water. That's what we wanted. We owned everything on either side of it. Anyways, Tommy says maybe Shel might want to live in it one day. Or Karen. That would be nice, wouldn't it?'

Actually, I can't imagine anything worse, but I'm grateful that they bought the place off me so fast, so I keep my mouth shut.

'I haven't changed too much in there,' Della's saying, as if I might be worried about that. 'It's pretty much the way Marina left it. I mean, I threw food out of the freezer and stuff. That was kind of a shame, because I'm sure a lot of it was expensive, but the kids won't eat that fancy stuff. You know, asparagus, and stuff like that. They're real plain. And I wouldn't know what to do with those things anyways. Tommy goes and checks around in there every once in a while. We have some trouble with kids. You know.'

'Yeah,' I say. 'I saw the mailbox.' Della nods. She drains her mug and gets up to reach for the coffee again.

'That,' she says, 'and a few broken windows, at first. Nothing really. They tell each other it's haunted, you know, like they see lights and things, but mostly they're 'fraidy cats and stay away. The video place in town is more interesting. You seen it yet?' She's offering me coffee, but I shake my head, and so she pours some more for herself.

'No,' I say. 'I haven't been into town yet. I figured I'd maybe go in tomorrow. Is the Coachstop still around?'

'With bells on,' says Della, 'and just the same. We got a new high school, the old one's offices now, if you can believe that, and there's the video place, but there's not too much to shock you. I don't think you'll get lost. Some of the old people are still around too. Well, most of 'em, really.'

'Like who?'

'Oh, I don't know,' Della says. 'Everybody, pretty much. BethAnn works in the bank. Dex Eames, he got married and owns the new pharmacy, and a couple of years ago he bought a food place too. He's done pretty well. Sonny comes back, from time to time. His Mom's still alive, but they don't have the farm anymore.'

'Don't tell me,' I say, 'you and Tommy bought them out?'

I mean it as sort of a joke, but Della says, 'Oh, no. It went to some new people. Tom would have trouble working this place and the Delrays' too. Only kind of help we can get is those migrant workers. They come all the way up from Mexico, and they don't even speak English.'

'Did you see Marina much?'

The question's out before I even meant to ask it and it's a second before Della replies, as if she's afraid that I might break down in tears, or that there might be a right or a wrong answer to this. Finally she picks up her half eaten Oreo and shakes her head.

'No,' she says. 'Not really.'

'But you guys were such good friends.' Della looks at me for a minute and then she takes a tiny bite out of her cookie.

'A few years back, four or five,' she says, 'I tried to be friendly, you know, when she came down, but she was real stand-offish. I just got the feeling she wanted to be alone.' The hurt's burrowed itself deep behind Della's face, but when she speaks I can see it move. It brushes the surface of her eyes like a fish rising from deep water.

'I'm sorry,' I say.

For a horrible second I think that Della's going to cry. There's no sound in the room. There's nothing between us except the distant echo of a cartoon gun being fired and some theme music, and then Della swallows her cookie and looks at me.

'You know, Susannah,' she says, 'even though I was mean to you sometimes, I never bought that stuff.'

'What stuff?' I have no idea what she's talking about.

'About you and Marina.' Della's voice has quickened and gotten louder. 'All that stuff about how you two were just alike. "Two peas in a pod".' She does a surprisingly good imitation of my mother as she says it. 'That was crap,' Della announces. A slight flush is creeping up her cheeks. 'Excuse my French, but I knew that even then. You were the nice one.' She is waving her hands in the air now, as if she's batting at imaginary flies. 'Oh, I know, you could fool Sonny Delray,' she says. 'You could make him kiss either one of you until he didn't know which was which, but you didn't fool me. I knew. She was mean. That Marina was just plain dirty mean, and they're the worst kind.'

I start to stand up. I try not to push the chair back because I don't want to make any noise. My mouth has gone dry and the sweetness from the Oreo is sticking to my tongue.

'Della,' I say slowly, 'I have to go.' There's a loud crack from the television upstairs and both of us jump. The chair almost tips over, but I grab it with one hand and reach for the keys with the other.

'Goodness!' Della exclaims. She shakes her head and laughs. 'Look at the time. I've got to make dinner. Will you be OK walking back? Do I need to drive you?'

'No, no,' I say, and in two steps I'm at the kitchen door. 'Thanks for the coffee,' I add. 'I'll see you.' The knob is slightly stiff, but it gives under my hand, and I step out on to the back porch just before Della reaches me. She looks as though she's about to try to give me a hug, or pat my shoulder, but I dive down the steps before she has a chance. When I look back, she's a solid bulk against the light.

'You take as long as you want now,' she says, 'at the house. And don't be a stranger!' Then she waves and closes the door.

For a second I stand there, staring at the house as if it might move, or as if something might jump off the porch at me. I can see Della moving inside the kitchen, but the rest of the windows are dark, except for one upstairs where the lights from the TV flicker and shift against the ceiling. In my pocket I can feel the keys. I finger them, and grasp the smooth-edged lozenge of the tag. Then I take a few steps backwards, and by the time I turn around I'm running. I'm out of Della's drive and into the road. I'm flying. I'm hitting pot holes, and stumbling and recovering, and running as fast as I've ever run in my life, while my eyes search out the road, fasten on its dark strip that splits the fields and disappears into the high, solid band of the woods.

NINETEEN

In the clear light of day, of course, the house looks perfectly ordinary. The first morning sun is spreading across the roof, and it's early enough that the white porch railings are still faintly tinged with pink. I've been up since before dawn, and by now the idea that I'm miraculously going to unearth some key piece of evidence seems absurd. I feel like I should just drive back up to Della's, and put the keys in the mailbox before anyone's awake. Then I should go off to Sea Island, or to Savannah. I could go to the beach. I could watch the sun set over the water and go out to dinner, and in the daytime I could look at nice houses. The idea is tempting, and maybe I'll even do it, but the pink plastic key ring in my hand is exerting a pull of its own. It's drawing me up the front path, and willing me on to the porch, and after all, it seems pretty dumb not even to go inside, since I've driven all this way.

The lock on the front door is stiff and refuses to turn, and finally I give it up and go around to the kitchen. The dew hasn't burnt off yet, and I leave dark little footprints on the raw wood of the step. I decide that maybe Della gave me the wrong keys, and that if the door doesn't open right away I'll leave. I'm actually half-hoping that this will happen when the key slides into the lock and turns instantly and the door swings open as if it's been recently oiled.

I have no idea what I thought it would be like, but the first thing I notice is that the house smells different. I hadn't realized it I guess, the way you don't miss things until they're gone, but when my mother was alive it always smelled slightly of ginger. Even if bacon or fish or something else was cooking, there was always an overlay of spice. It's gone now, and the place smells empty. There's a cool, disused feeling about it. Without even stepping into the kitchen, you can tell that nobody lives in this house anymore.

Blinds are pulled down over the windows, and I realize that this must have been what made them look so blank and empty last night. The curtains have been taken down, and I can imagine Della doing this. I can imagine her slipping them off the rails and piling them in a laundry basket to take home. I can see her ironing them and folding them and packing them away in plastic sleeves in case Shelby or Karen wants to use them someday.

I open a couple of the cabinets, but they're empty. The food's all been taken away, just like Della said, and the red flowered contact paper has been wiped clean. I close the cupboard quickly, and yank a drawer open. There are a couple of old wooden spoons and a can opener inside, and I rattle them, and then bang the drawer closed, which makes me feel better. A radio/CD player is sitting on the counter, but when I try to switch it on it's dead, which makes sense, since the Herveys would hardly keep the electricity on in a house that nobody lives in. The phone is dead too. There's no sound on the line, but I stand there for a second anyways, holding it to my ear like a kid pretending to make phone calls. Then I lift the window blind with one finger and through the crack I can see the garage wall and the lilies, and I think that this must have been where Marina was standing when she called me that last time.

'What were you going to tell me?' I start to ask her, but I stop the words in mid-sentence when I realize that I'm speaking out loud.

There's a jar on the window sill full of pens and a couple of paper flowers on green wire stems that I think I made. Marina and I went through a heavy duty origami phase when we were about twelve, and neither of us ever really outgrew it. When they finally let me clean out her townhouse, her desk drawers were full of little white paper swans and animals. They must have been her form of doodling while she was talking on the phone: her answer to hearts, and arrows hitting bullseyes, and endless shaded chains of interlinking squares. There's what I recognize as one of her creations tacked to the wall above the phone, and I put the silent receiver back and reach for it. It's a red and white flower, and it's only when I untack it and let it unfold in my hand that I see that it's a menu from a Chinese restaurant. I fold it back up and stick it in my pocket.

I don't know what I expected, but somehow it wasn't this. I thought somebody would be living here, that I'd have to stand on the step and ask nicely if I could come in, and that when I did everything would be changed. I didn't expect this strange, hollowed out shell still littered with the pointless bits and pieces of our past. I imagined the rooms alive, and I imagined noise: a radio, TV, kids. I imagined that I would have to peel back the layers of someone's new life in order to get a glimpse of our old one. I didn't think it would be presented to me quite so whole. Or quite so dead.

As far as I can tell, Marina didn't change anything in the living room either. The two couches are still here, and the matching armchairs, and my mother's old rolltop desk. White shades are pulled down the same as the kitchen, so the light is thick and murky. It makes me feel as if I'm underwater, as if I'm swimming in a big aquarium or a tank, a fishbowl where, instead of shipwrecks and mermaids' castles, the whole of my childhood is strewn across the fake ocean floor.

When I sit in Momma's desk chair and open the top drawer, I see her glasses looking up at me. They still have a goofy-looking sort of fake blue crystal chain attached to them, and underneath are a couple of pictures in frames. They're of us: of Marina and me, and of Grandma, and Uncle Ritchie, and Momma. They used to sit on top of the desk in a row, and I guess Della must have dusted them and put them away in case anybody wanted them later. I thought that there was another one too, one of Marina and me in our tutus and ballet shoes, but I can't see it. It probably got lost a long time ago. I can hardly believe that anyone will mind if I take them, and so I drop the pictures into my bag, along with Momma's glasses, and then I slide the rolltop up and it makes a clacking sound, like a train running on tracks.

I assume that the police went through it after Marina was killed, because there's no phone book here, or date book, or anything like that. I know that they came down and looked around, but Mark Cope told me that they didn't find anything useful. There's a stack of envelopes that are curling a little, and a couple of flyers in one of the pigeon holes. One's from a garden center and has a few things circled in red on it, and there's another take-out menu. This one's from somewhere called Red's. 'Easter Special,' it says, 'Ham Dinner and Biscuits, Two for One!' A couple of dishes are underlined, and across the top Marina's written what looks like 'Halibut', so maybe she was trying to get them to send her a special order. I wonder if she persuaded them, or if it wasn't on the menu so they told her to get lost. The idea makes me smile a little, which is mean, but I've always liked biscuits, so I fold the leaflet into a tulip and stick it in my pocket too.

There used to be carpet on the stairs, but for some reason it's been taken up. I suspect that that was one of Marina's improvements. I'm pretty sure that we thought it was ugly, and it might even have been one of the things she was talking about on the afternoon after the funeral when she suggested that the two of us could live here forever in perfect domestic bliss. The polished wooden steps are steeper than I recall, and without the carpet they're slippery. The tenth step creaks loudly, just like it always did. I can imagine Marina stamping on it every night on her way up to bed, just for auld lang syne.

The upstairs hall is almost totally dark. There's a colored shade as thick as a black-out blind pulled down over the single window, and I trip on the edge of the hall runner. For the first time, I feel the hair on the back of my neck stand up a little, and even though I tell myself not to be silly, I also think that after I've taken just one look at Momma's room, I'll leave. Then

I bang into the hall dresser, which I'd completely forgotten about. There's a crashing noise of something breaking, and just in time I catch one of a pair of antique hurricane lanterns before it hits the floor.

I remember them now, they were pretty, with etched glass funnels, and so was the glass plate that sat between them. It, however, is in two pieces at my feet. My eyes have adjusted by now and I can see well enough to pick it up. I think it might have been my grandmother's, and I feel a sudden flash of irritation. Why the Hell doesn't Della change this place around. Or sell all this stuff. Or give it to the Morgan Memorial. Or something? I'll suggest it when I drop off the keys. I'll tell her it's fine, and that nobody will care. I'll suggest she get one of those charities that come and clean out old houses and auction stuff off and keep the proceeds – if she isn't in jail. If Mark Cope doesn't come down and arrest her for cutting Marina into itty-bitty pieces with a carving knife. I put the two halves of the plate back and kind of push them together, hoping nobody will notice.

Momma's room is just the same too, although, thank God, none of her clothes are hanging in the closet. Marina must have gotten rid of those, but, I think waspishly, probably not before she'd taken to wearing them around the house. Some dust sheets have been thrown over the furniture, which is at least slightly more normal for an abandoned house, but it gives me the creeps anyways, and I decide that I've had enough of this. I don't know what I thought I was doing here in the first place, or what I thought I'd find. All our old papers, if there are any, will probably be up in the attic, and I am definitely not going up there. Mark Cope can come down and do it. He can go rooting for clues. It's his job.

I close the door to Momma's room, and I'm on my way down the hall when I stop. The door to our room is closed, and I want to walk past it, but I can't. It's as if she might be standing behind it, as if I can hear her moving on the other side of this thin panel of wood. I almost call out to her over time, whisper her name in this darkened hallway, as if the nightspinning might still work. Then, with a kind of detached interest, I watch my hand as it reaches out and slowly turns the knob.

There are no dust sheets in here. It looks as if I could have walked out and left for Chapel Hill yesterday. Our beds are still on either side of the room, and our matching bureaus, and our desks and chairs. The cushions that our Grandma made are in the window seat, and a thin strip of sunlight creeps through the edge of the blind and makes a stripe across one of her ugly afghans that's folded there. I run my hand down the quilt of my old bed, and plump the pillow.

The bulletin board above Marina's desk is empty. There are brighter squares and patches where things must have hung before the police, or someone else, took them away. Mine still has stuff on it, and I get a better look, I see some drawings that I must have done in high school. There's a pastel of flowers. A galloping horse. There's a photograph of my mother, and of Grandma, and there are a couple of pale patches here too, although I can't remember what they might have been. The police must have thought they might have held a clue and taken them away. There's a tack on the board in the shape of a daisy, and buttons that say,

'I Believe Anita', and 'Solidarity'. My hands are shaking when I start to take them down. All of a sudden I don't want them left here. I don't want this adolescent self of mine exposed.

I put my bag on the desk, and I'm pulling the tacks out of the drawings gently because the paper's brittle with age, when a voice behind me says, 'Anything I can do for you?'

I spin around so fast, I almost fall over.

'Jesus!' I yell. 'Goddamn it!'

He's a big man, and I don't recognize him, and it takes me a couple of seconds to realize that he's backing up, out of the doorway, holding both hands in front of him like a surrendering prisoner, and not coming towards me with a butcher's knife.

'I'm sorry,' he's saying, over and over. He looks as scared as I feel. 'I'm sorry, I didn't mean to scare you. Della told me you might be over here, and I just wanted to see if you needed anything.' He's wearing overalls and a T-shirt, and I realize that he must be Della's older brother, Tommy.

'I didn't hear the stair squeak,' I say.

He smiles at this uncertainly and says, 'I always step over it. Sorry.'

'That's OK,' I say. My breath is coming back now, returning in choppy little bites. 'I'm Susannah. You must be Tom.'

Now he comes forward rapidly and shakes my hand

'I'm sorry I frightened you,' he says again. 'You dropped all your stuff.'

He's right. My bag has gone flying off the desk and all the things in it, my glasses and lipsticks and keys,

and the pictures of us that I've pilfered from downstairs, are all over the floor. Before I can stop him,
Tommy's on his hands and knees picking things up,
and I end up taking them from him awkwardly, and
thanking him, and telling him that he really doesn't
have to do this. When his hand lights on one of the
photographs, I can feel myself blushing.

'I'm sorry,' I say, when he looks up at me. 'They
were in the desk downstairs, and I didn't think Della,
or you, would mind if I took them.'

I feel as if I've been caught stealing, which, I
suppose, technically, I have. Although this is absurd
because it's my family after all and I can't see what the
Herveys would want with a whole bunch of pictures
of us. Even so, I feel sneaky and terrible, and to my
utter horror I'm afraid that I'm going to start to cry in
front of this huge man with his balding head, and his
fat reddened hands, and his overalls.

'That's everything,' I say. 'Really. Thank you.
Thank you, so much.' Then I grab my bag and dash
for the stairs, going down them two at a time.

'Not funny, Susannah,' Detective Mark Cope says
when I finally get him on the phone.

It's just past seven a.m., and he's really angry. In
fact, he sounds as if he'd be happy to save our psychopath the trouble and wring my neck himself, if he
could get hold of me. Not that that's going to happen,
since I have no intention of telling him where I am.
The last time I did that I'd ended up with a basket of
violets.

I've even taken the precaution of driving to a White

Hen Pantry to use a payphone, a good five miles from the motel where I checked-in last night under the absurdly uninventive name of 'Mrs Farmer'. My voice had gone all nervous and squeaky when I'd done it, but the teenaged desk assistant could hardly have cared less. She wouldn't have noticed if I'd checked in as Snoop Doggie Dog. A tiny toy sized TV was half hidden under the counter and she was watching reruns of *Buffy the Vampire Slayer* while she took the cash I counted out and grunted as she handed me the key.

Of course, taking into account that Mark Cope is the police, I know that sooner or later he'll figure out where I am — and probably sooner. It won't exactly take Einstein, but I'm still freaked out by what happened at the Marriot so I'm not going to help him out in the meantime. He knows this, and he's not happy about it.

'Susannah,' he hisses into my ear while I lean against the grubby Plexiglass wall of the phone booth and watch pick-up trucks pulling into the Dunkin Donuts across the road, 'you can't honestly think that I. Or Phil. Or Becca Aaronson. Or Paul Donovan. Murdered Marina? Or that we have more than an academic interest in murdering you?'

'Is that the vampire's real name?' I ask. I had him made for at least some kind of Eastern European: a Pole, or a Latvian, maybe, but not an Irishman.

'What?' Cope asks.

'The flowers,' I say. 'The lovely little basket and the note. Sent to my room, that only the four of you knew about.' Mark Cope sighs.

'OK,' he says. 'I don't know. We found them, obviously.'

'What are you going to do?' I ask, and he sighs again.

'Well,' he says, 'they've gone to the lab. We don't have any fingerprints on the note, so we're trying to work through the florist, but it was an FTD order made online, so it's going to take some time.'

I think about this for a second, and then I ask, 'Is Phil there? I mean, is he right there? Can I talk to him?'

'No,' Mark Cope says, and he sounds momentarily confused, as if I've thrown him off his game plan. 'I mean, he's not here. He's in court this morning. Why?'

'Could a woman have killed her?' There's a silence on the other end of the line. 'Can you ask him?' I say. 'I know that we went over this before, and I know he said it was possible, but can you ask him again if it's likely?'

'What's going on Susannah?' Cope's voice quickens and I can almost sense him leaning forward. I can see those fine hands of his, the lean fingers splaying out across the blotter on his desk, or playing with a pen, tapping it angrily and then pausing in mid-air.

'I have a name for you,' I say. 'Della Hervey. I think her real name might be Adele. She comes from Petamill, Georgia.'

I expect Mark Cope to be thrilled with this piece of news, so I'm surprised when his voice goes flat and not very interested.

'Who is she?' he asks, and he sounds as if he couldn't care less.

'I sold the house to her,' I say. 'We all grew up together. She and Marina used to be close, a long time ago. They seem to have had a falling out.' I remember the sound of Della's voice and the shape of her body as I say it. The power in her arms and shoulders. In her back. The way she had moved through the kitchen without making a sound.

'Susannah?' Mark Cope's voice in my ear makes me jump.

'I should go now.' The phone booth is getting claustrophobic and I've been on here too long.

'Wait,' he says. His voice has turned barky, and the pissed off tone is back. 'You know, I can't make you cooperate. I have no jurisdiction over you at all. I don't even have the right to trace this call, incidentally, in case that's worrying you. You can do whatever you want. Frankly, I think you're a pain in the ass, and I don't have time for silly, fucking, little games, but I also don't need you dead. You hear me?' I don't say anything, and a second later he goes on. 'Do you have my new home number?' he asks. 'I moved and it's unlisted. It's not the same one as before, so I'm going to give it to you.'

Part of me wants to hang up on him, but I resist the impulse and jam the receiver between my ear and my shoulder. I mumble at him to wait a minute, and finally I fish the electronic diary that Lolly gave me for Christmas last year out of my bag. I've had to rely on it since Detective Aaronson impounded my Filofax, and I barely know how to use the thing. It hasn't had the organizing effect on my life that Lolly had hoped for, but it seems better than scribbling Mark Cope's new number on the side of the phone booth.

'Shoot,' I say, trying to make my voice sound normal, and he reads the number out twice and then makes me repeat it back to him.

'Anything,' he says, 'anything at all strange, and you call me.' I can tell he's giving me this because he feels bad that he yelled at me earlier. It's a peace offering, and I thank him.

'I mean it Susannah,' he says. 'If you need me, you call. OK? I know this is rough for you, but it is going to be over soon. We might be closer than you think. What did you do with the dog?' he asks. 'If you want, I can arrange—'

'It's OK,' I say. 'I put him in a kennel. He's fine. Actually, I told them to give him to you if I get killed.'

There's just a second before Mark laughs at this, even though it's true, and then he says, 'Thanks Susannah, you're a peach.'

'What did you mean?' I ask, 'about being closer?'

He pauses for a second and then he says, 'Look, I don't want to get your hopes up, because I'm really not sure about this yet, but we're taking another look at Kathleen Harper's alibi for the Friday night when you think Marina was killed. It turns out she was in Philadelphia the day Jake was poisoned. She didn't get home until late. She says she had a doctor's appointment and that she went out to dinner, but there are a few hours missing in there. We've got someone who's placed her near your apartment, and we're talking to her again. At the moment it's all circumstantial. We're taking another look at her divorce, too, but I am not saying that she did it. You understand?'

'You mean it's not over,' I say.

'I mean,' he says, 'I still need you to be careful, if you insist on running around on your own.'

Kathleen Harper's face swells up in front of me, and the phone booth is filled with the warmth and smell of her breath. I can see her hand, the long, strong fingers, reaching out, grabbing at the edge of my car window as she leans towards me.

'Susannah,' Mark Cope says, as if he can tell what I'm thinking, as if he too can see the broad, flatish bones of Kathleen Harper's face, 'we're watching her. She's not going anywhere, and if it's of any interest to you, she's nowhere near Georgia.'

After I put the phone down I sit in the car. I'm holding the organizer that has Mark Cope's number in it as though it's a good luck charm. I'm turning it over and over, rubbing its smooth sides against my palms, while through the convenience store window I watch people buying coffee and cigarettes. There's a woman in there and she's tall, and for half a second I'm sure that she's Kathleen Harper. She turns to look at me through the glass and I close my eyes. I squeeze them shut. When I open them again, she's gone.

TWENTY

No ex-presidents or Civil War generals were born in Petamill, Georgia, and when I was growing up it didn't even have an exit sign off the highway. It was a small, passably pleasant town surrounded by not very prosperous farmland, and it was on the way to nowhere. I suppose that it was like a thousand other places with Memorial Day parades, and town picnics, and Fourth of July fireworks. Even in the 1970s it was the kind of town where almost everybody knew each other and went to church on Sundays.

A country club and famous sons are not the only things that Petamill lacks. There is no Spanish moss, for instance, and the one plantation house in the area had been half-burned in a fire in the 1920s, and stood derelict on the outskirts of town until a medical services company finally bought it and turned it into a nursing home. So, as Southern towns go, the Petamill of my memory, the place that I regarded as the prison camp of my teenage years, never was especially picturesque. Even so, I'm a little startled by the mini-miracle mile that has sprung up on its outskirts. There's a four-screen movie complex, and a sort of low level mall. It's flanked by a smattering of chain food places: an Appleby's, a Taco Bell, a Waffle House.

I've driven into the far side of town, so I don't follow the route that is burned into my memory, the one the school bus used to take, and that my mother drove every day, going back and forth to the Coach-stop. Instead, I come in over the railroad tracks, bumping over the old level crossing, and passing the hardware store building with its rickety staircase up to what had once been the Shall We Dance Studio. The sign with the toe shoes and the star on it is no longer there, so I assume that no more ranks of hopeful little swans spend the afternoons turning their toes out and grasping the barre while the teacher claps her hands in time and the freight trains run by.

When I stop at the lights I notice a brand new sign that's mounted above badges for the Rotary and the Lions Club. It reads, 'Welcome to Petamill's Historic Center'. A pile of pumpkins and a confederate flag have been arranged in the stone water trough in front of the town offices, and sawn off barrels planted with chrysanthemums have been placed at the base of every lamp post on the main street. 'Halloween Parade and Mini-Spook Disco', an announcement in front of the Post Office reads, 'Prizes for The Best Costumes'.

I've pulled into one of the spaces facing the town square and I sit there for a minute, feeling vaguely as if I'm a time traveler, somebody who's wandered, or in my case been shoved, straight out of one life and over a precipice into another. The Coachstop Restaurant is directly across the square from me, and from the outside at least, it hasn't changed at all. The sign with the four black horses and the red stagecoach still hangs over the door, and there's still the same gauzy, ruched, white curtain across the big front window. Momma

hated that thing. She said flies buzzed in there against
the glass pane and got trapped in the folds of the
material and died, and that it was very unhygienic. I
can't read the red sign on the door from here, but I
know what it says. 'Open Lunch and Dinner. Noon
Until Late. Monday through Saturday. Join us for
Southern Hospitality Everyday. Cocktails.' I sit staring
at it, as if maybe I'm waiting for my mother to appear.
As if maybe I've only been over to the Library or up
to the Farm Store, instead of gone for fifteen years,
and any minute now she's going to come swinging
through the door, her dark hair bouncing, and her
peter pan collar bright in the sunshine.

I haven't eaten grits in decades, but I felt like it was
the least I could do, a small gesture to mark my return
to the South, and suddenly I was hungry for them.
When I got out of the car, I'd patted my pocket for
quarters before I'd realized that a dime buys you an
hour in towns like this, and so I'd dropped in two, and
then I'd gone searching for somewhere that served
breakfast. I found it fast, and it seems to be the local
hot spot. It's called the Chicken Fried Café, and it
wasn't here when I was a kid.

The front door is lacquered scarlet and has a little
bell above it that rings every time somebody goes in or
out, just like the souls going to heaven in *It's A
Wonderful Life*, and the walls are lined with paintings of
chickens. There are big fat roosters crowing, and red
hens scratching, and sitting on fence posts, and on
golden straw nests of bright white eggs. Actually it's

not bad. I'm wondering how Lolly would like the idea. Retro diners are really hot, and this is the sort of place that college students and professors love. Booths make them feel both furtive and innocent at the same time, and the diner part reassures them that they're still cheap and honest. Blue collar. Connected. Salt of the Earth. That kind of thing. I am stirring my third cup of coffee and seriously considering this as a proposal when BethAnn Evans walks through the door.

I haven't seen BethAnn since my mother's funeral, but you can't miss her. She looks just like those drawings of *Alice In Wonderland*. She did when we were kids, and later when we were in high school, and she still does now. Her blonde hair is tied back in a headband and a bouncy pony tail, and she's even wearing a blue dress and flat shoes that match. She waves to the cashier, and when she pauses to let one of the waitresses pass, she's so close to my little booth that I could reach out and touch her. She looks right at me for a second and her brow puckers a little, and then, as she decides that she doesn't recognize me after all, I say, 'Hey, BethAnn. It's Susannah.'

Since Della rumbled my disguise last night it seems pointless to pretend that I'm not here. BethAnn stares for a second. She widens her big blue eyes until they look like marbles, and then she breaks into a smile, and gives a little squeal like Southern girls do when they meet somebody unexpectedly.

'Oh my God!' she says 'What did you do to your hair?'

★

BethAnn says she can't stay and that she's in a big hurry, but she's ordered a chocolate chip muffin and coffee anyways, and she can't stop staring at me.

'I'm sorry,' she says. 'I'm really sorry. It just looks so strange. No,' she reaches out and touches my arm, 'not strange. I mean great. It looks great, really. It's just so different from how I remember you!'

'That's OK,' I say. 'I'm different. I'm fifteen years older.' BethAnn rolls her eyes and breaks off a piece of her muffin.

'Aren't we all,' she says. 'So what have you been up to, Susannah? Marina told me you were living in Philadelphia? Is that right? Or was it New York?'

'New York first,' I say, 'and then Philly.' BethAnn's already told me how sorry she is about Marina, and I'm grateful to her that she can say her name normally, that she can mention her in conversation without lowering her voice to a melodramatic hush. 'What about you?' I ask. 'What are you doing?'

'Small town housewife,' she replies. 'No, that's not totally true. I work in the bank. I'm the loan officer.'

'Yeah, Della told me something like that.'

'Della.' BethAnn rolls her eyes again. She's stirring sugar into her coffee, and I notice that her nails are painted baby pearl pink. 'Now there is one sad story,' she says.

'Oh?' Something inside me quickens, and I wonder if BethAnn has heard the interest in my voice. She looks at me and shakes her head.

'That Harley guy she married was a real no good,' she says. 'A serious red-neck. He was just all kinds of trouble, although those two little children are darling. Still, if you ask me, him walking out on Della was the best thing that could have happened. Of course,' she says leaning forward and lowering her voice, 'she has Sonny Delray and her brother Tom to thank for that.'

'She does?'

'Sure.' BethAnn nods, and eats another piece of her muffin. 'They went and had a little talk with Mr Harley, one weekend, when Sonny was back visiting his Momma and noticed that Della had a black eye, and right after that, "Poof".' She snaps her fingers, and I imagine the unseen Harley exploding in a little ball of fairy dust. 'At least Sonny did that much for her,' BethAnn adds. I don't understand her last remark, and the look on my face gives me away.

'Well, you know she was sweet on Sonny for years,' BethAnn says, 'and I think it just got her hopes up again when he rode in like a white knight and finally got Tommy to kick that rat on out of there. Rumor says that Della had high hopes that something would come of it, but, no surprise, it didn't.' She nods and takes a sip of her coffee. 'Mr Delray has moved on. He's very city-fied now, and you should see the presents he gives his Momma. He is not about to marry poor Della.'

I find the idea of the chubby moon faced boy with a grubby baseball cap permanently jammed on his head hard to reconcile with the picture BethAnn is painting, and I'm about to ask exactly how it is that Sonny has been 'city-fied' when she winks at me and says, 'Am I wrong in thinking that it was someone in your family who had sole possession of Mr Delray's heart?'

'Wrong one,' I say.

'Oh,' she says. 'Well, I was just teasin' you, but I still think Marina did not have to go and make things so bad for poor Della. I'm sorry,' BethAnn says, wagging her finger at me, 'but that was a naughty thing of your sister to do. I've never heard such nonsense. I can't imagine what got into her.'

My stomach is sinking a little, and I'm torn between nodding and pretending that I know what she's talking about, and asking her to explain. In the end the latter wins out.

'What did Marina do?' I ask.

'Oh Lord,' BethAnn says, 'of course she wouldn't have told you because she was probably embarrassed when she came to her senses.' I doubt it, I think, but I don't share this with BethAnn.

'It was the craziest thing,' she is saying, 'even for Marina, who, I seem to recall, could be a little crazy.'

'That's right,' I say, 'but I still don't know what you're talking about.'

'Oh,' BethAnn says. 'Well, she accused Della of stealing things.'

'Stealing things?' This seems so strange that it's almost impossible to believe, but BethAnn nods.

'That's right,' she says. 'You know, Della had a key to the house, in case of a fire or something while Marina was away, and Marina insisted that Della had gone in and taken things. I don't know what all, exactly.' She picks at her muffin, pulling a chocolate chip out of it, and adds, 'Marina made one big stink out of it. Went to the police and everything. Of course no one could believe it, and Chuck Hancy, he's the new police chief, he finally convinced Marina that nothin' had happened.'

This story seems so bizarre that at first I can't think of anything to say.

'Could it have been the husband?' I finally ask.

'Oh, no,' BethAnn says, 'this was after he was gone. This all happened about two, maybe two and a half years ago.'

Six months to a year before Marina was killed, I think – right around the time she started getting flowers and phone calls.

'I told you it was crazy,' BethAnn is saying, and she's shaking her head. 'But anyways it all died down, although I think it was awfully hard on Della.'

'Yes,' I say, 'I'm sure it was. What did you say the new police chief was called?'

'Chuck Hancy,' says BethAnn. 'He was hired about three years ago, used to be down in Naples, Florida, but said it got too big. You know, he was looking for somewhere to raise his kids that was civilized.' She is digging more chocolate chips out of the muffin, and eating them one by one as she talks. 'We were just so lucky to get him,' she says. 'And his wife is just the sweetest thing, too. We take yoga together at the gym. I bet you are way too smart for that sort of thing, Susannah deBreem, you and Marina with all your gold stars. You girls were just too smart. The Straight As, that's what we used to call you behind your backs at school.'

'You did?' I say. 'I didn't know that.'

'Oh, we didn't mean it as mean.' She reaches out quickly and touches my arm with the tips of her fingers. 'Really. I think we were just jealous, if you want to know the truth.'

'You didn't have anything to be jealous of BethAnn,' I say. 'You were the most popular girl in the class.'

'Oh, pooh,' she says. 'Look at me. Married and living in my home town and working at the bank – how exciting is that?'

'Oh, I don't know,' I say. 'Excitement's relative. Who did you marry? Anybody I know?' BethAnn shakes her head and her pony tail bobs.

'The bank manager,' she says, and starts to laugh again. 'Well, somebody had to. He'd just come to town, and there he was all sad and lonely. And besides I needed a job. That is a joke,' she adds. 'Sort of.'

She finishes the last remnants of the muffin, scrunching up the butter colored crumbs, and looks at her watch.

'Oh, Lord!' BethAnn exclaims, jumping to her feet, 'Susannah deBreem, you are making me late. I had not counted on you, and now I will get fired and my babies will starve.' She's gathering up her purse, and although it's only one small item, she manages to look as if she's in a flurry of activity.

'Now don't you be a stranger,' BethAnn is saying to me. 'You come by the bank sometime, you hear? We can go to the Coachstop.' She winks and adds, 'I will buy you a cocktail.'

Then BethAnn blows a kiss into the air, and vanishes through the shiny red door, leaving nothing behind her but the bill and the bright tinkle of bells.

Chuck Hancy has a prominent Adam's apple. He has agreed to see me only because he happened to walk out of the men's room and across the police station lobby as I was asking for him. I had not planned to do this, but what BethAnn has told me is so strange, that

I can't leave it alone. I used her name flagrantly, giving the distinct impression that she would consider Chief Hancy's talking to me as a personal favor. Although he's agreed, and has called me 'Ma'am' and asked me if I would like a glass of water or a coke, I can tell that he's not altogether happy about being button-holed like this.

His uniform looks as if it's too big for him, but it's so stiff, and so precisely pressed that the seams stand out in lines, and the heavy looking badge on his chest that says, 'Chief Of Police' doesn't even drag his pocket down.

'Miss deBreem,' he says, as he ushers me into his office, 'I want to tell you how sorry I am about your sister. That was a terrible thing.' He shakes his head. 'Terrible, terrible thing.' He gestures for me to sit down in one of the chairs in front of his desk. 'We did everything we could to cooperate with Alexandria,' Chief Hancy adds, as he sits down himself, 'but I haven't heard that they've gotten anywhere.'

'No,' I say, 'they haven't, really.'

He blinks at me and smiles, and for the first time it occurs to me that I'm making him nervous. He can't figure out why I'm here, and it's making him jumpy.

'Cities are horrible places,' he says, 'you never know what's going to happen.'

There are a lot of things that I could say in reply to this, but I don't bother. I'm not here to engage Chief Chuck Hancy in a debate on the relative merits of rural and urban life.

'Actually,' I say, 'I wanted to ask you about something else, I mean not the murder itself. I understand that my sister made some allegations, that she accused Della Hervey of breaking into the house.'

'Oh, not breaking in, exactly,' he says quickly, 'Della had a key.'

'All right,' I say, 'but she did think that Della had taken things?'

'Yes, yes, that's right,' Chief Hancy says. He pinches the bridge of his nose between his thumb and forefinger and closes his eyes for a second, and then he opens them and nods. 'It was about two and a half years ago,' he says, 'almost a year before your sister was murdered, I think. She hadn't been down here in a while, and when she did come down, oh, sometime before Easter, she came in and swore out a complaint against Della Hervey. Della was awfully upset, naturally.'

'What was it that she said was missing?' I ask.

He looks at me for a second, as though he's summing up how much trouble I might be, and then he says, 'Nothing of any value, really. Some photographs, I think. A scrapbook. Things that could easily have been misplaced, Miss deBreem.'

'But Marina was sure she hadn't misplaced them?' I say.

'Well, yes, I did suggest that to her, of course, but she was emphatic. Very certain,' he says, frowning at me, as if certainty is a serious character defect. 'She didn't strike me as an irrational woman,' Chief Hancy adds, 'although I understand now, of course, that she was under great pressure.'

I don't really know how he figures this, since I doubt that Marina had any inkling that in a year's time she was going to get murdered, but I let it pass, and try not to let my new found dislike of Chuck Hancy show on my face.

'Is there a list?' I ask as quietly as I can, 'of the things that she said were missing? Could I see it?'

I can tell that he's about to say 'no', or to remind me that the police are very busy, or that they have to respect confidentiality, but then he remembers that Marina was murdered, and that I'm from out of town, and the combination of these things somehow makes me special, so instead he smiles and says, 'Of course.'

He pushes a button on his intercom and asks for a file, and then he leans back in his chair and looks at me.

'We did tell the Alexandria police about this, of course,' he says.

'But they didn't think it was important?' Chief Hancy shrugs, and when he docs his shoulders appear to move while his shirt stays still.

'Ms deBreem,' he says, 'there was really no evidence that anything was missing. I went to talk to Della myself. You can imagine how upset she was. Reputations are still important things in a town like this, especially for a single woman. We looked all over Della's house. We didn't need a warrant, Della insisted. There was nothing there.'

He stares at me and I stare back at him, and although he does not say it, he wants me to know that Petamill had nothing to do with Marina's murder. This is what happens, his eyes say, to women who go up to the city, to places where reputations are not important. They step out of the safe circle. They stray too far, and then some lunatic hunts them down and kills them.

The file, which arrives a few seconds later, is just a couple of pieces of paper in a buff colored envelope.

The sheet that Chief Hancy passes to me is an official looking form with a list of items on it filled in in Marina's handwriting. It feels strange, and I imagine her standing in the old-fashioned lobby of this building, writing out these words with a fountain pen, itemizing the pieces of her past that had been taken from her. 'One photograph, girl, aged fourteen, silver frame'. 'One scrapbook, blue vinyl with yellow flower on cover'. 'One diary, with lock, 1981'. 'One photograph, gold frame, girls, aged ten, in ballet clothes'. After this last item, in parenthesis, Marina had written 'twins'.

'Thank you,' I say, and I hand the list back to Chief Hancy.

The florist is called KaBloom! It's in a row of shops a few blocks back from the police station, and its window is filled with large sprays of evergreen and yellow chrysanthemums and orange ribbons. A little black witch rides a broomstick that leaves a trail of baby's breath and a tissue paper ghost hovers over a bowl of paperwhites and says 'Boo'.

I should have taken flowers to Momma and Grandma earlier. I should have done it first thing when I arrived yesterday. I tell myself that I haven't had time, and that they'll forgive me. I also tell myself that I've intended to do this all along, and that it didn't just occur to me now because I happen to be passing this window, happen to be staring into it, the way I've been staring into the Petamill General Store, and the Kitchen Shoppe, and about half a dozen other places, studying displays of candles, and dishtowels with pictures of Tara on them, and trying to figure out if Della

Hervey really could have killed Marina. And if so, if she's now trying to kill me. And if not, why Marina would have accused Della of stealing diaries and scrap-books and photographs of us, and what Della might have done with them if she did.

None of it seems to make any sense, and when I open KaBloom's door I'm relieved to be bathed by a cloud of cool air. It's as chilly as a morgue inside, which I suppose is appropriate, since most of the flowers in here are technically dead and only being given a semblance of life by their buckets of water and little sachets of plant food.

There are roses and chrysanthemums, lilies and delphiniums, and small, highly scented freesias and spice carnations, all stuck into silver metal buckets. On the whole, I'd prefer to take something living out to Momma and Grandma, but I'm told that the bowl of paperwhites under the ghost isn't for sale, and there's not much else, apart from a small ficus tree and a couple of spider plants, which don't seem especially suitable. So, instead I pick out two bouquets. I pluck the stems one by one and lay them on yellow patterned paper. The nice middle-aged lady who wears a pink apron and rubber gloves shoves their ends into little plastic tubes that she promises will keep them fresh, and when she's done she ties each bouquet with a bow and loads me up. She fills my arms with flowers, so I leave the store feeling like I'm going to a wedding.

I put the bouquets carefully on the front seat beside me, and I turn the air-conditioner up, which doesn't do much good because the Unitarian Church is only a couple of miles outside town, and it's still blowing hot air when I get there. There is only one other car in the neatly graveled car park, and I pull in beside it, nosing into the shade of a tree. I had forgotten that the church was quite so desolate. It's a brick and glass box that was badly added on to in the 1960s. When I was a kid it was the only alternative to the raucous hymn singing and dunking baptisms that went on in the Baptist Chapel across the street. Even then the Unitarian Meeting House, as they called it, was so neat and so meticulously kept that it was hard to imagine people here at all, much less people praying, or weeping, or feeling anything as disorderly as exaltation, or grief, or joy.

My mother made us come here occasionally, at Easter and sometimes Christmas, but she never really went to church, and even as a child I had the vague suspicion that this had something to do with us. I don't mean that we wouldn't have been welcomed because we didn't have a father, I just grew to suspect that our birth might have convinced Momma that life was not as high-minded, or as orderly and benign, as the pastor liked to suggest. The Baptist Church across the street was altogether more rowdy, and potentially more interesting, but we didn't go there. When I asked her why not, one Sunday morning when I was about ten and the Delrays and the Herveys had just driven by in all their best clothes with the kids waving from the back seat, Momma had yanked a weed out of the garden and replied sharply that she didn't believe in Hellfire, or, for that matter, Salvation. 'Dressing people up in night gowns and dunking them in a bathtub never saved anyone. But when you're older and have a brain of your own,' she had added, 'then you can decide for yourself.' I had slunk off after that, rebuked, and spent the afternoon wondering whose brain I did have, if it wasn't my own.

Now, standing and looking down on Momma's grave, I wonder if she still feels the same way. Or if she's anywhere at all, feeling anything at all. Marina and I had been uncertain about what we should put on her headstone, since both of us were afraid of sentimentality. In the end, in one of our increasingly rare moments of agreement, we had done what she did for Grandma, and had put nothing except her name and the dates that had formed the borders of her life.

My grandfather is here somewhere too, but I am not certain exactly where. I do remember that when Grandma died we discovered that there was no space available for her to be next to him, because through some mix up one of his sisters had ended up with the spot. Momma had said at the time that this was typical, and she had not been at all happy about it, which had been what had prompted her to buy her own space when she bought Grandma's.

I'm pleased with the way the flowers look, even though I know that in a few hours they will wilt, and I think that I should bring some for Grandpa too, but that will mean finding him first. I don't think that there can be many deBreems, and I wander backwards across the neatly clipped grass, running my hand along the top of the white stones and keeping my eye open for names that are familiar. Sometimes I pause to read the inscriptions. 'Beloved Forever', they say. 'Dear Wife and Loving Daughter'.

A brick wall runs off from the side of the church, and the oldest graves rest there in the shade, along with the memorial plaques for those who could not make it home, or were cremated but still remembered. I wander in this direction, making for a series of more weathered stones that look likely. Some of them are for boys who died in battles. Iwo Jima, one says, and another reads Danang.

I can't see any deBreems, and I think I must have missed Grandpa altogether, and that I'd better start again up towards the front and be more systematic, and then it occurs to me that he might not even be here. He might be across the street, and it might well have been my mother, with her lack of enthusiasm for Hellfire and Salvation, who decided that since there was no room for Grandma there anyways, we would take up residence, so to speak, with the Unitarians. The more I think of this, the more likely it seems, and so I walk back up the lines of stones and cross the gravel car park, making for the white clapboard house of God on the other side of the road.

This graveyard is more interesting. It's more haphazard in its design. The stones range across the thick green grass as if they've tumbled there from Heaven of their own accord, or simply been wedged in where there was room for them. A lot of them have flowers planted around them. Roses seem popular, and some of the more impressive ones have calla lilies and little pots of trailing ivy. There are more monuments here too, mainly angels, their faces turned to Heaven and their hands held out. I see some Herveys and Charlie and Dex Eames' parents right away, and I really have to wonder whether Momma was right or not, and whether maybe Grandma wouldn't have been happier buried here with these people she'd known all her life.

I weave my way through the stones, looking for Grandpa and his sister, and every once in a while I have to be careful not to step on one of the small, flat ones that are just rectangles sunk into the earth. It's well past noon now, and hot, and I'd kill for a beer, and when I find that I've come the wrong way and ended up among a whole bunch of newer stones, I think that probably I'll give this up and let Grandpa rest in peace. Then I see our name, which is weird, since these dates are more recent.

It's one of the plaques, down in the ground, and I just catch it out of the corner of my eye, so I have to look again to be sure. I have to crouch down in this crowded space, so my back scrapes against a white cross and my shoulder rests against a tablet that proclaims, 'He will rise again'. It's only then that I can see the whole inscription, that I can be certain of the name. There are capital letters carved into the pale marble, and they're garish, bright and shiny with gilt. 'Rest In Beauty,' they proclaim. And underneath they say, 'Marina deBreem, Born into this world, August 30, 1965 – Called to God, March 17, 2000.'

TWENTY-ONE

It's the heat, I tell myself, that's making my head swim. It's the bright sun that I'm no longer used to. I close my eyes, but when I open them, the bright, gold letters are still there, sunk into the ground in front of me. This is Marina's grave, here in the Baptist cemetery in Petamill, Georgia, even though I buried her ashes myself in Reston eighteen months ago.

I get to my feet too quickly, and back up, anxious to get away. I bang into the marble cross behind me, and trip on a pot of flowers that falls over. It takes me a few seconds to right it, to stuff the plant back into its pot, and when I'm done the moist, dark loam clings to my hands. I wipe them down the sides of my jeans, rubbing them against my thighs as I weave back through the forest of stones. Then, when I finally reach the front of the church, even though the parking lot is empty and I know that there's probably nobody here, I go up the steps, and bang on the door, which is locked.

There's a notice board in a glass fronted case on the wall. An advertisement for a domestic abuse help line, a couple of flyers, and a schedule of services and events are pinned to its cork board. A diet group meets in the basement every Tuesday at noon. 'Slim For Him!' the

notice exhorts. Beyond that there's nothing, not even
the Pastor's name, or a phone number, or any clue
when he, or she, might be back.

The car that I noticed before in the Unitarian
parking lot is still there, but when I cross the road and
try the church doors, they're locked too. I think about
driving into town and going to the Chamber of
Commerce, or looking for an information booth, or
even going to the bank to ask BethAnn who runs the
Baptist church and where I can find them, but the
inside of my mouth has a thick, sour taste, and my eyes
are gritty, so instead I unlock the Taurus and get in
and turn the air-conditioning on full.

It clicks and whines in protest, and I lower my face
to the vent. I bend over until I'm half lying across the
furry gray fabric of the front seat, and I wait for the
stream of warm air that blows on to my eyelids, and
on to my forehead, to turn cold. I move my face in it,
twisting so it blasts first one cheek, and then the other.
Then I open my mouth and I breathe the air in. I gulp
and swallow, as if, somehow, it can fill me, as if it can
rush down my lungs and into my stomach and make
me clean.

'Well, I don't know,' the girl sitting at the front desk
of Sweet Memories is saying. 'How would you expect
me to know? What do you think I am, Lennie? A
mind reader?' She's tapping her fingers on the desk in
exasperation, but when she sees me standing in the
doorway she lowers her voice and says, 'Lennie, I have
to go. I'll see you tonight.' Then she puts the phone
down and smiles.

'Welcome to Sweet Memories,' she says to me. 'My name is Laurel. How can I help?'

Actually, she's good at this, and I'm a little surprised. In about two seconds she's gone from haranguing the unfortunate Lennie, to being a model of sympathy and discretion. Even her eyes have turned from hard to limpid, and when she reaches up to straighten her hair, giving it just the slightest pat, she does it with a demureness that suggests not vanity, but modest deference to the presumed depth of my grief, as if it would be in bad taste to look messy in front of the recently bereaved.

'I don't know if you can help me,' I say. 'I'm trying to find out who bought a headstone for my sister.' At this Laurel looks momentarily confused, but I sit down in her chair and help myself to one of her Kleenexes.

Sweet Memories is the third memorial store that I've been into this afternoon, and I'm hoping that the number will bring me some luck, because so far I've drawn a complete blank. The first place that I tried was Gulliver's, where Momma bought Grandma's stone, and where Marina and I bought Momma's stone. It's a dark little store front down by the old railroad depot in Petamill, and once it used to belong to an old Mr Gulliver who did all of his own carving and engraving, and who wore suspenders and had eyes that looked perennially sad and hands as callused and as hard as hooves. He must be long gone now, because the young man I talked to today looked at me blankly when I asked after him, and had hands so pale and so fine that they hardly looked as if they'd ever done a dish, much less picked up a chisel or a mallet. Even so he had eventually, and grudgingly, led me into the office and let me sit there while he very slowly turned the pages of the company's order books, and made clicking sounds with his tongue, and finally told me that they had no record of anything remotely like the plaque that bears Marina's name.

The second place I tried, Millets Memorials For All Occasions, in Sefton, which is the next town over, had borne basically the same results. Although that time it had been a middle-aged woman who had searched the back orders, and she had done it on a computer.

There are six names of local memorial places that I got from the *Yellow Pages* I consulted at the Appleby's in the mini-mall, where I stopped to wash my face and get a coke. I had considered a beer, but I'd been afraid that if I sat down in the electric twilight of the bar and started eating chips and drinking Heinekens I might never move again. My first thought, once I had gotten over the shock of seeing Marina's name there, had been Kathleen Harper, but surely she would have told me – not out of consideration for my feelings, but because she wouldn't have been able to resist it. Besides, she knew where Marina was buried, she had stood there while the urn was lowered into the ground. If she had not done it, then I had no idea who might have, but I had to try to find out.

Sweet Memories is hidden in the back of an office park in the middle of nowhere, one of those places that house FedEx depots and tax accountants, and have buildings that look so temporary that you imagine them erected or removed overnight. Stunted little fir trees are placed around the parking lot in tubs, and all of the offices have plate glass doors and signs that look new. I've worked in a radius, moving steadily farther

away from Petamill through the course of the afternoon, and sitting here at Laurel's desk, toying with her
Kleenex, I'm really hoping that my luck has changed,
because it's almost five and the other places on my list
are much farther away, which means I'll have to wait
until tomorrow to check them out.

Despite my best efforts here, and my story about
how I really want to thank whoever did this for my
sister, Laurel is looking a little dubious.

'Well, I don't know,' she's saying. 'I mean, I
understand what a dilemma this must be for you, but
we do have to respect our client's privacy.' She looks
at me and blinks. 'Death is a very delicate matter,' she
adds.

'Look,' I say, taking out my driver's license and
putting it on her desk. 'This is me. I know my hair
looks different, but really, it is. And here's my Mastercard too.' I slide my credit card, which is one of those
ones with a picture on it towards her. 'deBreem is not
a common name,' I add, 'and it's the name on my
sister's headstone. Marina deBreem. Couldn't you
possibly just look through your records for the last
eighteen months and see if there's a stone that had that
name on it?'

Despite their earlier tiff, Laurel wants to get home
to Lennie, I can tell. She's eyeing the clock behind my
head. I take the twenty-dollar bill that I've had ready
in my pocket and slide it under the edge of her desk
blotter.

'I know it's a lot to ask,' I say, 'but I'd be really,
really grateful.'

She looks away from the money, and then she picks

up the credit card and the driver's license and inspects them carefully.

'Philadelphia,' she says, 'that's a long way away.' Then she puts them down again and swivels her chair around to her computer terminal.

'Two Thousand, you said? March?' I nod and Laurel clicks the mouse a few times. Without taking her eyes off the screen, she reaches out and pulls the bill from under her blotter and slips it into her pocket.

She spends the next few minutes scrolling through what I presume are back orders and squinting at the screen so closely that I wonder if she needs glasses. Then she stops.

'Hmmmn,' she says. 'This is it. A plaque, white marble, twelve by twenty-four inches. Gold lettering.'

'That sounds right,' I say.

'Marina deBreem,' she goes on, and then she pauses. 'Oh,' Laurel says, 'Rest in Beauty.' She looks at me and smiles. 'That's so nice. Is it part of a poem?'

'I guess so,' I say, forcing myself to smile. 'I don't really know. Now you can see why I'd like to know who it is that did this for her. I'd really like to thank whoever it was, and I can't call all her friends asking if it was them, can I? I mean—'

'No,' Laurel says. 'I see what you mean.' She turns back to her screen. 'Let's just see what I can do.'

She clicks the mouse a few more times and types in some numbers. The twenty and the mushy epitaph have touched her heart.

'Here we go,' she says. She looks at me and beams while the screen's loading. 'That's one of the beauties of Sweet Memories,' Laurel tells me. 'We have outlets all up and down the east coast. Some people think a chain is tacky, but it means you can order your own personalized memorial in any one of them, and then the outlet closest to the cemetery of your choice orders the stone and installs it for you. It makes it a lot easier on people, you know,' she says. 'So,' she looks back at the screen, 'here we go. Your sister's stone was ordered in Washington DC. Then we fulfilled the order and had it placed in Petamill.'

I guess this shouldn't surprise me, but even though it's muggy in this office, and Laurel doesn't have the air-conditioning on, I can feel myself going cold.

'Washington DC?' I hear myself say.

'That's right,' Laurel nods. 'Does that help?'

'She worked there,' I say. 'She had a lot of friends. Can you give me anything else?' I push another twenty across her desk. This time I don't bother to hide it, and she doesn't make any pretense about not seeing it. She picks the bill up and folds it in half. Then she makes a few more clicks.

'Um,' she says, 'it was ordered on the eighteenth of March, two thousand.'

'The eighteenth,' I ask. 'A Saturday? Is that right?' Laurel shrugs.

'I guess so,' she says. 'We're open on Saturdays. Nine to five. Sunday's the only day we close.' Through the open window I hear a door slam, and a car starts and backs up.

'Does it say who bought it?' I ask.

'Well,' Laurel says, 'it was paid for in cash, and—' Her voice falters. She stops talking and she frowns at the screen, then she turns and looks at me. 'Is this a joke?' she asks. 'Are you trying to set me up or something?'

I shake my head. The cold feeling is getting worse. There's a sound, like the patter of running feet, in my head.

'What does it say?' I ask. 'Please tell me.'

Laurel frowns, and then she sees the look on my face, and she looks worried. She turns back to the screen. 'Susannah deBreem,' she says. She looks again at my driver's license that's lying on her blotter. 'Our records say you bought this stone on March eighteenth, 2000. In Washington DC. You paid in cash.'

'She said she was me,' I say, and my voice is high and whiny, as though this is the worst affront, the worst thing that this person has done, walking into Sweet Memories on K Street the day after Marina was killed and pretending to be me.

Mark Cope makes a kind of a humming sound.

'OK, Susannah,' he says. 'Good. This is really good. The name of the place is Sweet Memories, on K Street. Right?'

'Right,' I say, and neither of us actually mentions Kathleen Harper, although I know we're both seeing her. We're both picturing the way she walks, what she wore, how she pushed the door open. We're both hearing what she must have said.

I paged Mark Cope and he called me back in about two minutes. While I was waiting, standing beside this phone booth that's bolted to a telephone pole across the parking lot from the Sweet Memories store front, I could see Laurel. She was closing up the office, and she kept glancing at me while she straightened things up on her desk and shut her computer down. I'd made her write down the K Street address of the Washington store, even though all she wanted to do was get me out of her office. By then she'd figured out that something was really wrong, and she still half thought that somehow I was setting her up, that I was going to get her fired for taking my money. When she closed the window, she stared at me for a minute through the glass, and then she pulled the blinds down.

'It's after five now,' Mark is saying, 'but we'll get somebody down there tomorrow, first thing. We'll try to get an ID. Why didn't *we* get this?' he mutters, more to himself than to me.

'Wrong graveyard,' I say. 'My family's all in the Unitarians. This is across the street with the Baptists. Besides, it wasn't there when you guys were down here. Apparently it takes as much as a month for the stones to get made, and placed. I'm going to talk to the pastor tomorrow, try to find out—'

'No, Susannah,' Mark Cope cuts me off. 'What you've done is great, but you let us do our job now, OK?' When I don't answer right away he says, 'Susannah, I mean it. Really. I don't want you messing around with this anymore.'

'OK,' I say.

'Promise me,' he says.

'I promise,' I say.

There's a pause before he says, 'Do you feel like telling me where you're staying yet?' His voice has softened, and the question makes me feel silly, as if I'm some stupid Nancy Drew character he's been indulging.

'Sure,' I say. 'The Green Hills Motel, in Sefton, Georgia. I'm Mrs Farmer.' He gives a low whistle.

'Inventive,' he says, and then he adds, 'Hey, Susannah, make me another promise.'

'What?' I ask.

'Take yourself out for a drink tonight,' Mark Cope says. 'On me.'

'Called to God'. 'Rest in Beauty'. I hear the words spoken out loud, and in my dream I run my fingers along the edge of the stone. I grab and scrabble for a corner that I can dig underneath, and when the marble tablet still refuses to move, still lies heavy and stuck, welded into the earth, I get up and run to the car, and find a jack and a tire iron so I can prise it loose. I wrestle and sweat and finally the gravestone pops free. It lifts into my hands as easily as the top lifts off a beer bottle, and when I carry it, it's light. It might as well be papier mâché as stone. There's no weight to it at all, and with the clear logic of dreams I understand that this is because Marina is not there, her body never anchored it to the earth.

I am barefoot, but I do not feel the heat that rises off the road as I walk down it, and I know I don't have far to go. The big sign rises ahead of me, filling the sky, and the blond man with his hands upraised stares vacantly. I throw the stone. I fling it, and it flies as easily as a frisbee, or a bird. Marina's stone arcs through the air, and when it hits the billboard the blond man shatters. His face crumbles and his hands fall to his side and on the road there is nothing but a heap of letters that once spelled 'Jesus Saves'.

The blood is rushing to my head, making me dizzy when I wake up, and when I close my eyes again, I see Marina. She revisits me as I saw her last: bruising around both eyes and across her cheeks, dull purplish against the putty color of her dead skin, broken nose, cut forehead where she fell against a table. The sheet, bright white against the graying color of her face, is pulled up tight under her chin. I can't see the broken nails, or the marks on her arms that I know are there, or the gash that stilled her voice. I can't see the long slice where the blade came across her throat, opening her like a sacrificial animal so the blood poured out.

Called to God. Rest in Beauty. I'm convinced that the words are going to make me sick, and I sit up in the double bed in the Green Hills Motel and wrap my arms around my knees. I only lay down for a moment when I came back, but now the room is dark and the electric clock on the bedside table says it's past seven. I'm queasy and my head aches, but I know that it's not this early nap that's left me feeling like this. It's not even the dream, the fury that coursed through me as I dug up that stone, or the vision of Marina in the morgue. It's not any of those things. It's the date. It's the gold letters reading 'March 17th' that make my stomach heave.

When I buried Marina, when I had a gray granite stone polished and cut for her, I told them just to write 'deceased' and the month of March, 2000. Because until last week, there was no time of death, and no date. Nobody knew whether it was the night of Friday,

March 17, or sometime on Saturday the eighteenth, or even very early in the morning on Sunday the nineteenth, when she was 'called to God'. Nobody that is, except the person who killed her, and me.

TWENTY-TWO

Red's is a big barn of a place set back off the road. Even before I open the door I can hear the noise from inside, a twangy beat of country-western music and the purr and hum of voices, and I'm glad that I ordered take-out and didn't try to reserve a table. I'd dug Marina's red and white origami flower out of my pocket first, and it was only after I'd started to dial that I realized that the restaurant, Mau's China Palace, was in Virginia, nor Georgia. Then I'd remembered the tulip that I'd made out of the menu I found in Momma's desk, so I'd dug that out and unfolded it to see if it was local, which it was.

When I get inside it's obvious that the place is doing pretty well. It looks like they have at least three dining rooms. They aren't doing the ham and biscuit special any more, but they have a whole range of Bar-B-Q, and things like catfish, and gumbos, and dirty rice, and sitting in my motel room just reading the names made me realize how hungry I was, so I've probably ordered way too much food. The hostess is wearing a cow girl outfit with a little fringed jacket, and when I give her my name, she apologizes for the fact that my order isn't ready yet and suggests that maybe I'd like to have a seat in the bar while I wait.

The bar is actually a little quieter, and I find a stool free and order a beer, which comes ice cold in a frosted mug. I realize, as I'm raising it to my mouth, that I'm thinking of Beau, and as I take the first, long, cold swallow I half wish I'd bought myself a pack of cigarettes. Then I remember that it's not as much fun if you don't have somebody to blow smoke rings at. I'll call him, I think. I'll finish my beer, and then I'll go find a payphone and call him while I'm waiting for my food. I wonder if he'll be at Sherlock's, or if he'll be home trying to figure out how to heat up a frozen pizza. Or maybe he has a choir practice tonight. I don't even know what day of the week it is anymore, and I'm just about to wave to the bartender and ask him when I see him looking at the space behind my shoulder, and a voice says, 'Lou, this lady's order is on the house!'

At first, I don't recognize Charlie Eames' older brother, Dex. It's not until he's taken my hand and is pumping it and saying, 'Hey there, Sugar, how are ya?' and the bartender's saying, 'Yes Mr Eames', that I realize who he is, and that this must be the 'food place' that Della told me he owned, and that that's why Marina had the menu in her desk.

'Dex, hi,' I say, and he beams at me and claps me on the back.

Dex is bigger than I remember, in all senses, and prosperity seems to have agreed with him. He's as round as a Santa Claus, and he's wearing round glasses, and a checked shirt and bolo tie with a silver cow's head at his throat. I can't see anything of Charlie in him. There's no ghost in his older brother of the tall skinny boy Marina once loved.

'You look great,' I say, 'really.'

'Well, so do you, Miss Susannah,' he says. 'Although I admit that I would not have known you without that red hair, if I hadn't been watchin' for you. Saw your name on the order list in the kitchen.' Dex winks at me. 'I haven't seen you in a coon's age, girl,' he says. 'Mind if I have a seat?' Without waiting for me to say anything, he pulls out a bar stool and slides on to it. 'Listen,' he says, 'I want to tell you, that was a terrible thing that happened to your sister. Just God awful. We all felt so terrible about it down here when we heard. We're just damn sorry, that's all.'

'Thanks,' I say. The bartender brings Dex something that looks like bourbon on the rocks with a twist and sets it in front of him.

'Another for the lady,' Dex says, and I don't stop him. 'Tell me,' he goes on, 'they ever get the son of a bitch did that?'

'Not yet,' I say, 'they're workin' on it.'

'Well, here's to 'em,' Dex says, raising his glass. 'Bastard like that ought to be wiped off the face of the earth. She was one beautiful woman, your sister.' We clink glasses, and on the sound system Linda Ronstadt sings Heart Like A Wheel.

'This place is great, Dex,' I say. 'It looks like you've done well.'

He nods his head a few times and pushes his glasses up on to the bridge of his nose. There's something about him that reminds me slightly of a fat Jerry Lee Lewis. I can imagine him singing Great Balls Of Fire.

'The Good Lord has been good to me,' Dex says. 'He surely has, Susannah.' He looks so serious while he says this, so totally convinced of God's personal benevolence, that for a second I envy him. 'Yes sir,' Dex adds, grinning, 'I am blessed with a wonderful wife who's smart as a whip and doesn't take any crap from me, and three wiseass kids. Oldest one's applying to colleges next year. Can you imagine that?' He shakes his head. 'Makes me feel old,' he says, but somehow I don't think he really minds.

'What about you?' he asks. 'Married? Kids?' I shake my head.

'Neither,' I say, 'but I have a great dog.'

Dex laughs at this as the bartender puts my second beer in front of me and slides a basket of popcorn shrimp down to us.

'What about your parents?' I ask, 'how are they?'

'Oh, Daddy died, about five years ago,' Dex says. 'A heart attack. Real quick. Hope I go like that. I sold the farm for Mom after that and moved her into one of those assisted living places. She was happy, I think, last years of her life. She died about a year ago.'

'I'm sorry,' I say.

'Well,' Dex says, 'I guess it happens to the best of us.'

'It looks that way,' I agree, and then, more by way of conversation than anything else, I ask, 'Did you guys ever hear anything from Charlie, after he went away?'

Dex shakes his head.

'No,' he says, 'and you know it's so strange you should ask that. Marina asked me the same thing. She came in here lookin' for me, oh, God, it must have been just right before she died, and that's the only thing she wanted to know about, whether we'd ever heard anything from Charlie.'

I don't know why this should surprise me, but it does. As far as I can remember, I never once heard Marina mention Charlie Eames after the week when he disappeared, and I suppose that I'd assumed she'd forgotten all about him, had consigned him to the graveyard of faintly embarrassing teen-aged romances, or had filed his memory away in the catalog of early loves that most of us keep well-buried, and only care to remember when we are drunk and weepy with longing for some imagined past. It certainly never occurred to me that he might still have been an active part of her conscience.

'You're kidding,' I say. 'She came here to find you? And to ask that?'

'Yup,' Dex says. 'I mean she was hardly what you'd call a regular, but she'd been in here a few times over the years. Never mentioned Charlie, not before that night. Then she turned up on a Saturday. I remember 'cause we had a big party on and she said she was down from DC for the weekend. And that was all she wanted to know about, whether we'd ever heard from Charlie. Whether we'd ever tried to find him.' He thinks about it for a second, and adds, 'Yeah, it must have been damned close to when she was killed. It was fresh in my mind when I heard the news. I mean I'd just seen her, just been talking to her a week or so before. Made it even more weird, you know?'

'Yeah, I do know,' I say, and Dex nods. He assumes that I'm talking about the strangeness of seeing somebody very much alive one week, and hearing that they're dead the next, but that's not what's going through my mind. What's occurred to me is that Marina must have come here either just before or just after she called me in Philadelphia on the Saturday before she died. I imagine her sitting at one of the tables in the bar, a beer in front of her, and a basket of nibbles on the table. The image is so real that I almost expect to look over my shoulder and see her. A sudden pulse of excitement runs through me, and if I still believed in nightspinning, I might believe that she'd just whispered in my ear.

'Can you remember what time it was, Dex?' I ask, 'when she came in that night?'

If he thinks this question is odd, he doesn't say so. Instead he just nods and says, 'Oh yeah, early. It would have been about six, I think. 'Cause I'd just gotten here, and I had time to have a beer with her. Things hadn't gotten busy yet.' He swirls the ice cubes in his glass and takes a swallow and I can smell the sweetness of the bourbon. I think about what he's just said for a second, and realize that it means Marina must have called me afterwards, possibly because of something she'd heard from Dex.

'Can you remember what she was like, that night?' I ask. 'I mean, if she was upset, or sad, or—'

'Well, she didn't want to eat anything,' Dex says, 'I can tell you that much. It's what restaurant owners remember, honey. Terrible isn't it?' He laughs and slaps me on the shoulder, and then his face sobers at the memory of Marina. 'I told her I could get her a table, even though it was a weekend,' he says, 'but she wasn't interested. So, I bought her a couple of drinks, and I finally got her to nibble on some wings or something. She was too thin, that girl. We talked about some other stuff, maybe her house, her grandma's old farm, but she kept comin' back to Charlie. I mean, I know they were sweet on each other and all, but it was kind of strange, after all this time. I told the police all about it. I mean they came in asking right afterwards, tryin' to trace her movements and all. Of course,' he adds, 'it would have been different if she'd been killed down here.'

I'm not sure quite why, so I let the comment pass, and instead, I ask, 'Did you ever try to find Charlie?' I slide my second beer towards me, and pick at some of the popcorn shrimp.

'Oh sure thing,' Dex says. 'Just as soon as Daddy died. Hired a private detective and the whole nine yards.' He signals for another drink, and turns to me. 'You see, Mom never did believe that Charlie burned that barn down, and neither did I. Hell,' he adds, 'I don't even think Daddy believed it.' He grabs a popcorn shrimp and tosses it into his mouth, diving for it a little so he looks like a terrier catching a treat. 'Dad and Charlie just didn't get along, is all,' Dex says, and a wave of sadness passes over his face.

'But he thought so at the time?' I say. 'I mean, your Dad thought he'd torched the barn?'

'Oh, yes and no.' Dex shrugs. 'You know what men are like. You know what teenagers are like. Hell, there are times when I want to wring my own boy's neck, but I just love him to death. Daddy had a lot wrapped up in that farm, times weren't too good, and he had to be mad at somebody, so he fastened on Charlie. Charlie was going through a bad phase that summer. Running around. Never where he was supposed to be when he was supposed to be there. Of course,' Dex is smiling at me, 'your sister probably had something to do with that, although we didn't know

it at the time. And then there were those weird little
brush fires that made everybody so jumpy.'

I can see my mother standing on the porch in the
summer dark, her body a still column of shadow, her
arms crossed, while she stared out over the field,
scanning the boundary of our woodland for any bright
leap of flame.

'They ever find out who did them?' I ask.

'Oh, I don't know,' Dex says, 'Dick-Head did
come around just before the barn went up and talked
to all the boys, Charlie and Sonny and Tommy Hervey
about playing with matches, which was of course what
stuck in Daddy's head, and there was gossip going
around about something called a "firebug club", but I
didn't pay too much attention to it. You guys were all
too young and dumb for me to spend my time on,
remember?'

'Oh sure,' I say, 'I remember.' Dex laughs and slaps
me on the back again and I narrowly avoid spilling my
beer.

'You always were a good sport, Susannah,' he says.
'Anyhow, after Charlie left everybody blamed him. So
that was the end of that, even if he didn't do it.'

'You know he didn't light the fires?'

Dex shrugs, pulls the twist of lemon rind out of his
drink and bites it in half.

'Well, not all of 'em for sure. I mean one time he
was with me over in Sefton when one broke out. I
figure it was a bunch of kids,' he says, 'that's how
things usually work.' And suddenly I can remember
Sonny Delray staring at Marina on the afternoon when
he told us that Charlie had disappeared and saying
'Crackle, crackle', and her opening her mouth and

closing it again, like a guppy. Maybe, I think, it wasn't just the boys that Dick-Head should have talked to.

'Did you ever find out anything about him? Where he went or anything?' I ask. Dex shakes his head and sighs.

'Nope,' he says, 'not a thing. Daddy wouldn't let Mom do anything about it while he was alive. Pride, you know. Although I think it hurt him plenty, inside. I think right to the end he always hoped we'd hear something, but we never did, not a peep, and then, pretty soon after Daddy died, I knew it was eating away at Mom, so I went and hired a private detective. Hell, I could afford it by then. A good guy, name of Hal Burton.' I start to laugh, and Dex looks at me.

'I'm sorry,' I say. 'You told Marina about that, didn't you?'

'Sure did,' Dex says, although he clearly doesn't get the joke.

'She wrote his name down,' I explain, 'on the top of one of your menus. I thought it said "halibut".'

'Oh,' Dex says. 'Well, halibut or not, he didn't find anything. 'Course it had been the better part of fifteen years then, and trails go cold.'

'So nothing?'

'Zippo,' Dex says. 'Not a trace. Damn sad thing. It's like one Sunday afternoon he just ceased to exist. No record of him anywhere. Of course that's not so unlikely with a sixteen-year-old. They can change their name, disappear into the oilfields, or out on some cargo ship, or God knows where. If a person doesn't want to be found, it's not that hard. We just never reckoned that was Charlie, that's all. You know how

Moms are, she just always thought he'd turn up. Truth
was, so did I.'

'I'm sorry,' I say.

'Yeah.' He pushes the last piece of the lemon rind
around the edge of his glass, and then he says, 'Funny,
him and Marina, isn't it, in a way? That God should
see fit that they both end in a mystery.' I'm not sure
what to say to this, but then Dex says suddenly, 'I
wonder if she knew, if she had some kind of premonition, or something, and that's why she came asking
for Charlie then, like she was tying up a loose end.'

I wonder too, but it's what sort of premonition she
had that interests me. Somehow I don't think Dex and
I are thinking of the same thing.

'You told Marina, right?' I ask, 'Everything you've
just told me?'

'Oh, sure,' Dex says, 'and then some. She could
have been a prosecuting attorney, your sister. She
cross-quizzed me like you wouldn't believe, but the
end result was the same. As far as we know, when
Charlie got on that bus, he vanished off the face of the
earth.'

Dex thinks about this for a second. His glass is
empty and he rattles his ice cubes around, but when
the bartender moves to bring him another one, Dex
waves him away.

'And you know what else is strange?' he says,
looking at me. 'After I told Marina, after she ques-
tioned me up and down and sideways, and after we
went 'round and 'round and came out at the same
place, it was like she was happy.'

'Happy?' I ask.

'Yeah,' Dex says, nodding, 'happy. It was like I'd told her something that she really wanted to believe.'

I'm still thinking about this last statement, and about what Kathleen Harper told me, when the Hostess comes over and mutters something in Dex's ear.

'Oh, right oh, Honey,' he says, and then he turns to me. 'Susannah, you are gonna have to excuse me. I have a big private party coming in. Now are you sure I can't get you a table?' he asks. 'Your order is ready and bagged and all, but we can serve it up for you right here if you want.' I shake my head. All I really want to do now is get back to my room.

'No, but thanks,' I say. 'I will next time, I promise.' I get up and start to walk back to the front of the restaurant with Dex, and then, after he's handed me the bright white bag with 'Reds!' written on the side of it, and refused to let me pay the bill, I ask him another question.

'Hey, Dex,' I ask, 'you all went to the Baptist Church growing up, right?'

'Well, sure thing,' he says. 'Everybody on our road, except for you Uni-tar-Ians.'

'But not that Sunday?' I ask, 'at least not Charlie. Not on the day he left?'

Dex looks at me for a second. 'Well, no,' he says. 'As a matter of fact, that was part of Charlie's actin' up that summer. One of the things that made Daddy so mad, that he wouldn't go to church.'

'And Sonny Delray too,' I say. 'I mean he didn't go to church either that day, and Charlie must have known that. Didn't he ask him for a ride, to the bus?'

'Yeah,' Dex says, 'I guess so.' I shrug, and smile at him.

'I just don't remember them as being real good friends,' I say. Dex laughs.

'Poor old Sonny,' he says. 'I don't think anybody was his real good friend back then, but that's what you get for being the fat kid. Doesn't youth suck? But no more!' he crows. 'No more!' He beats out a little tattoo on his stomach. 'Bigger is better, and that's the truth of it. Now you get on the other side of that Bar-B-Q! All you city girls are way too skinny!'

Dex is right about the barbecue, it's delicious, and I'm not surprised that his place is a success. By the time I'm finished with it my room smells like a giant sloppy joe, and I open the windows, and go sit on the little plastic lawn chair that's outside my door while it airs out.

I've been thinking over my conversation with Dex Eames, and sitting in the dark it's clear to me that Marina must have believed that it was Charlie who had come back into her life. I wonder what it was that tipped her off. Some special signal? Some private thing that she remembered and that reappeared in one of the gruesome gifts he sent her? Maybe it was the wording on the valentine, or something about the flowers, but clearly she thought she'd figured it out and she came down here that last time to try to find out if anyone knew for sure where he was.

However, none of that explains why she should have been happy after talking to Dex, and I can't figure that out for the life of me. Surely her conversation with him would just have increased her frustration, not been something she really wanted to believe, as Dex said, or filled her with the calm sense of determination that Kathleen Harper described. Nor does it explain the headstone in the Petamill Baptist cemetery, unless Charlie Eames has taken to wearing a wig, or has become a transvestite and was able to walk into Sweet Memories on K Street and pretend that he was me.

I get up to go back inside. The night air is turning chilly now, and it's late enough in the fall to want a jacket on after dark. I think next week is Halloween, and I remember how Momma and Grandma used to work for days when we were little to dress us up as lions, or witches, or princesses, or whatever it was Marina and I fancied ourselves as that year. Then Mr Delray, or Mr Hervey, or even Uncle Ritchie sometimes, would collect all us kids and load us into the back of one of their farm pick-up trucks, and drive us around from house to house so we could ring the doorbells and yell 'trick or treat' and make all our mothers pretend they were scared and didn't know it was us.

I can't remember when that stopped, but I do remember the sadness of it, the strange empty feeling of being at odds with your own body when you realize that you're too big to dress up anymore, when painting whiskers on your face, or pinning a tail on your pajamas, and carrying a fairy wand just makes you feel dumb instead of magical. I wonder now if that's the moment when we all start to get mean, that moment when we start to figure out that we're stuck, and that there's no magic, no costume that we can put on, that releases us from what we are.

When I go back inside I lock the door, and the windows. After I put the chain on, I prop a chair under the door knob. Then I go into the bathroom and pull back the shower curtain, and loop it up and tie it in a knot. I leave the closet door open too. I've done this in strange rooms for years, not just since Marina was killed. Life's tough enough without having to wonder who's behind things if you have to get up and go to the bathroom in the night. When I get into bed the sheets are cool, and the pillows smell slightly of pine and fabric softener, and after I turn the lamp out, I hear the occasional 'whoosh' of a car going by on the road and see the reflection of headlights on the ceiling.

It's not long, then, until I fall asleep. I hear a voice in the parking lot. A dog barks and a door slams, and then I'm dreaming. I'm floating above a darkness that stretches out below me as thick and dense and soft as the sea. All through the night I hover there. I hang above the ocean, and above fields, and above thick tangles of trees and brambles and rose bushes. When eventually, I come to earth, I walk, but my feet do not touch the ground. I am surrounded by the bright flicker of fireflies, and lured onwards by distant, yellow, leaping tongues of flame.

TWENTY-THREE

'It's over.' Bars of white light are seeping between the edges of the curtains and the wall. They form stripes and fall into the room. 'They brought Kathleen Harper in early this morning, and they're going to charge her later today.' The electric clock on the bedside table clicks and the green letters read nine-thirty.

'I said it was over. Did you hear me, Susannah?' Mark Cope asks, and when I finally say, 'Yes', my voice is thick and furry with sleep.

Something that I can't quite grab is lingering in my mind. It's shifting in and out of focus like the hang over from a dream. Pictures and bits and pieces of information that all meant so much in sleep are receding and threaten to mean nothing in the mundane light of day. Somewhere in Alexandria, I can hear what sounds like a car alarm going off, or a telephone ringing.

'Did you get the ID?' I ask.

There's an infinitesimal pause before Mark Cope answers, and then he says, 'Not yet. But we will.'

'So—' I'm trying to understand the implications of this, but my mind seems to be fat and sluggish, unable to turn itself in any useful direction. Before I can finish the question that I haven't asked, Mark Cope answers it for me.

'We're not charging her with Marina. Yet. But it's only a matter of time. In the meantime, Becca Aaronson can hang on to her because we've got her tied to you.'

'To me?' The room comes into sharper focus, and I reach for the second pillow to stuff it behind my back and sit up.

'Yup,' Mark says. 'She talked her way into your building the night your hair was cut. One of your housemates let her in. She claimed she was a really good friend of yours, and that you'd called her. Knew all about you and even produced a key to your apartment, but said she didn't have one to the front door.'

'My apartment?'

'Yes, Ma'am,' Mark says. 'She's even admitted it. Says she was there about nine p.m. and wanted to talk to you. Claims she knew that you wouldn't let her in, so she lied. Then says you wouldn't answer the door, so she left. But we know she didn't. We've got forensics in the basement now. We think she was down there, waiting, until it got late enough to come up and give you a haircut.'

I'm trying to understand how Kathleen Harper could have got hold of a key to my apartment. I'm trying to remember what I did with my bag while I was at her house, where, exactly, I put it down, and for how long. I'm trying to figure out how she could have taken a key without my noticing it. Or did she somehow take an imprint of it, press it into playdough, or silly putty, the way people used to in the movies. I shake my head quickly. Most probably she just flashed any old key at the front door, and banked on the fact that she could get me to let her into the apartment once she got upstairs. Or that she could jimmy the lock, or use a credit card, or something. Then she got lucky, and I took a sleeping pill and forgot to lock the door.

'What time did you say this was?' I ask.

'She turned up at about nine, nine-fifteen,' Mark Cope says.

I'm imagining how easy it would have been for Kathleen to convince Cathy, who is always so concerned about the poverty of my social life, that she was an old friend, when I realize that Mark Cope is still talking.

'Breaking and entering,' he's saying, 'we've got her on that, and assault, maybe. Probably the stalking stuff too, but that depends on Pennsylvania law, which isn't my specialty. Anyways, I wanted to be the one to call and tell you.'

'Thanks,' I say.

'You're going to have to come back. The DA's office is going to want to talk to you,' Mark says. 'And we're going to need you too.'

'OK,' I say. He pauses, as though this is easier than he'd anticipated, as though he'd thought he was going to have to fight with me, and he's about to say something else. I can hear him thinking about it, and when he doesn't, I ask, 'What? What is it?'

I can almost see him shake his head. 'Nothing,' he says. 'It's just,' his voice lingers for a second and then he says, 'why didn't you tell me? About Marina?'

'What?' I ask. There's a silence, and then his voice rises in exasperation.

'Why didn't you tell me she was gay?' Mark Cope asks.

I think about this for a second, turning it over in my mind the way you finger a stone. I'm watching the sunlight that's reached the carpet and crawls across the end of the bed, and finally I say, 'I didn't know.' Which is the truth.

I can hear him breathing on the other end of the phone. It's a faint rasping sound, and for the first time I wonder if he smokes.

'It would have helped,' he says. He clearly doesn't believe me.

'I'm sorry,' I say.

'Well, apparently she was,' Mark says. 'Certainly according to Kathleen Harper's ex-husband.'

I think about this for a second, and then I say, 'It's not something I ever really thought about.'

Dust motes are drifting through the bars of sunlight, and there's a silence while Mark Cope considers this. Then he says, 'OK, Susannah. You drive carefully, all right?'

In the dark, I hadn't been able to tell what color Della Hervey's house is painted. Now I can see that it's dark green with white trim, and this surprises me because most of the houses down here are white. I guess because of the heat. I can't see anybody in the yard when I drive up, although there's a car parked in the driveway that I figure must be Della's. I haven't really thought about what day it's been, and so I was faintly surprised, when I went to check out of the Green Hills Motel this morning, to discover that it's Saturday. Which probably explains why Dex's was so busy last night, and why Della's car is in the drive at eleven in the morning. It also means that her kids must be home from school. As I get out of the car and walk to the kitchen door I can hear music playing through one of the upstairs windows that's open.

Della's waiting for me, standing just behind the screen, and she has an apron on over her jeans.

'I'm making a Halloween cake,' she says, as she pushes the door open, 'for Karen to take to school on Monday. They're having a bake sale for the class dance.'

The kitchen is warm and smells of cinnamon, and a pile of bowls and the beaters from a mixer are in the sink.

'I just came to give back the key,' I say.

'Oh,' Della's opening the refrigerator, and she turns and looks at me, 'so you're going? That was fast.'

'Yeah,' I say, 'I have to go back to Philly.'

I put the key on the counter, in an uncluttered place beside the telephone, and I watch Della while she moves eggs and butter and a carton of milk from the kitchen table back to the fridge.

'Della,' I say, 'I'm sorry.'

She stops and stares at me for a second, and then she fingers the back of one of the kitchen chairs.

'I'm sorry about what Marina did,' I say.

Della looks up at me and says, 'I didn't steal nothing. Never. I don't know where those things went, but I didn't steal them.'

'I know that,' I say. 'I know you didn't.' She nods and looks down at the chair again, and I'm not sure what else, if anything, I can say to make her feel better, to salve the hurt and humiliation that she must have felt.

'Listen,' I say, 'I saw Dex last night. We talked some about Charlie, and about that summer, the one when he took off.'

'Charlie,' Della says. She shakes her head. 'I never knew him real well, did you?'

'No, not really. I mean, I guess I was kind of out of it that summer. I wasn't really hanging around with you guys. Dex said something about a "firebug club", do you remember that?'

Della laughs, and pushes the chair away from her. 'That was Sonny,' she says. 'I thought everybody knew that. That was his secret club.'

'Was Marina part of it?' I ask, and suddenly the answer seems incredibly important to me, even though I know what it's going to be.

'Sure,' Della says. 'Marina, and Sonny, and me, and Charlie, and a couple of other people, I guess. The Firebug Club. We had a club house and everything. Up in the woods. We all signed in blood. Well, made an X.'

The sting is as sharp as if I was fifteen again. Where was I? How come I didn't know? Della's laughing, chuckling to herself at the memory.

'So you all set those fires that summer?' I ask.

'Sure,' Della says. 'That was the initiation rite. You had to set a brush fire, just a little one, and not get caught, in order to become a member.'

'And the Eames' barn?'

'Oh, I don't know,' Della says. 'I don't know 'bout that. I guess that must have been Charlie, but things got a little out of control.'

''Cause the other fires were all at night,' I say. Della nods.

'Oh, yeah,' she says, 'that's when we'd meet. You'd have to go off and set your fire, and the others would watch, like from far away, to make sure you did it, and didn't just say so. Then we'd put 'em out and scarper before the police came. We didn't mean no harm. Not like the Eames' barn. That was different. We were just havin' fun, you know, the way kids will, but I guess that's where Charlie got the idea.'

'Yeah,' I say, 'I guess so.'

'Things might have been different, you know,' Della says suddenly, 'if he hadn't gone away.' At first I can't figure out what she's talking about, and then I remember what BethAnn said.

'Della,' I say, 'you know, there was nothing, ever, between Sonny Delray and Marina.' She's staring at me and a stubborn look comes over her face. I can remember it now from when she was a kid. 'Honestly,' I say. 'There wasn't. Really.'

'That's not what he thought,' she mutters.

'Well, it's true,' I say. 'Believe me. I know. And it was a long, long time ago.' Della stares at me for a second, and then she smiles. Her mouth stretches over her teeth in an arc.

'Well, you are right there,' she says, and something goes out of the room, dispels, like a breath that's been held. Della wipes her hands quickly on the front of her apron and brushes past me and into the hallway.

'Karen!' she yells up the stairs, 'you come on down now. Like we talked about. Miss deBreem is here!'

I can't imagine what this is about, but a second later, a thin little girl with dark hair comes down the stairs. At first I can just see her feet, and the legs of her jeans, and then she walks ahead of her mother down the hallway and into the kitchen where she stops in front of me. She's carrying a book, about the size of a photograph album, holding it in two hands a little away from her, the way you might hold a tray, or a present.

'Go on, Karen,' Della says. She's standing in the doorway, as if to block any escape that this child might try to make back up the stairs. Karen herself is over-come with shyness. She's staring at the floor intently, and I'm about to say something to her, when she shoves the book towards me.

'This is yours,' Karen says. 'I took it out of your room.'

It's a turquoise colored vinyl album. On the front there's a pink flower, and the words 'My Scrapbook by Susannah', are spelled out in purple letters that I stuck painstakingly on one afternoon shortly after my thirteenth birthday when Uncle Ritchie gave this to me. Marina had been given a matching one, with a yellow flower on it, which is one of the items that was on the list I read in Chief Hancy's office yesterday afternoon. I do not believe, however, that she stuck her name on to the front of her album, and that was something that I later felt she did on purpose, and only after I had finished mine, so I would regret it and wish that I could peel the purple letters off.

Karen's looking up at me now.

'She took it when we were cleaning up the house,' Della says. 'After we bought it. I told her she could. But she thought maybe you might want it back.'

'Thank you,' I say, and I take the scrapbook out of Karen's hands.

Della walks me out to the car.

'They're good kids,' she says. She kicks a stone in the drive and it skitters away into a flower bed that's thick with violet-faced asters and edged with pieces of driftwood that Della's kids must have collected on trips to the beach or down on the creek. 'They mean the world to me,' she adds. 'Even if their daddy was a son of a bitch.'

'Will you thank Karen again, for me?' I say. 'Will you tell her how much I appreciate it?' Della nods. I'd tried to thank Karen myself, but without much success. She'd looked at the floor and nodded a few times, and then she'd asked her mother if she could be excused and had run back upstairs. Now the music's playing again, and this time I recognize Sheryl Crow because I'm pretty sure Cathy has the same CD.

I zip the album into my duffel bag, and when I slam the hatch down and look back at her, I see that Della's dug both hands deep into her jeans pockets and is staring off across the field towards the big low barn where we can hear the whine of Tommy's tractor.

'You do whatever you want with the house, Della,' I say. 'It's yours. All of it. I mean, I appreciate the scrapbook, but don't worry about what I'll think. There's nothing there I want anymore.'

'OK,' Della says. She smiles, and I open the car door. 'You drive carefully, Susannah,' she says. 'And you come back and see us.'

'I will,' I say, although both of us know that this isn't true, and then I slide into the front seat and start the Taurus. I roll the window down so I can wave, and then I back out of the drive and start down the road. It's a clear, bright day, and in the rearview mirror, I watch Della. Her apron blows a little in the breeze, and just before I reach the band of the woods, she raises her hand to wave.

TWENTY-FOUR

Jake leaps into the air. He lands, and wheels and then races back to me. He shoves his face into my stomach and wags his tail so hard that his whole body swings back and forth. Ever since I picked him up from the kennels this morning, he's been reluctant to let me out of his sight, and although he's thrilled to be back here at the dog park, he needs to keep coming back to me, to keep flinging himself up against me just to reassure himself that I'm solid, and not someone he's imagined. Now he turns his face up to me and speaks in his low singsong dog voice, telling me how happy he is to see me. I grab him on either side of his face and shake him until he growls. I bury my hands in the deep fur of his ruff, and kiss the black triangle on the top of his head.

The sun is setting, and the sky behind Penn is turning orange and then crimson as the darkness bleeds into it. By the time we leave the dog park the streetlights are coming on. A nimbus of light hovers around each one and picks up the faint chilly mist that is gathering in the air. All day long it's drizzled, but it hasn't yet been able to work itself up to rain.

The street that Jake and I walk up is quiet, but far away there's a background cacophony of honking and the buzz of rush hour traffic. The houses here are tall

and narrow and old. Each of them is three floors high
and two windows wide, and their front doors are
painted glossy greens and blues and reds. The houses
are larger than they look from the street. They are
two, and sometimes even three rooms deep, and many
of them have been remodeled and have fancy basement
kitchens that open through French windows on to tiny
walled gardens that trap the sun and shut the city out.

I know all of this because when the lease for our
apartment came up for renewal, George and I briefly
considered buying. For several weeks we trailed from
house to house in the wake of a real estate agent called
Marge who was half Portuguese and spoke with an
accent so thick that it was almost unintelligible. Now,
as I walk Jake up the cobbled street, I find myself
hoping that a For Sale sign will be posted in front of
one. For the first time since Marina was killed and
George left, I think that perhaps I would like more
than one room and a bedroom, and that Jake should
have a garden, no matter how tiny, and that I won't
mind the yoke and harness of a mortgage. Beau will
laugh at this, I know, when he hears. He will tell me
that I am getting old and bourgeois, and then he will
ask me if my new home has an attic where maybe he
could leave some of his things, and if it's anywhere
near a decent bar.

I haven't been able to get hold of him since I got
home last night, and when I look at my watch and see
that it's past five, I decide that Jake and I could both
use some more exercise. We'll walk up town and bang
on Beau's door. We'll throw a pebble at his window,
stand in the alley and call his name. He should be
home from work by the time we get there. We'll send

out for pizza, or, if he invites us, we'll watch *The
Simpsons* with him.

I can hear music as Jake and I come up the stairs. It's
the piano, something with a faint boogie-woogie beat,
and I can picture Beau playing. He'll be perched on
the old fashioned piano stool, bent over, his big back
slouched, his forehead creased with concentration, and
a sooty lock of blond hair will be falling into his face.
Jake pushes ahead of me, impatient to see if Beau has a
new tennis ball or a frisbee, and the music pauses. Beau
plays a few notes over, and then he starts the piece
again. This is why he hasn't been answering the phone.
I've called four times and all I get is the answering
machine. Sometimes, when he's playing the piano,
Beau puts his telephone in his sock drawer and leaves
it there for days at a time.

The music breaks, and I knock on the door.

'Beau,' I call, 'Beau, it's me, Susannah.'

He hits a few notes, high and plinking, and then he
yells, 'It's open.'

I push the door and see that the two lamps on
either side of Beau's big disorderly couch are on. The
light they cast is so bright that the rest of the room
seems unnaturally dim, and in the white pools I can
see an overturned shoe, a plate with a fork on it sitting
on a side table, and the sleeve of a sweater that hangs
over the edge of a chair like a disembodied arm.
Housekeeping has never been Beau's strong point.

Jake gives a little yip of joy. He jumps away from
me almost as soon as I have the door open, and rushes
towards Beau's wide back. The shades on the big loft

windows haven't been pulled and the wall of the warehouse opposite is black and shadowed with a streetlight from the alley below. Beau says something to Jake that I can't quite make out and reaches down with one hand to rub his ears while with the other he picks out a little tune of single notes. He doesn't turn around and look at me.

'Hey,' I say, coming as far as the couch. 'How are you?'

'I'm fine,' Beau says. 'How are you?' His hand still moves over the keys, and he seems to be watching it intently. I expect him to make some smart ass comment about my hair, but he doesn't even look at me.

'I'm OK,' I say.

I've never seen Beau behave this way before, and I'm not certain what's going on.

'They've arrested Kathleen Harper,' I say. 'I left a message on your machine. Maybe you didn't get it.' In that second I look down at the coffee table and see Beau's phone sitting there on top of an old newspaper. The little red message number says '4'.

'Beau,' I say, 'haven't you listened to your machine? Didn't you get my messages?' His hand stops moving across the keys and he nods, but he still won't look at me. I wonder, suddenly, if something bad has happened at work, or to his parents, and if he's been drinking, and the reason he didn't pick up the phone was because he was down at Sherlock's.

'Sure,' he says. 'I got them.' His hand stops moving over the keys and the last note he hit hangs in the room. 'I got the ones from today, anyways,' Beau says. 'If there were others, I guess I missed those.'

So that's what this is about. He's mad at me because

I didn't call him while I was down in Georgia. A flash
of anger runs through me. I see the basket of violets on
my breakfast tray at the Marriot, and the lock of hair
taped to my bathroom mirror. I feel the cold thing that
happened to my heart when I saw Della Hervey standing in the driveway at the house, and remember the
metallic taste that came into my mouth. I see the sharp
bright edges of the gold letters that spelled Marina's
name out on a headstone that I didn't buy for her.

'For Christ's sake, Beau,' I say. 'Somebody was
trying to kill me!'

At this he swings around on the piano stool so fast
that Jake jumps backwards in surprise.

'Yeah,' Beau says, 'well it wasn't me!' We're staring
at each other like two kids in a playground in the
second before they start hitting and pulling hair.

'I know that,' I say.

'Do you?' Beau asks. The words are hard and clear,
and even in this half lit room I can see that Beau's face
is mottled. His color is high, as if he has a fever or has
been running in cold air. 'Is that why I found out
about it from the police?' he asks. 'Because you trust
me so much? Is that why they came to my office and
started asking where I'd been, and who saw me, and if
I could prove it?'

'I'm sorry,' I say. 'I guess that's what they have to
do.'

'And what do you have to do, Susannah?' Beau
asks. 'Did you have to just disappear? Just vanish off
the fucking face of the earth without saying a word?'

A groundswell of anger is rising between us, and
like an earthquake it shakes the air.

'Yeah!' I realize that I'm yelling now. 'Yeah,' I

shout, 'that is exactly what I had to do, as a matter of fact.' Jake whines at the level of my voice. He pins his ears back against his head and looks from me to Beau. 'Beau,' I say, and I take a deep breath, 'somebody tried to poison Jake. They almost killed him. Somebody came into my apartment and cut my hair off while I was asleep. Somebody—' but I don't get to finish my litany. Beau cuts me off before I can go on.

'And you thought it was me,' he says.

The words hang in the air between us, and Beau stares at me. 'You thought I could have done that,' he says. 'To you.'

We look at each other for a long time, and I don't know what to say. Jake creeps across the floor and shoves the tip of his nose into my hand.

'You didn't even trust me enough, Susannah, not to think that I was trying to kill you,' Beau says, and he turns back to the piano. He picks out a few notes. 'Well,' he says, 'I'm glad they got whoever it was.' Then he starts to play again.

The music ripples out of the shadows and dances across the room. It reaches me and flows on either side of me as if I'm an island in a river, or a stone. I can feel tears rimming at the edge of my eyes, and I stand there for a second, watching Beau's back, and the way his head bobs, and his hands move, and then I pick up Jake's leash. When we get to the hallway, I pull the door shut behind us. The music swallows the sound of our footsteps as Jake and I go back down the stairs.

'Are you all right?' Gordon asks, and his voice makes me jump. I'm sick of people hanging around in shadows and sick of them asking me if I'm all right all the time. I've been sniveling on the way home and wiping my nose on the arm of my jacket, and I feel irritable and slightly embarrassed.

'There's not enough light in this goddamn place,' I say, and Gordon laughs.

'Yeah,' he says, 'but it's very authentic.' Without meaning to, I smile, and Gordon grins too and reaches down and rubs Jake's ruff.

We're standing in the entry hall, and Gordon's obviously just come home from work. He's carrying a briefcase and wearing a long dark overcoat and a suit, and he looks so ordinary and familiar that I'm happy to see him. This surprises me, and I turn around quickly to lock the vestibule door, so he won't see the look on my face.

'You've got some mail here,' he says, 'you want it?'

'Do I have a choice?' I ask.

'Sure,' Gordon says. 'We can throw it out. Or write "no known address", and go outside and stick it back in the mailbox.' He's smiling at me and it occurs to me that I've never really been very nice to him.

'Listen,' I say, awkwardly, 'I, I wanted to thank you.'

This is the first time I've seen Gordon since Detective Aaronson told me earlier today that it was he who let Kathleen Harper into the building. I had been so certain that it had been Cathy that when she told me I had simply stared at her until she finally stopped talking, and tilted her head a little to one side and asked me if I was all right. Then she'd explained to me that I'd be hearing from the prosecutors at the DA's office, and that they had already spoken to Gordon who had agreed to testify if Kathleen pleaded 'not guilty' and we went to trial.

This is essential to our case and, in fact, makes Gordon our star witness, since the guy who works in the video store down the block only saw Kathleen Harper standing on the corner when he went out for a cigarette that night. He didn't actually see her come up the steps and into the house, which, Becca Aaronson tells me, is crucial. Gordon's the only person who can place her inside, and she says we should love him for it.

It's even more important because forensics didn't turn up zip in the basement, and the police in DC haven't been able to get a firm ID, well actually, she admits, any ID, from Sweet Memories, and they never will. The order was placed over the phone, in my name, and the payment was sent an hour later by FedEx, in cash. So, she explains to me, apart from the circumstantial evidence, which is very strong, Gordon is virtually our whole case. He is, so to speak, the linchpin, Becca Aaronson says. Now he's blushing, as if he can read my mind, and for the first time it occurs to me that he's shy.

'I'm sorry,' he says. 'I just feel so awful that I let her in.'

'Don't,' I say, quickly, 'really. Don't. You couldn't possibly have known, and I'm sure she was very convincing.' Gordon nods.

'That doesn't make much difference, though, does it?' he says, and then, before I can reply, he gestures towards the stairs. 'Susannah,' he asks, 'would you like a drink? I've got a cold bottle of wine, and I hate to say this, but you look like you could use one.'

I'm sure I do, I think. I'm sure my eyes are red-rimmed and my face is blotchy, and, although I've now moved on from feeling sorry for myself to being mad at Beau for being mad at me, I still don't feel like being alone. The fact that forensics couldn't find any evidence that Kathleen Harper had ever been in our basement has been sitting in my mind since this morning when Becca Aaronson told me about it. She didn't elaborate. She didn't have to. She'd just taken a deep breath and glanced at me to see if I got the implication. I did. It meant that it was possible that Kathleen had let herself in at nine p.m., while I was still sitting in Bruges with Shawn, and that she'd been there the whole time. The idea that possibly I poured myself a drink, and wandered around, and took my clothes off while Kathleen was standing in my closet, or lying in the dust bunnies under my bed, is too awful to imagine.

The net result is that I'm a little less than eager to be home alone, to think about what forensics did or didn't find when they swept the place this afternoon. Besides, I'm supposed to be grateful to Gordon, who's offered me wine before, which I've turned down. If I keep doing it, it's going to look deliberate. So I say, 'Sure. Thanks. That would be really nice.'

I had started to take Jake upstairs, but Gordon told me he was invited too, so now he's sprawled at my feet and I can see that he's leaving a pale nap of hair across Gordon's rug, which is a newer, and much more expensive, variation on mine. In fact, this newer and more expensive look is true of his whole apartment, and I wonder if he insisted on additional renovations before he moved in and paid for them, or if Zoe just did them herself, and charges him a lot more.

The walls of Gordon's living room are painted bright white, and this makes the wooden paneling on the window seat and the ornate fireplace look buttery soft and almost black, as if carved from shiny, dark chocolate. The lighting fixtures are more modern than mine too. They're bounce lights, little up-turned dishes of frosted glass, and they don't really do enough for the two big abstract canvases that hang on either side of the massive mantel. The furniture is leather, and all at once I can see Gordon buying it. It's a set, and I imagine him picking it out from one of those already arranged living rooms that are displayed at the malls in King Of Prussia. I can see him standing there with a young salesman who shows him how the couch, and the loveseat, and the two armchairs, were featured in the latest edition of *Esquire*.

I know I'm being mean, but there's something about Gordon that eggs me on, something that positively invites me to do this. 'Stop it,' I tell myself, and Jake lifts his head from the rug and glances up at me as if he can read my mind.

A phone starts to ring, and it's a second before I realize that it's mine, and that the sound is coming from upstairs. It's Beau, I think, and I almost start to get to my feet, but that would be impossibly rude, so instead, I start to fidget. I count the rings. There will be five of them before the machine kicks in.

'Do you hear me much?' I ask Gordon, as the last ring dies above us. My living room is directly overhead and I've never even thought to ask before. He's been in the kitchen, where he's doing something that I can't see, so I'm not sure if he's heard me, but then he replies from beyond the door.

'Oh, not much. Just the odd patter of footsteps, or should I say paws, sometimes.' He comes out of the kitchen and he's carrying a tray that has two glasses on it, and a bottle of white wine stuck in an ice bucket, and a little bowl of olives and another one of macadamia nuts, and suddenly I feel utterly self-conscious. I remember that my face is probably grubby from crying, and that I haven't combed what's left of my hair, and that these are the jeans that I wore to the dog park, and that Jake spat on.

Gordon sets the tray down on the glass coffee table, which doesn't have a speck of dust on it. He lifts the bottle out of the ice and pours the wine. When he hands me my glass it's heavy in my hand, and I realize that it's crystal.

'Cheers, Susannah,' Gordon says. 'Welcome home.'

TWENTY-FIVE

The bars of the security grille are a black criss-cross against my pale paint, and from inside the apartment it looks like you could play tic tac toe on the door. I don't know if Zoe and Justin have seen it yet. At the moment they're on their way to Paris. They left this morning, very early, and Cathy and I stood on the front steps, and promised that the house would be fine, and waved while they drove away. When they'd gone Cathy'd turned to me and sighed. 'Paris,' she'd said, 'Wow. I love Paris.' I'd nodded, and thought that before they got back, I'd have to get the security grille taken down.

After all, I don't need it anymore. I've even got the locksmith's number out. I've opened the *Yellow Pages* to his ad and underlined it in red pen, and I should be calling him now, or working on the drawings for the Museum Tea Room, or seeing if I have anything to wear to the lunch I'm having with Lolly this afternoon. Instead I'm sitting at my desk and leafing through the scrapbook that Karen Hervey gave to me.

There are photographs pasted on to pages made of thick colored paper. 'Swamp!' I've written under one in green felt tip pen, and I've decorated the letters with drippy tendrils, and drawn an alligator with big teeth.

The snapshot is from a school trip to the Okekenofee. We stayed overnight in a motel and ran up and down the halls and ate peanut butter snack-crackers that you bought from a vending machine.

In the picture a group of kids whose faces I can't make out line up against the railing of a walkway that spans greasy water. They're sticking their tongues out and waving, and behind them long ropes of Spanish moss fall from the top of the frame. There are some pressed flowers on the next page. Almost all of the color has left their petals, which look translucent and threaded by tiny veins, and I can't remember where they're from, or why they were important to me.

On the next pages six valentines are glued side by side in a center spread, and I've written 'February 14!!!' and drawn a bow, and an arrow that pierces a heart. Only the backs are glued, so I can still open the pages of the cards. One is in the shape of a heart with silver writing on it, and another has a wreath of flowers and a fat cupid with wings that look far too small to keep him in the air. One says 'Be Mine!' in block letters on the front, and I remember it because it was not given to me. It was sent to Marina by Sonny Delray, who left it in our mailbox in a red envelope. When she'd opened it, standing in the middle of our bedroom, she had thrown it into the air, laughing, and said, 'Here, you might as well keep it, since he doesn't even know which one of us is which!'

When the phone rings, it's so loud that I jump. I start to answer it, but instead I let my hand hover over the receiver. Last night when I had come back upstairs after finishing Gordon's wine, I had seen the message light as soon as I came through the door. I had hit the button, certain that I would hear Beau's voice, but there had been nothing there, just the sound of the tone and empty air.

For half a second I had thought that I had heard someone speaking, had heard the sound that a voice makes when it is cut off, and I had wondered if it was Beau, and if he had started to say something to me and then had changed his mind. I'd played the tape back three times then, bending over it, as if I could sense him there, as if his reflection was somehow imprisoned on the little box on my desk, and I could divine it if I tried hard enough, but in the end I'd decided I was wrong, and that there was nothing, and I had erased the tape.

Now the voice is Benjy's. He doesn't ask if I'm all right, which I'm grateful for. He'd done that just once when I returned the Taurus. When I'd said, 'Yes', he'd just looked at me and nodded. 'You're a smart cookie, Doll,' he'd said. 'You know how to take care of yourself.' Now he's telling me that he has a new door for me, one that will actually match, and that I should bring the car in ASAP. I listen to his voice, and then, when he hangs up, I close the shiny covers of the scrapbook with a snap.

'Do not, I repeat, do not, be late,' Lolly had said. 'Do you hear me?'

'Do not pass go. Do not collect two hundred dollars,' I had replied.

'What?' her voice had sounded genuinely confused

and then she had sighed. 'Susannah, I should kill you, but I won't because I'm glad you're back. This reservation was very hard to get,' she had added.

And so I am making a special attempt not to be late. In light of this, and because I'm dressed up, I've taken a cab uptown instead of walking, and I've allowed enough time for it to drop me at 'Stratus', which is one of the better toy stores in the city. 'Toy', in so far as it relates to children, is a misleading term. This place is filled with all sorts of stuff, from every Stieff animal ever made to enough science kits and telescopes to keep most adults I've ever known happy. They sell the best kites I've ever seen, birds and airships and dragons in wild, bright colors with streamers attached to their tails. George and I went through a kite phase, and I'm tempted to walk through that department now, but I don't have time. I head for art supplies instead.

It only takes me a few minutes to find what I'm looking for, and I try not to get sidetracked amidst the endless rows of stickers and fluorescent pens. There are scrapbooks in all sizes here, and they range from plain to very fancy. Finally, I pick out a big one that comes in a box with a silver pen and a gold pen, and press on letters, and colored glitter that you can use with a glue stick. Then I take it down front, and stand in line, and when I pay for it, I arrange to have it wrapped and shipped to Miss Karen Hervey at 727 Rural Route One in Petamill, Georgia.

The lunch, Lolly had told me, is so we can 'size up the competition', which, in this case, is a very expensive new Thai restaurant that's just opened on the roof of one of the huge waterfront blocks, and is getting excellent write-ups. Which gives Lolly fits.

Normally Richard, her husband, or whatever he is, would go with her on one of these expeditions into enemy territory, but he has a meeting today, so Lolly's asked me. We're going for lunch rather than dinner because, Lolly insists, lunch is when you can really tell what a place is about. 'Everybody puts on the dog for dinner,' she had said to me on the phone, 'but lunch is when you can tell whether or not it's really a quality act.' Buffets are the kiss of death.

'I hope it revolves,' she hisses at me as we get into the elevator. 'If it revolves it will be really tacky.'

'Even if it doesn't,' I say, 'maybe there will be Buddhas.'

There are, but they're not as bad as they could have been. They're small and carved out of dark wood, and made into kind of a screen that hides the register. The place is called Chaing Mai Orchid, and the waiter, who is almost certainly a kid from Penn wearing a Thai silk cummerbund, leads us to a table by the far wall, which is entirely made of glass. The view of the river is stupendous, but I wouldn't advise this seating arrangement for anyone who suffers from vertigo. Before she sits down, Lolly moves her chair imperceptibly inwards.

'The "Orchid" is too much,' she mutters, leaning towards me after the waiter has gone. 'Chaing Mai would have been much better left alone. They couldn't help gilding the lily.' The thought of this makes her happy and she orders us a bottle of champagne.

'What's this for?' I ask, after the waiter has fussed around with an ice bucket and the bottle.

'For you,' Lolly says raising her flute to touch the edge of mine. She takes a sip, and then she says, 'Now, does buying you a bottle of Moët give me the right to know what the Hell's going on?'

'No,' I say, 'but I'll probably tell you anyways.'

Her eyebrows, which appear to have been recently plucked into two perfect half moons, are raised, and they almost disappear into her bangs. She's had her hair cut since I saw her last, and it makes her look a little like Doris Day.

'I had a visit from a Detective Aaronson,' she says, 'who, incidentally, has all the charm of a prison warden. Some other specimen came to visit Richard. Reminded him of something out of *Tales Of The Crypt*.'

'Philadelphia's finest,' I say. 'They were only doing their job.' There's a terrible inevitability to this, and I wonder if Lolly's mad at me too now, and if she's going to fire me, and that's why she ordered champagne. Little bubbles fizz and explode on the back of my tongue.

'I'm sorry, Lolly,' I say. 'I'm really sorry. I should have told you myself.' Then I tell her about the phone calls, and the flowers, and Kathleen Harper, and my hair, and someone singing Shoo Fly in the basement.

'Jesus Christ,' Lolly says, when I'm finished. She reaches for the bottle and pours us both another glass, and this brings the waiter running. He pretends to be full of remorse, but secretly he's very irritated with us for touching the bottle on our own, because now the maître d' is glaring at him.

When he finally goes away, Lolly points at my head.

'That, by the way,' she says, 'is hideous. Where did you have it done? Some place on the campus?'

'Just about,' I say. She shakes her head, as if this confirms her worst fears about me.

'Well,' she says, opening her menu, 'at least you won't need a costume tonight.'

'It's not that bad,' I protest. She raises one eyebrow at me.

'I'm taking you to New York,' she says, 'next time I go.' I realize I should maybe be insulted by this, but I'm not. Actually, it sounds fun.

'Lolly,' I say, 'are you going to make a fashion plate out of me?'

'Well,' she says, flipping a menu page, 'there's always hope.'

We've finished off a plate of a confused cross between dim sum and sushi, and we're on the last glass of the champagne and picking at a selection of marzipan-like little cakes when Lolly pats her lips with her napkin and drops it on the table.

'So,' she says, 'are they sure it's this woman?'

'Kathleen Harper,' I say. 'I think so. I mean, they think so.'

'What do *you* think?' Lolly asks, and I realize that it's the first time that anyone's asked me this question.

'I don't know,' I say.

The words have an unsettling effect on the insides of my stomach, and at the same time it's a relief to actually say them. I look out at the river, at the piers and at the tiny shape of the Moshulu, which was once a schooner and is now a restaurant and a night club for tourists. When I look back at Lolly, she's watching me.

'I was so certain that it had to be something in Georgia,' I say. 'I was so sure that she must have found something out down there, come to some big realization, but maybe the only reason I believed that was because it was the part of her life that I knew. Maybe I couldn't really grasp the fact that she had another life, one that I knew nothing about, because I made it that way. I don't know. Maybe, in the end, even I wanted to believe that no matter what happened between us, somehow we'd always know about each other. We'd always be the nightspinners.'

Lolly looks at me and raises her eyebrows. 'Nothing,' I say, 'it's just a name that we had for ourselves when we were kids.' I drain my glass and shake my head. 'I was wrong, that's all. I mean, the only person who ever led me to believe Marina discovered anything in Georgia was Kathleen herself, who may not be exactly reliable.'

'Not just Kathleen,' Lolly says. 'There was the conversation with Rex—'

'Dex.'

'Rex, Dex, whatever. It still sounds like a dinosaur. But more importantly, Marina too. She called you from down there, didn't she?'

'Yeah,' I say, 'she did.' I can hear the sound of her voice, first demanding, and then, whispering, 'You know it won't do any good, Shoo.' Well, she was right, I think. Nothing I've done has done any good.

'You could not have saved her,' Elena has said to me, how many times, leaning through the dusty air in her office. 'There is nothing you could have done to save her.' But now, looking out through this glass wall with the waterfront and the hundreds of tiny cars and people scurrying by below, I wish that I could be as sure.

'I just thought,' I say to Lolly, 'that it must have been someone she knew, and that when she went back there, she figured out who it was. I thought that that reassured her, made her think that she could handle them, and that that's why she opened the door.'

'Well probably it was,' Lolly says. 'Probably it was this Kathleen. Maybe that's what Marina figured out down there. Maybe she needed to get away from her to see it. I mean, this guy says he let her into your building, right?'

'Yes,' I say, 'I know. She even admits to being there. So it must have been her. And why would she fasten on me if she hadn't killed Marina?'

'They're sure it's the same person?'

'I'm sure,' I say. 'I can feel it.'

'Well, anyways,' Lolly says, 'you don't have to worry anymore.' She reaches out and covers my hand with her own. 'You've got to try to move on, Susannah. It's over now.'

It's three-thirty by the time we get in Chaing Mai Orchid's express elevator. The insides of the compartment are paneled halfway up and padded the rest of the way with blue and green striped Thai silk, so the effect is slightly like being inside a small aquarium. We're joined by a party of four middle-aged men in

dark suits and overcoats. They murmur amongst themselves and suck on toothpicks while the doors snap
shut and we fall back down to earth.

Lolly offers me a ride home, and for one guilty
moment I think of Jake, and I'm tempted to accept it,
but then I feel the soft mist of a drizzle that's started
up, and I decide to walk instead. The champagne's
gone to my head a little, and our lunch was so
fashionably light that I feel the need to sober up. We
kiss the air beside each other's cheeks, and I watch
Lolly as she darts across the street, and jumps on to the
far sidewalk, landing like a bird on a branch.

I'm only three blocks from Beau's apartment, and
at first I don't mean to go there, but as I start walking,
I can't help it, and suddenly I'm filled with an urgent,
almost weepy need to see him. I know, of course, that
he's at work, and that he won't be home, but I cross
at the lights and cut into his street anyways, as if I
think that standing outside his door will somehow
make me feel better.

The florist company that Beau lives above is going
out of business. It was a big place, a wholesale supplier
with just a small shop in front that I guess sold the
leftovers, the odd groups of stems and pieces of foliage
that they couldn't fit into those towering arrangements
that go in hotel lobbies and on the front tables of places
like Tiffany's. On some weekend mornings when I've
been here, the warehouse doors have been open
revealing a cave of blooms, bright blobs of color that
melt back into a cavern of brick. This afternoon,
however, the doors are closed, and through the plate
glass window of the shop I can see a woman packing
pieces of styrofoam into a box.

I push the security code on Beau's street door, and
it occurs to me briefly that I'm trespassing, but since
he's not here, I can't see that it makes any difference.
Inside, the fluorescent light above the hall buzzes, and
when I start to climb the stairs I pause, almost as if I'm
hoping that I'll hear music, but there's nothing, only
dead silence, and then the sound of my shoes on the
stairs.

By the time I actually get to his door, I'm feeling
foolish. I have a key, and I could go inside, but I don't.
Instead I decide that I'll write a note, but when I dig a
pen out of my bag, I don't know what to say. So
finally I just fold the piece of paper into the shape of a
dog that might be Jake, and then I wedge it in the
crack of the door and leave, quickly, before anybody
knows that I was here.

There are no cabs in the street. Four o'clock is a quiet
time of day. People who have been coming and going
for lunch are back at the office, and the rush hour
hasn't started yet. I want to get home in time to take
Jake for a good run in the park before it starts to rain
properly, and I decide that the fastest thing to do is cut
down the alley beside Beau's building which will bring
me out on a busier cross street where I should be able
to find a taxi.

It's too early for the streetlights to come on, and
the high brick walls of the warehouses rise so high that
when I look up it seems like there's just a narrow
wedge of cloud above. If I stood with my back pressed
against the opposite wall and looked up I could see
Beau's line of windows. I could check to see if light is

shining through, and if maybe he's hiding up there after all. Once, when I was drunk, I threw gravel at them and actually hit some of the thick, wavy panes, but there's no gravel lying around today, and I'm not about to lean against the warehouse wall, which smells of urine and rain.

There are no sidewalks in the alley and it's barely wide enough for a car. I suppose that originally it was nothing more than a passage, and that it dates from the days when people used horses. Now it feels as if I could brush my fingers along both walls if I spread my arms out wide enough. I pass an old door that looks like a coal hole, and the first heavy splashes of rain plummet down through the gap between the roofs and hit the pavement in front of me. Looking up, I can see them, big, soft, gray drops, and I realize that I'm going to be walking Jake in the rain, which he hates. He folds his ears down and slinks, and sometimes I have to coax him even to come out of the vestibule and on to the street. I am thinking about this, and wondering what effect the rain will have on trick or treating, and what I will say to Beau when he finds my origami dog and calls tonight, when I hear the footsteps.

At first I think that they're an echo, just a trick the high walls of the alley play, a reverberation that I haven't noticed before, but then I realize they're not. I hold my breath and I can hear them. They're measured, and not loud, but they're there, a little ways back, and constant, as if someone entered the alley a minute ago, and is slowly gaining on me.

I'm about halfway down now and the walls ahead of me seem to converge and draw in on each other, like the end point of a tunnel. I don't know if I can reach it, even if I run, and I'm trying, desperately, to remember what's on the cross street ahead. There may be stores, and there should certainly be traffic, although I can't hear it. All I can hear is the sound of my heels on the pavement, and the echo underneath them that moves in perfect time. I don't want to make an obvious motion, but I pull my bag in front of me and reach for my keys. I know that I could scream, but there are no windows in the wall of the warehouse opposite Beau's, and his is the only loft in his building, and he isn't home. I walk faster, and the steps behind me speed up.

They sound as if they're drawing in. I'm sure they're getting louder, and growing closer, and the end of the alley seems just as far away. I slip the strap of my bag off my shoulder, and grab it halfway down. It's not heavy enough to do damage, but I might be able to swing it once. I might be able to hit someone in the face hard enough to confuse them momentarily. Inside the soft leather, I wrap my other hand around the keys so their points stick up through my fingers. The eyes, I think, you aim for the eyes. Then, in mid-stride, I stop and wheel around. In one motion, I brace my feet and swing my arm back. My breath comes out in a long rush.

But there's nothing there. The alley is empty. No one stands between me and the gray block of light on Beau's street.

TWENTY-SIX

'I'm a martini!' Cathy announces as she twirls across the landing in front of me. 'This is the rim of the glass,' she says, holding out a circle of silver wire that hangs from her shoulders, 'and my lipstick's pimiento. What do you think?'

She is wearing a silver leotard and silver spray-painted ballet shoes. Silver sparkles dust her cheeks and the bridge of her nose. Her hair is covered by a fuzzy green hat that has a cardboard dowel sticking out of either side of it, so her head looks like an olive impaled on a giant toothpick.

'It's great.' I say. 'Are you gin or vodka?'

She stops twirling and puts her hands on her hips. Now she looks like an angry martini.

'Come on,' she says. 'Don't be a party pooper. Come with us. Jill is going as a daiquiri, it'll be fun.' I make a face at her.

'I don't have a costume,' I say.

'I have an extra one,' she counters. 'Shawn was going to wear it before he went off to poopy old Mexico. You can come as a tequila sunrise.'

'Beau's coming over,' I say, which as far as I know he isn't, but it's a trump card anyways. In Cathy's world boyfriends take precedence. She looks at me and narrows her eyes. She suspects that I'm lying, but she doesn't want to say so.

'Well,' she says finally, 'then you get to be on Trick or Treater duty.' She picks up the big mixing bowl of Tootsie Rolls and mini Snickers bars that's sitting on the landing table and thrusts it into my hands. 'Gordon is hopeless,' she adds. 'I tried to get him to do it last year, and he wouldn't even go downstairs after the first few times. Besides, I think he ate all the peanut butter cups.'

'OK,' I say. 'I don't even like Tootsie Rolls.' Cathy's intercom buzzes, and she pulls her door closed and starts down the stairs. Then she stops and looks back at me.

'Are you sure?' she asks. 'You don't even have to wear a costume.' She's frowning with concern because I'll be left out, sitting home on Halloween by myself, when I could be at a United Airlines party dressed as a cocktail.

The buzzer goes again, and she raises her eyebrows.

'Trick or Treaters,' I say, and I follow her down the stairs, hefting the giant bowl of candy, and telling Jake to 'stay', because he gets too excited and barks and knocks little kids over.

The rain has slowed to a drizzle, and a coven of tiny witches are standing on the top step. I lower the bowl so they can grab handfuls of candy, and over their heads I watch Cathy skip towards the waiting cab. The back door opens, and I get a glimpse of someone inside dressed in yellow, who I figure must be the daiquiri. Cathy squeals when she steps in the edge of a puddle by the curb, and for a second she has a problem adjusting her wire hoop and ducking her head low enough so her toothpick doesn't get caught on the cab's roof, but then she slides into the backseat, and slams the door, and they're gone.

The mother of the little witches thanks me, and as I close the heavy front door, they run down the steps and join a mini Darth Vader and an angel with pink wings. I stand for a minute in the vestibule, looking out through the etched panels on to the street. The pattern of swirls and arabesques and a garland of flowers superimposes itself on the dark band of the sidewalk and on the colored bulks of the cars that cruise past. People appear as fuzzy outlines in the frosted glass, and then they come briefly into focus and vanish again, moving silently in and out of sight like fish swimming back and forth in an aquarium.

Inside the house the front hall is so quiet that I almost feel like I should tiptoe, and instead of closing the big doors to the vestibule and shutting out the glimpse of the street, I prop them open. Zoe would frown on this. The inner doors are always supposed to be locked, as a security measure, so if some bad guy makes it through the front door, he can be locked into the marble-floored entry, trapped in the high cage of Zoe's midnight blue walls until the police can arrive and take him away. In so far as I know, however, this has never happened, and, I think to myself as I wedge the door-stop home, it certainly didn't deter Kathleen Harper on either of her visits. This makes me wonder if I should go down into the basement and check the back door to the garden. One look down the stairs decides me against it. It's dark and spooky down there, and I content myself with locking the door that leads up into the hallway instead. It's uncharacteristically flimsy, compared to the rest of the house, but it makes me feel better.

I'm only wearing heavy socks, and so I slide across the polished parquet floor like a kid. I collide with the stairway, and grab the rails and bend my neck all the way back, looking up to the big square of the skylight that glows fuzzy white above me, and to the flame-shaped lights on the landings that seem to flicker a little and then go still, as if they might actually be lit by gas instead of electricity. I hang like this until I see stars, and then I climb the stairs, running my hand along the banister and stroking the apples, and the leaves, and the clusters of grapes that hang like petrified fruit from the newel posts, and I don't make any noise at all.

The buzzer goes three times in the next twenty minutes, and each time I take my bowl and run dutifully down the stairs and stand on the damp top step in the misty rain and offer Tootsie Rolls to wizards and little monsters. In between trips, I find a bag of Mars Bars and some Hershey's Kisses on top of my refrigerator, and so I add those to the bowl too. The second time I let Jake come with me, but he barks at a tiny green dinosaur, who recoils against his father and looks as if he might cry, and so after that I close the security grille and leave the door open so he can sit in the apartment and watch me through the bars as I go down.

Beau doesn't call. It's almost eight o'clock, and I wonder if he's out at a Halloween party too, dressed up as a doctor, or a pumpkin. I could call him, I think. I could leave a message in case the paper dog got blown into the stairway, or stepped on, when he opened the door. I could make up some silly pun about Trick or Treats. I'm thinking about what this might be when the buzzer distracts me, and I take up my bowl again and go skittering down the stairs.

This time the ghosts and princesses are a little older and the mother waits at the bottom of the steps and waves to me when they leave. I notice when I close the door that there seem to be fewer of them now, and I suppose that soon they'll all be hustled home, and that only the bigger kids who throw eggs and spray shaving foam, and the cops who watch them, will be left on the streets. My bowl is half-empty, and as I go back up the stairs, I wonder if we'll get though it all, or if some will be left over for Cathy to use next year. The Snickers bars have been going the fastest, and I'm counting them up, trying to figure out how many Tootsie Rolls there are for everyone left, when Gordon pops his head out of his door like a jack-in-the-box and says, 'Susannah. Hi!'

He's been so quiet that I didn't even know he was here. I'd assumed that I was in the house alone, and seeing him is momentarily disconcerting.

'Hi,' I say, and I realize that I'm holding the bowl out in front of me like an offering. 'I've been doing the trick or treating. For Cathy,' I add. 'She went to a party. As a martini.'

'I know,' Gordon says. 'Last year she went as a zebra.' I imagine this. I can see Cathy covered in stripes with a pair of ears made of wire and tissue paper mounted on her head. 'It was an African party,' Gordon adds. 'The guy who went with her was a Masai warrior.' He pauses and looks at me, and then he opens the door wider and says, 'Come on in.' I think of Jake, and of whether I'll be able to hear the buzzer. 'They're tailing off anyways,' Gordon says, reading my mind. 'Do you have any peanut butter cups in there?'

'No,' I say, and just to make sure he doesn't steal the last of the Snickers, I put the bowl down on the stairs before I step inside.

He's got the gas fire lit in his big fireplace, and it's much more impressive than mine. His actually looks like flames. The bright red tongues climb up over a pile of painted glass logs and make them glow from inside. The lights must be on dimmers, because the room is more shadowed than it was last night, and the low light suits it. The walls don't seem as white, and the paneling looks clubby, and very male.

'This house must have been magnificent,' I say, 'don't you think?'

'Oh yeah,' Gordon says. He's pulling the curtains across the bay window and the windowseat, shutting out the sparkle and glare of the streetlights. 'I love these places,' he says. 'I've always dreamed of being able to afford one. You know, the whole thing, to do it up. I used to walk down these blocks, picking out which one I'd want.' He smiles at me, and I imagine him as a little boy, looking into lighted windows.

'Did you grow up in the city?' I ask. I realize as I say it that I know absolutely nothing about him, that in the year I've lived here, I've never bothered to ask. He looks at me for a second and then he shakes his head.

'No,' he says, 'well, not this one anyways. I was born in DC. We didn't have nice things. Not like you, I bet.'

There's an awkward pause. I can't think of anything

to reply to this, except to say that we didn't have nice things either, but before I can get the words out Gordon says, 'Can I get you a drink? Some wine?' He seems excited and kind of fidgety, like a child who has a secret. I hesitate for a second, and then I remember how good the bottle of Chardonnay that he opened last night was. A glass won't hurt, I think, and besides, it'll help me get my nerve up to call Beau.

'Sure,' I say. Gordon grins and ducks into the kitchen. A second later he reappears with a bottle and two of the heavy crystal glasses. I take the glasses from him and while he pours Gordon says, 'This is getting to be a habit.' Then he says, 'Happy days!' raising his glass. While I take a sip of the chilly, straw colored wine, he vanishes into what I guess must be a hallway, or his bedroom.

The lights are on in Gordon's kitchen, and I wander over to the door and look in. It's about the same size as mine, but much more modern and expensive. The whole room is white, with a tiled floor, and a white refrigerator, and a fancy halogen stove that's set into a white wood island and looks like it's never been used. In fact, the whole kitchen looks like it's never been used, and it occurs to me that I can't remember one cooking smell ever wafting up from Gordon's apartment. I imagine that there's a microwave somewhere in one of these white cabinets, and that if I opened the fridge, I'd find bottles of white wine and beer, and rows of jars of olives, and things like salsa and pickled herring treats, and gherkins.

The walls are empty, except for a calendar from the Sierra Club, and a magnetic strip that holds a pristine set of knives whose blades are so new that they sparkle under the lights. The phone is one of those sleek panel things with what looks like a little computer screen on it and lots of buttons for stuff like speed-dial. I remember what Shawn said about him probably calling porn lines, and now it seems slightly ridiculous. I can't imagine Gordon phoning anyone more sinister than L.L. Bean, but even so, I take a look at the frequent number panel on the phone. There are no names penciled into the little white slots, and when I look around I realize that there's not even a menu for a Chinese restaurant or a pizza delivery service stuck on the refrigerator. Suddenly, the place makes me uneasy. Gordon's loneliness permeates it, and I feel embarrassed that I've noticed, as if I've opened a door and found him with no clothes on, or sitting on the john.

'Here!' Gordon says, 'I found it!' His voice startles me and I spin around more quickly than I mean to. Some of my wine spills over the edge of my glass, and I wonder if I look guilty. I can feel my cheeks begin to color. Gordon doesn't seem to notice. He's standing in the kitchen doorway holding a round orange card in his hand as if it's a trophy, and he's put a jacket on. It's an obviously new, expensive looking, mossy tweed, and it's not quite right over his black turtle neck and his jeans. He waves the card at me and I can see now that it's supposed to be a pumpkin. It has black slit eyes and a snaggle toothed grin.

'It's a party, uptown,' Gordon announces, 'I was going to ask you, you know, if you wanted to come? We could go for a while and then go get some dinner. I made a late reservation,' he adds, 'at Monique.'

I know Monique. It's a wildly expensive French bistro up in the historic district that features things like

open fireplaces and overly cosy little tables frilled with
that flowery neo-Provençal material that gives me a
headache. It's frequently billed as 'Romantic' in the
tourist guides, and is the sort of place where bankers
take their girlfriends on first dates, or when they're
going to propose. I can't imagine sitting in one of
those stuffy little rooms across from Gordon, and I
have no idea what to say. He's watching me, grinning
in expectation, and I notice for the first time that when
he smiles, his face is as round and smooth as a child's.

I start to say something, something about the Trick
or Treating, or Jake, or Beau, but before I can get the
words out, Gordon's talking again. He has switched
now from excited to sincere. He creases his brow and
lowers his eyes a little bit, and when he looks at me
again there's something sneaky in his face. He has a
secret, and he's about to share it with me.

'I'm really, really, sorry about your sister,' he says.
'It must have been horrible for you.' I stare at Gordon.
I've never told anyone in the house about Marina. A
thin prickle of sweat spreads across my chest, and when
I speak my tongue feels thick.

'How did you know?'

Gordon looks at me for a second. 'The police-
woman,' he says. 'She told me why it's so important
that they get this conviction.' I look at him and try to
decide whether he's lying, whether Becca Aaronson
really would have told him this. Before I have a chance
to make up my mind he adds, 'I knew there was
something, anyways. I mean, I guessed. I can tell,
usually, you know, like when someone's been really
hurt. I think people recognize that in each other. I

mean, I believe in that stuff,' he says, 'you know, destiny. Fate. I think it brings people together.'

The air in Gordon's kitchen seems suddenly condensed. It's thick between us, and I feel faintly queasy.

'I don't really want to go to a party,' I hear myself say, but Gordon isn't paying any attention. He's talking about fate again.

'I mean, when all that stuff started happening to you. It was like I was supposed to be here. I don't know how to say this, Susannah,' Gordon says, 'but I want to take care of you. I really do.'

I put my glass down on the island and step backwards. I can feel the cool white tiles of Gordon's kitchen wall through my sweatshirt.

'Gordon—' I say, and my voice sounds strange, as if I'm talking from far away.

'I won't tell anybody,' he says quickly. 'I mean, I wouldn't do that. I understand about stuff like that, really.'

I nod, and Gordon takes this as a signal that everything's OK.

'It's not a fancy dress thing,' he says. He's smiling to reassure me. He's holding the pumpkin out, offering it to me as proof that I won't have to put a sheet over my head and say 'Boo', or wear a witch's hat, but all I can see is his arm coming towards me, backing me up into the corner of the kitchen. 'It's just drinks, and maybe a random vampire or two,' he adds. 'Then we can get away, and talk.' His body blocks the door. I try to take a deep breath, but even so, I feel as if, any second, I might begin to scream.

'I have to go!' I say.

I push past Gordon into the living room. As I move towards the door, I try not to dart. It seems important to go slowly, to keep my eyes on him, and I try to make myself walk, although I'm aware that I must be sidling like a crab.

'Susannah,' he says, 'please.' He's following me, with his hands stretched out and I step away from him and into the open doorway.

'I can't, Gordon,' I say. 'I'm—' I want to say that I'm involved with someone, that I don't want him to care about me, or even want him anywhere near me, but before I can get the words out, he takes my arm.

'Susannah,' he says, 'please. I don't want you to be upset. I just want—'

'No!' I say, and I try to jerk away from him, but he hangs on to me. 'Let me go, goddamn it!' I yell, and I wrench my arm away and spin around, and that's when I see Shawn coming up the stairs. He's taking them two at a time.

'Let go of her! Right now!' Shawn yells. 'What the fuck do you think you're doing?' Upstairs Jake barks once in alarm, and Gordon drops my arm and his face colors.

'Why the Hell don't you mind your own goddamn business, just for once?' he says. 'She's just fine. Ask her.'

Before I can say anything, Shawn grabs Gordon by the lapels of his new jacket and pushes him against the wall. I jump backwards and knock the candy bowl off the stairs. Snickers and Tootsie Rolls spill out on to the red rug. Shawn is sticking his face in close to Gordon's, twisting the lapels of the jacket in his fists.

'You stay the fuck away from her, you pervert. You hear me?' he hisses.

I start to step towards them, to try to stop Shawn from punching Gordon, which he looks like he's about to do, but before I can do anything, Gordon reaches out and shoves Shawn away from him.

'Get off me, you asshole,' he says. 'This'll cost you your job!'

'My job?' Shawn jabs Gordon in the chest with his index finger. 'I know all about you, you fuckin' weirdo. You've got a prior for soliciting and harrassment.' There's a moment of dead silence, and then Shawn says, 'It's true isn't it? Go ahead, tell her.' Gordon is turning sheet white, and I feel my stomach contract. 'I've seen the note from your old community service officer in Zoe's files,' Shawn says. 'The one that he wrote so you could rent this place. The one that says you're not "a danger to society". Well, maybe they'd like to think again. Maybe they'd like to talk to Susannah.'

'I don't have to put up with this,' Gordon says. He steps away from Shawn and, although his skin has blanched pale and I can't swear that he isn't shaking, he looks right at me. 'I'm going out to dinner, Susannah,' he says. 'I'd like it very much if you'd come with me.'

I shake my head. I can't stop staring at him, can't stop wondering if this round baby face is what Marina saw when she opened her front door.

'No,' I hear myself say.

'There,' Shawn says, 'you've got her answer. Now leave her alone.' Gordon is still staring at me. He starts to say something, but decides not to. Instead, he steps past me and reaches inside his apartment and flicks off the lights. Then he closes the door.

'You have a good night,' Gordon says to me, and then he pulls his jacket straight, and steps past Shawn and goes down the stairs. A second later we hear the front door open and close.

'Shi – it,' Shawn says. The word comes out as if he's been holding his breath. 'Are you OK?' he asks, turning to me.

'Yeah,' I say, 'I'm fine.' I can hear Jake whining upstairs, and I call up to him. 'Jakey,' I say, 'it's OK, good boy.' The whine fizzles out to a moan, and I hear him thud down on to the hall floor.

Shawn and I stand there, staring at the stairway as if Gordon might materialize out of thin air any second. 'Is that true,' I ask finally, 'about the prior conviction?' Shawn nods.

'Yeah,' he says. 'I didn't find out until this after-noon, or I would have warned you sooner. I found it in Zoe's files while I was looking some stuff up.' I don't ask why Shawn was going through Zoe's files on her tenants, or why he's here at all, for that matter, since he's supposed to be in Mexico. Right now I really don't care. I'm just glad that he is.

'The conviction came up when they ran a security check on him. They have one of those services do that before they rent to anybody,' Shawn is saying. I try to remember if Zoe and Justin informed me about this before I considered signing a lease, but I can't. 'His community officer squared it,' Shawn goes on, 'or at least he must have convinced Zoe and Justin that

Gordy was a reformed man, and them being them, they decided to give him a chance. Admirable, I guess,' Shawn adds, 'but maybe none too smart. That's why I'm here, incidentally,' he says. 'Zoe called from Paris just before I was due to leave. They've screwed up some big bid, FedEx has messed up the delivery, and she offered me enough money so I said I'd stay and fix it for her.'

'I'm glad you did,' I say.

'Yeah,' says Shawn. 'So am I.'

'Should we have let him go?' I ask, nodding towards Gordon's apartment.

'What?' Shawn says, 'we were going to detain him? Tie him up with the light cord? You and me? Besides, do you want him in the house?'

I shake my head. 'I should go call Mark Cope,' I say. 'He's the Detective. The one who's handling all this.'

Shawn nods. 'OK,' he says. 'But come on down after. I'm going to stay at Zoe and Justin's tonight and get this thing fixed for them.' He turns and starts to go down the stairs. 'You don't want to be alone,' he says.

I figure I should pick up the Snickers bars and the Tootsie Rolls, and I bend down to start collecting them, then I let them drop on to the rug again. I'll do it later. Right now, what I want is to hear the sound of Mark Cope's voice. I'm not sure even what I'm trying to tell him, what it means about Gordon, what the implications are for Kathleen, but, I decide as I start climbing the stairs, I'll let him figure that out. All

I can figure is that Becca Aaronson didn't tell me this because she thought it didn't matter anymore, or because she never bothered to find out.

Jake is lying flat on the hall floor of my apartment with his nose and front paws shoved as far through the bars as he can get them. He wriggles and moans at me while I turn the locks.

'Good!' I say. I get down on my knees and kiss him on the top of his head while I pull his ears, 'Good, good, boy!'

All of a sudden, I'm feeling shaky, and a little giddy, the way you do when you've just skidded in a car and narrowly missed running into something or going off the road. I pull the security grille closed behind me and Jake, and go into the bedroom to get my bag. My 'organizer' is buried in the bottom of it, and it takes me a second to open it, and then to figure out how to retrieve what I want, but eventually, sure enough, I pull up Mark Cope's listing. I prop the thing against my alarm clock so I can see it, and punch his home numbers into the bedroom phone, but when I hold it up to my ear there's nothing but silence.

I look at the phone and see that its little battery light isn't even on, much less green.

'Damn,' I say out loud. I probably pulled the plug out by mistake when I was making the bed this morning. I put it down and take the organizer and go into the living room, but when I pick up that phone there's no dial tone there either.

Halloween, I think. Some jerk's screwed with the wires somewhere, and now the phone's dead. Cathy's been telling me to get a cell for ages, and so has Lolly, but I hate the things. I'll have to walk up to the video store, I think, and use their phone. Then it occurs to me that I won't. Shawn's here, and he's definitely the sort of person who will carry a cell. I close the organizer and slip it into my sweatshirt pocket and then I unlock the security grille. Jake follows me out on to the landing, but when he gets to the top step, I turn around and tell him to stay. I think Justin's allergic to hair or something, and even if he isn't I don't want Jake shedding all over the apartment. I've already had to pay to have Zoe's overcoat cleaned.

'Good dog,' I say, 'you stay.' Jake gives me a long look, but he flops down on the landing like I tell him. 'Good,' I say. 'Good boy! I'll be right back.' Then I start down the stairs calling, 'Shawn? Hey, Shawn, are you there?'

TWENTY-SEVEN

Zoe and Justin's apartment is bigger than I expected. I've been in their downstairs office, which is on the other side of the main hallway, but I've never been in here before. The living room and kitchen must have been the original dining room, or possibly even a ballroom. It runs across the back of the house, and between its big sets of bay windows that look over the garden there is a set of French doors that open on to a deck. White blinds hang above the black panels of glass, and the effect, combined with bright white walls, makes the room look monochrome, as if the color's been bleached out of it. I would have added some red, I think, or maybe even a deep purple for contrast. Anything to lift it out of this expanse of black and white that is supposed to look minimalist and trendy but in the final analysis is dull.

The lights don't help. They're spots that fall in pools and leave shadows washed up in the corners like splashes of dirty water. There's music playing, something classical, maybe Brahms or Beethoven, and I don't see Shawn right away. I step inside and the door swings shut behind me. It's not until I call him that he appears out of what I guess must be a bathroom, or maybe a bedroom, and by that time I've already picked up the telephone that's sitting on a table by the couch. It's dead. I'm still holding it in my hand when he walks in.

'Hey,' he says, 'that was fast. Have they put out an APB? I've always wondered what that stands for, APB. They say that a lot on cop shows. You want a beer?'

'All Points Bulletin,' I say. 'Sure. And the phones are dead, so I couldn't call. Do you have a cell I can use?'

He's wearing motorcycle gear tonight, a black jacket with lots of pockets and complicated looking zips, so his color scheme fits right in with the rest of the room. It crosses my mind that maybe he planned it that way.

'Have a seat,' he says, and waves at the high half back stools that are pulled up to the breakfast bar. They're stainless steel, and go with the rest of the kitchen, which is open plan and takes up the back of the room. Shawn opens the shiny fridge and takes out a couple of bottles. I slide on to a stool, which is uncomfortable and probably cost a fortune, while he rummages in a drawer for an opener. Watching him, I remember what he said about being Zoe and Justin's wife. He moves around this place like he owns it.

'Pretty weird about our friend Gordy, huh?' he says. 'I actually tried to tell you earlier, but you weren't here.'

'When was it?' I ask, 'the soliciting thing?'

'About two years ago,' Shawn says. 'I couldn't tell too much about the details from the letter. Just that he got community service, really, and that it happened. Obviously.'

'Well, I'm glad you showed up when you did,' I say.

'Think nothing of it.' He grins at me over his shoulder. 'I'm just glad I poked my nose into those files.' The music swells and falls again, and Shawn pops the caps on the bottles.

'Thanks,' I say, when he hands me one. 'Here's to being nosy.'

'Here's to the Day of The Dead,' Shawn says.

I get my organizer out of my pocket and try to figure out how to find Mark Cope's number again.

'I can never work these damn things.' I take a sip of the beer and press the right button, and as if by magic the number flashes on to the little black screen. 'Eureka!' I say. When I look up he's leaning against the edge of the stove watching me. He raises his bottle and starts to dig around in his pockets for what I presume will be his cell phone, but when he finds what he wants and pulls it out, it's a pack of cigarettes instead.

'Want one?' he asks. Somehow I don't think Zoe would like us smoking in here and I shake my head. Shawn lights up and blows a thin stream of smoke towards Zoe and Justin's beautifully restored ceiling.

'Cell phone?' I ask.

'Oh, right, the cell phone. Sure.'

He stands there smiling at me and holding the beer, and the cigarette, and for the first time I wonder if maybe he's stoned, or high on something. There's a funny glazed look in his eyes that I didn't notice when he was upstairs before, and I wonder what exactly he was doing in the other room before I came down. It occurs to me that I really don't know very much about him, and I feel a little ripple of unease and think that maybe this really wasn't such a great idea. Besides, stoned people are a pain in the ass.

'You know,' I say, taking a swallow of the beer, 'don't worry about it. Jake needs to go out anyways, so maybe we'll just walk up to the video store.'

'Oh, no,' Shawn says quickly. 'I'm just not sure what pocket it's in.' He smiles at me, and then he puts his bottle down and starts to unzip his jacket. 'Maybe it's in here,' he says, and all at once I understand.

There was no call from Paris. The dead phone line isn't a Halloween trick. And he isn't here to fix a bunch of papers. What he's here to do is kill me.

I know I should run. I should at least throw something. Or kick. Or scream. But I can't. I can't move. My whole body has seized up. My muscles have clenched. My mind has too. Like a clock whose hands have been stopped, I've come to a complete halt. I'm frozen in time. All I can do is stare at the necklace.

He's wearing a black T-shirt, which makes the gold chain glitter, and the medallion that hangs from it seems smaller than a quarter. Its wavy edges look like someone drew them in with an unsteady hand, but even from where I am sitting, some ten feet away, I can see the picture clearly. It's exactly as I remember it. The big man stands in the river, one leg extended beyond the other, as if he's feeling for stepping stones, and might fall. Which would be a bad idea, because on his shoulders he carries the baby Jesus.

The last time I saw it, I felt a similar rush of paralysis and confusion, because then, like now, it was not

where I had intended it to be. It was not guarding
Marina, guaranteeing her safe journeys as Mrs Pease in
the jewelers had promised me it would. It was hanging
from the neck of the boy she had loved.

'Charlie?'

I say the name almost without meaning to, but
even before the man standing in front of me shakes his
head, I sense that I am wrong, and that the St Christopher medal had not guarded Charlie any more than
it had guarded Marina.

'Ironic,' he says, 'isn't it. Now you're the one who
can't tell us apart.'

But I can. All at once the pieces slide into place,
just like chessmen on a board, and the past is recon-
structed in front of me.

When did she guess, I wonder. Did a card come
with the flowers? Was there something in the wording
of the valentine? Or was it just a hope that turned into
a conviction? A hope that Charlie Eames would never
do this to her, would never torment her like this, even
after all these years, and a conviction that blossomed
and grew into certainty, that if it wasn't Charlie it still
had to be someone we'd known a long time ago.

I see Marina sitting with Dex Eames. I see her
smiling because he's confirmed what she already suspects. And then I see her calling me. She stands in the
kitchen and twists the phone cord around her hand.
She's calling to discuss the board with me, to discuss
which move she should make next, and to tell me that
she believes that Charlie Eames never left Petamill at
all.

Shawn's watching me the way a cat watches a
beetle. He caresses the neck of the bottle and his lips

curve upwards. I can remember kissing them. I can remember the soft, mushy feel of those lips, and the voice that whispered through them at that Memorial Day Picnic twenty years ago, 'I love you, I love you.' My sister stops in the alfalfa field just before dawn, her head coming up fast, like a deer's when it scents a hunter. A tiny light glows in the dark by the tangle of old rose bushes. The bright blob of a dandelion head lands at my feet

'You followed them.' I say. 'At night. And you watched. Then you killed him.'

He sighs, as if this story is boring.

'I told him to leave her alone, but even after the barn, he wouldn't listen to me,' he says. 'That Sunday morning, I was down digging a ditch by the silo, and I saw him coming. He stood there and said he'd tell about the barn, and about the rest of the fires, about everything, unless I stopped following her.' The man who used to be Sonny Delray shakes his head at how unbelievable this was. 'I could never do that,' he says. 'Even then, I knew that somebody had to take care of her. Somebody had to make sure she was saved.'

Saved? I think, saved from who? From what? And I see the Delrays driving by our house in their best Sunday clothes, and the billboard with its promises from Jesus.

'Is that why you bought her the plaque?' I ask. 'So she'd be saved?'

My body seems to be thawing and possibly capable of moving again. I tighten my grip on the beer bottle's neck, and wonder if I can use it as a weapon. My keys are in my jeans pocket, and I can't get to them without standing up. I don't want to look away from him, but

I don't think that I saw a knife block, or a set of boning shears, or even a skewer, in the pristine kitchen behind me. Even Jake can't get to me, because Zoe and Justin's apartment door is closed. I slide my feet down from the rung of the stool, feeling for the floor, and he smiles at me as if I've said something clever.

'I'm glad you liked the inscription,' he says. 'I thought of it. I didn't want to take the chance that God would forget her.'

'No,' I try to force myself to sound normal, 'I can understand that.'

I'm gauging the distance between me and him and the door to Zoe and Justin's balcony, wondering if it's locked, and if I could get to it before he could grab me. Even if I could, I don't know how I'd get over the garden wall. I'd be trapped. I can't tell where his knife is, but I'm betting on the pockets of his jacket.

'How did you know where to find her?' I ask. My toes brush Zoe's polished floor.

'I always knew,' he says. 'I kept track. I'm good at that.' I bet, I think, and I imagine Sonny keeping track of us for years. Looking our names up in the phone book. Walking by the apartments where we lived. And later, I imagine him romancing poor Della the way he romanced Cathy, getting up close so he could find phone numbers, and ask questions, and get inside.

'I saw her a couple of times,' he's saying, 'in Petamill. I even ran into her once, on the street. I asked her if she wanted to go for coffee, but she said she was in a hurry. I don't think that was very nice, do you?'

'No,' I shake my head.

'After that, I watched her,' he says, 'when she was home. I kept an eye out for her, just to be sure she was OK. Oh, she never knew,' he answers the question that must be in my face. 'But she looked so sad, up there all alone. I couldn't let her be like that. I knew that then. I couldn't abandon her, not like you did.' I hold my breath, but he doesn't move. There's no flash of a blade, or lunge towards me. Yet.

'I didn't tell her,' he says. 'I had to get ready.'

I don't want to hear this, but I know that if I'm going to have any chance of staying alive, I have to keep him talking. His pauses are terrifying.

'Until you were ready,' I prompt, and he nods.

'I mean,' he says, 'I had to have something to offer her. Something good enough. I went to college, you know. Voc Tech. Not like you guys did, but I did better than anybody thought.' He's proud of this, and he preens a little as he says it. Then he takes a drag on the cigarette, and drops the butt into the beer bottle. 'And I got a job too, a good one.' I remember BethAnn calling him 'city-fied', and saying he'd never marry Della. 'A condo,' he's saying, 'in Falls Church. I had it all ready for her. Furniture and everything. I got a blue rug. Blue was her favorite color.' I nod, trying to choke down the nausea that's rising in my stomach.

'When I called her, I used to sit on that rug,' he says. 'I used to imagine how happy she'd be when she saw it. I liked to hear her voice.' I remember the shrill, empty ringing of the telephone in my apartment, and I don't want to know where he was sitting when he called me.

'I sent her flowers. And a valentine. A big one. I

wanted her to know that she wasn't alone on Valentine's Day. That she shouldn't be sad, because she'd never have to be alone.'

'That was nice of you,' I say. He shrugs.

'I wanted her to be happy.'

'So, why?' I ask. 'Why did you kill her, if you wanted her to be happy?'

My voice barely comes out at all, and for a second I think it's lost in the music and that he hasn't heard me. Then he says, 'You know.'

I stare at him for a second, before I shake my head. 'No,' I say, 'I don't.' As much as I'd like to look away from him, I can't. I have to encourage him to keep going.

'Because,' he says, 'you know, because of what she was doing.' Color is rising up his cheeks, and he can barely say the words. It takes me a second to realize that he's talking about Kathleen Harper.

'Because of Kathleen?' I say. 'You killed her because her friend was a woman?'

'She wasn't her friend!' He's twisting the beer bottle in his hands so the swill slops out of the neck and beer and bits of tobacco spill on to Zoe's kitchen floor.

I don't know if what I'm doing, deliberately throwing this in his face, is a good idea, but I can't seem to stop myself. My heart has suddenly gone from being dead to hammering, and my mouth seems to be working on its own, possibly without too much advice from my brain. Maybe, if he gets worked up, he'll get distracted, which is the only chance I've got.

'You, of all people, should understand,' I say. His face colors again, and he laughs.

'What?' he says, 'What?' He slams his bottle down

on the counter and pulls on his jacket collar. 'You think this is all there is to me?' he asks.

His voice goes soft, it's almost seductive, but the anger underneath it radiates until I can feel it on my face.

'You thought about it, didn't you?' he asks, and I remember the night in Bruges, the mixed signals, the smell of sex that hung in the air. 'You wondered, just like Cathy,' Shawn is saying. He has his face down close to mine and I can feel tears welling. They spill over and dribble down my cheeks. 'You didn't know whether all that talk about weight lifting made you want to fuck me or tell me all about your sad little love life. And that's the trick,' he says, 'that's where I'm so good. I keep you giggling behind my back. Keep you wondering what you're gonna get, and not what I'm doing. You think it hurts me to dye my hair and discuss your make-up?' His voice rises now and he's almost yelling. 'Well, I'll tell you a secret, Shoo Fly,' he shouts. 'Women never take men who talk to them about their make-up seriously, you know that? They don't pay attention to guys who borrow their earrings, and make them squeal.'

Shawn's face is red and the cords in his neck are standing out like taut strings. He stops and takes a breath and it's shallow and ragged, like somebody who's run a long way. Then he gets a grip on himself.

'The joke is,' he says, 'you're so fucking stupid. You either spend all your time wondering if you'll finally be the one to bag guys like me, or you think we're all so cute that we could never, ever, be dangerous.'

I've slid my rear end forward so I'm almost off the stool, but when he starts talking again, I freeze.

'Don't get me wrong,' he adds, 'I wouldn't put up with that sort of shit, even from her. I wouldn't put up with her flaunting around like that, with her being a goddamn queer.'

He's shaking his head back and forth, as if he still can't believe that Marina could have done this to him, and this time when he starts to talk again his voice almost quavers, as if he might cry.

'It's a sin,' he says. 'You go to Hell, you know. I couldn't let that happen. Not to her. I told her. I told her I couldn't. I told her I had to save her. And do you know what she did?'

He's leaning towards me, he's so close that I could reach out and touch him. Spit trembles at the corners of his mouth, and I can see what might be tears on the edge of his eyes. I try to move round and the breakfast bar bites into the small of my back. 'She laughed,' he whispers. 'I told her I could save her, and she looked right at me, and she laughed.'

I see Marina. I see her thinking that this is only Sonny Delray, and that even if he did kill Charlie all those years ago, he's nothing she can't handle. In fact, as far as she's concerned he's nothing at all. Never has been. I see her looking right at him. I see her listening to his offer of a blue rug, and of salvation, and then I see her laugh.

'I'm sorry.' My voice doesn't want to come out properly, but I force it to, and for half a second I think that maybe, maybe if I can make a connection with him, I'll survive this. 'I'm sorry,' I say again, 'I'm so sorry, Sonny—'

But they're the wrong words.

'It isn't even my fucking name!' he yells. 'You

never even knew my fucking name!' And then he hits me, hard.

The breakfast bar holds me up, and I swing my arm back and aim for his head with the beer bottle. At the same time I scream as loud as I can, and I go on screaming. I scream and scream, forcing the noise out of me, hoping that somebody, somewhere, will hear me.

The bottle connects with the side of his nose. It probably startles him more than anything else, but automatically he raises a hand to his face. It gives me time to kick the stool towards him, and run, but not before I see his other hand reach into his pocket and come out with a knife.

My socks slip on the floor, and as I reach the couch he grabs at my leg, and I feel a sharp pain. A lamp falls over and crashes, but I get to the door just before he does. I yank it open and I feel his hand on my waist. He grabs for my head. I feel his fingers slipping, and I scream, twisting and throwing myself forward, my arms flailing, but he's got me around the neck.

There's pressure, sharp pain, and a choking feeling, and when I try to scream again, no sound comes out of my mouth. My feet are still moving, though. They're slipping and scrambling, and the two of us lurch forward into the hallway. I hit the sideboard and a pile of magazines spills on to the floor. Shawn's yelling something, but I can't tell what, and then, out of the corner of my eye, I see Jake.

He's bounding down the stairs, coming as fast as he can, and in the brief glimpse that I get of him, I see that his ears are pinned down and his lips are curled back, exposing his big canines in an ugly grin I want to yell at him, to stop him, because I know Shawn will kill him too, but I can't, and in the next second he leaps, and I fly sideways.

I need to keep both hands on my throat. It's hard to breath, and I can't see Jake. I'm afraid he's been stabbed, and that he's lying somewhere, and I can't help him. A lot of blood is seeping through my fingers. It keeps coming no matter how hard I press. I can feel it on my arms and running down my chest, and I know that I have to get to the door, and out on to the street. Because Shawn's cut my throat, and I'm dying.

I get up and take a step and almost fall. Black smears rise and shift in front of my eyes. My legs don't work, and I grab for the edge of the sideboard. I'm aware of broken china, a piece of something that must have been a vase crunches under my hand. I can see the white panels of frosted glass in the front doors ahead of me, and when the sideboard ends I feel for a split second as if I'm falling into nowhere. Then I half step and half slide across the parquet, and collide with a chair, and the marble of the vestibule floor swings up to meet me.

My head is too heavy to lift. Something moves beside me, and I feel Jake's fur against my face. I see flashes of light, and then there's a loud ringing, and a child's high voice shouting 'Trick or Treat'. Someone is hammering on the glass and yelling, but I can't breathe, and I feel myself getting smaller and smaller, as though I'm shrinking, as though I'm being sucked backwards out of time. In the second before I disappear, I hear Jake bark.

TWENTY-EIGHT

I can smell flowers. Something lingering, and sweet. Freesias. Their perfume clouds my dreams. It drifts across the fields to the farm, where I can see the sun lighting the steps of the front porch and the windows thrown open. As I come closer I see the white curtains pushing against the gray mesh of the screens as if they're trying to escape. They flutter and throb to the hidden pulse of fans. By the garage the lilies are blooming in a bank of flame, and the glider rocks, restless in the wind. The front door opens, and someone is standing there, beckoning me in, but before I can make out who it is, I am awake again.

That is how it happens every time. The nurses say that this is because of the morphine that they are dripping into my blood, but I am not so certain. For in the last moments on the vestibule floor, as I was growing smaller and smaller, shrinking to nothing but a point of light, I heard Marina's voice. 'Come home,' she whispered, 'come home.'

Lolly bends over me.

'I have Jake,' she says. 'He's fine. Don't you worry.' She squeezes my hand.

The perfume is coming from my nightstand, and I can see color out of the corner of my eye. Bright purple, and gold, and a velvety magenta splash against a pale square of the wall.

'I don't know who they're from,' Lolly says. 'There's no note, but they're beautiful. Somebody's spoiling you.' She picks up the vase that is crowded with freesias and holds it in front of me so I can see. 'There's just this,' she says, 'taped on. I wonder who did it. It's so cute. It looks like Jake.'

The door opens and a nurse in pink scrubs swims into my vision.

'I'm sorry,' she says to Lolly, 'but you'll have to leave now.' The nurse is plump and blonde, and with her apple cheeks and blue eyes, she looks like something out of a children's story. I can hear the wheels of the cart she's pulling. She parks it beside my bed, and ducks out of sight as she locks it into place.

'We have to change the dressings,' she announces when she pops back up. Lolly nods and puts the flowers back on the bedside table.

'I'll be back tomorrow,' she says to me. 'I have to go now because Richard and I are taking that dog of yours out to Fairhill. Richard bought him a frisbee.' Her hair tickles my face as she kisses me on the forehead, and I hear the click of her heels as she slips out of sight. The door closes with a whoosh, and there's a snap as the nurse pulls on plastic gloves. Out of the corner of my eye, I see the flash of steel.

'Don't worry,' she says, 'this shouldn't hurt.'

I feel a tug and I hear a snipping sound. I roll my eyes sideways until I can see the edges of the flowers. I breathe in their smell and watch their melting blur of color. Even when I feel a sharp tear of pain across my neck, and hear the nurse mutter under her breath, I keep concentrating on the vase of freesias, and on the little origami dog that's taped to its rim.

That was this morning. Now, Mark Cope is standing by the window in my room. His shirt is a crisp, bright blue against the gauzy white rectangle of the sky, and he's moving his hand back and forth along the window sill, tracing its edge with his finger as if he's found dust there and is going to complain to housekeeping. When he looks at me, he frowns, and I know what he's going to say before he says it.

'They found the body a couple of hours ago,' Mark Cope says. 'Right where you said. Near the old silo hole.'

I had guessed that Charlie would be there because the Delrays had torn the silo down that summer, and the hole, and the rubble, would have been ready made, a grave waiting for him when he walked across the summer fields to find Sonny Delray that Sunday morning twenty years ago.

I had whispered this to Becca Aaronson yesterday, croaked it in her ear when she bent so close to me that I could see the stitches on her white silk collar and smell the mix of shampoo and perfume that clung to her hair. She and the vampire were here when I woke up, and she was the one who told me about the Trick or Treater who had peered through the glass panels of the door, and about his father who had had a mobile phone and dialed 9–1–1.

'You were lucky,' she'd said.

Now I look at Mark Cope, and close my eyes. I see Chief Hancy. And Dex Eames. And blue lights flashing down the farm road. I see a group of men standing over the sink hole of the Delray's old silo, and I think of Charlie, who never made it to the Gulf, or to the oilfields, or anywhere else, despite the medal that he wore tucked inside the collar of his shirt.

'They say they think the Delray kid burned a barn down,' Mark Cope says. 'Does that make any sense to you?'

I nod and open my eyes.

'He did,' I whisper. 'It was a warning. For Charlie to stay away from Marina.'

'Well—' Mark Cope says, 'it's all unrolled like a ball of string. Sonny – his real name actually is Shawn, by the way – never got over her. He went off to the Vocational College at Macon and did pretty well. He was a smart kid, made his Momma proud. She still doesn't believe this, of course. Says her boy never hurt a fly. Anyways, he got a job in Atlanta first. We're trying to see what we can find out there. He doesn't actually have a record, but there's a spate of peeping tom incidents that happened at around the time he was in town and stopped about when he left.' Mark Cope shrugs, 'Might have been him,' he says. 'All of the women were single and several of them had red hair.'

He looks out of the window as though he's studying something or has seen someone he knows in what I guess must be the parking lot or the street below. Then, without turning around, he goes on telling me about Shawn.

'He left Atlanta after more than five years at the same company, where he had a good record. I spoke to a personnel guy on the phone yesterday. He said they were sorry to lose Shawn but he insisted that he

needed to move to DC. The guy says Shawn told
them that his fiancée had just started a job there. They
gave him a great reference and a modest golden handshake.' Mark Cope thinks about this, and then he says,
'We figure he watched Marina for maybe a year,
possibly two before he ever did anything. He had
another pretty good job in Bethesda, and that's when
he started to get a little funky, the hair and all. He had
a friend he played squash with, a guy, who never
bought the gay stuff and called him on it. Shawn said
he liked it because it made things "easier". He had a
female boss at work, who I guess he cosied up to, got
to be pals with. Anyways, he told this guy that it "oiled
the wheels". He said women were never threatened by
gay men.'

I close my eyes again and Mark Cope goes on
talking.

'We haven't turned up any trace of a boyfriend,' he
says, 'so I don't know what his trip is. Phil says that, in
that respect, probably neither does he. Anyways, he
got his promotion. Actually, he got the lady's job
altogether, and a pay rise along with it. He bought the
condo in Falls Church in August, and we figure he
made his first call to Marina about a month later. Della
Hervey thinks she might have given him the number.
And the new one after Marina changed it. She's sure
that he must have used her keys to get into your old
house. Incidentally, when he went down there, he
ditched the tight jeans and the earring. I don't know
what he did about the hair.' Miss Clairol Temporary, I
think. Wash in. Rinse out.

Mark's words flow over me, and even though I
close my eyes he knows that I'm listening. He's talked

to me this way before in the day and a half since I've
been here, swaddled like a baby in my hospital gown
and wearing my white turtleneck of gauze. He's come
every couple of hours, and he's told me everything.
He's laid out every last, minute detail that the police
have discovered about Shawn as if he owes it to me, as
if it is the least he can do for failing to protect me.

Now he says, 'He sold the condo a year ago, and
quit his job. In fact, they wanted to downsize, so he
took voluntary redundancy and got paid for it. That's
what he's been living on in Philly. He found out
where you were from Della, too. He asked about you
after Marina was killed. Said he wanted to send you
flowers.' He pauses while this sinks in, and then he
says, 'We think he must have watched the house a
while, trailed Cathy, joined her gym. Then all he had
to do to get inside was make friends with her. The rest
is history. After Zoe hired him, he had keys to everywhere. We found a screwdriver in his apartment that
we expect to have paint traces from your car on it. He
knew where you were working. He'd been following
you.'

There's something else he wants to say, I can tell,
even with my eyes closed, and I wait. After what seems
like a long time, I hear his voice again.

'Phil thinks it was Marina's relationship with Kathleen Harper that tipped Shawn over the edge,' Mark
says. 'The mother's heavy duty Baptist, and I guess,
given his questions about his own sexuality, thinking
about Marina with another woman would have really
freaked him out. Phil thinks that, maybe, if she hadn't
rejected him so totally, if she hadn't laughed at him

when he said he wanted to save her, maybe he wouldn't have killed her.'

'No,' I say, but I don't open my eyes.

'That's what I think too,' I hear Mark say. 'I think he was going to kill her anyways. Or try to, sooner or later. It was the only way he was ever going to be able to keep her.'

'Save her,' I say. 'What he wanted was to save her.'

'Right,' Mark says, 'I forgot. The only thing is, I should have known with you. I should have picked it up. He was playing it all out again, only this time it was more accelerated, and it was when you got serious with Beau, when Shawn saw him spend the night, that his wire tripped. The hair cutting was a warning, a final call. Just like the barn burning and Marina's trash cans. I should have figured it out. I was so wound on Kathleen Harper that I didn't see what was right under my nose.'

'Neither did I,' I say.

'Yeah,' he says, 'but you're not a policeman.'

At first I thought that it was unfair, to let him go on this way, to let him feel so guilty for the blossoming of something that had set its roots so long ago, something that had been growing, creeping, through the years, its buds of envy, and love, and pain finally swelling to the bursting point. Then I realized that it's the only thing that he can give me now, and it seemed churlish to turn down the gift. It's all Mark Cope has left. This talking, this testifying, is his atonement for the fact that Shawn has got away.

I first suspected this yesterday when neither Becca
Aaronson nor the vampire mentioned him, and my
suspicions were confirmed by the cop that they posted
outside my door. I was not supposed to know he was
there, but I glimpsed the uniform, and I heard Becca's
lowered voice when she spoke to him. I didn't know
the details, though, until Mark Cope told me how Jake
had apparently attacked Shawn, and how he had fled
into the basement where he got out through the
garden door and climbed the wall that we never did
top with razor wire or broken glass. They had found
blood on the basement stairs, and on the garden door,
and yesterday Mark had assured me that they would
catch him, that now that they knew who he was, and
had gone through his apartment, and were questioning
his friends, and tracing his movements, it was only a
matter of time, of hours even, before Shawn would be
in custody. The fact, Mark had said, that, in all
probability, he had more than one serious dog bite
which would need treating, would only make the
search easier. Every hospital, every clinic and drugstore,
had been alerted.

But the day had passed. And this morning had
passed. And when I finally open my eyes, Mark Cope
has his back to me. 'I have bad news, Susannah,' he
says, 'I didn't want to tell you until we were sure.' He
sits down in the plastic armchair at the foot of my bed
so I can see him, and for the first time since I've
known him, I realize that he looks tired.

'He was one step ahead of us,' Mark Cope says.
'He got a plane out of Kennedy early yesterday morn-
ing. To Mexico City. He bought the ticket here in
Philly three weeks ago.'

Something is rising inside me, and it's so unfamiliar that it takes me a moment to realize that it's laughter. It's painful, and when it hits my chest and my throat, it brings tears to my eyes. Mark is talking about extradition, after they find him, which of course they will, when he notices that I am making small, strange sounds, more like a gerbil, or a bird, than a human being.

'Susannah,' he asks quickly, 'are you all right?' His hands move towards me, although they don't know what to do. He jumps up. 'Do you need a nurse?' he asks, but I shake my head.

He watches me, as the sound subsides, and then, when I gesture, he hands me the pad and the blue Bic pen that has been left by my bed. I can talk, sort of, but it hurts, so I've taken to writing things down. 'Water,' I've written, and 'Beau'. Now I write 'November 2' and hold the pad out to Mark Cope.

He looks at me, and he doesn't understand.

'Yeah,' he says, 'that's today.' When I don't say anything more, or gesture for the pen again, he decides that I must be getting tired and puts the pad down.

'Listen,' he says, 'you get some rest. I'll be back later.' I watch him as he gets up and walks to the door. He pulls the cuffs of his shirt down in a fussy little gesture, as if he's straightening himself up before he faces the world again.

'Kathleen Harper wants to see you,' Becca Aaronson says. 'She's outside. Do you feel OK about that? You can say, no.'

Becca's dropped by to tell me that they don't know

anything new about where, exactly, in Mexico Shawn might be, but that they do know that he must have been in the house and followed my cab when I went to the Marriot. A girl in the newspaper kiosk had ID'd him from a photo. She thinks Shawn hung around and bought a bunch of fitness magazines on the afternoon when I checked in.

'He followed you to the hair place,' Becca had said. Then she told me how he poisoned Jake. 'It was ordinary household mouse killer,' she'd said. 'We found it in his apartment, and two sausages laced with the stuff that he hadn't even bothered to throw out were in his freezer. That afternoon, he knew you'd go to the park sooner or later, and so he just waited and followed you. Jake knew him, so it wouldn't have been so tough. We think, maybe, he practiced on some strays,' Becca had added, 'to get the dosage right. Luckily, he blew it with Jake. My dog was a stray when I got her, and I hate that kind of shit.'

Until she'd said this, I didn't know Becca Aaronson even had a dog. We hadn't exactly been big on trading confidences, but since I almost got killed, she's been downright cosy. I can't figure out if this is a guilty conscience or genuine concern, but I'm not thinking about that. I'm thinking about Jake, and the way he struggled when Shawn had picked him up to carry him to the car. He'd even growled. I'd been too stupid to guess, but Jake knew. The idea of this brings tears to my eyes, and I reach for a Kleenex.

Becca thinks I'm worried about Kathleen, and she says, 'I can stay, while Kathleen's here. If you want. Or I can tell her to leave.'

'I'm OK,' I whisper in my strange non-voice.

Becca nods and straightens up. I can tell that she doesn't like this much, that she's afraid that Kathleen might do or say something to upset me even more. If talking was easier, I'd point out that I'm pretty much on the far side of being upset. Becca goes to the door and opens it. My guardian cop is gone now, he's back on traffic duty since we know Shawn is in Mexico. She looks back at me, and says, 'I'll be right out here if you need me.'

A second later Kathleen Harper is standing at the end of my bed. She's holding a bouquet of asters. Their stems are bound up in Saran Wrap and tied with a ribbon.

'They're the last from the garden,' she says, and she puts them down on top of my fake wood bureau. She's wearing a suit. It's navy blue and it looks like it fit her once, but now it's all loose and baggy in the wrong places because she's lost a lot of weight.

'That night,' she says, 'the night I came to your house. I lied to get in. I showed them some old key and said you gave it to me. I didn't think you'd let me in, and I needed to see you again.' She pauses and looks at me and for a moment I think she's going to cry, but she doesn't. 'I wanted to apologize,' she says, 'for being such a total bitch to you when you came out to the house. And I wanted to explain, about me and Marina.'

I look at her, nod a little bit, which hurts, and gesture to the chair, telling her to sit down. She shakes her head.

'I can't stay,' Kathleen says. She fingers the bunch of asters, and suddenly I wonder if Marina planted them, or if they planted them together. 'It was her first time,' she says, without looking at me, 'with another woman. Not for me,' she adds. 'I mean I'd fooled around in college, but then I met Allen and got married, and had the kids. We were happy. Sort of. But then Marina came to work at the bank, and I just knew.' She looks at me. 'You know what she was like. She was, well, amazing. Scary even. She pulled you in, made you feel like everything else was pale in comparison. I really loved her, you know. I wanted us to be together. I felt like she owned me, but I never felt like I owned her.'

I watch her. I don't know what I would say, even if I could.

'I was so jealous of you,' Kathleen says. 'I still am.'

She goes to the window and stares down. The tips of her fingers rest on the sill, tensed and waiting, as if she's a pianist who's about to play. From behind, she looks as if she might be holding her breath.

'He killed her because of me, didn't he?' she says, and I realize that in some horrible way she needs this to be true. She needs to believe that if she could not be utterly central to Marina's life, then at least she was utterly central to her death.

When I don't answer she turns around and looks at me. She's willing me to give her this last thing, this last piece of Marina.

'I don't know,' I whisper, and the words hurt. Each one of them.

Cathy comes to see me. Beau is here when she arrives, and we're watching *The Simpsons*. 'Du'uh!' Homer says, and the door pops open and a bunch of mylar balloons fly in. Cathy's still wearing her United uniform which means that she came straight from the airport, and she's trying to be perky, but she's having a hard time. Finally, she starts to cry. Beau puts his arm around her and makes her sit in the plastic chair and brings her a glass of tepid water from my bathroom.

'I didn't know,' she says over and over again. 'He was so friendly at the gym, you know, I mean, he seemed harmless. He was funny. I didn't know. I just didn't know.'

Beau tells her that it's OK. He pats her shoulder and says that nobody could have known.

'Susannah didn't know,' he says, 'and she knew him.' At this, Cathy laughs a little bit and nods. Beau gets her some toilet paper from the bathroom and she blows her nose and then wads it up into a little ball.

'I know,' she says, 'but it's different. I mean, I made friends with him. He even let me have a crush on him. He let me think maybe—'

'He's an asshole,' Beau says. 'Honey, he's a fruitcake psychopath. Manipulating people is what he does.' When he's not killing them, I think. Cathy and Beau look at me, and I know that they just thought the same thing, but none of us want to say it.

Instead Cathy sniffs and says, 'Well I feel like an asshole for letting him use me. I mean, I gave him the keys to my apartment. I convinced Zoe to give him a job. What the Hell is wrong with me?'

'You're a nice person,' Beau says.

'Well screw that!' Cathy bangs the arm of the chair so hard that I wince. 'I just hate the fucker!' she says.

★

Zoe comes with Justin. They bring roses, and a split of champagne, with a straw, that I can't drink. Zoe twists her hands back and forth, and says she's sorry for hiring him, over and over, and Justin says they should never have given him keys. Later that night, Lolly arrives and drinks the champagne.

'Don't you worry, Kiddo,' she says, waving the straw at me, 'we're going to get you all fixed up in no time. I have got this dynamite plastic surgeon.'

My neck still hurts, and I whisper, and write things down a lot, but they've moved me off morphine and on to percodan, and this afternoon they are letting me go home. Lolly is picking me up, and taking me to Beau's, where Jake and I are going to be staying for a while, and where he and Cathy are serving a dinner that is supposed to be a surprise. Lolly has told me this because she knows that I won't be able to eat any of it, and I don't like surprises. She says she'll get them to call it off, if I want, but I know that Zoe and Justin are coming and that Beau's even invited Benjy, and I tell her it's OK. She is still worried though, and she has bought me a pair of Chinese silk pajamas, and a kimono wrap so I'll have something to wear. They're gorgeous, and I am fingering the heavy silk, tracing the pattern of chrysanthemums and dragons, and wondering if I can actually wear anything this beautiful, when Mark Cope comes into the room.

He is carrying a large paper bag from somewhere like Saks Fifth Avenue or Filenes, and he smiles at me and says, 'Hey, looking good!'

It is not the sort of comment that comes naturally

to him, and I grimace and push the kimono away. I'm a little surprised to find that I'm happy to see him.

'So, you're going home,' he says. 'That's good.' He holds the bag out to me. 'If this ever gets to trial this will be material evidence,' he says. 'We found it in Shawn's apartment, and I thought you'd want to see it.'

I take the bag, and when I look inside I see photo frames, and recognize the pictures that were taken from Momma's desk in Petamill. Under them is something wrapped in white plastic that feels like a book. I catch a glimpse of bright turquoise, and when I unwrap the parcel Marina's scrapbook lies on my lap, the bright yellow daisy on its cover staring up at me, as round and unblinking as an eye.

The album's covers are smooth and slightly puffy under my fingers. I notice that the binding is cracked, as though someone's opened it over and over again, and the edges of the thick colored paper pages are soft and worn and slightly grubby from being turned. The words 'BALLET'and 'RIDING' are written at the tops of facing pages. The letters are a childish attempt at calligraphy, in green ink, with too many swirls and tails. A silver ribbon that has 'Level II' printed on it in blue letters is glued down on the ballet page and below it there's a picture of all the girls from that dance class clustered around our old teacher. Marina smiles from the center of the group. On the other page there are pictures of Uncle Ritchie's old horse, Jewel, and of Marina and me riding double. In one we sit back to back like a push-me-pull-you. Marina holds Jewel's mane, and I rest my hands on the horse's rump, laughing.

A few pages later there is a Junior High School portrait of Marina. It's one of those bad studio pictures, the kind that are taken against a cloudy blue background which makes the subject look as if they are giving off steam. I don't remember ever having seen this picture before, but from looking at it I would say that it must have been taken just before the summer of the fires, and I'm surprised that she was still putting pictures in by then. She stares straight at the camera. Her long hair is combed, uncharacteristically, straight back in a headband, and she is scowling. She almost looks as if she has a widow's peak.

But it's not Marina's face that holds my eye. It's the small gold necklace that she's wearing. I look at it, lying in the indent of her collarbone. I touch it with the tip of my finger, and I think that this photo must have been taken just weeks before she gave it away.

Marina was not the chronicler I was. She didn't have my belief in souvenirs, and many of the pages in the album are blank. I flip through them, almost mechanically, and then, towards the end, I see that there are more pictures. These are grainy, and black and white. The quality is poor, but even so, they've been arranged carefully on the pages, and the fuzzy images are held down with professional mounting tabs, as if they're valuable.

At first I don't understand, and I look at Mark Cope for an explanation, but he's turned away and is staring out of the window. I look back at the top picture. There's something blurry at the edge of the foreground, and beyond it is what looks like a stage with two figures on it and columns down one side. I squint a little, and then, suddenly, I see. It's Marina and me on our front porch.

We used to practice ballet out there sometimes, in the evenings. Momma would turn on the stereo for us and let the music drift through the open windows, and we'd use the porch rail as a barre. Our pink leotards would become damp with sweat and as soft as flesh as we sank on our knees, and rose, and pointed, our toes flicking up and down in our shiny black slippers. If we were being swans we would wear our tutus, and they would rustle like dead leaves when we moved.

The other pictures are as fuzzy, and as distant, but there's the same strange intimacy to all of them, and I understand that they were taken without our knowledge. They're moments that were snatched from us long ago without permission, and now they're pinned down on this page like butterflies. When he took these Shawn must have been hiding behind the corner of the barn, or possibly even crouching in the dense bank of the lilies.

There's a single shot of one of us, I can't tell which, sitting on the glider, reading, but in all of the others, we are together. There are several pictures of us on the porch, and in one we stand at the bottom of the steps, obviously quarreling. Marina reaches for what looks like a book in my hand, and I am caught in the moment of swinging it away from her. Looking at the picture now, I can hear the tone of her voice. I can almost feel the warm air move with the swipe of her hand, but I cannot recall what we might have been fighting about, or why.

I imagine the comfort that Shawn must have taken

in studying these pictures, these stolen glimpses of my sister. It was the best way he had of getting close to her. Undisturbed by reality, he must have spent hours alone with them, planning her salvation. Then, after he'd saved her, when he could no longer hear her voice on the phone, or follow her through the streets, there was nothing left. Nothing but these photographs and me.

These blurred little moments of possession that Shawn had hoarded so carefully and for so long are giving me a strange feeling in the bottom of my stomach.

'He watched us,' I say. 'Always.' The words come out in my croaky whisper, as loud as I can make them, and Mark Cope turns around from the window.

'We'll get him, Susannah,' he says. 'I promise you, we'll get him.'

That was a year ago. Now, Beau, and Jake, and I, live in another city. It's a smaller place in the flat mid-West, somewhere where strangers will stand out. I still work, but I have changed my name, and I fly from city to city. On the whole, I don't like to be away from home for long.

Lolly was as good as her word, and I'm sure her plastic surgeon would have been excellent. I met with him twice, but in the end, I decided not to have anything done. So for now, I wear high collars, and turtlenecks, and sometimes scarves, but I don't really like them. They're inclined to slip. Elena would say that this is a sign that I am not ready to part with my past yet, and perhaps she would be right. Beau says that we'll do something about it when I'm ready.

I still hear from Mark Cope. He calls from time to time, usually every couple of months, and before he hangs up, he always repeats his promise. 'We'll get him,' he says, 'we'll get him.' But nothing has been seen or heard of Shawn for a year now. He has vanished, or transformed himself into someone else. Perhaps he has buried Shawn-Like-The-Dawn in a new persona and a new body, just as surely as he buried Sonny Delray in the punky weight lifter with the purple hair who I once drank beer with in Philadelphia. This, naturally, presents me with a problem since, beyond a medal that assures safe journeys, I have no idea who, or what, I should be watching for.

It is cold now, and soon the snow will fly. Two nights ago tiny witches and ghouls made their way up the lighted path to our front door by the dozens, and Beau and I handed out Hershey's Kisses and mini bags of M&Ms. Today, I saw a Christmas tree in the drugstore window, and next week they're turning on the lights around the Madonna and the shepherds and the baby Jesus in the park. The phone rings, and downstairs I hear Beau go to answer it. Seconds later I hear his footsteps again, and when I lean over the stairwell and ask who it was, he stops with his newspaper in his hand, and smiles up at me and says, 'Just someone trying to sell us something, Doll. I hung up on them.'

I am running the water for a bath. It steams slightly and bubbles, and when I get in I let my hands float across the top of it. I make swirls on the blue soapy surface and imagine that my hands are not my own, until they gravitate to my collarbone and rise and finger the tapering edge of the scar that I wear like a jewel, like a necklace that is so precious that it can never be taken off.

I lean my head back, and through the skylight above me, I watch the dark patch of the sky. There's a thin veil of cloud tonight, and the lights from town reflect off it and make it shimmer like smoke, but up above it, somewhere, there are stars and, possibly, a moon.

It's the Day of The Dead today, and I wonder if Shawn can see the stars where he is now. I wonder if he is buying sugar skulls. I imagine him preparing for his 'annual second chance' with the dead, laying out his feast, and inviting Charlie and Marina to his table. Then I wonder if all the places are taken, or if, when Shawn makes his plans, he still thinks that, someday, he will lay a place at his table for me.

extracts reading groups
competitions books new
discounts extracts events reading groups
competitions extracts discounts
books new extracts reading groups
new events extracts discounts
reading groups events books
new extracts books
reading groups new titles reading groups
interviews new events
events extracts books reading groups
reading books events extracts interviews books
discounts new books events interviews new books extracts
events new events books extracts
discounts extracts discounts books
www.panmacmillan.com
extracts events reading groups
competitions books extracts new books